Praise for *The Most Likely Club*

"Endearing and immensely readable, Elyssa Friedland's *The Most Likely Club* is an ode to female friendship, second chances, and the people who are 'Most Likely' to love us the most."

—Laura Dave, #1 *New York Times* bestselling author of *The Last Thing He Told Me*

"Elyssa Friedland writes with heart, depth, and humor in this story of four friends exploring what they wanted in high school and what they have today. Utterly delightful and uplifting!"

—*New York Times* bestselling author Kristan Higgins

"A fun and satisfying romp through the journey from imagining we will have it all to realizing we don't want it."

—*New York Times* bestselling author KJ Dell'Antonia

"A hilarious, delectable, and much-needed time machine back to the nineties."

—Jo Piazza, bestselling coauthor of *We Are Not Like Them*

"[A] hilarious, feel-good saga."   —*Woman's World*

"A high school reunion sparks new life for a group of best friends in Elyssa Friedland's winning novel *The Most Likely Club*. . . . Through their triumphs and failures, the group cherishes the bond of their friendship and honors their childhood selves in this hilarious and heartwarming tale."

—PopSugar

"We love this book about a group of girls who graduated in the '90s and are coming up on a milestone high school reunion. Full of nostalgia and surprises, the 'Most Likely Girls' will discover that it's never too late to make their dreams come true." —Medium.com

"Get ready to be in your feelings—especially if you read this from your childhood bedroom while home for the holidays. It follows four washed-up fortysomethings attending their high school reunion. As they look back at their yearbook superlatives and are reminded of their old hopes and dreams, they collectively decide to jump-start their lives and become the people their high school selves would be proud of. Aww." —theSkimm

"Perfect for fans of Emily Henry and Gail Honeyman, *The Most Likely Club* is a celebration of embracing all the ways your life derails—and the friends who help you along the way." —PureWow

Praise for *Last Summer at the Golden Hotel*

"Two families agonize over whether to sell their once-successful Catskills resort. *Last Summer at the Golden Hotel* promises snark, sass and sunshine-filled fun." —Bustle

"You will laugh out loud at the antics of two delightfully dysfunctional families as they fight, share secrets, and fall in love in the once-prosperous Catskills hotel that they own. Once again, Friedland brilliantly wields her rapier wit—if Dorothy Parker and Joan Rivers wrote a book, this would be it!"

—Fiona Davis, *New York Times* bestselling author of *Magnolia Palace*

"Friedland brings two families full circle over the fate of a storied hotel they've owned together for three generations. . . . Old tensions and new romances arise as they decide if the nostalgia and storied legacy of the hotel can save it, or if they're having their last summer at the Golden. . . . Episodes of intergenerational disconnect contrasted with unshakable family bonds make *Last Summer at the Golden Hotel* a great choice for fans of *Schitt's Creek* and feel-good family dramedies."

—Shelf Awareness

"In *Last Summer at the Golden Hotel*, Elyssa Friedland creates a broad cast of characters who are at once touching and hilarious. Their fears, their secrets, and their dreams come together in a moving story that balances nostalgia for the past and hope for the future. A perfect book for a family book club."

—Jill Santopolo, *New York Times* bestselling author of *Stars in an Italian Sky*

"Long known for her humor and wit, Elyssa Friedland has penned a charmer of a novel in *Last Summer at the Golden Hotel*, a story about two families who own a resort in the Catskills, which was a crown jewel in its heyday but is now in decline. Fans of *The Marvelous Mrs. Maisel* and *Dirty Dancing* will revel in the nostalgia of a bygone era and the richness of this intergenerational tale, which manages to be smart, funny, honest, and poignant all at the same time."

—Pam Jenoff, *New York Times* bestselling author of *Code Name Sapphire*

"Chock-full of charm and wit, Elyssa Friedland's *Last Summer at the Golden Hotel* is the only family drama you need this year! Set in a ramshackle Catskills hotel and featuring a vibrant cast of characters, it's a laugh-out-loud-funny novel with a heart of gold."

—Karma Brown, international bestselling author of *What Wild Women Do*

"Prepare to laugh. Take a trip to the Catskills with *Last Summer at the Golden Hotel* and bask in the hilarity and chaos that make Elyssa Friedland the queen of the family drama."

—Jane L. Rosen, author of *On Fire Island*

"Written with Friedland's signature wit and sharp dialogue, *Last Summer at the Golden Hotel* is an incisive novel that touches on family legacies, nostalgia and multigenerational dynamics. Readers not content with armchair immersion will want to book their Catskills getaway immediately."

—*Booklist*

"The vanished history of the Catskills is evoked with love and plenty of schmaltz. A high-spirited party of a book. BYOB: Bring your own borscht."

—*Kirkus Reviews*

"Friedland brings laughs and nuance to the family foibles and demonstrates a wide range in her convincing narration from the many points of view. Breezy and charming, this is great fun."

—*Publishers Weekly*

Praise for *The Floating Feldmans*

"When Annette Feldman decides to celebrate her seventieth birthday with a family cruise, drama—and hilarity—ensue." —*People*

"Family reunions can rock the boat. This one does it on a cruise ship. When the Feldmans hit the high seas for their matriarch's seventieth, a lot of drama and laughs come out in tight quarters. Think *This Is Where I Leave You* meets *The Family Stone*." —theSkimm

"*The Floating Feldmans* is a hilarious romp on the sea that is perfect for your poolside reading this summer! I read this book with a wide grin, and I know that you will too! Highly recommend!"
—Catherine McKenzie, bestselling author of *Have You Seen Her*

"Friedland uses multiple perspectives, witty dialogue, and complex characters that are incredibly relatable to deliver a funny, astute look at the family dynamic and the relationships shared within. Whether on a cruise or taking a staycation, contemporary readers will want to have *The Floating Feldmans* on deck." —*Booklist*

"*The Floating Feldmans* is a fast, funny, surprisingly heartwarming ride on the high seas." —Shelf Awareness

"Friedland creates vivid characters with distinct voices, from the outwardly critical matriarch to the insecure teenager. . . . A fun look at family drama on the open seas." —*Kirkus Reviews*

"*The Floating Feldmans* is a story about an estranged family's wild vacation. This book is so dramatic that it might actually make your fam feel normal . . . even if you're losing your mind on day five of your own trip."

—*Cosmopolitan*

"Long a master of insightful books about modern life and relationships, Friedland turns her formidable talents to the family cruise. Uproariously funny, yet heartfelt and true, *The Floating Feldmans* will have each reader seeing her own family fun and foibles in the choppy waters, laughing and crying at the same time to the very last wonderful page."

—Pam Jenoff, *New York Times* bestselling author of *The Lost Girls of Paris*

"An intelligent, insightful, touching novel about the secrets we keep and the family that loves us anyway."

—Abbi Waxman, *USA Today* bestselling author of *Adult Assembly Required*

"Elyssa Friedland's premise is perfect. Take three generations of an estranged family, put them on a boat—a forced cruise to celebrate the matriarch's seventieth birthday—and let the dysfunction fly. A pleasure to read."

—Laurie Gelman, author of *Smells Like Tween Spirit*

"Such a smart, honest look at the modern American family. Elyssa Friedland has written a book that feels both up-to-the-minute contemporary and, somehow, absolutely timeless."

—Matthew Norman, author of *Charm City Rocks*

"All aboard! *The Floating Feldmans* is for everyone who's ever thought their family is absolutely crazy . . . but loves them anyway. Sibling rivalries and skeletons in the closet all come to a head in this fun, quirky family saga."   —Georgia Clark, author of *Island Time*

"*The Floating Feldmans* was a blast: funny, moving, and immensely readable. Friedland's all-you-can-eat buffet of quirky characters walks right off the page and into your heart."

—Jonathan Evison, author of *Small World*

"Take a big, dysfunctional family, reunite them for the first time in ten years on a Caribbean cruise ship they can't escape, and add end-less buffets, blindfolded pie-eating contests, and impromptu conga lines on the sundeck. What could possibly go wrong? Both cruising fans and skeptics alike will get a laugh out of this story of a family trying to stay afloat."   —*National Geographic*

"Friedland's well-executed and smartly structured novel features chapters from each character's point of view. The simple but clever premise lets the author explore the complicated tensions of family relationships in a compressed and directed way. . . . There is dry hu-mor and a certain sweetness as well."   —*Library Journal*

Praise for *The Intermission*

"The snappy dialogue makes this an effortless page-turner, almost a movie treatment more than a novel. . . . Intelligent commercial fiction."   —*The Wall Street Journal*

"*The Intermission* is a thoughtful look at the complexities of marriage, delivering deep truths about how we share a life with another person. It will have you wondering: How well do I really know my spouse?"
—PopSugar

"A multifaceted look at the difficulties and rewards of marriage."
—*Kirkus Reviews*

"Entertaining marriage saga. . . . Friedland insightfully dissects motives, lies, and love in this engrossing deconstruction of a bad marriage."
—*Publishers Weekly*

"Expertly paced and eerily realistic, this novel will make readers think twice about the line between deception and mystery in any relationship."
—*Booklist*

TITLES BY ELYSSA FRIEDLAND

Jackpot Summer

Elyssa Friedland

Berkley
New York

BERKLEY

An imprint of Penguin Random House LLC

penguinrandomhouse.com

Copyright © 2024 by Elyssa Friedland

Readers Guide copyright © 2024 by Elyssa Friedland

Excerpt from *The Most Likely Club* copyright © 2022 by Elyssa Friedland

Penguin Random House supports copyright. Copyright fuels creativity, encourages diverse voices, promotes free speech, and creates a vibrant culture. Thank you for buying an authorized edition of this book and for complying with copyright laws by not reproducing, scanning, or distributing any part of it in any form without permission. You are supporting writers and allowing Penguin Random House to continue to publish books for every reader.

BERKLEY and the BERKLEY & B colophon are registered trademarks of Penguin Random House LLC.

Library of Congress Cataloging-in-Publication Data

Names: Friedland, Elyssa, author.

Title: Jackpot summer / Elyssa Friedland.

Description: First edition. | New York : Berkley, 2024.

Identifiers: LCCN 2023050027 (print) | LCCN 2023050028 (ebook) |
    ISBN 9780593638545 (trade paperback) | ISBN 9780593638552 (ebook)

Subjects: LCGFT: Novels.

Classification: LCC PS3606.R55522 J33 2024 (print) |
    LCC PS3606.R55522 (ebook) | DDC 813/.6—dc23/eng/20231024

LC record available at https://lccn.loc.gov/2023050027

LC ebook record available at https://lccn.loc.gov/2023050028

First Edition: June 2024

Printed in the United States of America

1st Printing

Book design by Ashley Tucker

This is a work of fiction. Names, characters, places, and incidents either are the product of the author's imagination or are used fictitiously, and any resemblance to actual persons, living or dead, business establishments, events, or locales is entirely coincidental.

For Karyn, the coolest Jersey girl I've ever known.
You are deeply missed.

Jackpot Summer

If I were a rich man
Ya ba dibba dibba dibba dibba dibba dibba dum
All day long, I'd biddy biddy bum
If I were a wealthy man
                    —*Fiddler on the Roof*

It's like the more money we come across
The more problems we see.
                    —The Notorious B.I.G.

Heaven looks a lot like New Jersey.
                    —Jon Bon Jovi

Los Angeles Times

CALIFORNIA MAN WINS $2B JACKPOT: HOMELESS THREE YEARS LATER

By Macy Roko

Billy Rockwell knows better than anyone what it feels like to go from rags to riches overnight. He's the winner of the largest jackpot in the country's history, a whopping $2.3 billion. And for a period of eighteen months, Rockwell was living large. But by the third anniversary of the historic win, the country's biggest winner was living in a homeless encampment ten miles from his foreclosed Beverly Hills mansion.

"Booze, drugs and women," Rockwell said, speaking from inside his tent, which he shares with three other homeless individuals. "They will get you every time." His only remaining possession of value is a rhino horn from Tanzania that he purchased on eBay for $2 million. "It was supposed to bring me luck," Rockwell said. The horn turned out to be a replica.

Rockwell isn't alone in falling on hard times after hitting it big. According to the National Endowment for Financial Education, a staggering seventy percent of lottery winners go bankrupt within five years.

"Most winners go hog-wild," Everett McPherson, an accountant with nationally recognized firm Ernst & Young, said. "And they don't realize just how large a slice of the pie Uncle Sam is going to take." McPherson explained that taxes can eat up nearly half the advertised value of the jackpot.

"Billy was no good with money from day one," his ex-wife, Jeannie Rockwell, said. "The Elvis who married us in Vegas swindled him out of three hundred bucks on our wedding night."

Des Moines Register

IOWA TOWN POOLS TICKETS AND WINS BIG

By Carson Roberts

The residents of Holly Springs, Iowa, a quaint hamlet with a population of six thousand, have collectively won the Iowa state lottery. The $40-million prize was divided equally among the town residents, each of whom contributed five dollars toward the purchase.

Holly Springs is a factory town where life centers around potluck backyard barbecues and celebrations at the town pool. The day the residents discovered their win, the mayor organized a parade and fireworks display.

"Our citizens are simple people," Mayor Julia Stillman said of how the lottery win will change life in Holly Springs. "I used my share of the winnings to build a man cave for my husband so he leaves me in peace."

LOCAL FIREFIGHTER WINS LUCKY BUCKS LOTTO: GIVES EVERY CHILD IN TOWN A FIRE POLE

By Emily Emerson

"There's nothing like hearing that 'Wheeeeeee!'"

That's what Dwayne Jenkins said when asked what prompted him to buy every child in his town of East Rocklin, Pennsylvania, a fire pole after he won $6 million in the Lucky Bucks lottery.

Jenkins has been a firefighter in East Rocklin for nearly twenty years. He said he knew he wanted to fight fires since he was a little boy. It was the pole that attracted him.

"I couldn't believe there was a job where I could slide down a pole," Jenkins said, arm around his wife, Nola, on the porch of their new house, a 3,000-square-foot ranch on four acres of pristine farmland. The house was the couple's biggest splurge after the win, but Jenkins seems far more excited about gifting the fire poles.

"Not all the parents are happy with me," Jenkins said. "There have been a few broken arms."

The Star-Ledger

LONG BEACH ISLAND SIBLINGS AND A RUMSON GRANDMOTHER OF 12 WIN BIG SLICE OF POWERBALL PIE
Drama Surrounds Sibling Win

By Jeanette Espinosa

It's time for people to stop thumbing their noses at the Garden State. Making lottery history, two of the four winning tickets of a $261 million Powerball were claimed by New Jersey residents who purchased their winning tickets over July Fourth weekend. The chances of winning the Powerball jackpot are 1 in 292,201,338, so having two winners from New Jersey is quite the reason to celebrate. Sources in Governor Phil Murphy's office are saying a ticker-tape parade is under consideration.

Mabel Collins of Rumson, an eighty-two-year-old retired elementary school bus driver, took home over $30 million before taxes. She said she plans to use the money to help her local church and shower her twelve grandchildren with gifts.

"I'm at Target every day now buying gifts for my babies," Ms. Collins said. "It's constant Christmas over here."

The other New Jersey winner is a set of siblings with a family home in Beach Haven on the south end of Long Beach Island. The three siblings, whose last name is Jacobson, were quickly dubbed the Jackpot Jacobsons. The nickname has been adopted by the local summer community where the family has owned a home for more than three decades.

Unlike Ms. Collins, each of the Jacobson siblings declined to comment on the win. Public records show that Laura Jacobson is in contract to purchase a 7,000-square-foot home in upscale Franklin Lakes, New Jersey. Sister Sophie is listed on LinkedIn as a public school teacher in Brooklyn, but calls to the school indicate she is no longer employed there. The third sibling, Noah Jacobson, works as a private tech-support specialist but appears to have no official business or property registered to his name. One Beach Haven resident who wished to remain anonymous but described herself as a close family friend was not optimistic about the Jacobsons.

"Drama, drama, drama," she said. "That's all that winning the lottery has done for that poor family. Well, maybe poor isn't the right word."

1

Sophie

"WELL THAT WAS DEPRESSING," SOPHIE SAID. "I'M SURPRIS-ingly hungry considering we were at Mom's grave less than ten minutes ago." She tilted the syrup dispenser and let it ooze over her pancake stack.

"I am too," Noah said, lifting a forkful of scrambled eggs. "But these eggs are awful compared to the ones at Chegg."

"You think everything is better at Chegg," Sophie said, referencing the Chicken or the Egg, one of the famous eateries on Long Beach Island.

"It is," the rest of the table responded, a chorus of voices that included Noah, Matthew, Laura, Laura's husband Doug and the patriarch of the Jacobson clan, Leo.

"For the hundredth time, you did not get food poisoning from Chegg," Laura said to Sophie, lowering the gigantic Kenilworth Diner menu she'd been using to hide her tear-streaked face. "You were puking because you drank too much of Dad's Chivas Regal. I saw you."

Leo raised an eyebrow at what apparently was coming as news to him.

Sophie considered Laura's claim. Maybe she had been conflating memories. The night of her alleged food poisoning was nearly twenty years ago.

"I thought the gravestone was very nice," Matthew, the oldest Jacobson sibling, said. His comment brought them back to why they were gathered in northern New Jersey on a sunny afternoon in June. It was for the unveiling of the gravestone marking the place their mother was buried. "I think Mom would have approved."

"She more than approved," Leo said, wiping Tabasco sauce from his mouth with a paper napkin. "She designed it."

The siblings' gasps quickly gave way to wry chuckling. They shouldn't have expected anything less from Sylvia Jacobson. Sophie considered the tombstone inscription with renewed appreciation, especially the line about canasta, the card game that was their mother's addiction.

SYLVIA ROSE JACOBSON
FEBRUARY 6, 1947–JUNE 30, 2023
DEVOTED WIFE, BELOVED MOTHER TO THE FANTASTIC
FOURSOME, BOOK LOVER, VOLUNTEER, JERSEY GIRL
"AWAITING SPECIAL HANDS IN HEAVEN"

"Did I ever tell you that Mom emailed me a detailed description of what the girls and I should wear to her funeral, including accessories?" Laura said. "Oh, and that Doug shouldn't wear a navy tie."

"And I didn't. I wore yellow," Laura's husband said proudly.

"When she could barely speak anymore, she managed to mime that pink lipstick washes me out," Sophie said, puckering her burgundy-painted lips. "I listened too."

"I added the 'devoted' and 'beloved' to the inscription," Leo said. "She didn't want it to be too schmaltzy. This may be the first argument I ever won."

"I can definitely see her finding a regular canasta game in heaven," Sophie said. "Where she will win many special hands."

"Did anyone feel like they were waiting for directions from Mom today? Like where to stand, what to do," Matthew asked. "It's so weird to all be together and not have someone boss us around."

Sophie knew exactly what her brother was saying. She'd been staring at the plot of earth under which her mother lay buried, expecting a wagging finger to poke through the dirt.

Their mother had been the protective force field surrounding them at all times, instructing their next moves, sharing her opinions whether they were welcome or not. Even Leo took direction from his wife as though he were a fifth child. Sylvia's departure from this world one year earlier still gave Sophie the constant feeling that she was forgetting something, like leaving the house without her keys.

"At least we'll all be at the house for July Fourth weekend," Noah said. "Mom would like that."

The Jacobson family celebrating the Fourth of July together was a tradition dating to Sophie's childhood, when cousins and friends would gather at their summer house on Long Beach Island for the holiday weekend. Over the years, it grew to a full-blown daytime party with an overflowing buffet—almost all the dishes homemade by Sylvia—and concluded with the town fireworks. That Sylvia died just days before the holiday last year, forcing them to trade hot dogs, burgers and Sylvia's famous coleslaw for shiva platters of deli meats and rugelach that barely anyone touched, was especially painful.

"Excuse me," Beth said, waving a hand toward the diner's counter. Sophie noted it was the first time Matthew's wife had looked up from her phone since they'd sat down.

A waitress with a pencil behind her ear and a bored expression walked over with two steaming pots of coffee. "More joe? I got regular and decaf."

Beth shielded the top of her mug. "Not for me. I was wondering if you could provide the Wi-Fi password. The service in here is terrible."

The waitress wrinkled her nose. "Back in a minute."

"Sorry, I'm just absolutely slammed at work," Beth said. "I have to get a brief out within the hour."

"Does she ever stop?" Laura muttered to Sophie, jutting her chin in the direction of their sister-in-law. Sophie rolled her eyes in return.

"I found the air mattresses," Noah said, bringing the conversation back to the holiday weekend. "I'll have them pumped up before you guys get there."

"I call a real bed," Sophie said. "I'll have just finished teaching and need good sleep."

"That's fine. The girls and Austin will take the blowups," Laura said, referencing her two daughters and Matthew and Beth's son, the third-generation Jacobsons. "Doug too if his snoring keeps up."

"I don't snore," Doug said.

"Oh yes, you do."

"No, I don't."

"Okay, I'll record you."

"Fine, I'll try the damn nose strips again."

"He needs a CPAP machine," Laura said to her three siblings. Sophie shrugged. Luckily Ravi, her boyfriend of nearly two years, only snored when he drank too much. They spent just two nights together a week anyway.

"Miss! Miss!" Beth called out. Sophie followed Beth's flailing arms to where the waitress was schmoozing with a line cook behind the counter. "The Wi-Fi, please?"

Matthew turned to Beth. "Can't you finish up after lunch? We'll be back in the city in an hour."

Beth looked horrified. "Absolutely not. And don't you have to turn around that offering memorandum by EOD?"

So there were people who actually said EOD out loud, Sophie mused. She pinched Laura's knee at the same time Laura kicked Sophie's ankle under the table.

Matthew's expression shifted. "You're right. Let me go speak to the waitress." He left the table as Beth continued to jab at her phone, clearly frustrated to discover the Jersey diner wasn't as technically equipped as her law firm.

"I can probably hook you up to a hotspot," Noah said. The youngest Jacobson sibling had always been a technology whiz.

"Thanks. Tight deadline," Beth said as she handed over her phone to Noah. "In fact, we've got to head out soon anyway. Austin's in the last round of his chess tournament. He's up a rook in game seven."

Sophie gave Beth a thumbs-up, assuming "up a rook" was a good thing.

"Us too," Laura said. "Hannah bought six prom dresses, and if I don't get home soon, she'll rip the tags off and we'll be stuck keeping all of them."

"Did we give her a budget?" Doug asked.

"Of course. But you know Hannah. She'll have some reason why she needs to spend more." Laura scoffed lovingly.

"I'll help her choose," Sophie said. "FaceTime me when you get home. This falls under the cool-aunt umbrella."

As the siblings started to collect their things, Leo held up his hand. "Hang on, everyone. I have something I need to tell you kids." The widower glanced at his lap, took a visibly deep breath, and righted his head. Looking at no one in particular, he said, "I sold the beach house."

"You what?" Sophie and Laura managed to sputter. Noah went white as a sheet and dropped Beth's phone into the puddle of ketchup on his plate. Beth let out a yelp.

"Got the password," Matthew said cheerfully as he reappeared at the table. "It's 'joysey'—spelled J-O-Y-S . . ." He paused. "Sheesh, what did I miss?"

Noah looked at their older brother with tear-filled eyes. "Dad sold our happy place."

THE NEXT DAY, ACROSS THE RIVER FROM WHERE HER MOTHER lay to rest, Sophie watched an open container of glitter topple on its side, roll down the entire length of the long metal craft table, collide with the floor and deposit miniscule red sparkles on the checkered linoleum of her classroom. She did not get paid nearly enough to do this job.

"Awesome!" Harrison, a third grader, said as he removed a finger from his nose to applaud the mess.

"Look at my sneakers," Lulu, another child in the class, said, shimmying a high-top in the air.

"I'm sorry, Ms. Jacobson," said Owen, the klutziest child at P.S. 282 in Brooklyn's Park Slope. Sophie, Ms. Jacobson between eight a.m. to three p.m., was one of two art teachers at the school and managed to get Owen Cullman-Romero assigned to her class every year. So far he had Krazy-Glued his fingers together, dropped crayons in the radiator and managed to get a paintbrush stuck in his ear canal. And now, glitter everywhere.

Glitter was the bane of Sophie Jacobson's professional existence. Sparkles from the autumn leaves project in October would appear in tissues when she blew her nose during a December cold. Specks clung to her sweaters and eyelids for weeks. As much as she couldn't stand it, the kids loved it, so at least once a month Sophie relented and let them glitter their papier-mâché birds, their self-portraits, their clay mugs. This incident though. A whole container. She would be sparkling for eternity.

"I can help clean up," Owen said. Fat tears were clinging to his mile-long eyelashes. Sophie couldn't stay mad at him. She couldn't stay upset with any of the kids, even though she typically left work with the makings of a migraine and crepe paper trailing one of her shoes.

"It's okay, Owen. Just means I owe Ronaldo another drink," Sophie said, referring to the head custodian at P.S. 282.

"What kind of drink?" Owen asked. "I like grape, but my parents said I can't have it because I'll spill it and ruin the carpet."

"Your parents are right," Sophie said. "Why don't you help Ella with her collage?"

Ella Cooper, eight going on eighteen, was the reliable kid who always got stuck with the annoying partner. *I owe you one*, Sophie mouthed to her, something she wouldn't have dared if it wasn't the second-to-last day of school.

"Fine," Ella said and turned to Owen. "Hold my glue stick."

Sophie made a note to email a note of praise to Ella's father, known as Divorced Dad Dave or Triple D among the teachers. While she was committed to Ravi, she couldn't help noticing how adorable Triple D looked with Ella's American Girl backpack slung over the shoulder of his leather jacket.

The bell rang and the third graders shuffled out as the first graders charged in. Only thirty-six hours to go and it would officially be summer vacation. To celebrate the close of another year, the staff of P.S. 282 would celebrate at a bar the next night at a party affectionately nicknamed "Survivor." That's where she'd buy Ronaldo a well-deserved drink. The man was a whiz at whipping up concoctions to undo the remains of Mod Podge, oil paints and whatever else the kids left behind.

As she walked toward the school's front doors after the final bell, thinking what the first summer without her family's shore house would be like, Sophie nearly smacked into the principal, Evelyn Garcia.

"Grades, Ms. Jacobson," Garcia snapped as Sophie mumbled "Excuse me."

"I'll have them for you next week," Sophie said, stifling her irritation. Grades! For an elementary school art class. *Billy is really improving his coloring-in-the-lines skills. Kate only cut herself once with the scissors this semester.* It was a colossal waste of time.

"Good. You have glitter on your shirt," Garcia said and brushed past her. Finally on the other side of the school building, Sophie spotted her closest friend on the faculty, Nora-Ann Crane, dressed in an orange neon vest, standing at her bus-duty post.

"One day more." Sophie belted out the ballad from *Les Miz* as she joined Nora-Ann.

"Maybe forever," Nora-Ann said.

"What are you talking about?"

Nora-Ann pulled Sophie in close. "I heard Garcia talking about budget cuts. Who do you think is going to be first on the chopping block? I teach yoga!"

Sophie was startled. She complained about her day job frequently, but she never imagined leaving it before she could support herself as a professional artist. If budget cuts were indeed coming, the arts programming would be slashed right along with yoga. The other art teacher, Winner Baker, had far more seniority than she did.

"Well that sucks," Sophie said. "Did you hear anything else?"

"Garcia is meeting the superintendent over the summer to go over numbers. I'll have to move back in with my mom. She just got her seventh cat." Nora-Ann moaned. Sophie considered who she would move in with if she could no longer afford the rent for the fourth-floor walk-up she currently shared with three roommates. Ravi and she hadn't broached the subject of moving in together yet. Laura and Doug's house in Jersey was tiny and too far from her studio. Maybe Matthew and Beth's antiseptic condo in the city? She couldn't remember if they had an extra room.

"Stop. We don't know anything for sure. Maybe we'll get more scoop at Survivor. I have to get to the studio now. See you tomorrow," Sophie said and headed toward the subway, suddenly feeling a hell of a lot more pressure to finish the painting she was working on.

She was ten paces from the subway steps when Ronaldo called out from behind the maintenance shed. "Glitter again?"

She threw up *mea culpa* hands. "Shots on me tomorrow night."

"I'm bringing Rosa. She wants to meet the person responsible for the sparkles on our couch."

"She's a good woman, your wife."

"Your man coming?"

"I'll ask him tonight," Sophie said.

"When's he gonna put a ring on it? How long have you two been dating anyway? I had three kids by the time I was your age." Sophie eyed the cartoonish five-person bumper sticker on his nearby pickup truck.

"First of all," Sophie said, drawing her lips into a dramatic *O*, "you don't know how old I am. And, second, you sound like my mother. *When's he gonna propose? You're not getting any younger.*"

"Your mother is a smart lady," Ronaldo said.

Was. She *was* a smart lady, Sophie thought. "Thanks again for your help. No glitter until October next year. My solemn vow."

"Anything for you, kiddo," Ronaldo said with a salute. "Looking forward to meeting the lucky guy tomorrow."

Her boyfriend, the "lucky guy," was a sculptor. A home goods store in Williamsburg sold his pieces for triple digits. He also sold a number of works directly through his website. That income, plus the fact that he lived and worked rent-free on the top floor of his parents' townhouse on the Upper West Side, allowed him to pursue his art full-time. She wished Ravi was more satisfied with his career, but he measured himself against the superstars. In contrast, it filled Sophie with childlike wonder—and a pang of longing—each time he told her about a sale.

Anytime he drank too much, Ravi was prone to wax on about their future as a power duo in the art world. Sophie happily indulged the fantasy of their works up for auction together at Sotheby's. When the haze of alcohol cleared, Ravi would pull the plug. "I'm already over the hill in the art world," he would mutter. Sophie refrained from pointing out that she was thirty-five to his thirty-two and routinely picking clumps of Elmer's glue from under her fingernails. She chose to forgive his tone deafness. Two of her three siblings were married and, from observation (most recently at her mother's unveiling), Sophie surmised it could be useful to be a bit deaf and a bit blind when it came to relationships.

AN HOUR LATER, SOPHIE ARRIVED AT HER COWORKING SPACE, SHART, or the Shared Home for ARTists, in Bushwick. It was located in an industrial building with a crumbling brick exterior and a rotating cast of homeless men gathered out front. Sophie handed a few singles from her wallet to the most sober-looking in the group and stepped inside, inhaling the familiar scent of paints, wet clay and wood shavings. As usual in the evening hours, the coworking space was abuzz. Most of the tenants held day jobs and used the after hours for their personal work.

Renewed by a meditation on the G train, during which she was neither groped nor mugged, she felt ready to work. She was rarely energetic in June, when the kids at school were practically feral and squeezed every last ounce of patience from her. Pushing aside Nora-Ann's warning of budget cuts, Sophie instead focused on the telltale tingle in her fingertips that signaled she was in the zone.

Walking to her station, she passed Pierre, who painted scenes of the French countryside on porcelain tiles. She tapped lightly on his wall.

"Hey, Pierre, I would appreciate it if you didn't take my paints without asking first," Sophie said.

Rather than deny it, he made a haughty face and said, "Zis is SHART. Zat means a *shared* space for artistes."

"Well, in English, a 'shart' is a fart that comes out with a little sh—," Sophie retorted but stopped herself from explaining. She walked on, making a mental note to buy a padlock for her supplies.

Farther down the hall was Victoria, a menacing figure who utilized bodily fluids and the occasional solid in her multimedia works. Sophie grumbled in vain to management, four permanently stoned recent college grads who believed every problem could be solved by tapping a keg.

Aside from Pierre and Victoria, most of the artists on Sophie's floor were pleasant and inspiring to work alongside. Florina, a landscape photographer from California, shared juicy stories about the posh weddings she shot on the weekends for extra cash. Andy, who drew with charcoals, taught elementary school by day like Sophie. They swapped tips on how to avoid germs and commiserated over how exhausting it was to work on their art after the school day.

When she reached her "studio"—as if three plywood walls and crappy ventilation warranted that name—she noticed a group of out-of-place-looking men gathered at the graffiti wall, huddled over floor plans. She was reminded of the time her brother Matthew showed up in a suit and tie to an outdoor art fair in Woodstock, New York, where Sophie was exhibiting. These fellows looked equally out of place at SHART.

"What's with the men in black?" she asked her studio neighbor, Yolanda, who was puffing on an e-cigarette while waiting for her paint to dry.

"Girl, we're in trouble," Yolanda said, motioning Sophie to enter her workspace. Sophie noted Yolanda's steady progress on her self-portrait, intended as a commentary on aging. From forehead to chin, she gradually increased her age, an ombre effect of time. Sophie was impressed by her skillful execution and clever idea, but mostly, she was jealous of Yolanda's progress. "Those guys are from Wall Street." Yolanda stuck her pierced tongue out toward the graffiti wall.

"Did they get lost on the way to Peter Luger?" Sophie asked. Often the only reason the suit-and-tie types came to Brooklyn was to eat at the fabled steakhouse.

"You wish. The frat bros are going into partnership with these guys. The good news is they plan to keep the building as a workspace for artists. The bad news is that they are making improvements. That's code for raising our rent."

The grilled cheese Sophie ate earlier did a loop-de-loop around her stomach. She was already stretched thin. And if Nora-Ann's intelligence indeed meant she could be laid off, any increase in rent would mean she'd have to leave SHART immediately. She had practically peanuts in savings.

"Well, shit," Sophie said to Yolanda, who was already back to work at her canvas.

Sophie studied her own work in progress. It was the first in what she hoped would be a series of paintings capturing New York City landmarks at sunset when the steel, brick and asphalt metropolis was cast in rainbow hues. Her unique twist was including a Disney princess in each painting, posed ironically. She had already drawn the series in a sketchbook—now she had to bring those drawings to life on canvas. Her summers on LBI had endeared the golden hour of sunset to her. Frankly, she was too intimidated to paint the Jersey Shore sunset. The view from the back porch of her family's home was so special to her, so precise in her mind's eye, she worried she wouldn't do it justice. It was hard to believe that view would soon belong to another family. The house, maybe her job, her studio . . . so many things might be in her rear view soon.

The Vessel at Hudson Yards was the first landmark she was transferring to canvas. Sophie was mesmerized by the beehive-shaped attraction which drew scores of tourists. Several people had jumped to their deaths from the top. The unexpected darkness lurking within the architecturally dazzling structure made Sophie eager to paint it. In her painting, titled *Look at this Stuff*, Princess Ariel was leaning over one of the Vessel's reflective railings wearing a ripped concert T-shirt and her signature iridescent fishtail.

"I love it."

Sophie turned toward the voice and saw that one of the suits had approached her booth. He was maybe fifty, with kind eyes looking out from behind tortoiseshell glasses.

"It's not done yet," Sophie said, flustered. It was one thing for her fellow artists to see her work in progress. They shared a tortured, it's-never-good-enough undercurrent that both crippled and propelled them. But a civilian?

"Well, I like what you have so far. I work at Hudson Yards in one of those huge office towers. I see the Vessel every day but never really see it, you know? I'm Tom, by the way."

"Sophie." She extended her hand, and though it was splattered with gold paint, he took it without hesitation. She caught Yolanda watching them and remembered she ought to be chilly to this corporate intruder, but it was rather difficult on the heels of his praise.

"All our friends are into NFTs these days, but there's nothing like the real thing." Tom produced a card from his wallet and placed it on Sophie's worktable. "Will you let me know when it's done? I'd love to buy it for my wife for her birthday. It would be perfect for the library in our apartment."

Tom had friends who invested in trendy digital art. He lived in an apartment with a library! She wished she could tell her mother, who worked as the town librarian for decades and was an unabashed bibliophile. Sophie glanced back at her representation of Princess Ariel. *Girl, you're moving somewhere fancy.*

"I definitely will." She wondered how much she could charge. Based on his impeccable suit and library in residence, Tom could cough up enough for her to cover three months of increased rent at SHART, six if she was gutsy enough.

"Is your wife also interested in self-portraiture that subverts the male gaze while also celebrating female sexuality?" Sophie and Tom turned to face Yolanda, who had slunk into Sophie's cube.

"Afraid not," Tom said, appearing sheepish. "But good luck." He smiled at Sophie. "Don't forget to call me. I don't want anyone else snapping it up."

Snapping it up? That was a laugh. If only Tom knew how little experience she had in such transactions. While a student at the Rhode Island School of Design, she donated a few paintings to local charity events to be auctioned or raffled off. The well-heeled guests raised their paddles or threw a ticket into the fishbowl because it was de rigueur at such events. She had a painful memory of learning that the couple who had won her painting at a charter school benefit had left it behind in the coat room.

"You should have asked him about the rent," Yolanda hissed

after Tom left. A FaceTime from Ravi saved Sophie from responding. She answered and smiled when she saw Iris, Ravi's greyhound, splayed on her boyfriend's lap. She'd like to have a dog, but there was no way she could afford a walker or the vet bills.

"Hey, babe. I have good news," Ravi said. Sophie took in his sexy, crooked-toothed smile. Why had she and her siblings spent a combined twelve years with incarcerated teeth when imperfection looked this good?

"Me too." Sophie lowered her voice, noticing Tom and company were still present. "Well, good news and bad news. But you go first."

"How do you feel about spending July Fourth weekend in Nantucket? A group of emerg—" Ravi stopped mid-sentence. The phrase *emerging artist* did not sit well with him. He wanted to be a household name, at least in households with a certain level of disposable income. "I met a gallerist arranging an artists' retreat on Nantucket. She's putting everyone up at this cute B&B. We can chill on the beach, drink good wine and network the shit out of the place."

"That sounds heavenly," Sophie said, meaning everything but the networking part. "But Nantucket? I don't think they do Jews or brown people there. It's for blondes." Part of growing up at the Jersey Shore necessitated hating other summer enclaves.

"Your brother is blonde," Ravi said.

"We don't think Noah's actually our blood relative," Sophie joked. "You know what I mean. Nantucket is hoity-toity. Next you'll be suggesting we go to the Hamptons."

"The Hamptons were good enough for Jackson Pollock. Why don't you focus on eating fresh oysters *avec moi* instead of worrying what your Jersey Shore friends will think of you experimenting?"

Sophie laughed. Ravi made sunning on a different beach sound as scandalous as swapping sexual partners.

"It's not just the Jersey Shore. It's LBI. The best part. I can't go, anyway. I'll be down the shore with my family for the holiday."

"I know July Fourth was your mom's favorite holiday," Ravi said, his voice dropping appropriately. "That was my first time eating barbecued brisket. This is a great opportunity though. Don't you think your family would understand?"

"That was two summers ago. The brisket . . ." Sophie's voice croaked. Last summer the family spent the holiday sitting shiva, hearing one Sylvia story after another from the many people whose lives she touched. "It's not just about being together. I need to help pack up the house."

Sophie and her siblings were still in disbelief that the house would no longer be theirs. There was a memory behind every sunbeaten curtain, a story buried in each sandy carpet fiber. She could hear her family's laughter and smell the ocean when she was still a mile from exit 63 on the Garden State Parkway. But their father had been firm in his decision. He said he couldn't manage the upkeep any longer, both financially and otherwise. It was true that charging a cell phone and running a blow dryer simultaneously could short-circuit the entire house. That their home lived to tell the story of Hurricane Sandy was nothing short of a miracle.

"The closing is at the end of July and packing is going to be hell. I wouldn't say my mother was a hoarder, but she definitely didn't have enough interaction with the trash in her lifetime."

Ravi chuckled. "I'm aware. I got hit in the head by a shoebox when I opened the coat closet. Why don't you see if you can go the weekend before to help pack and then you can come to Nantucket with me." He paused and Sophie listened to Iris's labored panting. "I want great things for both of us."

She knew she ought to swoon, but something gave Sophie pause.

Maybe she wasn't romantic by nature. Maybe she didn't want to jinx her good luck. Maybe, maybe, maybe. The word swirled around her brain like a swizzle stick.

"Come on, Soph," Ravi said. "Just say fuck it and come to Nantucket."

Could she skip out on the family weekend? She imagined lying on a fluffy beach towel while Ravi rubbed SPF 100 on her back—she was a redhead after all—and day-drinking Negronis at an oceanfront bistro instead of unearthing Manischewitz a decade past its expiration date.

"Let me text my siblings. I'll call you back," Sophie said. She opened the Fantastic Foursome chat. Their mother nicknamed her children the Fantastic Foursome when Noah was still a baby. Sophie liked knowing the name would live in perpetuity carved into the marble of Sylvia's headstone. The affectionate moniker made the Jacobson kids sound like a superhero squad, which they adored as children and appreciated the irony of when they got older. Noah created an icon for the group chat, a superhero cape with the letters *FF* and a Jewish star.

> I'm not sure I can make it to LBI for the 4th . . . major opportunity for me (🎨🖌️🖼️) same weekend.

Sophie reread the text and exhaled as she hit send, her sharp breath sending a drip of wet paint careening down her canvas.

As she waited for the first sibling to reply, she gave herself a pep talk. Packing would be so exhausting there would be little time for family bonding. Nobody was counting on her to run the show. Organization was Laura's domain. Noah, the only Jacobson capable of running a mile without passing out (some superhero squad they made), could maneuver the heavy furniture, even if he bellyached the entire time about losing the house. And if Matthew wasn't stuck on work calls, a big if, he would provide another set of useful hands. Nobody would even miss her.

Sophie's phone pinged.

LAURA

R u fucking kidding me?

NOAH

Last wknd in house together!!!! U have to come

MATTHEW

Even I'm coming and I'm drowning in work

SOPHIE

Was just joking. Sheesh. Already tasting the Bird & Betty's

LAURA

Not funny

Sophie had clearly miscalculated. She called Ravi back. "Nantucket's a no-go. Major guilt trip from the sibs."

"That's a bummer but I promise to brag about your paintings the entire weekend," Ravi said. "So what was your news?"

"I'll start with the good. I may have sold my Vessel painting. Some dude with a library in his apartment wants to buy it. The bad news is that he's part of a group that might be buying SHART and raising our rents. Which will be especially hard considering Nora-Ann said our school is going through budget cuts, so who knows if I'll keep my day job."

"You could move in with me," Ravi said.

Her heart skipped a beat. "That's not why I—I wasn't saying it because . . . you know—"

"Don't answer now," Ravi said. "Why don't we swing by Franz's show and get some champagne with Lupita. If we have time, we can hit the *ARTnews*—" Iris's barking escalated and drowned out Ravi. He had endless energy to network in person and online. Sophie's social media presence was ghostlike, her attendance at openings spare. Fortunately, a SHART pal had dragged her to the gallery show of a mutual friend and that's where Sophie met Ravi. Sometimes it paid to leave the house. If only leaving the house in New York *actually* paid; excursions on the town were always a wallet drain.

"It's a date," she said. When she looked down at her phone, there were eight new messages on the Fantastic Foursome chat, most of them food-related. Her siblings planned to eat their way through the holiday weekend. Laura wanted the saltwater taffy at Country Kettle Fudge. Matthew was craving the lobster gnocchi at Black-Eyed Susans. Noah said they should order pizza at Bird and Betty's and play cornhole while they waited.

Sophie had no appetite. She reviewed the dizzying events of the past twenty-four hours. She was possibly out of a job. Out of her studio. About to say goodbye to her family home. She might have sold her first large-scale painting, if she had time and space to finish it. Her boyfriend asked her to move in with him out of nowhere, but maybe only because he felt obligated. Still, it couldn't hurt to feign enthusiasm for the family weekend. She picked up her phone to text her siblings.

I want butter pecan ice cream at skipper dipper after I demolish u all in mini golf 🤙

FANTASTIC FOURSOME 🧑‍🦲 🧑‍🦲 ✡ 🧑‍🦲 🧑‍🦲

SOPHIE

Did anyone else get a text from Myrna Shapiro?

LAURA

I did. WTF? She said Mom owes her sixty cents from their last game

MATTHEW

Who is Myrna Shapiro?

NOAH

Mom's canasta friend. You don't remember Myrna, Betty and Arlene?

SOPHIE

omg eww arlene. She yelled at me for being too loud while they played

LAURA

She accused me of cheating and i wasn't even playing

NOAH

Arlene's a good player. She counts the sevens

LAURA

Creepy u know that

NOAH

Whatever

MATTHEW

What did Myrna want

SOPHIE

"Just checking in"

LAURA

She asked me if we're having people over for the 4th. And the sixty cents thing which i'm praying is a joke

NOAH

We should invite people

MATTHEW

Def not. Beth and I are swamped at work. Need to be in and out

NOAH

That's what she said

LAURA

Huh?

NOAH

It's a joke

SOPHIE

The sixty cents?

NOAH

Nevermind. C u guys next week

2

Laura

LAURA JACOBSON COHEN WINCED AS THE KNIFE SLIPPED AND pierced the skin of her thumb. The cut was superficial but stung nonetheless. She licked the trickle of metallic-tasting blood. A nick was unusual after two decades of carving strawberry fans and kiwi stars for school lunches. Laura had not inherited her mother's cooking skills, to both her and Sylvia's chagrin. Everything she made benefited from a generous sprinkling of salt and the free flow of condiments. At least she was a pro at whittling fruits. Usually. Laura retrieved a Band-Aid from the first-aid kit and resumed hacking away at a ripe pineapple. She couldn't help thinking that she wouldn't have nicked herself if she could afford the high-quality Wüsthof knives instead of the knockoff Voosthofs.

The rumble of a hair dryer upstairs confirmed Hannah was up. Her younger daughter's beauty routine was a daily assault on the house. Pungent spray tans, sticky lip glosses, noisy dryers—eighteen-year-old Hannah beautified like an animal marking her territory. Laura would miss the sensory overload when Hannah left for college in the fall. At least she had the entire summer to spend with her baby. Emma, Hannah's sister, was leaving in two days for an internship on an organic farm in Vermont. She wished Emma would stick around longer, but Laura was accustomed to her eldest's independent ways. Emma and Hannah, only sixteen months apart, were close despite their differences. Emma packed herself for sleepaway camp and counted the days until she got there; Hannah cried every night from homesickness. Emma created a "life goals" poster that she hung over her bed; Hannah had a poster of Justin Bieber until recently. Still, the girls cuddled to watch movies. They exchanged knowing glances that might as well have been a secret language. Laura liked to think she was as close to her own sister, Sophie, though she was feeling less than charitable toward her since Sophie tried to bail on LBI.

Laura shook her phone to life and scrolled back to reread Sophie's text on their chat, shaking her head in disbelief. Laura had expected Matthew to bail. He and stuck-up Beth would claim their jam-packed schedule of conference calls and whatever else fancy-schmancy lawyers did prohibited them leaving their desks. Noah, her baby brother (ten years between them) wouldn't bail, but that was because he had nowhere else to go. Sophie though? That stung, worse than the slip of the knife. Didn't she recognize that as the female half of the Fantastic Foursome, she and Laura had to pick up the slack where the men disappointed? Especially with the gaping hole left by their mother's passing.

Fortunately, Sophie had backed down immediately. Hannah would have been especially bummed if her aunt didn't come. Laura's girls shared a special bond with their aunt Sophie, which typically manifested in eye rolls when Laura did something uncool, like chastising their short skirts or suggesting the girls read a book. Yelling "Your grandmother was a librarian!" did little to convince Laura's girls that anything interesting existed outside of their cell phones.

Laura heard the hair dryer quiet. She eyed her watch and frowned. Her daughter was going to be late for her first day lifeguarding at the Westfield town pool. And for what? Her hair would bloom into the signature Jacobson-Cohen frizz the moment it contacted humidity. When Laura was a lifeguard at the LBI Foundation pool, some twenty-plus years ago, she learned quickly it was a tight braid or disaster. Now that Laura and Hannah were done with applications and were enrolled at George Washington University (the "royal we" appropriate since applying to college had been a collective endeavor), Hannah had a relaxed summer ahead. She'd earn a decent wage lifeguarding from nine to three and hang with her friends in the evenings. Hannah promised to eat dinner at home at least once a week. Laura knew from experience that they'd have a ton of shopping to do in the weeks leading up to college. Extra-long twin sheets, shower caddies, wall decor, a humidifier, a reading lamp, a rug for the foot of the bed, not to mention the new wardrobe she was sure Hannah would demand—they'd be combing the stores for weeks. She couldn't wait to get to IKEA. Laura was wistful recalling her visit with Emma. Hannah didn't yet know how much fun inexpensive Swedish cabinetry could be. This time Laura wouldn't let Doug attempt assembly of the Billy bookcase. The only thing worse than an unhandy husband is an unhandy husband who believes he's handy.

The toaster dinged and Laura pincered the piping hot bagel carefully, avoiding a second hand injury. From the fridge she pulled the chive cream cheese, Hannah's favorite, but held off spreading it so it didn't melt.

"Han," she bellowed up the stairs. Doug was out of town and Emma was a sound sleeper, so Laura could yell freely.

Hannah bounded down in jean shorts and a GW cropped tee, her shiny brown hair pin-straight and reflecting the rays pouring through the skylight. Her dewy makeup was flawless. Laura and Doug were still waiting for Hannah to find a passion beyond TikTok eyeshadow tutorials.

"This for me?" Hannah grabbed her plate before Laura had time to embellish it with pineapple flowers.

"Don't you have to wear the lifeguard tank?" Laura cast a wary glance at Hannah's getup.

Through a mouthful of bagel, Hannah said, "So . . . Mom, we need to talk." Seeing Laura's obvious panic, she added, "Relax, it's good."

The reassurance took away Laura's immediate concerns: drugs and pregnancy. But it was her experience of raising teenage girls that the phrase "We need to talk" was rarely followed by something that both the speaker and the listener would be happy about.

"Okay," Laura said, her neck suddenly prickled with sweat.

"I'm not going to be a lifeguard this summer. I got an amazing opportunity and I accepted."

Laura was stunned. Hannah never made major moves without talking to her first. She wanted her daughter to be more independent, like Emma. She knew Hannah ought to be able to get a meningitis shot without holding her mother's hand in the pediatrician's office. By seventeen, Emma had traveled to three continents through exchange programs. She was a serial monogamist, currently entwined with a grad student named Tomas she claimed she would marry. Hannah had always been needier and less mature. She lasted all of four days at sleepaway camp; Laura drove five hours to New Hampshire in the dark to scoop her up. She wouldn't entertain applying to a college that required an airplane ride. Neither Laura nor Doug minded. The cost of air travel was an added expense they didn't need. Two college tuitions at once was enough to make them sweat. The Cohens didn't qualify for financial aid, but they were hardly rich. Neither daughter wanted to go to Rutgers, the New Jersey state school where Laura and Doug met. They said Laura would show up at their dorm every weekend to check in. That was ridiculous. Maybe once a month. Emma was entering her sophomore year at Colgate, where she'd earned a modest academic scholarship, and Hannah was off to start GW in the fall. Both girls were four hours away, apparently a sufficient buffer to keep maternal visits at bay.

"Mom, are you listening?" Hannah asked. Laura wiped away the dot of cream cheese above her daughter's lip with the back of her thumb. How much more obvious could it be that she was needed?

"I'm sorry. Why aren't you lifeguarding?"

Hannah readjusted her sitting position so that one foot was folded underneath her bottom and the other bent practically behind her back. Laura had once been limber like that, but her Gumby days were ancient history. Her back perpetually ached from doing laundry and she hadn't worn heels higher than an inch and a half in a decade.

"So you know how I've been Snapping with my roommate, right? At first I thought Amaya was kind of annoying, but then I discovered we have some mutuals and I found out she's actually cool. Anyway, she's doing a program in DC tutoring high school juniors, helping them with college applications and test prep. These are kids from low-performing high schools where, like, not everyone goes to college and, like, has the opportunities that I had—"

Laura put a hand on her daughter's bobbing knee. "That sounds very worthwhile. But you're committed to—"

"Amaya's older brother did it. He got paired with this awesome girl and they even hooked—" Hannah stopped short. "He helped her write her essay and she got into, like, a dozen schools on scholarship."

Laura puffed out her cheeks as Hannah practically vibrated with enthusiasm. This was the passion Laura wanted to see in her daughter—she just wanted it to emerge at the end of the summer, after eight weeks of family dinners, shopping and, yes, even Laura handwashing Hannah's chlorine-soaked bathing suits.

"We still have so much to do," Laura said. I do at least, she thought. *Print coupons for Walmart. Prepare your favorite meal for your last dinner at home. Choose a color scheme for your dorm room.* She had to give Hannah "the talk" about campus safety, never drinking from an open container, and being vigilant about taking the pill (one forgotten day and that's how Emma came to exist). Then there was maintaining good nutrition. Getting enough sleep. Laura still hadn't googled Hannah's roommate to make sure she wasn't a serial killer. "When do you need to be there?"

"Today."

"Today?" The kitchen tilted off its axis and began to spin. "Are you crazy? I don't think you have enough clean underwear to get you through the week. And we're supposed to visit Grandpa Leo for July Fourth in Beach Haven. You love the shore. Aunt Sophie is coming."

Hannah slid off the stool and Laura took in just how little clothing was covering her daughter's body. She added rape whistle and pepper spray to her mental shopping list.

"I know this is sudden, but it's an amazing opportunity to help people. You know how that's always been Emma's thing more than mine? The environment, animal rights, blah blah. Now I found something I care about. And Amaya says because we'll be on campus early we get to choose our dorm room."

"What about your boss? The innocent children of Westfield will be left to drown because you want a bigger room?"

"Mom! No one is drowning. Donna said she'll be fine for this week. She was overstaffed anyway in case someone had a change of plans. Like *moi*." Hannah cupped her chin like Shirley Temple charming a photographer. "Amaya's dad is going to drive us to school and help us get set up."

"He's probably a creep," Laura said, but Hannah was already FaceTiming with a guy whose voice Laura didn't recognize and, just like that, her active role of mother was kaput. Hannah's dirty plate sat abandoned on the counter. Soon it would join the others Laura had to wash in the sink before she went grocery shopping. Some retirement party.

"What about your dorm room? We haven't bought anything yet." Laura cast a Hail Mary. "I was going to take you to Bloomingdale's in the city for new clothes. Saks too." She wasn't, but now she would. "And sheets. You need sheets."

"Oh my God, Mom, seriously? Ever heard of Amazon?"

MINDY WEISSBERG SCRUNCHED HER FACE IN CONCERN WHEN Laura ordered a second glass of sauvignon blanc at lunch.

"Laura, didn't you drive here?"

"I'll be fine." She waved Mindy off. They were eating on the patio of an Italian place in a strip mall, and Laura assured her friend she'd browse the stores until the alcohol worked its way out of her system.

"Besides, as you know, I'm in no rush to get home." Laura tore a large piece of focaccia, searching for comfort in crusty bread seasoned with rosemary twigs and salt crystals.

"Can't you see this as a good thing?" Mindy said, raising her sunglasses to look at Laura. "No responsibility for the summer. You and Doug can relax. Sleep in. Not worry about keeping the fridge stocked or having your head handed to you because you said the wrong thing. I'm jealous. Zoe asked me to pack her lunch every day for work because the snack bar at the pool isn't up to her standards. Oh, and it needs to be vegan."

Laura wondered if it was because Mindy, her closest mom friend, had two younger children at home that she found the task of making daily lunch so reprehensible. Laura wouldn't have minded six more weeks of lunch assembly, even if she had to source cashew cheese. "I guess," Laura said. "It's just going to be a huge adjustment. Doug and I haven't lived alone since college, and even then we were surrounded by friends."

Mindy leaned across the table with a conspiratorial smile. "Think about all the sex you're gonna have. You won't even have to close the bedroom door."

Laura shifted in her chair, hoping Mindy couldn't intuit the mental calculation she was running. How long had it been since she and Doug had last had sex? A month? No, there was no way they had slept together in June. Laura was crazed with Hannah's graduation and the six trips they made to tailor her prom dress. It couldn't have been in May when Doug had an awful stomach bug that lingered for weeks; he'd spent days on the toilet and had slipped her Mother's Day card from under the bathroom door.

"C'mon . . . you know I'm right." Mindy poked Laura's arm with a giant breadstick and winked.

"Of course," Laura said feebly. "Gimme that." A bawdier version of Laura that existed only in her mind would have suggestively licked the breadstick before taking a bite.

Laura had always been prudish about discussing sex, even with Mindy, with whom she shared zoomed-in pictures of varicose veins. The moment the topic came up at book club, and it usually did within fifteen minutes since no one ever had time to read the book (Sylvia would have poo-pooed that excuse), she would quickly shift the topic or move to another cluster of women talking about things she felt more comfortable with—how to find a trustworthy driving instructor or where to buy organic broccoli that didn't cost $5.99 a bunch like at Whole Foods. Having successfully dodged the topic for more than a decade, she had no idea how much sex was "normal" to have.

She and Doug were due for quality time. Their lives ran on parallel tracks, two trains barreling full steam ahead toward some indeterminate finish line. They rarely raised their voices, just bickered at a simmering volume over how early to get to the airport or Doug's refusal to follow Waze. And they fought over money, a perennial source of tension. Money might as well have been a third person in their marriage, creating the least sexy ménage à trois imaginable. Laura and Doug had different spending priorities. He wanted to update their audiovisual system and subscribe to every streaming service. She wanted to stop staring at the damn cracks in their ceiling and using a medicine cabinet with a broken handle. They lived in a land of "or" instead of "and." A new roof *or* finish the basement. A vacation *or* re-sod the grass. Just once, Laura wanted to experience what "and" felt like.

"What you need is vacation sex." Mindy smacked her hand on the table, sending the silverware rattling. She said it like it was a brand, like Old Navy leggings or a KitchenAid blender. *Vacation Sex. On sale for a limited time only.*

"Doug and I are spending the Fourth of July at the shore, helping my dad clean out the house. We could go early and make a little getaway out of it. Stay at an inn. Originally, I thought Hannah would be with us, but now, well. Hopefully rates won't be too high."

She remembered the last trip she and Doug were meant to take five years ago with Mindy and her husband and some other couples in town. It was a no-kids getaway to Nashville. Laura didn't love country music and she'd look moronic in cowboy boots, but she liked the people going and was excited to dump the girls at her parents'. Then, a month before the trip, a storm blew through the Northeast and blew through a chunk of their roof as well. There went the money for Nashville. The Cohens had gracefully bowed out, citing Doug's work as the excuse.

"Love it," Mindy said. "We might be there too. Harry and I want to use his mom's place in Ship Bottom. But not if she wakes up from her coma first."

"Mindy!" Laura chastised her, but she adored her friend's irreverence. "I'm going to tell Doug the plan tonight when he gets home from Tucson."

"What's in Tucson?"

"Dental convention." Laura felt the need to add, "He doesn't mind these things."

Truthfully, Doug seemed to relish the break from routine. He always attended the American Dental Association annual meeting, bounding off to a Courtyard Marriott in Anytown, USA, with a spring in his step, returning a few days later with a tote full of Crest and Colgate swag. In the early days of their marriage, Laura tagged along, leaving the kids with her parents in East Brunswick or with Doug's folks in Morris Plains. While Doug listened to a lecturer speak about fiber-optic crowns and swapped tips on billing best practices, Laura sipped a wine spritzer at the hotel pool. She couldn't exactly remember why she stopped going. Had Emma gotten the flu one year? Had the sponsors stopped covering partners' meals? Was remembering anything clearly after age forty this hard for everyone?

Mindy smiled. She had a mouth of poorly executed veneers that gave her face an equine quality. In their less-charitable moments, Doug and Laura called her National Velvet. They had their inside jokes. They had special moments together, giggling while watching Jay Leno in bed after the kids went to sleep. Although, come to think of it, hadn't Jay Leno been off the air for almost a decade? Was it Conan now? Jimmy Fallon? A Jersey Shore getaway sans the kids would be the kick-start they needed.

Mindy's phone dinged.

"Oh, for fuck's sake. It's Zoe. She needs me to bring her tampons because she can't find any in the employee bathroom. I'll Venmo you for lunch. And if I don't see you before the Fourth . . ." Mindy lowered her voice and playfully smacked her lips together. "Enjoy your fuck fest."

LAURA STOOD NAKED IN HER AND DOUG'S SHARED CLOSET, "GW Mom" sweatpants puddled at her ankles. She shivered as she surveyed her choices. A row of abandoned denim hung on the lower metal rod. Half the pairs probably didn't fit or were totally outdated. She ought to drop the whole lot off at Goodwill. Laura favored cotton pants in neutral colors with elastic waistbands. They matched everything and were perennially fashionable by suburban housewife standards. Westfield, New Jersey, was a modest town and the only "fashion plates" were the whimsical cookie platters at book club. An array of blouses in floral patterns she couldn't remember being drawn to created a sartorial botanical garden on the upper rod. Choosing an outfit was proving more difficult than she expected. She started to feel silly for making an effort. Wasn't the point of marriage that you didn't have to try?

Doug would be walking in the door any minute from his flight. She slipped a scoop-neck top over her head and stepped into black jeans with enough stretch to almost qualify as leggings. Then she quickly glided a mascara wand through her lashes and applied shimmery gloss to her lips just as Doug's footsteps sounded in the entryway. Laura was nervous. It was the first time she could remember feeling anything toward Doug other than a desire to recite her to-do list and complain about the girls.

"Welcome home," she called out over the second-floor railing. Her voice sounded three octaves higher than normal and cracked on the third syllable.

"Thanks," he said, barely looking up. "I'm starving."

Laura joined him in the kitchen, feeling even more the fool for expecting Doug to notice anything different about her. She didn't exactly greet him in a negligee. Besides, Doug didn't realize today was the day their sex life got rejuvenated. For him it was just Thursday. Meatloaf night.

"How was Tucson?" she asked, watching Doug scarf down an apple and a yogurt, his go-to between-meal snack. He was as predictable as her period used to be before she hit perimenopause.

"Fine. The usual," Doug said, his mouth full.

"Learn anything new?" Laura leaned across the island and propped her elbows on the scuffed countertop, prepared to feign interest in biodegradable floss if necessary.

"Actually, yes. There's mounting evidence to suggest a daily serving of turmeric can be effective at preventing gingivitis. I'm going to tell my patients to add it to their diet."

"Wow," she said, hoping her enthusiasm sounded genuine. "I'll pick some up at the grocery store."

"How are you holding up?" Doug asked. He didn't have to explain that he was referring to Hannah's unexpected departure.

"Not too bad. She seems happy. The program hasn't started yet so I'm not sure why she was in such a rush to get down there. Probably some boy. Either way, she had to leave the nest sooner or later. I just wish it had been later." She toyed with the neckline of her top. "Want a drink or anything? I can pour you a scotch."

Doug's spoon froze midair. Finally, she had his attention. This wasn't business as usual for the Cohens. Routines were being broken left and right.

He scratched his chin thoughtfully while Laura wondered if they even had scotch at home. "Nah, it'll just put me to sleep." He brought his spoon to the sink, rinsed it and placed it in the dishwasher. "But thank you."

As disappointment threatened to overtake her, Laura gave herself a metaphorical pinch. How many of her friends complained their husbands never cleaned up after themselves? That they weren't appreciative?

Doug's cell phone vibrated in his pocket, not exactly the action in his pants Laura had been hoping for.

"I have to take this," he said, looking at the screen. Laura could hear his voice faintly as he moved down the hallway toward the other end of their house. "I'll see if I can fit you in tomorrow . . . Yes, yes, I will . . . Feel better." Then he laughed, a real hearty chuckle. Had his patient made a joke? A priest, a rabbi and an imam walk in for a root canal?

She listened to him climb the stairs, the sound of his carry-on clattering against the treads. If their house wasn't already falling apart, she would chastise him for scratching the wood. Instead, she followed him upstairs a few minutes later.

Predictably, he was holding his electric toothbrush. He was meticulous about brushing after eating. Less predictably, he had undressed and had a towel wrapped around his waist.

"The plane was gross," he said. "Gotta rinse off."

Laura channeled Mindy's bawdiness as she poked her with the breadstick. *Here goes.* "Want company?"

"Are you serious?" It was hard to tell if he was amused or shocked. He ran his fingers through the salt-and-pepper hair that skimmed the rim of his glasses, ostensibly contemplating the offer.

"Yes," she said, wondering if this was the moment she was meant to start unzipping her jeans.

"I think I'm going to just quickly wash up. But, um, thanks." He pulled his glasses off, making her practically invisible to his legally blind eyes, and stepped into the stall. The ancient showerhead sputtered to life, drowning out the potential for further discussion.

For a hot second, Laura thought about updating Mindy on the flop. But what was Mindy supposed to do? Take her lingerie shopping? Instruct her in the art of seduction? Laura would sooner die of embarrassment. She had less-bawdy friends to confide in, but instead of calling them, she went back to the kitchen and grabbed a pint of mint chocolate chip from the freezer. After scraping off the freezer burn, Laura dropped a spoonful onto her tongue and sighed with pleasure. Who needed sex?

Doug came downstairs freshly showered, wearing running pants and a slim V-neck undershirt. When they first started dating—what felt like a lifetime ago—Laura was the looker between them. She had thick, wavy hair as a college coed, which lost luster and fullness with each pregnancy. The chestnut color faded with age. She maintained it with salon visits and used a drugstore coloring wand in between, but it seemed like a new gray hair emerged every time she blinked. Her skin sagged at the chin if she wasn't vigilant about keeping her neck taut. In contrast, her husband, who had been lanky and awkward throughout his twenties and thirties, had blossomed in middle age. He'd discovered exercise at forty and now filled out his clothing like a freshly pumped tire. He looked venerable, not old, with gray hair.

There was probably a brief period when she and Doug met on the ladder of attractiveness, as Laura hobbled down and Doug swiftly climbed. Maybe it happened while they were distracted by the implosion of Doug's second dental office in Springfield. Or when

Emma was being bullied in eighth grade and Laura could think of nothing but pummeling the twats tormenting her daughter. Doug wasn't demonstrative, one of those "you're so beautiful" gushing husbands. He'd said such things early on in their courtship and Laura had waved him off. She didn't need that kind of assurance back then. Now she wondered what he thought about her appearance. If he thought about it at all.

"Want?" She handed her spoon to Doug.

He accepted it, but stopped short as he was about to dive in. "I don't need it."

Laura returned the pint to the freezer, realizing she missed the comfort of Doug's once-pouchy stomach.

"So, I was thinking, since we have to get down the shore to help my dad, why don't we go early and make a little vacation out of it? I looked online and the Sea Shell has one room left. It's always a slow week at your office. We can go, like, three days early, before my siblings descend, and enjoy some R and R, just the two of us."

Doug looked up from his phone. "Sounds expensive."

What they could and couldn't afford trailed them like a stinky fart. "It's not that bad. And we can stay somewhere cheaper. Here, I'll show you." She went to grab her laptop from the kitchen, where the Tripadvisor page was open. Earlier in the day, she had gotten lost in the comments. *So romantic . . . Best anniversary trip . . . Peaceful and restorative . . . Worth every penny . . .*

"Laura, we need to talk."

She didn't recognize her husband's tone. The cut in her finger began to throb. Of course the slip of the knife was a bad omen—when was the last time she was that careless? We. Need. To. Talk. It was the second time in a week someone in her family had used that phrase.

"We do?"

"We do."

She should have known. His practice was in trouble again. Doug was normally a good sleeper. Thanks to his volcanic snoring, Laura could always tell when he was out. But ever since the dental clinic, SMILE, with the flashy sign visible from a block away and the all-white-leather-upholstered waiting room, opened in Westfield, Doug tossed and turned. SMILE offered thirty-minute whitening sessions you could schedule through an app. The hygienists featured in their ads looked like supermodels. Laura, wearing a baseball hat pulled low, had gone inside to check it out but fled when she spotted a patient of Doug's—a real Benedict Arnold—in the waiting room.

"I'll post some bad reviews for SMILE on Yelp. I can get the girls to do the same. Sophie and Noah too. Don't worry." Laura had always been a good problem solver. She wished the people in her life would take advantage of her services more often.

"It's not that," Doug said. "I'm not threatened by a factory cleaning teeth on an assembly line. Did you know they offer packages? Like at the car wash." He snorted.

Laura blanched. Clearly she had struck a nerve. A dental pun she might have expressed out loud if the mood was lighter.

"My practice is fine. That new X-ray machine cost me an arm and a leg and I'm dealing with a few insurance disputes, but my patients are loyal."

Not Benedict Arnold, Laura thought. If the problem wasn't financial, then . . .

She felt the weakness first in her knees, forcing her to clutch the kitchen counter for support. It rose to her stomach, which felt tingly like it did when the roller coasters her daughters forced her to ride climbed to the peak. And then the wooziness hit her head and her vision streaked with a terrifying aura. That tone of Doug's. It contained a note of something she'd never encountered before in their interactions. Pity.

He sat across from her and took her hand in his. She felt the clamminess of his palm, though that might have been her own. When had it mattered before, what was hers and what was his?

"I wasn't going to do this now. I figured when Hannah left at the end of summer. Or maybe I'd never say anything at all. Maybe I would feel differently. But hearing you talk about going away together . . ." Doug's voice trailed off.

Laura noticed he was pulling his wedding band on and off, a standard fidget of his, but at this moment it seemed telling.

"What are you saying?" she asked.

Doug fiddled with the salt shaker, spilling a few granules. That was known to be bad luck.

"Laura, I haven't been happy for a while. We've grown apart. You see that, don't you?" Doug removed his glasses, wiped the lenses with his T-shirt and replaced them, as if to convey that everything would be obvious to Laura if she was willing to see things clearly.

"You want to get a . . . a divorce?" Laura heard the way the D-word came out, like it was a federal crime. She might as well have said, *You want to commit murder?*

"No. Not at all," Doug said. He released her hand. "I was thinking a trial separation. Nothing formal."

"Nothing formal, I see. Casual dress for the implosion of our marriage?"

"C'mon, don't pick my words apart. I mean we don't even have to tell the kids. Laur, we've been together since we were kids. Got pregnant with Emma when we were only twenty-one."

Why was he reciting their history? As if she didn't know it better than he did. She was the one who puked every morning in the bathroom in the Rutgers dorm. She had a C-section scar with the texture of a raisin bisecting her lower abs from her nether region.

"We never got to be young," he went on. "To see who we are as individuals."

She was no longer hearing him, not the kind of hearing that involved processing and digesting. That was probably what listening was. And she wasn't capable. She thought, oddly, of her father's hearing aids, how sometimes no matter how much he adjusted them, words wouldn't penetrate.

"Who is she?" A kaleidoscope of gorgeous younger women in skimpy clothing suddenly blinded her, dental hygienists with bleached hair and fake tits wearing heels with their scrubs. Maybe it was the patient that had made him laugh earlier. Did she not mind his yogurt breath? Did she know he built up a nauseating volume of earwax during the winter months?

Doug shook his head. "There's no one else. It's not about that. Do you even know who you are without me and the kids? Don't you want to find out?"

"No!" she exclaimed. "I'm happy. I thought we were happy. We have a beautiful family. I don't need some self-indulgent midlife crisis the minute the kids are out of the house. Are you bored? Because that's not my fault! I suggest we do things. You're the one who says no. We can take up golf. Do you want that? We should have a hobby together."

"Golf!" Doug snickered. "Do you know how much a round of golf costs?"

She shrugged. He was missing the point. "Who cares?" she finally whispered.

"I care. You care. Do you remember what we did on our last date night?" He air-quoted "date night" and she braced herself. "We brought our laptops to the couch and reviewed our credit card bill. Sure, we had wine and sushi. But we spent the evening trying to figure out how to cut expenses."

"So what? That's real life. Grow up!"

Doug tugged at his shaggy hair. He was wearing it longer these days and it was working for him. Was this happening because he was better looking than her now?

"Laura, for our anniversary, you told me not to get you a gift. You said you just wanted two hours of my time to review the loan options for Hannah's tuition."

"And we found a great plan! Besides, you worry about money more than I do." What the hell was he complaining about? Hadn't they had sex after they signed up for the Sallie Mae loan with the three percent APR and deferred payback plan? She could swear they had.

"Laura. I repeat, I'm not asking for a divorce. I'm asking for a little time to myself. To think. To figure some shit out." He looked annoyed, his expression one of disbelief that she hadn't seen this coming a mile away.

Laura backed away abruptly and almost knocked over a kitchen stool. Doug grabbed it before it banged into a cabinet filled with ceramic mugs, most of them made by the girls over the years. Did he not care about drinking his coffee from the "#1 Dad" mug with the backward *D* anymore? Because Laura would be damned if he took anything but a suitcase of clothes with him if he left.

"Well, then you're not coming with me to Beach Haven for the Fourth. I don't want you around when we pack up the house. Clearly, you don't care about family anyway."

"That's not true," Doug said. "I'd like to be there. Your family is my family too. Don't you think you'll need me? Matthew will be on his phone the whole time. And Noah?"

Doug wasn't wrong. But if he came, could she possibly pretend things were normal between them when they went with the whole gang to get saltwater taffy and picked up their to-go order from Uncle Will's diner?

"I don't know, Doug. And right now I have to make dinner. We can't all just shirk our responsibilities, can we? By the way, we're having salmon, even though it's a Thursday. And I splurged on the organic."

FANTASTIC FOURSOME 🥷 🥷 ✡ 🥷 🥷

SOPHIE

Is Dairy King still open? Craving . . .

NOAH

The poor man's Dairy Queen is open. Arlene Katz's grandson is working there for the summer

SOPHIE

Why do u know so much about Mom's canasta friends

NOAH

I'm a friendly guy

MATTHEW

DK was my first job . . . I remember getting in so much trouble for dropping a scoop and putting it back on the cone

NOAH

That was MINE

MATTHEW

Well u didn't have to tell my boss

NOAH

I didn't! He saw. It doesn't seem to have hurt your career moneybags

SOPHIE

Yeah, seriously, M.

MATTHEW

Guess so. I miss my scooping days though. Laura—didn't you work there too?

NOAH

She did and she didn't charge me like you did, a-hole

SOPHIE

She charged me! WTF, Laura?

NOAH

Laura??? Does that mean im ur favorite?

SOPHIE

No chance. She felt bad for you because—ya know. Right, Laura?

SOPHIE

Laura, you dead?

NOAH

Um, Laura . . . we need to know who you like more

LAURA

Sorry. Been busy. See u guys tomorrow

3

Noah

"YOU KNOW," MRS. HARRISON SAID, STUBBING OUT THE REM-
nants of her skinny cigarette into an amber ashtray etched with exotic cats, "they don't call this place Loveladies for nothing."

Noah looked up from his client's iPhone, which he was in the
midst of repairing, and caught a cloud of her smoke in his mouth.
The sash of her silk robe was coming dangerously close to undone.

Rita Harrison, one of his tech-help regulars, had gotten logged
out of her Hotmail account for the second time that week. After
Noah entered three possible passwords, the phone had gone into
lockdown mode for thirty minutes. Which meant he too was in
lockdown. At least he charged by the hour. He could certainly use
the money.

"What was that?" Noah asked, his eye catching the red lipstick
stain on her coffee mug. He had refused a cup earlier, which had obviously displeased her, but he really didn't want the caffeine. Noah's
plan for after he wrapped up with Mrs. Harrison's phone was to return home, watch a little porn and take a good, long nap before his
family descended en masse.

"I said, there's a reason they call this town Loveladies. Do you
know what it is?" Mrs. Harrison set her coffee mug on the desk and
traced the lace trim of her robe with her index finger. Her nails were

pink and polished in a shiny coat that resembled car paint. He focused on the bird print on her robe. There was something avian about Mrs. Harrison herself, beyond the talon-like nails. Was it her nose?

"I don't," Noah said, even though he did. If Mrs. Harrison decided to tell the story of her hamlet's unusual name, it would eat up at least five minutes of the time remaining for her phone to unfreeze, and maybe spill over into charging her for another hour. Loveladies was one of the fancier neighborhoods on LBI and Mrs. Harrison owned one of the many mansions that lined the beach. The area was far tonier than Beach Haven, with houses spread out on generous portions of land and no noisy commercial district. Noah far preferred the vibes on his end of the island. To get to Loveladies meant taking a left once over the bridge to LBI; Beach Haven meant a right. The entire island was only eighteen miles long, but there were major differences depending on which way a person turned after the bridge. A reporter once said of the island's split: "It was a case of the haves and the have-mores."

"Because the women are lovely. And . . ." Mrs. Harrison paused to ensure she had his full attention. "They make excellent lovers." She placed a hand lined with bulbous veins on Noah's shoulder. "Isn't that something?"

It was something alright. "That's a cute theory," he said, standing to relieve himself of the light scratching of Rita's nails on his T-shirt. "But I'm pretty sure that's not the real story. There was a man called Thomas Lovelady. He owned an island in the bay and the area was named after him. This was, like, a hundred years ago or something. Maybe even earlier." He was no scholar, but every homeowner on Long Beach Island knew how Loveladies got its unusual name.

"Well that doesn't make sense," Rita said, looking perplexed. "'Lovelady' ends in a *Y*. And our town ends with *IES*. Why would they have made it plural? And if his name was Thomas, then surely they would have chosen to call this place Thomas Bay or something like that. I'm pretty certain I'm correct."

"You may be," he said, stopping short of agreeing with her. Rita was a steady customer and tipped generously. Her connections had him installing modems, organizing photos in the cloud and downloading software updates pretty consistently in the homes of her rich friends. Serving as a traveling IT provider on LBI was far better than any of his previous stabs at employment, which included selling office supplies (ironic given he'd never had an office job), assistant manager of a gym (fired for too much flirting) and customer service for Peloton (there he was a victim of layoffs, but Noah didn't miss the explosive tirades from the six a.m. spin class set). Doing tech repair, he could set his own hours and spend the bulk of his time in the fresh air, biking between clients and collecting cash for fixing the most basic technical issues. He couldn't count how many times his clients gushed, "You're a genius!" when all he'd done was a hard reset.

"So how do you feel about your family home being sold? I heard it went for over asking." Mrs. Harrison was as interested in gossip as she was in young flesh. Rita moved across the room and perched on a frilly sofa covered with tasseled throw pillows. Every type of jungle cat was represented in the decor; Noah considered making a joke about being allergic.

With her at a safe distance, Noah sank back into his chair. The thought of packing up twenty-five years' worth of books, photo albums and memorabilia, labeling boxes "Sophie's artwork," "Matthew's soccer trophies" and "Mom/Dad wedding pics" made his heart ache. And yet that was exactly what he would be doing for the next two days. A week later, the home would be subject to a final inspection and the new owners would retrieve the keys at the end of the month. Unless he had the guts to go through with The Plan.

Even if he did, he'd have to pretend everything was normal with his family over the weekend, which meant bubble-wrapping cherished items and sentencing them to oblivion in cardboard boxes.

"I'm sad," he admitted to Mrs. Harrison. There was no point in putting on a brave face. "We've made a lot of great memories there." He was tempted to list them. The night Matthew raced to answer the phone because a girl he liked was calling and he fell down the stairs and needed twenty stitches in his knee, but it all worked out because his crush was a candy striper in the hospital and they started dating. Or the time Sophie, maybe eleven at the time, decided to surprise their parents by painting a mural on their bedroom wall and their father grumbled the rest of the summer about the cost of re-painting. It was the place where Noah first held his niece Emma. Noah had many other firsts there. The Jersey Shore was where he learned to ride a bike. To swim. He smoked his first joint at fifteen behind Tuckers Tavern, where his best friend Joe was bussing tables for the summer. It was where he'd lost his virginity the summer after sophomore year of high school to the most beautiful girl he'd ever seen at that point, Lizzy Markowitz. They were now Instagram friends. Lizzy, still gorgeous, was married and expecting her first baby.

"I'm sorry, honey," Mrs. Harrison said softly. Noah could imagine laying his head in her lap. "About your mother too. She was such a nice woman. I always enjoyed chatting with her at temple. I'm a mahj player, not a canasta gal, so we didn't really interact all that much. But I loved the adorable little free library she put outside your house. Is that still there?"

"It is." The lending library at the edge of their property was Sylvia's brainchild when Noah was in high school. She'd paid the handyman at their temple to make it (it was essentially a wooden post with something that looked like a birdhouse on top, filled with books that neighbors could borrow and replace whenever they wanted).

There was always a "Sylvia Selection," which she marked with a yellow Post-it note, and that would be the first book snapped up. "It's not quite as up-to-date as when Mom oversaw it."

"I'll bring over some books," Mrs. Harrison said.

"That would be nice." He had misjudged this woman as a cougar. At most, she was part feline.

"By the way, Myrna Shapiro is very eager to get the end-of-summer card party at the temple going again. We all are. It was your mother who insisted on adding a room for mahj players. Boy, did she run a great event."

"She was a very capable person," Noah said. She even managed to teach him canasta despite the fact that he was math challenged, at least according to every school teacher he ever had.

"She was. I'm sure your family is having a tough time letting the house go."

Some more than others, he thought. But Noah had his reasons for the strong attachment. His siblings were already teens and tweens when his parents purchased the house in the late nineties. He was an "oops" baby, though his parents would never admit it, born six years after Sophie. And so he spent many summers in the house well after his siblings had gone off to college and visited only for the Fourth of July, Labor Day and the occasional weekend when they brought friends and only used the place as a crash pad. Noah's experience was entirely different.

While his father worked out of his North Caldwell accounting office during the week in the summer months, Noah and his mother parked themselves at the shore full-time. They would putter around the house together, playing cards, throwing jacks and building sandcastles right outside their front door. The Realtor who got the listing said that the house had "good bones." It sure did. His mother's bones. Her essence was practically the home's foundation. Many of the prospective buyers who'd checked out the property would say some version of, "We're planning to tear it down anyway." They might as well have stated plans to dig up Sylvia's body and dissect her.

"It's just too much for your father to maintain this property and his new place in Florida," Mrs. Harrison said.

She was right. Leo was firm that on his fixed income, composed of the pensions from his accounting firm and Sylvia's library job plus a modest boost from Social Security, he could only maintain one property. Noah had suggested refinancing the Jersey Shore property—he remembered Matthew's eyebrows climbing in surprise when he made the suggestion—but Leo had dismissed the idea outright. Besides despising financial risk, Leo lacked the capacity for the home's upkeep, especially from afar.

I'll take care of the house, Noah thought more than once about saying, but he could predict the reaction. It was true he'd been living there for a year and hadn't fixed the warped floorboard on the steep entry steps. Nor had he nailed down the loose shutters or repainted the mail slot. And that was just the exterior. The wallpaper inside was stringy and discolored from years of exposure to the sea air. The air-conditioning system was so erratic that the ground floor could be tropical while the upstairs arctic and then, lo and behold, the next day it would be the opposite.

Noah nodded.

"I heard he got a nice condo in Boca." Mrs. Harrison sighed. "I hope the new people moving into your family's place won't be . . . you know."

The LBI community was a tight-knit, trusting one, but a tad judgmental. For decades, families left their doors unlocked and literally borrowed sugar from each other, along with beach umbrellas, wagons and even substantial sums of money that were never in doubt of repayment. During and after the pandemic, an influx of new families started buying up the properties, raising property values while also changing the character of the place. Wall Street types were moving in, and with them came BMWs and loud cell phone conversations as they walked along Long Beach Boulevard. For the first time, reservations were needed for the more upscale restaurants. You couldn't go everywhere barefoot anymore. His mother hadn't been a fan of the change, though in the last year of her life she wasn't out enough to be bothered by the newcomers swarming the island with their New York license plates and expensive haircuts.

"I don't know much about the buyers," Noah said. He had deliberately avoided hearing about them. They would be casualties of The Plan.

The timer dinged and Noah was relieved to return to Mrs. Harrison's phone. It took about fifteen minutes for him to set her up with a Gmail account to use the next time she got locked out of Hotmail and a password she wouldn't forget. He suggested she use her birthday, but she provided her husband's. "A lady never reveals her age," she kidded, and her hand crept back onto his shoulder.

"Have a nice holiday weekend," Noah said, his hand poised on the brass doorknob. "Let me know if you have any other issues."

"You're a doll," she said, handing him a crisp hundred-dollar bill and planting a kiss on his cheek. "I'm going to miss you when your family moves out. You're not having people over the Fourth, are you? I heard some chatter that you might."

Noah shook his head. "Nah. We're pretty swamped with the packing."

Mrs. Harrison patted his arm. "I hope you'll rent something nearby. It'd be a shame not to see that handsome *punim* of yours, and heaven knows I can't manage my devices without you."

"I'll try," Noah said.

With any luck, he wouldn't be going very far at all.

ON A GORGEOUS DAY WITH THE ATLANTIC AT LOW TIDE AND the waves blissfully mellow, Noah would have far preferred to bike home from the Harrisons than pile into the family Volvo. He'd always preferred getting around on two wheels. The wind in his hair, tousled by the saltwater mist, his T-shirt flapping against his chest as he rolled down the narrow streets with the occasional leaf falling on him, nothing could be better. Noah hated how biking was associated with little kids, unless you were a serious *cyclist*, the kind wearing a skin-tight onesie and special shoes who biked in packs to show off their new BMCs. Those dudes were now descending upon LBI in droves. Noah would honestly have preferred the invasion of a motorcycle gang.

He was stuck driving the sedan because of an ache in his right knee from a fall he'd had a month earlier when some LBI newbie completely disregarded bike lane etiquette. The doctor had prescribed physical therapy, which helped, but the sessions were expensive and he'd had to stop. Freelance tech support meant his only health insurance was a don't-get-hurt credo.

Happily, the driveway was empty when he returned home. Laura was in Manhattan for the day with their father, shepherding him through a medical pub crawl. Leo was in good health, but at seventy-three, routine appointments were necessary. On their last pilgrimage, Laura had described the experience like a relay race, the gastroenterologist handing the baton to the neurologist who handed it to the orthopedist who handed it to the podiatrist (bunions were a family curse). If his bum knee was any indication, Noah was terrified of his other body parts quitting as he got older.

Sophie was meeting Laura and Leo in the city and riding down with them. Matthew and Beth were also coming that route, but wouldn't appear before dinnertime, not if they could squeeze out an extra billable hour. The family planned to use the outdoor grill one last time that evening. The next morning, JerzeyGurrrrrl123, the Craigslist buyer of the ancient Weber, would come collect it. The new homeowners expressed zero interest in keeping the free-standing barbeque, even after Leo had offered it gratis and assured them the grill had fed hundreds of satisfied bellies over the years. "We're planning a full outdoor kitchen with a built-in Viking and a pizza oven," the wife, a perky yogi who probably didn't even eat meat, explained. It was that moment when Noah decided he didn't need to know any more about these people.

A few other things in the house had already been sold on Craigslist or donated to the JCC. His father wasn't interested in taking the remaining furniture to Florida, much of which had taken a beating from the corrosive salt air. "Movers are crooks," he insisted with curious certainty. "I'm better off getting new stuff." Their father had always been tight with a buck. Noah wondered if his desire to leave everything behind was actually because he preferred to begin his next chapter without furniture and knickknacks saturated with Sylvia's memory. Noah could still hear his mom say, "Use a coaster!" when he brought a drink into the living room, and it filled him with sadness. What he wouldn't do to be yelled at again.

Laura had it all figured out. "The ladies in Boca are already primping. Dad will have new furniture and a full fridge in no time." His father, sought after? With the fringe of hairs jutting past his nostrils, thicker than what remained on his head? His sister was probably right. What did Noah understand about senior romances? Even less than about relationships between people his own age. Just ask his ex, Paola, or the voodoo doll she created from the things he left in her apartment after they split.

"Hiya, Noah," called a familiar voice, and he turned to see Stanley Archer waving from his next-door porch, the enormous American and Giants flags hanging from the second story flapping above his head. If the new buyers were Eagles fans, it would put Stanley right into the grave. Stanley was fond of hiking argyle socks to his knees and clunking around in orthopedic sneakers, and today was no exception. It was the same uniform favored by Leo. "Everyone coming this weekend? Let me know if you need any help packing."

Mr. Archer was one of the old-timers. Like his parents, he bought his house decades earlier for a fraction of what it was worth now. Considering Stanley was blind in one eye and occasionally used a walker tricked out with tennis balls for wheels, he was unlikely to be of much use packing, but Noah appreciated the offer.

"I think we'll be alright. Come over later if you're hungry. We're grilling."

"I just might," the old man said, patting his belly. "Ruth is visiting the grandkids in Colorado for the week so I'm a bit low on rations."

"We'll have plenty," Noah said. Mr. Archer saluted kindly and stepped back into his house, the sound of the swinging screen door banging against the frame hitting Noah hard with nostalgia. Their house had the same door. All the original houses on the block, the ones not yet torn down and resurrected as McMansions, had a similar wooden door with a brass knocker positioned behind a mesh screen meant to keep out the bugs. The summertime soundtrack of their neighborhood was a medley of waves crashing, chirping birds and front doors swinging open and shut.

Noah looked up at the house, trying to memorize the details of its architecture the way he once tried to commit the contours of Lizzy Markowitz's body to memory. The Jacobson home wasn't large by new-build standards—about 2,200 square feet on the interior, 2,600 if the porches were included (and included they ought to be—the front boasted a swinging sofa on one side and three Adirondack chairs on the other; the back porch was screened in and offered incredible sunset views and ocean breezes). Though it wasn't grand, it had a presence, appearing two stories tall perched on the stilts that were essential to minimize flood damage. Technically, it was one-and-a-half livable floors since the top was an attic with a steeply sloped roof. The three dormer windows that stood out on that level were Noah's favorite detail. The Cape Cod–style home was painted a light gray, like many of the cottages in the neighborhood, but unlike most, the trim and shutters were navy blue instead of white. While the house had been symmetrical for most of its time in the Jacobson family, about ten years ago his mother had insisted on a small addition for the grandchildren. At the time, there were three of them and the house was busting at the seams on a summer weekend, stuffed animals spilling out of closets and LEGO bricks hiding in shaggy rug piles. Noah remembered his mother nagging his father, "We have three now. Before you know it we'll be up to eight grandchildren. Where will they sleep? On the beach?"

It was reasonable for Sylvia to assume that with four children of her own, her grandchildren would at least number a multiple, if not an exponent, of the base. It hadn't happened and now she was gone, though the home expansion she successfully lobbied for (did Leo ever say no to Sylvia?) was put to good use by Laura's girls. They claimed the space with a Crayola sign that read, "Private Property of Emma and Hannah Cohen" (spelled "privit proportee").

Sadly, Noah's now-grown nieces weren't coming for the weekend. His nephew, Austin, would be in tow, but he was no fun when his parents helicopters at close range. When Sylvia was healthy, no one dared turn down her invitation to visit for July Fourth weekend. Sylvia took orders for everyone's favorite foods weeks in advance, put fresh flowers in every room and spent the entire weekend doting on all of them. It meant eleven people sharing two and a half bathrooms and at least one or two guaranteed blowups. Arguments were equally likely to break out between parent and child, spouses, or siblings, but the overall feeling at the end of the weekend was always one of fullness, both emotional and gastrointestinal.

Entering the house, Noah cast a wistful glance at the place where his mother's cone-shaped hydrangea had once bloomed into puffy white clouds. She would hate seeing the pile of dirt and mulch that lay wanton in place of her cloudlike flowers. Hydrangeas were perennial; it was a sign of how little care the house and surrounding earth was receiving that they no longer burst forth in spring. It had been in Noah's mind to replant them but now there was no point.

He flung himself onto his bed and teed up his favorite porn site on his phone. In seconds, his screen was populated by a classroom with two girls in plaid miniskirts and a "teacher" with bleached hair and a double sleeve of tattoos, naked save for a striped tie. The dude was not handsome, but Noah wasn't there for the guys. He slipped a hand down his pants as he settled in to watch. There was a storyline in this one. Not lengthy enough to recommend popping popcorn, but enough that Noah turned up the volume.

"What is that noise?"

Before he could hit pause, his two sisters appeared in his doorframe. And by the fact that they were both giggling hysterically, their question had been rhetorical.

"Knock first?" Noah choked out, fumbling to lower the volume on his phone but accidentally raising it. Their threesome (admittedly an awkward way to think about Noah and his sisters) listened to escalating moans and screams and finally a throaty "Did I get an A?" before Noah managed to power the phone off.

"Can I help you?" Noah hopped up from the bed and yanked up his fly.

Laura composed herself first. "We were coming up to say hi. Didn't realize you were, um, busy. One of the doctors canceled at the last minute so we wrapped up early. Dad's downstairs having something to eat."

Sophie, still giggling, asked, "Why do you have lipstick on your cheek?"

Noah lifted his palm to his cheek, which even without the lipstick was surely red. He wiped away the sticky remnants of Mrs. Harrison's kiss.

"I was fixing a client's email earlier," Noah said matter-of-factly.

"Good to know you take payment in kisses," Laura said.

As the three of them filed down the stairs single file, Noah was flooded with déjà vu. He was probably around six, and his sisters dressed him up in their clothes, made up his face and covered his hair in bows. Proudly, they marched him down the stairs to show their parents. Sylvia cried out, "Noah would have been the most beautiful girl," and his sisters gushed in agreement. To this day, they lamented that he got the best hair and bone structure.

"I get paid in cash," Noah said, pulling the hundred-dollar bill from his pocket. He didn't add that he *was* fooling around with another one of his clients. Technically two, if he counted the groping session with Patty Lauffer, interrupted because the landscaper showed up. Patty left him to tend to a pesky "rotten bush" and Noah had to stifle a laugh, which even he recognized spoke to his maturity level.

Robin Miller, on the other hand, he'd been messing around with consistently. When he first went to her Harvey Cedars home, Robin did present with a genuine problem. No matter what she searched on her laptop, the results returned images of Nicolas Cage. "I'm not a Nicolas Cage stalker or anything," she said, burying her button-nosed face in her hands. "Though I do love *Honeymoon in Vegas*."

When Noah looked blank, she said, "Oh gosh, I've dated myself." Robin was younger than much of his clientele; he guessed she was around fifty. She had two children and an ex-husband who was unreliable with child support. Robin and Noah tumbled into bed pretty quickly and he visited her about once a week for a romp.

"Hi, Dad," Noah said. Leo was at the kitchen table with a deli sandwich spread before him, struggling to open a mustard packet. Noah opened another packet and handed it to him. "I heard you escaped having to see one of the docs."

"He sure did," Laura said. "Still a long day though."

Noah was startled by the fatigue on his father's face when he looked up. His aging process had sped up rapidly since losing his wife, so much so that a busy day of appointments appeared to age him a year. This was the opposite of what he and his siblings expected. Caring for their mother, who was diagnosed with lung cancer despite having smoked exactly two cigarettes in her life (both stories she could tell in vivid detail, one of which involved the weekend she met Leo at the Golden Hotel in the Catskills), was more than a full-time job. Her diagnosis coincided with Leo's retirement from the accounting firm, so he went from a demanding job to caretaker without a breath in between.

After Sylvia succumbed to the disease, the silver lining was supposed to be their father finally getting a much-deserved respite. Their mother, whirling dervish that she was, was a shell of herself toward the end. Leo said goodbye to the force of nature he married months before she died. That was supposed to make the actual goodbye easier, even a relief. How wrong they had been.

Florida, they all hoped, would revive him.

Specifically the Boca Breezes condominium complex to which Leo was moving, with its six soaring towers filled with similarly situated retirees, eighteen-hole golf course, brightly lit card rooms, full-service dining room with a sixteen-foot-long buffet, twenty-four-hour coffee shop, maid service, water aerobics, book club, gardening club, politics club, sports (possibly betting) club and eight newly installed pickleball courts.

It had been Leo's dream to retire to Florida. He craved the sun and the cool shade of palm trees. Dinners at five thirty that wouldn't send fire up his intestines. A community where all his needs could be met within one square mile. He was tired of caring for a house—two houses—dealing with frozen pipes and shoveling snow in the winter, only to mow the lawn and clean the gutters come spring. Leo, in his seventies, wanted to pick up the phone and call the super when there was a problem. That, paradoxically, was his definition of a real man.

He'd pushed the Florida life on Sylvia as though he worked in the Boca Breezes sales office. He suggested swapping the Jersey Shore home for a Florida condo, or getting rid of their primary residence in East Brunswick and dividing their time between Florida and Beach Haven. Sylvia resisted. "Why do I need to rush to God's waiting room?" she was fond of saying. She claimed she was too busy in New Jersey to spend meaningful time in Florida, which was true. Noah's mother worked as a librarian in their town for more than thirty years, the "loudest librarian on earth" as she was often described. She also volunteered extensively for their temples (yes, plural; one in East Brunswick and one by the shore because "God doesn't take vacations"—another Sylvia-ism) and still found time to yack for hours on the phone with countless friends and play hours of canasta with Arlene, Myrna and Betty. And then there was the matter of raising four children, which Sylvia Jacobson would be the first to say didn't end when they turned eighteen, nor when they graduated college or got married. There was no prying Sylvia away from her cubs, which included everyone from her children and grandchildren to the members of the Ladies Auxiliary of her local Hadassah chapter.

Leo's Florida dream didn't stand a chance.

Finally, he was getting his chance to live in the Sunshine State. The condo was purchased and ready. All that remained was to pack up the Jersey Shore home. The East Brunswick house had sold in February, furniture included, to buyers with a penchant for the mustards and avocado greens of 1970s decor. Since then, Leo was living full-time with Noah at the beach, something Noah could hardly resent given he was technically a squatter. He didn't mind Leo's company, especially knowing that soon he would be in Florida full-time and they would see each other two or three times a year at most. Projecting how the future nexus points of the Jacobson clan would play out, Noah envisioned Passover in Boca and Leo flying up north for the Jewish holidays in September; though without Sylvia as the magnetic force pulling them in, nothing was certain. Noah had been relishing watching baseball with Leo in the evenings. He liked grilling for two. He'd gotten over his father's unfortunate habit of not fully closing his battered terry cloth robe and his flatulent digestive tract.

What Noah minded most was losing the house altogether. He'd been living at the beach for a year already, even in the off-season when the place was a ghost town. While most of the stores and restaurants shuttered, and naturally his business waned, Noah appreciated the natural beauty of LBI the way only the year-rounders could, without the masses crowding Schooner's Wharf for their iced matchas.

By the end of July, he would officially be homeless. He had a few viable options before he needed to resort to a cardboard box. He could convince Paola to take him back as a platonic roommate or crash in his pal Timmy's shed behind his bike shop, which smelled like grease and kitty litter, but also had an Xbox. There were other friends he could call upon, who owed him favors for when he saved their IT asses. Plus, he had three siblings he could lean on. Even if Sophie had too many roommates, he could finagle his way into Laura's basement or ask Matthew for a loan. Or, he could stay right where he was if he executed The Plan.

"Which doc did you miss?" Noah asked.

"The orthopedist had to cancel because of a surgery. But this man got a clean bill of health from the other docs," Laura chirped, stepping into their mother's shoes as Leo's mouthpiece.

"And we stopped off at the Second Avenue Deli for hot pastrami sandwiches before driving back," Sophie added, dropping a slice of meat that matched the color of her tongue into her mouth. Why hadn't anyone texted to see if he wanted one? He ought not to be surprised, seeing as no one had expressed concern over the far more pressing matter of his housing status.

"Except these girls made me get the lean pastrami," Leo said in disgust. "What's the point?" He held up a slice of meat that, to Noah's eye, still had ample portions of fatty deposits.

"The point is so your blood pressure stays low, your arteries stay clear and—" Sophie tried.

"My father, may he rest in peace, ate pastrami and chicken in schmaltz almost every day of his life," Leo said.

"Wasn't Grandpa Jack's cholesterol the highest his doctor had ever seen?" Sophie asked. "He had a heart attack at fifty."

"That was for other reasons," Leo said curtly and without elaboration.

When the girls had their heads tucked in the refrigerator gathering dinner provisions, Leo flashed a black-and-white cookie at Noah, miming *Shhhh*. Noah delighted in his father's secret, safe in the pocket of his cardigan. There was the spark of life that reassured Noah the old man would do alright on his own in Florida. Maybe more than alright.

"Where's Doug?" Noah asked and both Laura and Sophie whipped around, their heads nearly colliding.

"Working," Laura said.

"On July Fourth weekend? Yikes."

"Yes, Noah. Dental emergencies don't take off for the holidays. People can't exactly plan when these things happen, can they?" Sophie said, a hand on her hip.

"A patient needed an emergency root canal," Laura said, more calmly.

Sheesh. He was sorry he asked. He caught his sisters exchanging a glance that he could only assume meant: *Obviously our idiot brother doesn't understand the concept of work.* "I'm just sorry to miss him. Was hoping to watch the Yanks with him."

"Shouldn't Matthew be here by now?" Leo asked. "Laura, have you heard from him?"

Noah observed a sag in his sister's shoulders; Laura was visibly straining from the weight of becoming the de facto leader of the family, responsible for a full fridge, clean sheets and knowing everybody's schedules.

"Any minute. Beth already sent me the list of Austin-approved foods for the barbeque." Laura waved a sad-looking package of watery tofu in the air. "It's such a waste because you just know they're going to show up with their own stuff anyway."

"No soy, no dairy, no nuts, no sugar," Sophie parroted their sister-in-law. "Preferably just a meal of air, so long as it's been purified and blessed by the EPA."

Beth wasn't Noah's favorite person, but he didn't find her as objectionable as his sisters did. They were always talking about how she changed Matthew, but Noah didn't really buy it. Matthew was a grown man, not a clump of Play-Doh. Beth Moore-Jacobson was a specific type, the polar opposite of the kind of woman Noah would ever desire, but that didn't make her the enemy. And who knew what Matthew really wanted or how his desires had evolved in adulthood? Noah hadn't expected to enjoy sleeping with a menopausal woman whose bathroom counter was cluttered with products labeled "Anti-aging," and yet it was in Robin Miller's bathroom that he happily got an education in eye creams.

The way Noah saw it, Beth made his older brother about as happy as a corporate lawyer who worked nonstop and had no hobbies or pleasures outside of work could be. They worked at the same firm, Matthew on the corporate side and Beth in litigation. Together they billed infinity hours a year and were heftily rewarded for their labors. They lived in a ridiculous apartment in Tribeca, a glass cube with glittering views of the Hudson River and a garage in the building with electric charging stations for their Tesla. When Noah visited them in the city, which wasn't often, he felt his presence alone left fingerprints behind.

The one area where Noah did agree with his sisters' criticism was the way Beth interacted with Austin, his thirteen-year-old nephew. At that age, Noah only cared about playing sports and stealing Matthew's dirty DVDs. Austin was a robot, or at least programmed like one. Nobody purely human could study that many languages and excel in chess, piano and Krav Maga. And his diet. Last summer, to give the kid a break from the shiva and the endless kisses from overly perfumed great-aunts, Noah took Austin out for ice cream. Beth nearly convulsed when she saw the evidence around her son's mouth. The chocolate hadn't been vegan and he had already hit his sugar limit for the day.

"Hello, all!" Beth called out as if on cue. "Austin, shoes off."

"Hi, everyone," Matthew chimed in.

"Where's my grandson?" Leo said. Noah could imagine Leo breaking his black-and-white cookie in half to share with Austin when no one was looking.

Matthew, Beth and Austin stepped into the kitchen. Noah nuzzled his nephew's head of dirty-blond curls. He was a perfect combination of his mom and dad. "Hey, kid." Austin looked up at Noah with a missing-tooth smile. Was it normal for a thirteen-year-old to have a missing tooth that wasn't the result of a hockey accident? Throw another log on the pile of things Noah didn't know.

"Hi, Uncle Noah. Hey, Grandpa," Austin said, hugging Leo with arms finally long enough to make their full way around.

"This boy has shot up since I saw him last," Leo said.

"You're just shrinking, Dad," Matthew said good-naturedly. "Hi, sibs." He pecked both his sisters' cheeks and exchanged a handshake-hug with Noah. The brothers were more than twelve years apart. Fewer years separated Noah from Laura's girls, which was probably why he felt he belonged more in the third generation.

"I'm coming around for hugs next. Just need to free up my hands," Beth said. She was carrying two large shopping bags. "Figured I'd bring over our own food, just to be safe."

"You don't say?" Laura sneered as she took the bags from Beth's hands.

"Where are your suitcases? Noah, help your brother bring his stuff in," Leo said.

"Actually, we don't have any bags," Matthew said. Beth appeared at his side.

"We rented a place of our own," she said. "It's in Harvey Cedars."

"Left after the bridge," Laura muttered. "Of course."

"The house is gorgeous. Right on the ocean. The kitchen was just remodeled with top-of-the-line appliances. The hood over the stove retracts into the ceiling. The bathrooms are all marble. Can you believe there are six of them?" Beth looked around for confirmation it was unbelievable that a house could have that much plumbing. Noah refrained from asking if a two-to-one toilet-to-butt ratio was something they looked for in a home.

"Funny, I would have pegged you guys for the Hamptons," Laura said.

"Next summer," Beth said, oblivious to the dig. "This will be our last Jersey Shore hurrah."

"So will Austin go to camp here?" Sophie asked. "We all went to sailing camp. Dad believes Jews don't boat, but Mom forced it through."

"We don't boat and we don't camp," Leo said. "Forty years in the desert was more than enough."

"Man, those were the days," Sophie said "I mean, one summer a kid was left at Barnegat Lighthouse and another summer the owner dated a fifteen-year-old CIT, but we had so much fun. Austin—you would love it." Addressing Beth, Sophie added, "I'm sure the place is totally buttoned up now. It was the nineties. Things were different."

"One summer I was a counselor there and a parent tried to tip me with an extra beach badge," Laura said. "Mom was upset I didn't take it."

"The camp is closed. It shut down by the time I was old enough to go," Noah said. "Sorry, kiddo." He jabbed Austin playfully in the ribs.

A laugh escaped Beth's lips. "Sorry, sorry." She clapped a hand to her mouth. "Austin is enrolled in a very competitive summer program run by NASA. Only ten middle schoolers nationwide were chosen and he got one of the spots. They meet on Zoom for four hours every day and the rest of the time is for independent study."

"So he doesn't go outside?" Laura asked.

"He can take his laptop outdoors anytime he wants, as long as he's careful with sunscreen." Beth patted Austin's head and Noah thought he saw the boy squirm. "He loves the program."

"It is really cool," Austin said. "We get to visit NASA in Washington, DC, at the end of the summer." Noah couldn't tell if he meant it. Maybe the program wasn't so bad. Astronauts were cool. The closest Noah had gotten to space was the collection of plastic glow-in-the-dark stars he stuck to the ceiling of his childhood bedroom.

"Hannah's in DC, sweetie," Laura said. "She's working there for the summer. Hopefully you two can get some cousin time when you visit. I'm sure she'd love to show you around the GW campus."

Beth pursed her lips. "Or Austin can show Hannah around NASA, if there's time. He's going to be very busy."

"Hannah will be quite busy too. I doubt she'd have time to see him anyway." Noah felt embarrassed for both women, jockeying for position in their invisible chess game.

"Let's get started on dinner?" Matthew removed his blazer and rolled up his sleeves, shedding light on his ghostly white arms. Old family photos confirmed he and Noah had once been the same color. "I can start the grill if someone can find the lighter. Hey, where's Doug, by the way? We need the grill master."

"Working," Sophie all but shouted. "Doug is working this weekend."

"I'll be working all weekend too," Beth said in response to no one. "I'm on a very big case. Huge, actually. Major banking client. I can't say who, of course, but these folks have been in the news quite a bit recently so I'm sure you know who I mean." Others nodded, but Noah had no clue who or what she was talking about. But if Beth was super busy at work, she'd hardly notice his presence if he slid into her beach rental.

Just then Noah felt his cell phone buzz. It was the text he'd been waiting to receive from his roach-killing, beehive-slaying buddy Joe, who worked over at Buzz Off. Dude, we doing this? Joe had written, including an insect emoji. Give me a few hours, Noah responded, tilting the screen to block it from view.

"Lemme help you with the grill, Matty." Noah clapped his brother on the back and reached for the jumbo tongs.

MASTER CHEFS WITHOUT THEIR MATRIARCH THE JACOBSONS were not.

Noah had forgotten to defrost the meat that morning despite Laura's multiple reminders. Austin's tofu skewers caught on fire and crumbled to a blackened pile of ash. And then, following a scary hiss and a terrifying burst of flames, the grill broke down entirely.

Everyone grew hungry and cranky at once. Leo, who had indigestion from the afternoon's pastrami delight, settled for oatmeal. Sophie threw a package of frozen hot dogs into a pot of boiling water, but Noah, who was rarely picky, couldn't bring himself to eat one of the pink logs after listening to Beth detail their chemical makeup. What was nitrate? It sounded terrible.

"What's the shelf life of frozen kugel?" Noah asked, palming a rectangular dish triple-coated in aluminum foil. "There's also a loaf of gefilte in the freezer but it's labeled "Do Not Eat" for some reason." He got nothing but apathetic shrugs.

Somebody, probably Laura, thought to order pizza. When the pies arrived, Noah dug around his pockets to tip the delivery guy. He only had the hundred-dollar bill from Mrs. Harrison.

"Matty, can I grab a five?" Noah asked his brother, who was seated on the living room sofa, Austin sandwiched between him and Beth. Their trio was hunched over numerous textbooks spread across the coffee table. Matthew fished a twenty from his wallet. "Smallest I have."

"Ten back," Noah said to the delivery boy, pleased to be generous with Matthew's money.

"Thanks, man," the pimply teen said, appreciation gleaming back at Noah. It must be nice to be rich, Noah thought, eyeing his brother. A shiny gold watch glinted on his wrist. Beth had a matching one. Probably a Rolex. Not that Noah lusted for brand names. He was happy enough to dispense a generous tip.

"Okay, people, we need to discuss the plan for tomorrow," Laura said. She had finished doling out pizza slices and was perched on a faded suede ottoman with a torn tassel border, clipboard in hand. Sophie, seated at the folding card table where their mother played countless rounds of canasta, was sopping up the oil on her slice. A younger Noah had subbed in on occasion when someone in the card foursome canceled. He'd loved when the women praised his card skills. Betty called him a genius the first time he got a special hand.

"I've divided the rooms and I think if we start early, we can get through the bulk of packing by dark. Then we can watch the fireworks." Laura consulted her pad. "Soph, you'll do the kitchen and living room. Noah, the room you're staying in and the porches. I'll do Mom and Dad's room, my girls' room and all the hallway closets. Matthew and Beth, you guys can take the attic. There are boxes, tape, labels and markers in the garage, along with all the crap we took from East Brunswick."

"The attic has no windows. We won't be able to breathe up there." Beth gulped for air as though she was already suffocating.

"How am I supposed to pack the kitchen up if we still need to use it for the rest of the weekend?" Sophie asked.

Noah wasn't loving his assignment either. "How do I pack up porch furniture? It's huge."

"Well, maybe keep some of it until the closing," Laura said. "Where are you going after anyway?"

Finally, someone was curious.

"Your basement? Hannah's or Emma's room?" Noah's tone walked the line between joking and seriousness. Laura didn't bite. In fact, she looked petrified. Was he that bad a houseguest?

"You should live at our beach house this summer, Uncle Noah," Austin said. "We can hang out when I come on the weekends. And I won't have to bring Polly back and forth."

"Polly?" Noah asked.

"My bearded dragon." Austin pulled up a picture of the scaly creature on his phone.

"I thought she was your girlfriend," Sophie teased and Austin tossed a pillow at his aunt. Noah launched a pillow at Austin's head, but his nephew impressively intercepted it.

"That's very generous of you, Austin," Beth said. "Daddy and I need to talk about that later though." Beth probably preferred hosting Polly, but it was nice that Austin wanted his uncle around.

"Laura, what time do you want us here tomorrow?" Matthew asked, clearly eager to shift topics.

Noah was also fine with ceasing discussion about his next residence. "I don't think Dad's armchair is going to make it down the stairs," Noah said, gesturing to the sharp turn at the midlevel landing. "Laura, any ideas?"

"Jesus, I'm not a professional mover," his sister said, flinging down her pencil. "I have enough crap on my plate. We should have done a tag sale."

"And have all those people trampling the lawn while they paw our stuff?" Leo piped up after being eerily quiet all evening. The "lawn" of which he spoke was a tiny square of neglected patchy grass.

"C'mon . . . let us have a lawn pawn," Sophie pleaded.

"Absolutely not." Leo folded his arms across his chest.

Noah flipped on the TV, an outdated flatscreen Leo acquired during the DVD era. He cranked the volume on the local news. They all needed the distraction.

"I didn't realize how late it was," Beth said. "Matthew, we have to get Austin home. You must be tired, sweetie." She looked at her boy.

Austin shrugged. He clearly relied on his parents to tell him what he felt.

Noah also hadn't realized the time. He found another text from Joe that read Hello??? He quickly marked the text unread and shoved the phone back in his pocket.

"Hey, she's on LBI!" Sophie exclaimed. "That's our 7-Eleven!" She pointed at the TV screen. They all turned to look.

"New Jersey residents are lined up for blocks for their chance to win a $261 million Powerball this holiday weekend," said the perky field reporter standing with a handheld microphone outside their local 7-Eleven.

The camera panned to a line of people waiting single file to enter the convenience store. Noah passed by it nearly every day when he went for his morning donut at Crust and Crumb. "There hasn't been a major Powerball winner from New Jersey in the past five years, but these folks are hoping to change the Garden State's luck. To boost lotto ticket sales in the state, participating 7-Elevens are giving away a free slushie with the purchase of a Powerball ticket. That's enough to get these folks out in the heat."

"What's the Powerball?" Austin asked.

"It's a tax on stupid people," Beth said. "Pack up your books."

"Okay, then what's a slushie?" Austin persisted.

"You're shitting me," Sophie said, crossing the room to cup Austin's chin. "A slushie is like the best drink ever. Imagine a milkshake version of a soda." Austin's eyes turned to saucers. "Your dad used to love them."

"It's pure chemicals," Beth said.

The reporter outside 7-Eleven was now in a split screen with the in-studio anchors, chatting about what they would do with the money if they won.

"Listen, guys, I'm beat," Laura said as she collected the detritus of their meal. "Let's just figure out the plan tomorrow. Most of the stuff is junk and can be tossed."

Junk? Noah noticed his father didn't even flinch. Why was he the only Jacobson who cared?

"Since the buyers are tearing the place down, do we even need to get everything out?" Matthew asked. "We can just take the photos and whatever else and let them trash the rest?"

Noah felt physically ill.

"I could ask the broker." Laura tied a double knot in the garbage bag. "Let me see if the dumpster in town is accessible tomorrow because of the holiday."

"It's probably closed the whole week," Leo said. "I don't know what the mayor does with our tax dollars."

"We can fill big trash bags in the meantime," Sophie said.

That was it. It was time for The Plan. Noah reached for his phone and texted Joe. Meet you in ten.

Where? Clock's ticking, Joe replied.

The flash from the TV caught his eye. A white-haired lady hooked up to an oxygen tank was being interviewed as she exited the 7-Eleven about how she picked her numbers.

7-Eleven, Noah texted Joe. Leaving now.

FANTASTIC FOURSOME 🥷 🥷 ✡️ 🥷 🥷

MATTHEW

Offer still stands re hiring movers. Happy to pay

SOPHIE

Why are U texting? We r all in same room

LAURA

Because Dad doesn't want us to use movers. Waste of $

NOAH

We could just not sell

LAURA

OMG Noah get over it

SOPHIE

M—why is B worried about A going to bed? It's 9 pm

MATTHEW

Mind your own biz

SOPHIE

Sheesh

MATTHEW

Sorry. Idk. she's into sleep

LAURA

Why is Mr. Archer looking through our window? OMG he's not wearing pants!

4

Matthew

MATTHEW, ANNOYED WITH EVERYONE AND EVERYTHING, ROSE to greet a partially nude and fully confused Stanley Archer on the back porch.

"When's the barbecue starting?" Stanley asked. "I brought drinks." In his hand was a two-liter bottle of off-brand diet cola. Matthew tried to look anywhere but at the old man's loose, threadbare skivvies.

"Unfortunately, the barbecue didn't work out," Noah said to Stanley. "Let me take you back."

"Probably for the best. My ulcer's flaring," Stanley said as Noah escorted him through the sliding doors on the ocean side of the house. Matthew could hear Stanley walking Noah through his Mylanta and TUMS routine.

"Ruth will be back in two days," Noah said when he returned. "I think Mr. Archer needs the supervision."

"He's not a baby," Leo snapped. Nobody dared to argue.

"I gotta run out for a bit," Noah said, scooping up the Volvo keys.

Out. Out sounded delightful. Matthew could use some fresh air and a break from calculating jet propulsion. Not that he wasn't overjoyed when Austin was selected by NASA for the highly competitive program. It was basically MIT-in-training. He wished his mother was alive to *shep nachas*. But his joy quickly receded when he realized Austin's enrollment meant more work for him. Monitoring Austin's extracurricular and summer programs was a full-time job, and Beth wouldn't hear of letting their son go it alone.

"Where are you going?" Matthew asked.

"Huh?" Noah said, looking up from his phone.

"You said you had to run out. I'll come with you. We can take the Tesla. You'll love it." The electric car glided like silk. Driving it was like playing a video game. It even had a button that made a fart sound, though Matthew only played it for Austin when Beth wasn't in the car. Noah would get a kick out of it. Matthew produced the key fob from his pocket. "You can drive. Where we off to?"

"I'm . . . I'm going to 7-Eleven," Noah stammered.

"Really? The line looked killer. Bring me back a pint of ice cream if you go," Sophie said. "Get a few, actually. I don't want to share."

"Good idea," Laura said. "Rocky Road if they have it. Also bring me—" She mouthed something that Matthew didn't catch. Laura made a head nod in Austin's direction.

"Hey, Austin, can you grab the bag of pretzels from the kitchen?" Matthew said. Once he was out of the room, Laura brought two out-stretched fingers to her lips, miming smoking.

"I got you," Matthew said. He'd love to join her for a smoke. He'd puffed his way through law school, Beth too, the two of them sharing a pack a day during exams. She'd kicked the habit by her final year, once her job at Meyer, Packer & Driscoll was signed in ink, but Matthew went on smoking until they started trying for a baby, when Beth flushed all his smokes down the toilet with no warning.

"Ready to go?" Matthew asked, giving his brother a friendly push toward the door. "What do you need at 7-Eleven?"

Noah was staring at the TV. The in-studio reporters were still chirping about the odds of winning the lottery, which were significantly lower than getting struck by lightning. "I want to buy a Powerball ticket," Noah said.

"You?" Matthew was dumbfounded.

"Yeah." Noah shrugged.

Sophie crawled over to her tote bag and fished out a few singles. "Count me in for the Powerball. They're jacking the rent at my studio and I may be out of a job come the fall. Budget cuts at school."

"Yikes. I'm in too," Laura said, handing a five-dollar bill to Noah. "I could use a cash infusion right about now."

"Two private college tuitions at once has to hurt," Matthew said, but he instantly wanted to jam his loafer in his mouth. He and Beth were in a totally different financial situation than his siblings and he usually found it best to avoid the topic of money altogether. As junior partners at the same top-tier law firm, they both earned enough that even with the exorbitant price tag of their Manhattan condo, the beach house rental and Austin's private school tuition, there was just enough left over to afford them many of life's daily comforts. They splurged on Juice Press shakes, a twice-weekly housekeeper and top-tier gym memberships, which admittedly Beth made better use of. None of his siblings were in that position, nor had his parents been.

Leo, who had been preoccupied reading the *Star-Ledger* with a magnifying glass, put down the paper. "Rutgers was good enough for you kids," Leo said. "And so was your kindergarten through twelfth-grade public school education."

"Austin is gifted," Beth said. "He needs special programming."

There were exceptional public schools for gifted students in New York City, but you had to test in. Austin would almost definitely have passed, but it seemed like Beth was too afraid to chance it. Further, these magnet schools, as they were called, often had close to a thousand students per grade. With those numbers, Beth couldn't as easily get the teachers' attention when Austin brought home a less-than-perfect grade.

"Two college tuitions *is* painful. Plenty of things in life are," Laura said, her face growing dark. She looked at Matthew. "Luckily, you don't have to sweat it."

"That's for sure," Sophie said. "Unlike the rest of us mortals about to lose their leases."

Don't have to sweat it? Sweat was all he did. Did his sisters have any idea how hard he worked? That he was haunted by deal memos in his dreams? That when he stood at his mother's graveside he imagined what his own tombstone would say? All he could come up with was: *Here Lies Matthew Jacobson. He died at his desk while reviewing an S-1 filing for a chemicals company whose products pollute the earth. His death occurred one minute before his next twelve-minute billing increment.* Would they like to trade? Would anyone who hadn't been schooled in the Beth Moore-Jacobson "more is Moore" way of life? He didn't think so.

"I'm leaving," Noah said, stepping into his Havaianas. He was still holding the Volvo keys.

"What about the Tesla?" Matthew asked.

Noah scratched the back of his neck. "I'm just gonna run out solo. One of my customers thinks she deleted an important file. I'm going to call her from the car to help."

"I bet you will." Sophie pantomimed a kiss and Laura giggled.

"Alright," Matthew said, trudging back across the living room to rejoin Beth, Austin and the pile of incomprehensible textbooks.

"You guys want in on the tickets?" Noah asked, turning back. "Matthew? Beth?"

"No thanks," Beth said. "We're good."

"Can't we buy just one?" Austin pleaded with well-executed puppy-dog eyes.

Matthew might have thrown in with his siblings, to appease his son, but he was feeling annoyed by them. *First, Noah rejects his company, then his sisters make it seem like his money just miraculously appears in his bank account.*

Beth whispered to Austin, "The chances of winning the lottery are lower than the chances of an asteroid hitting the Earth. And I know my smart boy knows how likely that is."

Austin didn't appear cheered. Matthew leaned in to add, "What your mother means is that we are very lucky people and already have everything we want and need."

"Suit yourselves." Noah waved goodbye. "We could be millionaires by the end of the weekend."

We could be millionaires by the end of the weekend. He and Beth were already millionaires. Just barely, but still. Was his kid brother so out of touch that he didn't have a clue what a partner in a law firm made in a year? The naivete saddened Matthew. He didn't wish for Noah to work at a place like Meyer, Packer & Driscoll, with its endless rows of offices and matching corporate furniture surrounding a bullpen of cubicles. Noah wasn't cut out for that kind of life. Matthew wasn't even sure he himself was. He just didn't like thinking of his kid brother roaming LBI like a lost puppy, earning a few measly bucks fixing laptops.

"More money for us," Sophie said and she fist-bumped Laura.

"*Buena suerte, tio,*" Austin called after Noah.

"He's studying Spanish, French and Mandarin," Beth explained. Normally Matthew's chest puffed when Austin flexed his linguistic muscle. Today, in front of his family, he felt embarrassment that made his skin itch. His siblings did little to hide their judgment about how he and Beth were raising their son. Beth—she was the main driver—wanted to harness their son's talents in a way that nobody had done for her. Austin was a precocious, brilliant boy and she wanted him to reach his potential. Nobody could understand the pressure cauldron of raising a child in New York City unless you were doing it yourself. Austin was thriving, so why did Matthew feel embarrassed when his family was around? Maybe because a part of him knew they were right. Gathered together in their summer home, where all they did was frolic on the beach and play sports and get ice cream as kids, it was hard to deny that Austin was missing out on pure, unadulterated, childhood fun.

But the world is way more competitive today than when we were kids, Beth echoed in his ear. *You only get to be a kid once,* his siblings whispered into his other ear. It was like having the devil and an angel perched on his shoulders.

"Did Noah actually go to buy lottery tickets?" Leo asked, putting down the newspaper again.

"Yep," Sophie said. "And ice cream."

Leo waved a hand with enough liver spots to give him de facto authority. Their father detested frivolity and any reward that came too easily. A win by default was no different than a loss. He had chastised a ten-year-old Matthew for celebrating when the opposing Little League team didn't show and his team got the win.

Accountants were apparently not held to the same confidentiality standards as doctors. While he didn't use names, Leo shared stories around the dinner table about the ways his clients were irresponsible with money, the silly things they bought, the risks they took investing, the disorganized accounts that led to late fees and ruined credit scores. It was no surprise that he took on the role of allowance tsar in the Jacobson household, one of the few areas in which their mother played only a supporting role. Leo insisted his children each keep a ledger to track their expenditures. If the ledger wasn't up to date, he would dock the next week's allowance. Sylvia was gentler. She would sneak them money for little things here and there, like bottles of

Sun-In for his sisters and a deck of trick cards for him. She had an uncanny way of convincing their father that the extravagances were necessities.

Leo grumbled that "money doesn't grow on trees" so often it became a family joke. It was Matthew who hatched the plan to attach dollar bills to the oak tree that held court in their front yard. Pooling bills from their allowance, the four Jacobson children used paper clips to attach the money to its leaves under the cover of darkness. Noah, the scrappiest among them, climbed up to reach the highest branches. Their mother had laughed hysterically when she discovered it the next morning. Their father, not so much. Leo went ballistic, appalled that they hadn't considered what would have happened if it rained or someone stole the money.

Matthew looked at the oak tree now, illuminated by automatic bistro lights strung from branch to branch, every other bulb burned out. He would love to climb it with Austin. That and about a million other things he'd love to do with his son but had no time for.

"On that note, I'm going to hit the hay." Leo gave a great yawn and, as he did so, his bottom dentures fell out. Sophie scrambled to pick them up as Leo mumbled something about needing better adhesive.

"Where's Doug when you need him?" Matthew quipped.

"Good question," Laura said sharply.

Their father slowly dragged himself out of his recliner. There was no denying old age had come for him. How long until Matthew's own body moved like that, muscles dragging through molasses? Would he spend the next thirty years stuck behind the dual monitors in his office until his body caved?

One step at a time. Matthew needed to get through the weekend. He needed to help with the packing. Look up astrophysics on Wikipedia. Sneak a cigarette with Laura.

"Night all," Leo called out when he reached the top of the stairs.

Florida would be good for his old man. Matthew would have difficulty carving out time to get down there, but maybe Austin was old enough to fly alone. Boca Breezes had three swimming pools, a full arcade and a screening room to entice grandchildren who would rather be anywhere but silver-hair city.

"Good night, Dad," Matthew called, holding his breath as Leo's footfall sounded on the warped floorboards. "I love you."

THE NEXT MORNING, MATTHEW DISCOVERED BETH HUMMING in the kitchen in between sips of coffee. Matthew quietly watched her from the living room. The rental house had an open plan that made it feel even bigger than it was. He absorbed the rhythm of her body as she moved around the kitchen, sorting groceries and cooking tools. It was rare to find Beth in domestic mode—he sometimes forgot she had that setting.

"Morning," he said, coming up behind her and kissing the dip in her neck just below her earlobe.

"Hey, you scared me." She held up a paring knife in mock threat. "Want coffee? The built-in machine is incredible. I had three Americanos. Feel like I could run a marathon." There wasn't enough coffee in the universe to enable Matthew to run 26.2 miles. Their law firm did a charity 5K last year and he'd faked a stomach bug to get out of it. Beth came in first place.

Matthew approached the stainless-steel appliance that supposedly dispensed caffeine. It was built flush into a wall of light oak cabinetry, flanked by open shelves holding gleaming white porcelain mugs. Beth, anticipating his confusion as he studied the options on the touchscreen, was instantly beside him to explain how it worked.

"I love this house," she said, pressing the necessary buttons to prepare Matthew's drink. Her green eyes looked iridescent in the sunlight. She ran her fingers through her pale blond hair, which she was wearing loose for a change. He hadn't even remembered that her hair went past her shoulders because it was always clamped into a bun. She caught him staring. "These are beach waves. From the actual beach." She pointed enthusiastically to the shoreline, visible through the floor-to-ceiling glass that made up one entire wall of the kitchen. His family's Beach Haven house was also on the ocean, but it had much smaller windows and tall dunes that often blocked the view. "We should make an offer on it at the end of the summer."

"It's very nice," Matthew conceded. "But I can't even imagine how much they'd ask for this place." His family home, a tear-down on an inferior plot of land, was in contract for two million. To think his parents had scooped up the coastal home for $150,000 in the nineties. He estimated what the mortgage on a place like this would be and got light-headed. If the number was anywhere in the ballpark, buying this house meant he could retire, well, never. No, he could not allow Beth to entertain buying a second residence this extravagant. "Anyway, it's too big for just the three of us. Speaking of, where's Austin?"

"Outside collecting shells. By the way, I gave him a talk about not extending invitations to houseguests without running it by us first. He understood."

"You know, it wouldn't be the worst thing for Noah to move in here and spend more time with Austin. He knows the area inside and out. I bet he'd take him stargazing."

"Hm," Beth said, and Matthew sensed her gears churning. He took a sip of his coffee, which really was outstanding. Matthew would love to help Austin sort his shells later. Shell sorting was something he used to do with his sisters, and he was curious how his identification skills had held up. Could he still tell a black bay scallop from a hungry moon snail?

"I found an online oceanography course run by the Jacques Cousteau Foundation that Austin can still sign up for," Beth said.

Matthew's heart sank. He should have known that shell collecting could never be just shell collecting.

"We don't want to pigeonhole his interests too early with the space thing. It could be great for him," she said.

Great for him or great for you? It was sometimes hard to tell where his son ended and his wife began. The last thing their twelve-year-old needed was more work, especially over the summer.

Beth, moving at turbo speed, had already moved on. She was thumbing through her emails on an open laptop while rinsing a cutting board with her free hand. "Want a smoothie? I bought a bunch of berries at Neptune earlier."

He absentmindedly nodded yes, though he had little appetite.

Austin's childhood was looking less and less like his own had. Austin attended Dalton, a rigorous and competitive private school, where doing only the work assigned in class meant you were falling behind. Austin belonged there. He was gifted, that much was obvious when he began speaking in complete sentences at fourteen months. At four years old, he was making change at the corner bodega before the cashier punched the numbers into the register.

Beth seized upon his promise, recognizing the brainpower she possessed as a young child but which nobody caring for her harnessed. Not her parents, who divorced when she was four and both drank too much. Not her grandparents, whom she barely knew, not the teachers at her shitty school on the wrong side of the tracks in a forgettable midwestern town. She attended Rutgers and paid in-state tuition by using the address of a relative in Ho-Ho-Kus, New Jersey.

Matthew attended an excellent public school with a deep bench of advanced placement classes, sports teams and clubs, but he lacked Austin's natural ability. The fact that Matthew and Beth ended up at the same college—she in the honors program—spoke far more to her drive than his abilities. Everything had been teed up for him whereas Beth had to chart the course herself. And so when his sisters, particularly Laura, rolled their eyes at Beth's brand of mothering, Matthew grew defensive. They ought to admire her, not judge.

"You know," Beth said loudly over the sound of the blender, "I think something's up with Laura and—"

Matthew waited for the blender to quiet before responding. The morning had a "chill vibe," to borrow a phrase favored by the younger lawyers who reported to him, and he didn't feel like shouting.

When the grinding ceased, Matthew said, "That's just Laura. She probably feels guilty that she never motivated her girls the way you do Austin." He was careful not to use the word "push."

Beth whirled around. "What are you talking about? I wasn't saying anything about Laura and me. I was saying that I think something is up with her and Doug. I've never known him to work on a holiday weekend. You can't tell me this is the first time someone needed a root canal on July Fourth. I hope everything is okay."

Matthew scratched his chin, marveling at the wonder of the female brain. It never occurred to him to question Laura's explanation of Doug's absence. Come to think of it, it had been Sophie who jumped in to explain. There was also Laura's face when Noah joked about moving in with her.

Leave it to Beth to suss out an issue where his brain felt gummy and blocked. She was a wiz at multitasking, coordinating Austin's Tetris-like schedule and, apparently, sensing where relationship problems might be lurking.

"It must be tough having both girls out of the house when she has no job." Beth handed him a glass filled to the brim with a creamy purple liquid. "I'd go nuts."

"I'm sure she'll find a way to keep busy," he said. More quietly, he added, "Not everyone needs to work eighty hours a week to be fulfilled."

"What'd you say?" Beth was rinsing her glass and turned off the faucet.

"Nothing."

He didn't know how his sister intended to spend her free time. They hadn't had a real catch-up in ages. Before their mother got sick, the entire Jacobson clan gathered at least three times a year. In September they would be together for Rosh Hashanah, taking up an entire row at B'nai Shalom in East Brunswick and then feasting on Sylvia's melt-in-your-mouth oven-baked brisket (not to be confused with her BBQ summer brisket), sweet apple kugel and gooey carrot *tzimmes*.

In spring they got together again for Passover, alternating between Laura and Doug's house in Westfield and his and Beth's apartment. Beth called Zabar's and had all the food delivered; Laura claimed to make the entire seder meal from scratch. Beth swore she spotted take-out containers in the trash bin in the Cohens' driveway though. Why she was poking around in Laura's trash Matthew didn't need to ask. He would rather focus on jokes he could recite at the table: *Where do you buy bran matzah? LetMyPeopleGo.com. How do you drive your mother crazy on Passover? It's a piece of cake.*

Then there was the famous July Fourth weekend at the shore. His mother invited anybody with a pulse to eat, schmooze and watch the fireworks. Each year the crowd grew larger, and when the police started to show up because of noise complaints and cars blocking traffic, Sylvia invited them too. All this while their father threw up his hands about the cost and the mess.

Matthew hadn't considered the effect losing his mother would have on the holidays when she first got sick. He was hardly an observant Jew—his favorite meal was a bacon, egg and cheese sandwich, a guilty pleasure only on account of its unhealthiness, not because God was wagging a finger at him from above. Beth had converted to Judaism to appease his parents, but her transition from nonpracticing Christian to barely practicing Jew had a drive-thru quality. How his family would celebrate Jewish holidays was rarely top of mind for either of them. And yet, he missed the forced gatherings.

Not only was Sylvia too weak to tackle marinating a brisket for twenty-four hours and peeling over fifty carrots—her cancer struck during a concurrent worldwide pandemic. It was risky for any of them to be around her, and even in a post-vax world, nobody stepped up to host—probably because to do so while Sylvia stayed home felt blasphemous. And so Matthew had no idea what was going on with Laura, Sophie or Noah. Really going on, that is. They had their group chat but the chain was mostly jabs and jokes. The deeper conversations happened in person, usually after a heavy meal.

"Can you believe Noah waited in that line last night to buy lottery tickets?" Beth said, with a head shake that made Matthew notice she'd clipped up her hair again. "And Laura smokes even though Sylvia had lung cancer? And did you hear Sophie say she's losing her lease?" She booped Matthew's nose and kissed him firmly on the lips. "I'm so glad I found this Jacobson."

It irked Matthew when Beth put down his siblings, even when she did so in a roundabout way. Shifting from taking offense on behalf of his siblings to taking offense on behalf of his wife felt like riding a seesaw, something he hadn't enjoyed even as a kid.

Beth clucked her tongue. "I was up until three a.m. reviewing depositions. You were out cold when I came in." Matthew almost apologized for being asleep, as if he should have been burning the midnight oil too. "I'm going to take a shower. Make sure Austin's feet aren't covered in sand when he comes back. It's bad for the travertine." Before he could blink, she was racing up the stairs, her footsteps hitting the carpeted steps like a brisk rainfall. "Let's talk more about buying this place," she called from the second floor.

Matthew threw up his hands. His father's voice bounced around his head. *Money doesn't grow on trees . . .*

A few minutes later, Austin came in through the sliding door with a dimpled smile and an overflowing bucket in hand.

"Dad, I found a sand dollar." He lifted a delicate, creamy white shell with the five-point pattern of a starfish and handed it to Matthew, who held it up to the light to admire its intricate design.

"Good job, bud. This is very cool."

"Belongs to the order *Clypeasteroida*," Austin added, looking at Matthew in expectation of praise. Matthew deflated. To think *he* planned to help Austin classify shells. The kid was probably already developing a thesis on beach erosion based on his findings.

"What are you going to do with it?"

Austin hesitated before shrugging. "Maybe look up how much it's worth? I could sell it on eBay."

"And what do you need money for? What do you want that you don't already have?"

"I dunno. A skateboard maybe." It felt like yesterday Austin learned to ride a two-wheeler. Beth had paid a kid working at Ron Jon to teach him because she and Matthew were too busy. "Is Mom right that buying a lottery ticket is stupid? Aunt Laura, Aunt Sophie and Uncle Noah aren't dumb, are they?"

Matthew rubbed his eyes. He was still shaking the sleeping sand from his eyes and already he'd discussed Laura's marriage, buying a house he couldn't afford, and his siblings' intelligence.

"Everyone is different, kid. Don't try to understand anyone else's actions but your own. It's a fool's errand."

"What's a fool's errand?"

"A fool's errand is attempting to relax this weekend." Matthew looked down at his son's feet, coated in sand so thick it looked like he was wearing tan socks. "Go wash up before your mother sees."

MATTHEW, FAMILY IN TOW, ARRIVED AT THE BEACH HOUSE AT quarter past nine. Harvey Cedars was a good twenty-five minutes to Beach Haven in holiday traffic.

"I gotta pee," Austin said, darting inside.

"Remember not to flush in case someone is showering," Matthew called after him.

"I'll be inside in a few," Beth said. "I've got to make a couple of calls." Matthew also had work to attend to, but he planned to be surreptitious about it around his siblings.

In the light of day, the house's crumbling facade looked even worse. He noticed that the mezuzah, a bronze tube attached to the doorpost containing ancient Hebrew prayers that Matthew didn't understand, was dangling from a single rusted screw. Matthew stepped into the living room and winced. A sharp staple supposed to hold the carpet in place had come loose and jammed into his heel. In the kitchen, he found a box of Cheerios from the Clinton administration. The tower of dirty dishes in the sink made him think the dishwasher was on the fritz again. Most of the appliances, like the pantry items, were past their shelf life. When they did work, it was only half-heartedly. Wet towels took three spins in the dryer to dry. Over time, the family started to drape them outside on the hammock, along with the wet bathing suits.

Still, Matthew wanted to give the house its proper due. It had stood up to Hurricane Sandy when so many others in their vicinity were destroyed. In reality, the Jacobsons were just lucky the strongest path of the storm hopscotched over their little street, but he liked to think there was something magical in the infrastructure.

Sophie bounded down the stairs. "That sounds amazing," she said into her cell phone. "I'm so excited for you. Yes, I mean us. Thank you for showing her my work. Fam's here, gotta go. I miss you."

"Just got off with Ravi," she explained. Sophie lifted Austin's backpack, which was propped against the wall, and visibly slumped under its weight. "You keep rocks in this thing?"

Austin smiled and his dimple, a centimeter wide and at least as deep, surfaced. It was the same dimple Sylvia was famous for, a one-sided wonder that she'd passed down to Noah and Austin. Matthew inherited her lactose intolerance. "Just books. Guess what? I collected shells this morning and one of them had a slug inside. And I found a sand dollar."

Austin had the slightest hint of a lisp, which grew more pronounced the more excited he became. Matthew appreciated the glimpse of fleeting youth from his son's trampled *S*s. Austin's extensive vocabulary and ability to sit still for hours reading could otherwise make Matthew forget he had only just completed the seventh grade.

"Sand dollars are cool. Maybe we can paint shells together later? Or make shell necklaces? Ooh, we can even tie-dye them. I'm doing that right now with my campers at the Y. My only rule is no glitter. I don't glitter in July and August." Sophie winked at Austin, who looked both excited and puzzled.

To Matthew, she said, "Remember when we—"

"Tie-dyed our sheets?" Matthew chuckled at the memory, though nobody was smiling when Sylvia discovered their mess.

"Yep! This morning I found the sketch I made for that mural I painted in Mom and Dad's room. On the back of the paper, I had drawn all these hearts with my initials and Josh Siegel's.

Remember him? He lived down the street. I was totally obsessed with him."

"Of course." Boy did Matthew remember the Siegels. He had been equally obsessed with Josh's older sister, Samantha. But since meeting Beth twenty-three years ago, Matthew's sole romantic and sexual focus had been his wife. Beth was nearly his height, with a firm figure she was religious about maintaining. Her olive complexion (the only really great thing she got from her parents) tanned to a golden brown in summer, unlike him, with his Ashkenazic pasty skin that turned lobster-red, ironically a nonkosher animal.

They had met in the early days of sophomore year and immediately started dating. Under Beth's tutelage, his GPA climbed four-tenths of a point. He went from undeclared to a political science major and made dean's list. Beth coaxed him into applying to law school along with her, something he never imagined having the gravitas for, nor the grades. He was far more enchanted by the idea of staying with Beth than he was of becoming a lawyer, not that he had an alternate future planned out. Thinking now of Samantha Siegel, who had been bubbly and frothy as a teen and wondering what she might be like as a woman, he felt a longing for the first time since he'd smashed the glass under the chuppah. The memory of his awkward yet magical kiss with Samantha at the Barnegat Lighthouse some twenty-five years earlier awoke a part of him that had been hibernating in Beach Haven. Goofy Matthew. Magician Matthew. B+ Matthew. He wondered briefly if he should see a therapist.

"What were you congratulating Ravi about?" Matthew asked, eager to shift the gears in his head. He nudged his son gently. "Austin, go sit with Grandpa on the back porch."

"He's in Nantucket for the weekend with a gallerist."

Matthew vaguely recalled Sophie's text about a big opportunity this weekend. "And how is your art coming along? What are you working on?"

"A multimedia landscape, with a twist." She smiled. "Actually, I may have sold it to someone like you."

"Like me?"

"You know, a fancy suit person who can use Excel."

Matthew chuckled. "Touché. Should we go upstairs? I hear Laura and Noah."

As they passed the sliding doors that opened onto the back porch, Matthew was pleased to see Austin's and Leo's heads bent together, attacking the *Times* crossword while Austin fooled with his grandfather's magnifying glass.

Upstairs, they found Noah flopped on their parents' bed and the hump of Laura's behind jutting out from the opening in the bifold closet doors.

"Mothballs," Laura said, crawling out backward. "Mom was really into them. I'm pretty sure I'm high from the smell."

"Mothballs are toxic." Beth announced herself to the room with this remark. "I better tell Austin to keep out. What can I do? I'm here to serve." She flexed her biceps.

Laura, now on her feet, yawned with her whole body. "Jeez, Beth, you are looking very fit. I just hope you don't get too hot in all that spandex."

Matthew cringed, praying Beth wouldn't repeat what she'd said when they came upon a walking group in Central Park: *Spandex is a privilege, not a right.*

"Oh, I'll be fine. Lululemon athleisure is very breathable. Maybe I'll get you a set for your birthday. Thanks for the compliment, by the way." She flexed again, this time to show off well-defined triceps. "I completed my thousandth Peloton class just last week."

"Did you ever call Peloton customer service by chance?" Noah asked.

"I sure did. The software updates are very frustrating. Why do you ask?"

Before Noah could explain, Sophie pulled a sparkly dress from the closet. "I remember this! Mom wore it to your bar mitzvah, Matty." She held it against her frame. "I need to try this puppy on."

"You were six," Matthew said. "How could you possibly remember what Mom wore?"

Sophie already had both legs enrobed and was shimmying her arms through the sleeves.

"It's hard to forget a masterpiece like this. I thought big shoulders were an eighties thing, but Mom dragged that trend right through the nineties." Sophie waddled in the unzipped sequin gown over to Beth, motioning for her to pound the shoulder pads. "Let's see those muscles again."

Inspired by Sophie's transformation into the Liza Minnelli of the Jersey Shore, Laura adorned herself with their mother's fake pearls and fastened a gold brooch to her "JCC of LBI Family Volunteer Weekend" T-shirt. "Loehmann's finest," Laura said, showing off her accessories.

"Or Daffy's," Sophie said as she and Laura recited in unison, "Clothing Bargains for Millionaires."

"Our mother loved a bargain," Matthew said.

"Enough to change in that gross communal dressing room at Loehmann's," Laura said with a shudder. "I saw body parts in there that I'll never unsee."

"At least we won't fight over the family jewels," Sophie said, retrieving a silver bangle that had tarnished to near-black in a Nine West shoebox.

"Most definitely not," Beth said, pulling a chunky cocktail ring from the box and slipping it on next to her updated engagement ring.

"Holy shit!" Sophie grabbed Beth's hand. "You could ice skate on that thing."

Everyone's gaze fluttered to the emerald-cut diamond on his wife's ring finger. The salesperson had sworn that diamonds shrink over time, but Matthew was pretty sure this one had grown.

"Thank you," Beth said. "Anniversary present from your brother."

Matthew, embarrassed, busied himself by emptying his parents' dresser.

"Speaking of ice skates," Sophie continued. "I found my old ones in the garage. I can't believe Dad agreed to the lessons. Mom must have convinced him. I had zero talent. Laur, remember you were into tap dance for a hot second? That was unfortunate."

Laura's gaze was fixed on her phone, her brows knit together like spiderwebs.

"Laura? Hello?" Sophie said, waving her hands in Laura's face.

"Sorry," she muttered. "Was checking up on the girls."

"How's Doug managing back home?" Matthew asked, attempting a "nice weather we're having" tone.

"He's fine. Replacing the crown later today," Laura said.

"I thought it was a root canal," Matthew said, catching Beth's eye as Noah trundled back into the room with a stack of flattened cardboard boxes tucked under each arm. "Doesn't matter. What room should I start in again?"

Though Laura had gone to the trouble of divvying up the house, the Jacobsons spent the day moving from room to room together, reminiscing and laughing until their sides hurt. Laura grew noticeably cheerier. By the time it turned dark, they were crowded into the attic, using flashlights to sort through boxes and plastic bins.

They found yellowed issues of *Bay Magazine* (LBI's "culture" rag), for which Sylvia wrote a book recommendation column, Sophie's headgear ("No wonder I never had a boyfriend back then," she mused), Laura's tennis trophies ("You were athletic?" Beth asked), Noah's report cards ("Mom was so much easier on you," Sophie whined) and Matthew's magic sets ("Abracadabradoo!" the four siblings chanted, citing his signature finish). Combing through the box of foam rabbits, trick decks, metal rings, stacking dice and wands, Matthew realized he couldn't recall a single trick.

"Hey, check this out," Sophie said. She had unearthed a stack of canvases tied together with twine. "I didn't paint these. I'd remember."

She held up the top one from the pile, a watercolor of the ocean with a lifeguard chair as its focal point. "L.J." she read aloud, making out the initials in the bottom right corner.

"Dad? No way," Noah said. Sophie was flipping over the other canvases. Each one was signed L.J. except the last one, where "Leo" was scribbled.

The discovery silenced them. Their father was so right-brained he was practically lopsided. He showed zero interest in the arts beyond mumbling "Nice job" to Sophie when her drawings got tacked to the fridge. He was a numbers guy through and through. Artistry, to their father, was a beautifully balanced checkbook. To imagine the man who taught his kids about Fannie Mae and Freddie Mac and why recessions happen taking a paintbrush to a palette and swiping it across a canvas was inconceivable. And yet, there was his name in a loopy script that tapered off by the *O* as the paint ran thin. Matthew looked at Sophie. She was mesmerized by one particular painting, a self-portrait done in the graphic style of a comic book. To her, this had to come as the greatest shock of all.

"Maybe this is the sign we shouldn't sell," Noah said. He was also looking at Sophie. "We're rushing to pack up. Who knows what else there is to find? I'm sure it's not too late to call it off. We barely discussed the possibility of renting the house out."

"The closing is around the corner, Noah. And Dad doesn't want to deal with renters every time the toilet is clogged," Laura said. "But I'll take the boxes back to my house and go through them carefully. The girls are gone. I'll have plenty of time this summer to sort through them."

A loud crack that sounded like a gunshot startled everyone as Austin burst into the attic.

"Guys, come outside, the fireworks are starting. I'm watching with Grandpa."

Matthew had forgotten it was the Fourth of July. Everyone went downstairs and onto the deck, but they could only hear evidence of the display.

"Too much fog," Leo said. "Looks like we're not going to see much of anything."

"Maybe it'll clear up," Austin said. "Cumulus clouds travel quickly."

"Guys, look up," Laura said, pointing to the sky. "I'm pretty sure I saw fireworks behind those clouds. Or lightning, but it was really pretty."

"Speaking of pretty," Sophie said, unscrewing a sweating bottle of wine. "Dad, we found these beautiful canvases you painted in the attic. How in the world did you not show those to us before? To me?"

Leo shifted in his seat. "Those are here?"

"Yes," Sophie said. "Dad, you were good. I love the self-portrait."

He waved her off. "It was a hobby a lifetime ago. Matthew, would you bring out my Alka-Seltzer? It's upstairs in the bathroom."

Matthew hopped up, catching Sophie's disappointed face.

When he returned, his family was discussing the Powerball.

"I bought eight tickets," Noah said. "They're two bucks each, if anyone was curious. You can either choose your own numbers or they get randomly picked for you, so I did half and—"

Noah was interrupted by a sudden outburst. Austin was splayed on the deck, clutching his leg. He'd stumbled over a loose plank while trying to glimpse the fireworks and his shin was bleeding. In Sophie's scrambling haste to locate Band-Aids and ice, a kitchen drawer came off its tracks and landed on her foot. She yelped as Laura slipped on an ice cube and landed on her behind.

"Austin! Are you okay?" Beth rushed to him. "I hope he didn't get a splinter on top of everything. I'm sure the wood is rotted."

Matthew crouched down and stroked his son's cheek. "It's okay, sweetie. We're going to fix you right up."

"Good riddance to this place," Beth mumbled, gesturing to the plank of wood that tripped up their son. Matthew felt strangely offended on the house's behalf.

"She's not so bad," Matthew whispered into his son's ear as he applied bacitracin to his leg. He meant the house, and it was only later when he replayed the evening in his head that he realized Austin might have thought he was talking about Beth.

THE NEXT DAY, MATTHEW WAS IN THE MIDST OF OBTAINING A Skee-Ball record when Beth came running over, interrupting his flow.

"Shit!" he bellowed, realizing he missed his shot at a personal best. He shouldn't have cursed at Fantasy Island, which despite its lascivious name, was very much a family establishment. It was a small amusement park in Beach Haven and had been around since the dawn of time. Matthew lost all control when he was competing against his sisters at Skee-Ball.

"Have you seen Austin?" Beth tugged at his free arm, her face in a state of total panic.

Matthew looked around instinctively, as though his son might suddenly materialize between the race cars and basketball shoot-out. "What? No? I thought he was with you."

"I thought he was with you!" Beth was panting, beads of sweat erupting from every pore. "Austin! Austin! Austin!" She was screaming, turning in circles.

"I don't understand," he said. "You said you were going to do bumper cars with him." Matthew's heart beat wildly as he realized that he might be living every parent's worst nightmare.

"I meant later. I had to make a work call. I never said I was taking him now. You said you were going to the arcade with your sisters and Austin said he wanted to do that." Beth was fumbling through her phone. She stopped on a clear picture of Austin and held it in the air. "Has anyone seen this boy? Has anyone seen this boy?" She was spinning around while Matthew remained frozen in place, his shoes glued to the carpet.

"I didn't hear that," Matthew said, though it wasn't the time to determine whose fault it was that their son was missing. Missing! Why hadn't he heard Austin ask to go to the arcade? Matthew had been voice dictating a response to a work email that couldn't wait. *Couldn't wait.* Of course it could wait! Everything could wait until the end of the world if it meant keeping Austin safe.

His sisters had gathered around.

"Soph, you stay in here and check every inch of this place. I'll go outside and do a sweep of the rides," Laura said. "Everyone, make sure your phones are on full volume. Matthew—you go speak to the people in the ticket booth. I'm sure they have a lockdown procedure. Beth, keep showing people his picture. And—you." Laura grabbed a uniformed attendant fixing the Frogger machine. "You check the bathrooms for this boy." She thrust the photo on Beth's phone in his face. "His name is Austin. Check for feet under the stalls. Go!"

Matthew blinked twice. This was actually happening. He needed to move, to transport his body the twenty or so yards to where the stoned-looking ticket takers gave out wristbands and explain that his world was ending and he needed their help.

Their group dispersed in a blur. Matthew managed to get his jelly legs to run in the direction of the ticket booth. He was about to push his way to the front when he heard Sophie scream: "I SEE HIM!"

Could it be true? Could it all be over that quickly? Or did Sophie see him, except he was tragically hurt or worse? He turned toward his sister's voice and found her, smiling, her hand in the air pointing to the top of the Ferris wheel, where in the highest cabin Matthew saw his son, his healthy, breathing, joyful son, sitting next to Noah. They were laughing.

"Oh, thank God," he said to himself as he collapsed onto a nearby bench. It was at least five minutes before his breathing and heartbeat slowed and he could swallow normally.

When Austin came off the ride, he was startled to be swallowed by tight hugs from his teary-eyed parents.

"I'm sorry. I thought everyone saw us go to the Ferris wheel," Noah said.

"We had so much fun," Austin said. "We threw popcorn at people from the top."

"It's not your fault, Noah," Matthew said quietly. "It's ours. We clearly need to go over our crowded-place procedures. Right, Austin?" His boy shook his head in agreement, still looking dazed and happy from the mischievous ride.

Back home fifteen minutes later—nobody except Austin felt like staying at Fantasy Island after the incident—the Jacobsons, minus Leo, who was next door at Stanley's, were sprawled out in the living room when the doorbell chimed. Before anyone could stand to open the door or say "Come in," it swung open and three older women charged inside.

"We heard what happened," one of them said. She was dressed in a purple velour jogging suit even though it was easily ninety degrees outside.

"Thank goodness you found him," the woman to the left of Jogging Suit said. She couldn't have topped five feet and looked like Dr. Ruth. "I told my daughter to get one of those leashes for her kids the next time she takes them to Fantasy Island."

"That's a good idea," Beth said. She pulled out her phone, clearly to send herself a reminder to order one.

"I'm not wearing a—" Austin began to protest, but the third woman in the trio cut him off.

"We're sorry to interrupt." She wore tennis whites and a sun visor that said "Cornell Grandma." "But we're here on business."

"Hi, Myrna; hi, Arlene; hi, Betty." Noah stood to hug each of these women. Turning to his siblings, he said, "You remember Mom's canasta group." Matthew nodded but in truth these three ladies looked indistinguishable from the dozens of other older women who had been at the funeral and shiva.

The one in purple—Myrna, based on Noah's greeting—marched over to the game table and picked up a pad of paper. "Look," she said. "Sylvia's last game. She got three special hands that day, I remember."

Tennis lady, Betty, spoke. "We wanted to catch you all together. As you probably know, Sylvia chaired the temple's biggest fundraiser every Labor Day weekend. It's a card party with canasta, mahjong and bridge tables and it brings in a fortune. For the past two years we didn't have it. The first year Syl thought she could do it but when it got closer, well, you know, she had no strength. And then last summer . . ." Betty's voice trailed off.

"We've got to bring the event back. The temple needs funds. There's a church on every corner, but you know the JCC is the only synagogue on the island. We'd love to have involvement from your family. Frankly, we've been waiting to hear from one of you. This was Sylvia's baby after all," Myrna said, pulling a bag of sucking candies from her purse. Matthew recognized the strawberry foil wrapping. He didn't know those candies were still available.

"What kind of involvement?" Laura asked.

"Well, your mother did everything. Made the groupings, found a speaker for the luncheon, dealt with the caterer, solicited the raffle items, decorated the tables." Myrna smiled. "She convinced Black-Eyed Susans to donate all the food one year—no idea how she pulled that off. Anyway, we've got to get going. Betty's got a tennis match in fifteen minutes, Arlene has aquasize and I've got a FaceTime with my grandson at sleepaway camp. We'll be in touch."

"Just a moment, Myrna. Noah, can you sub for Linda Solomon next Tuesday? She's having a hip replacement," Arlene asked. Noah flashed a thumbs-up.

As they were leaving, Betty turned around and her gaze swept over the mountains of boxes scattered on the ground floor. She made a *tsk* sound. "Such a shame."

"You'll be hearing from us," Arlene said, poking her head back inside not a minute after the three women left.

You'll be hearing from us . . . Matthew suddenly remembered Arlene. She said that exact phrase to the poor caterer who dropped off the shiva food and forgot to include toothpicks with the gefilte fish bites.

"Sheesh, they're like the three witches from *Hamlet*," Laura said after their car pulled away.

"You mean *Macbeth*," Beth said. "The three witches are in *Macbeth*. *Hamlet* has the ghost."

"Whatever," Laura snapped.

"How about the three witches of LBI?" Matthew suggested.

"They're not so bad," Noah said. He was shuffling the cards on the game table. "Just don't screw up the count when you play cards with them, or things will get ugly."

FANTASTIC FOURSOME 🥷🥷✡️🥷🥷

LAURA

I have 64 boxes of Mom and Dad's crap in my garage if anyone's curious

SOPHIE

I wasn't curious

LAURA

MATTHEW

I can rent a storage unit if you want. Or two. No big deal

LAURA

Maybe. Are they $

MATTHEW

Doesn't matter. Just tell me

LAURA

K. I'll think on it. I'll start poking inside the boxes soon

SOPHIE

omg we could be on that show Storage Wars

MATTHEW

Except nobody wants our stuff

NOAH

That's not true. Matty— I think i might have broken your fancy coffee maker

MATTHEW

U better fix before the weekend

NOAH

Also does anyone know a good carpet cleaner on LBI— asking for a friend

SOPHIE

Who did mom use when Emma spilled the Manischewitz in the dining room?

LAURA

I have #—Noah, i will send 2 u

NOAH

🙏

MATTHEW

Noah, do you think you could refrain from burning the place down? It's a rental.

LAURA

Anyone talk to Dad?

NOAH

Yeah. He's all set for the move

SOPHIE

omg some kid in my camp group just painted a penis and balls

NOAH

Send pic

MATTHEW

Please don't. This is also my work phone. Unsubscribe

5

Sophie

TWO DAYS AFTER RETURNING FROM THE JERSEY SHORE, Sophie was stretched out on the daybed in Ravi's home studio listening with envy as he detailed his visit to Nantucket.

"You would have loved it, Soph." He sat on the low stool behind his potter's wheel, his brown palms and elegant, long fingers covered in gooey clay the color of slate. As the wheel turned, he moved his hands up and down to narrow the neck of the vase, stopping periodically to add water. It was a scene straight from *Ghost*. Sophie loved watching Ravi at work, from the first moment when he threw the slab on the wheel to when he used the tip of the scraper to etch the fine details. "Harriet's the real deal. She has two galleries already—one in London and one in Chicago. She wants me to advise her on building out the Nantucket space. Her other galleries focus on paintings, so they're all about wall space, but she's really into my work and wants to think more about how to display objets d'art."

Sophie sat up. "Is she old? Harriet's kind of an old-person's name."

Ravi took his foot off the pedal and the spinning wheel came to an abrupt stop, the lip of his vase collapsing. He frowned briefly and said, "She's young. I thought she'd be in her fifties but she's closer to our age. Harriet is a family name." Ravi went back to work, sturdy palms fixing the vase's mouth and nimble thumbs shaping the rim into a wavy flare.

Harriet is a family name, Sophie mimicked in her head.

"She has a really great eye," Ravi said.

I'll bet she does, Sophie thought, imagining Ravi through another woman's eyes. He wore snug T-shirts in dark colors, a knit beanie and a bad-boy wallet chain. Sophie ought to be more mindful of having Ravi out of her eyesight. She was on alert after spending three days with her devastated sister, who had filled in Sophie about Doug whenever they had a moment alone. Sophie was as shocked as Laura by Doug's behavior.

Given Laura's state of mind, Sophie was glad she had chosen to be with her family rather than go to Nantucket, even if Ravi was now infatuated with a young gallerist who, if he played his cards right, could mount his first solo show.

Sensing her insecurity, Ravi rinsed his hands and joined her on the daybed.

"Tell me about your weekend. How's your father?"

"My father, it turns out, is an artist! We found a stack of his paintings in the attic. I had no idea. His stuff is actually good. I asked him about it, but he totally brushed the whole thing off like, *Oh, that was a lifetime ago. Just a hobby.* It's so weird. Remember I told you how he insisted I get my teaching certificate at Bank Street? I know nobody wants their kid to be a starving artist, but you'd think he'd have mentioned—'Hey, by the way, I paint too.'"

"I can't imagine your dad painting," Ravi said. She understood what he meant. Leo the artist was as unlikely as a butcher composing poetry in between carving up a cow. "Did you bring any of his work back with you?"

She smacked her forehead. She needed to be more proactive

about preserving memories of her father while he was alive and had his marbles. She'd missed too many chances with her mother.

"No, but all the boxes are at Laura's." Sophie scooched closer to Ravi and threw a nearly bare leg over his lap. Harriett might be a hot gallerist, but Sophie knew exactly how to rev Ravi's engine. He was very much a leg man. He started to play with the fringes of her jean shorts and she felt herself heat up. Had she shaved her underarms or the other area? Showers were limited to three minutes at the shore, given the hot water situation. And since being back, hygiene had taken a back seat to working on her painting for Wall Street guy.

"Sounds like nice family time," Ravi said. His index finger was circling her navel, teasing her.

"It was like finding a time capsule of the Jersey Shore, digging through piles of beach badges, swim caps and sand toys. I found an award I got at camp for 'Most Improved Tetherball Player' and a participation certificate Noah got from a sandcastle competition. We are not a family of winners."

"I'll get you a '#1 Girlfriend' ribbon if you want," Ravi said.

"I would like that." Sophie laughed. "Remember those folding chairs with the vinyl strips that stuck to your skin when it was hot out? We found like a dozen of them, all with at least one strip missing. Did I tell you that Noah is crashing at this ridiculous house Matthew and Beth rented in the fancy part of LBI? All they do is work, so I'm not sure why they need a beach house, but who am I to judge?"

Ravi raised an eyebrow.

"I know how I sound," she said. "But it's normal for siblings to judge! It's done with love, I swear. You're an only child . . . you don't get it. Judging one's siblings is a responsibility, not a choice. Speaking of which, did I tell you about Laura and Doug?"

"Not yet." Ravi was lightly blowing on the back of her neck. She turned to straddle him.

"You know what?" She was entranced by Ravi's caresses. "I'll tell you later." Just then her cell phone dinged.

"Check it," Ravi said, sliding out from under her. "I have to glaze anyway."

She looked down at her phone and found a message from her SHART neighbor Yolanda: Read your email, bitch. We r @#$%&!

Buried in a slew of P.S. 282 messages about lost-and-found items and end-of-year evaluations, which fortunately mentioned nothing about budget cuts and her ass getting fired, Sophie found the message Yolanda was referencing. The sender, Ajax Group, meant nothing to her, but the subject, "Rent Increase—Important," got her attention.

The men in suits, formally called the Ajax Group, had announced a forty percent rent increase for all tenants effective immediately upon each lease renewal. *Undermarket for some time . . . increased costs of operation . . . yada yada . . .* Sophie couldn't give a fig about their bullshit reasons. She was out on her ass.

Ravi was reading over her shoulder. He took the phone from her hand and placed it on the chair. "Soph, you can live and work here."

She was wondering if and when he was going to bring that up again. The holiday weekend in Beach Haven was too hectic for her to obsess over his initial offer, which, having been made casually over the phone, didn't feel totally genuine.

"Look at all the extra space I have." He swept a toned arm around the room. Chic decorative objects rested on sophisticated coffee table books. There were armchairs and side tables whose sole purpose was to look pretty. A potted ficus thrived thanks to ample natural light.

In comparable square footage, SHART crammed in ten artists

who fought over the slop sink and elbowed each other if their brush-stroke was too wide. She felt bad shitting on SHART. There was plenty to love about the place. The energy that tended to peak around ten p.m. thanks to somebody's Red Bull run. The excitement when a resident sold a piece. The collective creativity mixed with the collective struggle made for an exciting atmosphere that felt like home.

She also didn't want to feel beholden to Ravi. Sophie was proud to set aside a portion of her teaching salary to pay for her studio and apartment share. Budgeting made her feel like a real adult—the sort her parents would be proud of. The problem was that she might not have a choice anymore.

She knew exactly who to call to discuss her predicament. The person who would stay on the phone with her until all hours of the night weighing the pros and cons, playing out various scenarios no matter how unlikely to occur. That person was Sylvia Rose Jacobson, and she was dead. Each time Sophie faced a moment where she wanted her mother's counsel, the reality that she was gone scalded her insides like hot soup. On the advice of a friend who had recently lost a parent, Sophie visited a medium. Maybe Madame Madeleine really did summon Sylvia from the other side, because when Sophie sat on a velvet tufted pouf in the medium's musty room in the back of a deli in Astoria, surrounded by hanging beads, tarot cards and candles burned to the wick, she could hear her mother loud and clear: "Why aren't you wearing lipstick?"

Laura would have been Sophie's natural next phone call, but she was dealing with her own relationship crisis, one much bigger and more consequential than Sophie's. She had her work friends, but their dating lives were a series of Tinder and Hinge disasters. Asking Nora-Ann to weigh in on "My sexy boyfriend wants me to move in rent-free and I don't know what to do" was not tone-deaf.

"What's your hesitation?" Ravi was back at her side, massaging her shoulders as if they were mounds of clay. Rent hikes were less stressful when the knot in her neck was being released by the pressure of Ravi's thumb.

"Would we get any work done if we're here together?" she asked, turning to face him. "I can be very tempting."

"No arguments there. But I'm sure we would manage. Listen, the offer is on the table. You don't have to decide today. My parents love you. They'd be thrilled."

Sylvia, too, had been a fan of Ravi. He charmed Sophie's mother by eating her food and asking for seconds and thirds. He promised her that he was on board with raising their future kids Jewish, which was awkward considering they'd only been together for a month when Sylvia brought it up. Leo's opinion of Ravi was less certain, but that was because he was quieter about everything.

Ravi stood and nudged open the drapes even wider before returning to the wheel. The space glowed. There was nobody using urine as a paint thinner or stealing supplies like at SHART.

"And if you sell a painting for five figures or win the lottery, I won't take it personally if you get your own studio," Ravi said.

"Ha, that reminds me. I bought some Powerball tickets over the weekend when I was with the fam. Noah was going out to buy some for himself and I figured, what the hell? Laura went in too. It's the first time I ever bought a lottery ticket. Not even a scratch-off." Sophie chuckled, thinking back to the weekend, Austin asking his mom about the Powerball and Beth basically calling them all idiots for getting in on the fun. "Better luck next time, I guess."

Ravi's foot left the wheel.

"You mean the $261-million Powerball? The winning number was drawn yesterday. That one?"

Sophie shrugged. "I guess. I think that's how much it was."

Ravi jumped up. "Sophie, two of the four winning tickets were sold in New Jersey. One of them at the shore. It's lottery history or something. One of the Jersey tickets was claimed already but there's one outstanding. I didn't mention it because it never occurred to me that you bought a ticket. Maybe you won. Sophie, holy shit!"

Sophie knew the odds were next to zero, but she felt herself getting light-headed. "How do I look up the num—" she started to ask, but Ravi was already reading them off his phone.

"They're 60-94-92-8-30."

The numbers sounded familiar, but she wasn't sure why.

"Wait a second, the Powerball is six numbers. I'm almost positive."

"I know," Ravi said. "I said, the winning numbers are 60-94-92-8-30-26."

Sophie scribbled them down. Looking at them on paper, seeing 609 and 492 instead of hearing "sixty," "ninety-four" and "ninety-two," she recognized the digits as the start of their home phone number in Beach Haven. The last four digits she couldn't figure out. But if the winning ticket was sold at the Jersey Shore, then it was entirely possible someone else had chosen the same area code and exchange. What had Noah said about the numbers he'd picked? Sophie tried to remember but all she could recall was Austin tripping and everyone scampering to soothe him.

The door to Ravi's apartment swung open and Iris bounded in as the dog walker unclipped her leash. She headed straight for her favorite place, Sophie's crotch.

"Not now," Sophie said, petting the dog. "When I'm rich, I'll give you all the treats you want. But right now, I have to call my brother."

"C'MON, NOAH, NOT NOW," A BREATHY VOICE SAID IN THE background when Noah answered Sophie's call.

"Robin, shh, it's my sister," came Noah's muffled voice. "Soph, what's up? I'm at work."

"Noah, I don't care what you're up to. I need you to focus. What numbers did you pick for the Powerball tickets?"

She heard the sound of covers swishing and the groan of the woman waiting on Noah's "customer service."

"My birthday, one ticket with Yankee player numbers, one with the Giants and our home phone number plus—" he said.

"The phone number one—you need six numbers, right? Did you do the extra digits before or after the phone number?" Sophie was asking questions that prolonged the possibility of them having won. She wanted to extend the fantasy that her life was about to change in a glamorous, unfathomable way, and the moment Noah said the wrong number, or the right number but in the wrong position, it was all over.

"I did it after," he said. He didn't appear to be catching on that there was a chance they had won. Maybe he already knew they hadn't and was irritated Sophie had interrupted him.

"What numbers did you pick?" This was it. The sink-or-swim moment. Her breath caught in her throat. Ravi motioned for her to put the phone on speaker. Together they stared at the screen, as if the digit would appear.

"I picked eight, because it's my lucky number. Then thirty, because I'm thirty. And twenty-six, for our house number. Yes, I know, I'm the only sentimental one that cares about the—"

"Noah Samuel Jacobson. I could freaking kiss you right now. WE WON! WE WON THE FUCKING POWERBALL!"

"Holy shit, holy shit, holy shit! No way!" Noah started screaming. Ravi and Sophie were hugging, jumping up and down until the phone clattered to the floor. Sophie dove to pick it up.

"What do we do now?" Noah asked. "This is so insane. Did you tell Laura?"

"No, I didn't know we won yet!"

"Noah, what in the world is going on?" Breathy Voice asked.

"Robin, I just won the Powerball."

The woman let out a glass-shattering shriek.

"Noah, Noah, focus," Sophie yelled. "Where do we turn the ticket in? What does it say on the back? Noah, read it to me."

Sophie waited for Noah's response, but there was only silence. Even his companion was quiet. It gave Sophie a moment to regain her faculties. Her heart was thudding so forcefully she put a hand on her chest to keep it from bursting out. To think she was worried about getting kicked out of SHART. Now she could buy the building! She could buy whatever she liked!

"Noah? Hello? Do you need me to help you with the ticket? I can come down now. We can celebrate at Black-Eyed Susans. I'm getting lobster. No, two lobsters. And champagne. Noah—are you listening?"

"Soph, I—" Noah's voice was strained, as if squeezing through a colander. She was antsy to call Laura. Winning the lottery ought to take the sting out of Doug's departure.

"I know. You're with someone now. That's fine. Do your business and just be ready for me when I get there. It won't be for another three hours anyway."

"Sophie, listen, there's—" Noah tried again.

"Noah, it's all good. I need to hang up to get an Uber."

"Sophie, let him speak." Ravi put a firm hand on her shoulder.

"Yes, let me speak," Noah said. "Sophie, I don't know how to tell you this, but I have absolutely no idea what I did with the tickets."

"ARE YOU TELLING ME THAT I LOST A HUSBAND AND MILLIONS of dollars in one week?"

Calling Laura had been a mistake.

In the seconds she deliberated before patching in her sister, Sophie reasoned that in the worst-case scenario—never finding the ticket—none of them was any worse off than before. But it was quickly apparent that the expression "It is better to have loved and lost than never to have loved at all" did not parlay to "It is better to have known you could have been a millionaire and not be one than to never have known at all."

"What do you mean, lost a husband? What happened to Doug?" Noah asked. "Is that why you were weird about me moving in?"

"Not now, Noah," Sophie snapped. "Laura, we need your help."

"Yeah, you're good at this stuff," Noah said.

Laura groaned. "Noah, walk me through exactly what happened from the minute you got to 7-Eleven until you got home."

Noah detailed his excursion in minute detail, down to the moment he stepped in gum upon leaving the convenience store. Something didn't add up. He'd been gone for well over an hour and yet the story—from grabbing the ice cream, choosing the lotto numbers and paying for the tickets, to collecting his free slushie with purchase—didn't add up to much. Even with the five minutes spent peeling the gum from his shoe, his story didn't account for the amount of time he was out. He hadn't mentioned anything about talking to his socalled client about her computer trouble. Maybe he'd gone to Breathy Woman's house for a quickie? A frisky roll in the hay could have landed the ticket any number of places.

He had no incentive to hide the whereabouts of the ticket—Noah, who would give the shirt off his back, would never steal the entire amount for himself. The man had the monetary desires of a teenage boy—unlimited fast food and the latest gaming console. Normally Sophie respected boundaries, which wasn't easy in a family of six. But in this case, every detail mattered. If Noah was kissing someone, perhaps the tickets fell out of his back pocket while his lover slipped her hand inside. If he pulled out his wallet to pay for a bag of weed, maybe the tickets got mixed up in the haste to do the exchange?

"I am like ninety-nine-point-nine percent sure that I had the tickets when I got back home. I remember seeing them in my wallet when I was looking for my rolling papers. Yes, I smoke the occasional joint."

So he wasn't hiding weed. Sophie still felt like there was something he wasn't saying.

"Then the next day we were all together packing. I didn't use my wallet at all. I didn't even leave the house. You guys know that. I definitely had my wallet when I went to get lunch at Tuckers. I remember because my credit card didn't work—guess I missed a payment or something. Charlotte just let me have my sandwich on the house."

"But were the tickets in the wallet? Think!" Laura's patience had gone from thin to nonexistent. While she was the most similar to Sylvia in terms of maternal instinct, she did not coddle Noah like their mother had. "Did you stop for gas? Did you make any pit stops?"

"No, definitely not. But I did transfer a bunch of things from my wallet when I moved into Matthew's house."

"You're living with Matthew?" Laura asked.

"Yeah, didn't you see our text? I broke his coffee maker."

"I still can't believe Beth okayed that," Sophie said.

"Yes, and all I have to do is take Austin stargazing and record what we see once a week, which I like doing anyway."

"Guys, can we refocus—" Sophie said, noticing Ravi tapping away on his device. She hoped he was googling "What to do about a lost lottery ticket" but the messages app was open. Squinting, she made out the name Harriet.

"Noah, why were you reorganizing your wallet? Since when are you Mr. Clean? I could smell your socks from down the hallway last weekend," Laura said.

"That's not helping," Sophie said. "Keep going, Noah."

"I am helping," Laura said, and it was then that Sophie heard the car horns in the background. "I'm driving to LBI. I'm going to turn the place upside down until we find that ticket. Help would be appreciated."

"Getting an Uber now," Sophie said, praying she was spending against a future windfall when she saw the price. She eyed her untouched bagel on the kitchen counter. Though her stomach was growling, she couldn't imagine taking a bite. She collected her bag and blew Ravi a kiss as she sailed out the door.

"I'm already looking for it," Noah said just as Laura interrupted with, "And, Noah, don't touch a thing until I get there. Sit on your hands if you have to."

SOPHIE'S UBER PULLED IN JUST BEHIND LAURA'S SUBARU, three hours after they'd hung up the phone. Sophie pulled her sister in for a frenzied hug. She took a step back to appraise Laura. She had deep purple sockets under her eyes and the tip of her nose was chafed, which meant she'd been crying. They all expected empty nest–hood to be rough on Laura, but having to navigate it without Doug was unfathomable. If the past three hours were any indication, sometimes unfathomable things become reality. The past year had been an exercise in disbelief. Sylvia dying before Leo had been an impossibility, and yet there they were.

"I thought you'd get here way ahead of me," Sophie said.

"I had to make a stop," Laura said, avoiding Sophie's gaze.

"Which was? I would think you'd want to hightail it here as quickly as possible."

Laura looked down and kicked at the pebbled driveway.

"Laura . . ." Sophie lifted her sister's face by the chin. "What did you do?"

"Fine. So you know I searched Doug's things after he came back from Arizona. Come to think of it, this makes today my second search operation in a week. Anyway, I went through every pocket, combed his suitcase, looked in all the obvious places and the less-obvious ones. He had a ton of names and emails scrawled on brochures and business cards. I looked up everyone—even the men, because, you know, I obviously don't know my husband at all. Anyway, I found a bunch of the women's profiles on LinkedIn—mostly dental hygienists. I know he needed a new person because one of his hygienists is moving. This one woman whose name he had written down, Alexis McPherson, lives in Manalapan. I found pictures of her, and let's just say I'm sure Doug wouldn't mind if she gave him a deep cleaning. So I drove by her house, which was on the way. More or less."

Sophie willed her face to remain neutral so Laura didn't clam up. "Manalapan is like a forty-five-minute detour at least. Were you checking to see if Doug was there?"

"No, he's at work. I wanted to see what Alexis looked like. It doesn't matter because she wasn't home. Her mailbox needs a paint job, I can tell you that much."

It was definitely not the time to point out that Laura and Doug's mailbox was also in disrepair.

"Laura, you have to get ahold of yourself. As soon as we tear this place up and find the ticket, you and I are going to have a long talk."

Noah appeared, walking gingerly across the pebbled driveway with bare feet and a noticeable limp. He wore a faded T-shirt that said "Beach (Haven) Bum" and ratty cargo shorts. His hair looked like he'd stuck his finger in a socket, something he'd done more than once as a child. Framed by the modern mansion, he looked like a rock star coming off a weeklong bender. She felt a pang of guilt at how little mind she'd paid to where Noah would go after the family house sold and Matthew's rental was up, but the guilt gave way to frustration pretty quickly. Why had she and Laura not insisted on keeping the tickets themselves? Obviously, they never expected to win, but Noah had always been the kind of person who would lose his head if it wasn't attached to his body.

"What's with the limp?" Sophie asked.

"Bike accident a while back. I was going for PT, but the sessions got too expensive," Noah explained. "My health insurance ran out after Peloton laid me off."

"That's not okay, Noah," Laura said. "You need health insurance. Mom would kill you if she knew."

Noah shrugged. "Yeah, well, I don't think I have to worry about that."

They followed Noah through a gray slate door into the uber-modern beach house. The exterior was a striking combination of white stucco and massive expanses of glass. It had a flat roof and three balconies with glass railings capped in steel. The inside matched the outside, all sharp lines and shades of white and gray. "Is Matthew here?" Sophie asked.

"No, they're all back in the city. I tried to keep Austin for the week but they didn't trust me to make sure he gets his work done. Considering I lost a winning lottery ticket, I guess they're right." Noah hung his head.

"Back to the ticket. Tell us everything you remember," Laura said. "Again."

Sophie looked around and noticed two distressed wooden signs hanging on an otherwise bare wall. One said "Beach Vibes Only" and the other said "Gone Fishin'!" Even in the midst of the chaos, she had to chuckle at the incongruity of Matthew and Beth living amidst these Jimmy Buffett slogans.

Noah took a deep breath. "Right. When I got here, I decided to clean out my wallet. I left everything on the dresser to organize later. The tickets were in that pile—it was a bunch of receipts and rewards cards and old credit cards I never use. And then Beth called me for dinner and I didn't want her to think I was messy, so I took all that stuff and shoved it in the dresser."

"So it's in the drawer!" Sophie reached on her tiptoes to hug her much taller, younger brother, but he backed away.

"Well, not exactly. It was the same drawer where I dumped all my T-shirts. The ones I sleep in."

"As compared to this fine specimen you're wearing now," Laura asked.

"Laura, again, not helping," Sophie said, shooting her sister a look. They could criticize Noah all they wanted *after* they found the ticket. "Take us to your room. It probably just fell behind the dresser."

"Actually, what happened was that after dinner I went to my room and opened the drawer to get a shirt but it was empty. I went back to the kitchen to ask Beth where my stuff was and she said she asked the housekeeper to wash all my things that had been in the other house because, you know, it was so dusty over there."

Sophie bit her lip. Beth-bashing would also have to wait.

"So basically our millions were put through a heavy-duty rinse cycle and tumble-dried on high heat?" Laura asked.

"What would that mean for the tickets?" Sophie asked.

"If they got the full treatment, I'd say there's about a fifty percent chance they're in good enough condition to be valid. I'm hoping the cleaning lady skipped the fabric softener. How do we get in touch with her?"

"I already texted," Noah said.

"You got her number from Beth? She's going to assume you destroyed something in the house. In which case, we gotta move fast."

"Relax, Soph. I had Jacinta's number because I thought she was cute, so I asked her for it. Anyway, she said she remembers seeing a bunch of things mixed in with the clothes and that she definitely didn't wash them. And that she never throws anything away. That's apparently in the housekeeping code of conduct."

"So where is the stuff?" Laura asked, her body poised like a jungle animal ready to pounce. She had been a modestly competitive swimmer when they were kids, and Sophie hadn't seen that look of determination on her face since her toes were curled over the edge of the pool waiting for the whistle.

"That's the problem. Jacinta can't remember. She's sure she put them in a drawer or cabinet for safekeeping, but she can't remember which one. She's new to working in this house and doesn't have her system down yet. She's really smart. You guys would like her. Also, her English isn't great and we were having a tough time communicating. And I didn't want to tell her that there was a winning lottery ticket in the pile, because, you know."

"That was actually smart of you," Laura said. "We need to tear this place apart. Luckily, we have the helpful tip from Jacinta that it could be anywhere."

The siblings divvied up the house and began to canvass. Sophie moved furiously from room to room on the top floor, her arms limp from tossing bulky couch cushions and shoving bed frames. Noah went out to the garage and storage shed where the outdoor furniture and pool toys were kept. Laura searched the ground floor.

After about thirty minutes passed, Sophie was ready to give up. They were looking for a needle in a haystack, the needle a small paper probably shredded to bits by now and the haystack the entire length of LBI, plus the ocean. She took a seat on a leather armchair and let her mind drift to whether she ought to move in with Ravi since the windfall was clearly not happening.

"I FOUND IT!" Laura's voice exploded from the ground floor, winding its way around the steel-and-glass staircase up to Sophie and out to the storage shed where Noah, they later learned, had just stumbled upon a trunk full of cosplay gear.

Sophie flung herself down the stairs, missing one and grasping the banister for support, reaching the foyer at the same time Noah busted inside, dragging a stiff leg and holding a Daenerys wig. Laura was in the center of the foyer, standing triumphantly with one hand in the air like the Statue of Liberty, clutching a stack of tickets.

"Hang on," Sophie said. "We need to triple check that the numbers are a match."

"This one's the winner," Laura said, staring down at the top ticket. "At least we hope so."

Sophie pulled up the screenshot she'd taken earlier of the winning draw. Slowly, she read each number out loud, after which Laura said, "Correct" in a firm yet nervous voice. When she said the final "Correct," the three charged each other, huddling into a sweaty mosh pit. "We won! We won!" they chanted over and over until their voices grew hoarse.

"Thank God we found it," Sophie said, stopping to catch her breath.

"Found what?"

They pulled apart and swiveled in the direction of a fourth voice. Matthew stood in the front door. Sophie tried to focus on his face, but she was only seeing stars and splotches of darkness.

"Guys, I'm not feeling so—" Sophie said just as her knees gave out and she sank to the ground.

6

Laura

"SOPH, CAN YOU HEAR ME?" LAURA BENT OVER HER SISTER and studied the green of her eyes. A quick Google search indicated that a concussed person may have dilated or uneven pupils. "Soph, keep your eyes open. We need to check you out, honey."

Laura beckoned Noah. "I don't know what I'm doing. Do her pupils look normal to you?"

He crouched over Sophie as Laura held her lids open. "I can't tell. What do normal ones look like? Maybe they are a little bigger. I need something to compare to."

Laura lay down next to her sister on the cold marble floor and widened her eyes.

"They look about the same," Noah said with meager confidence. "Soph, how do you feel?"

"Huh?" Sophie muttered. "Where am I?"

Matthew, who still had no idea what he'd stumbled upon, had thoughtfully reacted to Sophie capsizing by grabbing ice from the kitchen. He knelt on the floor, applying a cold pack to Sophie's forehead. Laura felt delirious as she stared into the bulbs of the bronze chandelier that hung over the two-story foyer.

"You're at the shore, with all of us," Noah said. "You fainted but you're going to be okay."

Matthew looked at Laura, clearly wanting an explanation for what was going on. She realized she had to get up. But how to function normally? She didn't remember how to do that. She had won the lottery. She was rich. She needed to tell Doug.

Doug. What did this mean for them? He was still living at home, where they tiptoed around each other awkwardly, with too much politeness. She saw, well spied, a website with condo listings open on his laptop, alongside another open tab with a live feed of the farm where Emma was working for the summer. *The girls.* She couldn't fathom how Hannah and Emma would react to the lottery or the separation, if that was still happening. Both would mean enormous changes for them.

"Laura, I'm speaking to you," Matthew said, and she realized how deeply she had zoned out. "Can you explain why everyone is here and why Sophie fainted? When I walked in the door you guys were screaming, 'We found it.' Found what?"

It was, strangely, the first time it truly hit Laura that only three-fourths of the Jacobson siblings had won. From her prone position, Sophie, red hair fanned around her head like a rooster's crown, mumbled, "I didn't eat or drink anything all day."

Laura cleared her throat. "Because we won the Powerball."

"Right. And I'm Kim Kardashian," Matthew said. Laura was surprised her brother knew who that was. Maybe his firm represented her underwear line.

"No, Matty, we really did," Noah said, putting a hand on his brother's shoulder. Noah was at least three inches taller than Matthew, but given that Matthew was older and more mature in every possible way, Noah's extra inches made for a comical difference. Except now there was another way Noah would tower over Matthew.

"How much did you win?"

Nobody answered. Laura, for one, didn't even know the answer.

The lottery had three other winners. She knew taxes would eat up a chunk.

"About twenty million," Noah said. "Give or take. I'm not really sure. I did a quick look online but didn't really want to think about it before we found the ticket."

"You're joking." The color drained from Matthew's face. "I need to sit down." He stumbled over to the Lucite bench by the entry and dropped his head between his knees.

"It's true," Sophie said. She had pulled herself to a seated position and shifted the ice to the back of her head. "Ravi told me there was one unclaimed winning ticket purchased at the Jersey Shore. Sure enough, it was ours."

"And I lost it somewhere in the house, which is why—" Noah started to say.

"Which is why you guys are all here and my rental looks like a family of raccoons ripped it apart," Matthew said. Had he said "rental" on purpose, Laura wondered? To emphasize that while he was living large, he didn't own the home? Or because as a renter, he was responsible for keeping the place in good condition, and the three of them had ransacked it?

"We'll clean everything up," Sophie said. "As soon as this bump on the back of my head calms down and I stop seeing double, I will make sure everything is put back in its place."

"Or we'll hire someone to do it. Now that we're lottery winners," Laura said. Too soon, she realized, when nobody dared to crack a smile.

"And I'll be able to get out of your hair and rent my own place," Noah said.

A phone rang and Matthew fished his cell from his pants pocket. "Hey, Beth," he said. "Yeah, I'm here."

The three other siblings locked eyes. Suddenly, everything was happening in double time. A week ago, they were crammed into their childhood home, contemplating how much a tag sale might fetch for some of the nicer things. Now, they were about to be millionaires, with money to—to what? What would Laura do with *millions* of dollars? She couldn't think beyond splurging on the fancy-looking laundry detergent sold in glass bottles that only the ladies wearing nice jewelry put in their baskets at ShopRite. Was laundry even going to be part of her life going forward? If not, would she send the laundry basket down the river like Moses to formally bid it adieu?

"What noise? Oh that, yeah. My siblings are all here," Matthew was saying to Beth.

Shit, Noah mouthed to Laura.

"No, not just Noah. All of them. I just arrived so I haven't had time to look for Austin's book yet. Yes, I know his assignment is due tomorrow." Matthew looked around, taking in the destruction. "It could take me a while to find it."

Sorry, Laura whispered to Matthew, but he shushed her.

"Beth, listen, there's been a development. Remember when Noah went out the other night to buy that Powerball ticket?" Matthew turned away from them. "Well, they won. They actually won the thing. Noah, Laura and Sophie won about twenty million dollars. They think, anyway. The number is still up in the—"

Beth, who had been inaudible moments earlier, could now be heard loud and clear. "ARE YOU KIDDING ME? YOUR SIBLINGS WON TWENTY MILLION DOLLARS?"

Matthew turned back around and gave the three of them a defeated shrug, as if to disclaim whatever Beth might say next.

"Yes. It's very exciting. Noah had the ticket in the house, which is why they're all here. It's before taxes of course, and they need to split it in three, but it's still pretty life-changing. Want me to put the phone on speaker so you can congratulate them?"

"Um, Matthew," Noah said, signaling with a swift cut to the throat not to put the phone on speaker just yet. "It's not twenty million total. It's twenty million dollars . . . each."

"Beth? Did you hear that?" He covered the mouthpiece. "I'd better take this in another room."

Matthew strode briskly into one of the ground-floor guest rooms and closed the door behind him. Laura beckoned Noah and Sophie with a jerk of her arm and the three tiptoed over and pressed their ears to the door. Their brother's voice came through in spurts.

"I know, it's crazy . . . I have no idea how Noah will manage it . . . I don't think my dad knows yet . . . We should be happy for them . . ."

For a few seconds, they didn't hear anything else. Laura was about to scurry away, pulling Noah and Sophie with her, but then Matthew's voice sounded again, this time louder.

"Beth, c'mon. You said the lottery was a tax on stupid people. I'm pretty sure everyone heard you. No, you were not whispering. Noah asked us twice if we wanted in. Beth . . . Beth . . . that's not nice. They will not lose all the money in a year. Beth, I gotta go. Let me find Austin's book. I have a two-hour drive back tonight. Beth, I love you. Let's talk when I get home. Okay, bye."

The three of them made a mad dash for the living room. Matthew emerged a minute later, clasping the cell phone in his hand. A flash of lightning illuminated the foyer, followed by the crack of thunder. A summer storm began pelting the large glass windows.

"Er, Beth says congratulations."

AFTER MATTHEW LEFT TO RETURN TO THE CITY, AUSTIN'S BOOK in hand, the three remaining Jacobsons sat for a while in stunned silence. Laura was physically and emotionally drained. From her slumped position on the sofa, she mumbled, "We need to tell Dad."

"Now?" Sophie asked. "It's ten p.m."

"I don't think he'll mind being woken for this news," Noah said.

Leo answered on the fourth ring, sounding wide awake. "Yello?"

"Dad, are you sitting down? I'm with Noah and Sophie and we have something pretty incredible to tell you," Laura said.

"What is it?" Leo asked. "I'm kind of tied up."

They exchanged a surprised look. Mr. Mylanta should have been in bed for at least an hour already.

"Are you sitting down?" Laura repeated.

"Leo! Pass me the flashlight. I'll hold the ladder for you next," came a man's voice. He had a distinct Brooklyn accent. "Ladder" came out as "ladda."

"What did you say?" Leo called out. "Hang on, I gotta adjust my hearing aid."

"Dad, what's going on? Where are you?" Sophie furrowed her brow.

"I know that voice," Noah said. "That's Stanley Archer."

"What's he doing with Stanley at ten o'clock at night?" Sophie's right eyebrow lifted in confusion.

"Dad, what are you doing with Stanley this late?" Laura enunciated each syllable, hoping to connect with the receptors in her father's hearing aids. "And, Dad, we really need to tell you something. It's pretty big news." *Bigger than whatever it is you're doing with Stanley Archer at this hour.*

"This flashlight's dead," they heard Stanley say.

"It's not dead. You're not using it right," Leo responded. "Press the top button."

"There's only one button. I'm not a moron, Leo," Stanley said. "Oh, wait, never mind. I got it on."

"Dad, what is happening over there?" Sophie demanded.

"The damn broker called me this afternoon. The buyer's inspector claimed there's a termite infestation in the attic. I said that's impossible but the buyers are demanding we knock twenty thousand off the purchase price for remediation costs. I told Stanley about this *mishegas* and we decided to investigate for ourselves. He's in the attic and I'm about to join him."

"Dad, Stanley can barely see. You can barely hear. You should have moved into Matthew's house with Noah until you left for Florida. The two of you have no business fooling around on ladders," Laura said. "Noah will drive over there and have a look." She looked at Noah, motioning for him to get moving, but he was ashen. It sounded like he was muttering "Oh no" and "Stupid idiot" to himself.

"Dad, hey, it's Sophie. We need you to focus. Can you please forget the termites for a minute?" She covered the speaker and whispered to Laura and Noah, "I can't hold it in any longer. Let's just tell him."

"Okay, I'm listening. What's going on?" Leo said.

"So . . . remember when the Powerball story came on TV that first night we were all together and Noah went out to buy a ticket? Well, believe it or not, we won! We're rich!"

There was a loud pop, then a rustling and finally the screech of static.

"Dad, are you there?" Noah asked.

"Hello? Dad? Stanley?" Laura said.

They heard a thud.

"Holy hell." Leo's voice came through just as they were about to hang up and try him back.

"I know, it's insane," Laura said.

"No, it's not that," Leo said. Laura locked eyes with her equally surprised siblings. "I gotta go. Stanley fell off the ladder."

———

"I DON'T UNDERSTAND," DOUG SAID FOR THE FOURTH TIME
the following morning. He and Laura were seated at the kitchen table, coffee mugs in hand. Neither of them were used to such an eerily
quiet house. Laura couldn't remember having time to sit with her
husband and drink coffee in peace. Normally, the girls were milling
about, fighting over a missing article of clothing or complaining to
Laura that she had bought the wrong brand of oat milk.

"I know. It's a lot to take in. But it's real. Noah, Sophie and I—
on a total whim, mind you—went in on a few lottery tickets after a
Powerball story came on the news. Sophie and I are turning the winning ticket in to the lottery office later today. This is really happening." She smiled and took Doug's hand in hers. "We're rich, baby!"

He returned her smile and she recognized it as his genuine one,
which was crooked and gummy and unmasked a chipped left inci-
sor. He loved when patients noticed his less-than-perfect teeth because he was able to respond, "That's what happens when the only
dentist you trust is yourself."

"What about Matthew?" Doug asked. "And Beth. She must be
having a conniption."

"I told you. They didn't want in on the ticket," Laura said. "Noah
asked several times. Anyway, it's not like they need the money."

"I guess that's true," Doug said, his chin cocked as though he was
running mental calculations. "But this is a lot of dough, to anybody.
Holy shit, Laura. We *are* rich." He stood spontaneously, pulling
Laura up with him, and swept her into a bear hug that nearly snapped
her ribs. Other than brushing up against each other in their small
bathroom, they shared little physical contact. It was something
Laura hadn't even realized until Mindy planted the bug in her ear.

She felt the weight of Doug against her, the quick patter of his heart-beat against her chest and the scratchy bristles of his preshave jaw-line against her cheek.

"We're not just rich," she said. "We're filthy rich."

At that, he pulled away and looked at Laura with consternation. She knew what he was about to say.

"Laura, this feels wrong. I asked for a separation last week. I don't want you to think that the money changed that. That because you won all this money, suddenly my doubts have vanished. What would you think of me if I was that kind of person?"

This, Laura thought, was exactly why she loved him and why she needed to fight for their marriage.

"I didn't win millions of dollars. We did. We've been married for twenty years and we've been separated for less than a week. We still live in the same house. We share daughters. And toothpaste. We drink from the same Pepto-Bismol bottle. This money belongs to both of us."

Doug looked at the floor. "I'd been looking for a condo to rent. I hadn't told you yet. I don't think I ever would have pulled the trig-ger, but still."

Laura feigned surprise, as though she hadn't combed through each bookmarked listing and cross-checked it against every dental hygienist's address she'd found. So far, there was no smoking gun.

"You had so much going on with packing up the Beach Haven house, and I know how quiet it's been with Hannah and Emma gone, that I figured I could wait a few weeks before even thinking of mak-ing a move. But it would be wrong of me to pretend that—"

She put a finger to his lips. If she could, she would have stapled them shut permanently. She respected his honesty and his unwill-ingness to sweep the past week under the rug, but did he have to say everything out loud? Couldn't they just silently agree to carry on as a married couple like before, except with nicer clothes, a bigger house and a fancy car?

"When you asked for, you know, the separation, you said my idea of date night was comparing our calendars and reviewing the family budget. And you're right. We had so little time together without the girls around that when we were alone, I pounced on the opportunity to do business. I'm the daughter of an accountant, what can I say? There is nothing sexy about reviewing college loans and taking out a second mortgage. Or discussing how we're going to pay for an SAT tutor and your office renovation at the same time. We were pitted against each other too many times in stressful situations. But those days are over. We have the money now to enjoy each other in a whole new way."

Doug closed his eyes, appearing to be in deep contemplation. "These winnings will definitely open up some new ways. So, what is that figure? Six million?" He shook his head in disbelief.

"I think so. After peeling Stanley off the attic floor and removing a splinter from his—well, it doesn't matter—we sat down with my dad for a talk. There's nothing like an accountant to throw a wet blanket on a Powerball win," Laura said.

"What did he say?"

"At first, he wouldn't say anything. He kept telling us that we needed to hire our own financial advisor, as if we'd sue him for malpractice or something. Eventually, he gave in. Turns out he had a client who won the lottery, but a much smaller amount. Still, there are some common factors. The biggest is that the sum you see advertised—the $261 million—is the amount of money you'd get if you took the thirty-year annuity option. He advised us to take the lump sum up front, which is roughly half. It's something to do with the present value of the money. Don't ask me to explain. I was an English major, remember?" She had been a good student, which is why it had really irked her when Beth called her out on the mistaken Shakespeare reference.

"I don't see your Dad advising that we take the lump sum. He'd be worried that it's too much, too soon, no?"

"Totally," Laura said. "I was shocked. But the lump sum is better for investing opportunities and can avoid long-term tax implications. I guess if the tax rate goes up? I stopped fully understanding halfway through his talk. But I got the main points, I think."

"So lump sum it is. Then what?"

"Then there's an automatic twenty-four percent taken off by the IRS."

"Taxes, that makes sense."

"That's just the beginning. The twenty-four percent is some special lottery tax. Come April, we pay income tax on what's left. And because we'll be in the highest tax bracket, that's another thirteen percent off. Uncle Sam is greedy, which is funny because my actual uncle Sam—you remember my mom's brother—was greedy too."

"Sam made us share the tolls on the Turnpike when he drove us to your cousin Jennifer's wedding," Doug said.

"Yep! And you didn't have any cash on you. Anyway, this Uncle Sam wants a lot more than two dollars back."

"I never thought I'd be annoyed to be in the highest tax bracket."

"I know, right? Then come the state taxes. Our dearly beloved state, that everyone in the country makes fun of, taxes the highest bracket at a whopping ten-point-seven-five percent."

Doug's face pinched. "I'm losing track of the numbers. Is there anything left? Kidding, of course."

"Plenty. Back-of-the-envelope calculation leaves us with about six million. Obviously, we need to hire our own accountant, a financial planner and an estate lawyer to confirm all of this."

"It's still a huge chunk of change," Doug said. "You know, Laura, I really wasn't seeing ano—"

"Stop. This is a day to celebrate." And she meant it. She wasn't going to obsess over why he was watching his weight or which patient made him laugh on the phone or why he needed a shower immediately after coming home from Tucson. Not today. Hopefully never.

She grabbed a step stool from the cupboard, remembering an expensive bottle of champagne a patient had gifted Doug for replacing a cap the night before his wedding. Laura had said they should save it for a special occasion, but in reality she planned to regift it, knowing Doug would never remember about the bottle and, if he did, he'd be happy she put it to better use.

Doug followed her into the kitchen.

"So who are the other winners?"

"A firefighter from Idaho. His wife is pregnant with triplets. The other winning ticket was sold in South Carolina, but I don't know any details yet. Plus the other Jersey winner. I'm sure we'll find out who that is soon enough."

"This is just wild," Doug said, shaking his head.

Laura retrieved two flutes from an upper cabinet, wiping a thick layer of dust from the rims. Doug took the bottle and popped the cork, champagne spraying over the counter and onto the floor. For once, the waste and mess didn't bother Laura. Doug didn't reach for a paper towel or even frown at the puddle. She wondered if this nonchalance was what rich people felt all the time.

Doug poured them each a glass and they moved to the den, where they cozied up under a fuzzy afghan with the bubbly.

"You're right about us," he said. "We can have fun together in a careless way, like we used to. Getting pregnant with Emma when we were still in college, I mean for God's sake, our entire lives changed from that moment on." He had already drained his glass and was pouring himself another.

She decided not to correct him. Sure, things were different from the moment she peed on the stick in the main campus library while Doug waited anxiously outside, but they had changed far more for her than him. He still went to dental school as planned. She, instead, was a mother at twenty-one, forced to put her career plans on hold so she could care for their infant while also working part-time to support his continued schooling. The plan to go for another baby shortly after Emma made sense at the time. Get through the diapers, sleep training, tantrums and car-seat stage all at once, so she could revisit her career plans when the girls were in school full-time. She'd be only twenty-six at that point. But endless cycles of strep throat and playground dust-ups evolved into more serious issues, like social exclusion and body-image issues, and Laura was scared to take her eyes off her girls for even an instant. There was never a day where she felt like, *Okay, now is my chance to think about my own future*. Each day passed in a blur, and if she was lucky enough to finish her errands and household work and get to sleep before eleven, it was a good one.

"When should we tell the girls?" he asked. "And what are we telling them? Laura, do we have trust-fund babies now?" He cackled and Laura joined in, giggling at the absurdity of telling their daughters they were millionaires after years of feuding over their spending habits. When Doug suggested Hannah get her jeans at Costco like he did, she started to cry.

Laura topped off her champagne and watched the fizz settle. The glass was less than half full once the bubbles died down. There was a metaphor in there somewhere, but she was too delirious to ponder it.

"It's gotta happen soon. Our TV appearance when we get that big, silly check is later this week. As for having trust-fund babies, all kidding aside, we have a lot we need to figure out. But we'll have a financial planner to advise us." She paused to rest her flute on the table. "I would have loved to buy my mom an amazing piece of jewelry. She always wore costume junk. Travel jewelry, she called it, even though they barely went anywhere." Laura rested her head on Doug's shoulder.

"Do you think she'd be happy?"

Laura could easily picture Sylvia slipping into a consigliere role when it came to how they should spend the money. A new house for Laura and Doug, for sure. An apartment in a doorman building for Sophie. And definitely a session or two with a top-notch makeup artist for both of her daughters. She wasn't sure what Sylvia would have wanted Noah to splurge on. Maybe one of those super-high-end celebrity matchmakers to find a woman good enough for her baby. "Of course, why not?"

Doug stared at her. "Laura, three of her four children won the Powerball. Don't you think Sylvia would have been concerned about how that would change the family dynamics? I mean, she literally called you guys the Fantastic Foursome. If it wasn't against Jewish tradition, she would have tattooed it on her leg or something."

Laura felt the champagne slosh around her belly, remembering how uncomfortable it had been when Matthew stumbled upon them after they tore up his house. But he had declined to go in on the tickets. He'd had plenty of opportunity to join them. Moreover, his wife had ridiculed the rest of them for doing so.

"You said yourself that Beth and Matthew don't need more money. I showed you pictures of their rental in Harvey Cedars. You've been to their apartment. They're already rich. Besides, they love to work so damn much. Even if they won the lottery, they'd still get their kicks from being in that *Best Lawyers* magazine. You know that thing Beth sends around every year. Honestly, I'd be afraid to give them any more money than they already have. They'd probably use it to hire a grandmaster to move in with them so Austin could take nonstop chess lessons."

"Well, did your dad say anything about Matthew?"

Why wouldn't Doug leave this alone?

"No. To be honest, he was so fixated on this termite situation it was hard to get him to process our news. I told you about that, right?"

"So gross." Doug shuddered. Plaque and tartar he could handle. Insects sent him ducking for cover. "I can't believe you slept in a house infested with termites."

"Yep. It's crazy. Especially because Noah has a really good friend who works for an extermination company on the island and he literally treated the house a month ago. So this termite thing is really weird. Noah seemed all upset about it. Maybe he feels responsible for recommending his buddy? Or because he was living there and didn't notice anything askew? Anyway, enough pest talk for now. Let's discuss travel."

Laura opened her laptop and typed "Luxurious vacations" into the search bar, balancing the computer on one of her legs and one of Doug's. She squeezed her husband's thigh and said, "Where to first, Moneybags? I hear Bora Bora is lovely this time of year."

THREE DAYS AFTER TELLING DOUG THE BIG NEWS, LAURA WAS at Starbucks to meet Noah and Sophie. She was exhausted from consecutive nights of staying up late with her husband, planning their first post-Powerball vacation—and, yes, having rather enjoyable sex.

The meeting between the siblings had been hastily arranged after a cryptic text from Matthew appeared on the FF chat earlier that morning. Laura had read her older brother's message at least a dozen times and could recite it by heart: Good luck on TV . . . occurred to me that Noah might have purchased the winning ticket with the money I gave him to tip the pizza guy. Crazy, right?

Doug and Laura had been busy looking at properties online when Matthew's text, and the attendant barrage from Sophie and Noah, came through. "You're dinging a lot," Doug had said. She was surprised to have missed six text messages. Normally, the ding triggered a Pavlovian response that her daughters needed her.

She had read the top thread first, an exchange between Noah and Sophie:

NOAH

Is he upset

SOPHIE

I really don't know

NOAH

We should talk about this in person

SOPHIE

Agree. Laura?

NOAH

Laura?

Laura then opened Matthew's message, the one that had sent Noah and Sophie spiraling, and immediately tilted her phone away from Doug. She wanted her husband focused on which posh golf club he wanted to swing his driver at and not concerned with Jacobson sibling drama.

"Everything okay?" he'd asked, sensing a shift in her mood.

"Totally." Laura had given Doug a reassuring kiss on the lips.

An hour later, Laura was in the city to meet her siblings. "Sorry I'm late," Laura said, shuffling to the back of the coffee shop, where Noah and Sophie were huddled at a small table. "Traffic was a nightmare."

"Was the helicopter not free?" Noah asked. Laura smiled weakly. The three of them had been amusing each other like this on a side chat, sending pictures of ridiculous mansions and making silly comments like "Looks cramped" and "You can do better" about a limited-edition Ferrari.

"Guys, what are we going to do about Matthew?" Sophie asked, whisking her cappuccino with a green plastic stirrer she'd chewed to smithereens.

Laura eyed the two untouched pastries on the table. She had no appetite either and had already pounded TUMS on the ride in. "I can't tell if he's upset or sort of joking."

"Me either," Sophie said. "But in the history of FF texts, has he ever initiated one?"

"He did give me money for the pizza guy and I forgot to give him back the change, but I also had a hundred bucks in my pocket from Mrs. Harrison. I used the change and some of the hundred bucks to buy the Powerball tickets, ice cream, and the cigarettes for you, Laura. I don't know whose money bought the ticket but—"

At the mention of cigarettes, a fresh craving bloomed inside Laura. The night Noah had gotten her a pack, Laura had chain-smoked on the outdoor patio after Austin departed, agonizing over the sharp turn her life had taken since Hannah flew the coop and

Doug asked for the separation. She had told herself she wouldn't touch another cigarette after that night. Sylvia had died of lung cancer after all. Where could she get some Nicorette gum now? Her knee-shaking grew more turbulent.

"This feels like a question of intent. Matthew didn't want a ticket, so it doesn't matter if it was his money. Does that make sense?" Sophie said. "I wish one of us was a lawyer."

"Matthew's a lawyer," Noah said, stating the obvious irony. "But are we missing the point?" He managed a nibble of his croissant. "Maybe it doesn't matter whether it was Matthew's two dollars that bought the winning ticket. Maybe we're supposed to cut him in because, you know, he's our brother. It could just be that simple. Besides, we're not taking our brother to court."

Sophie pouted. "That's NOT what I meant."

Laura stepped in before another sibling conflict erupted. "Should we reread the text together? Do we think Beth put him up to this?"

"What if we cut him in for a portion of what he would have won—like half?" Sophie suggested.

Laura wrinkled her nose. "I don't like that. That's like saying he's our half brother, not a full one."

"So it's better to give nothing?" Noah asked. "I'm not disagreeing. I'm asking seriously."

Just then a teenager in line for the bathroom crashed into Sophie from behind, spilling her coffee and his on their table. He mumbled a barely audible apology from behind the cell phone covering his face.

"Isn't it weird that we're lottery winners and no one knows?" Sophie swiveled to look at the kid, his half-spilled mochaccino far less interesting than whatever he was watching on his phone. "Like that kid just spilled on a Powerball winner and has no idea. Not that we're, you know, above getting spilled on. It's just—"

"I get what you mean," Noah said. "I keep forgetting myself. Yesterday I lost my sunglasses and was stressing about having to buy new ones."

Laura nodded along, but she couldn't chime in in good faith. The money had been front and center for her since she found the ticket at Matthew's house. The money was going to save her marriage.

"Back to Matthew," Sophie said. "Let's talk in real numbers. It's roughly six million for each of us if we don't cut him in, and four and a half million if we do. That's still a ton of money."

"Does Matthew even realize we're not getting as much as we initially told him? Like does he get the lump sum thing?" Laura asked. "And taxes?"

"Matthew's pretty sharp," Sophie said. "But, I don't know, maybe it's not something you think about unless it directly affects you. Or maybe he doesn't *want* to think about it."

Laura knew—they all knew—that siblings weren't reducible to numbers. Their feelings about Matthew couldn't be punched into a calculator or run through a spreadsheet. That's what made the whole matter so unwieldy. Guilt had tugged at Laura before Doug raised the issue and before Matthew had sent that text, but it had gotten eclipsed by the state of her marriage. Besides, she was in a very different place than Sophie and Noah. She and Doug had a mortgage and two dependents with sky-high college tuitions, who might want to go on to graduate school or need help buying a house in the future. She had scrimped and saved for twenty years to raise her family. Noah's and Sophie's expenses were minimal by comparison. She assumed her siblings could see that. But maybe it was true what Sophie said. It was easier not to take the time to evaluate someone else's situation.

"The thing is, Matthew and Beth are already wealthy. And they weren't absent when we decided to get the tickets. They actively said no. And they were smug about it. That's the part that bothers me the most. Matthew thinks he's smarter than us. Do you know he called me Dopey Sophie when I messed up making change during a Monopoly game? And when I got a B- in English, I remember he saw my report card lying around and said 'Who gets a B- in Ms. Bender's class? She's the easiest grader ever,'" Sophie said. "On the other hand, considering I make forty thousand dollars a year after taxes and accepted a gig drawing caricatures a few weeks ago for a child's birthday party, I'm sort of disgusted with myself for being this petty and greedy."

"Isn't Matthew's office only a few blocks from here?" Noah asked. They were outside the Starbucks now, clustered on the sidewalk while the corporate crowd bustled around them. "He and Beth work in one of these buildings I'm pretty sure."

"Not too shabby," Sophie said, looking up. "Some of the parents at P.S. 282 are partners at big law firms. They make serious coin."

"I know our main concern is Matthew, and this shouldn't be about Beth, but I just hate how superior she acts," Laura said. "She's always talking about how hard they work, as if the rest of us just chow on bonbons all day. I bet it *was* her that put Matthew up to sending that text. She doesn't even need the money. It just bothers her that we might have more than she does, especially since we don't spend eighteen hours a day behind a desk."

"I showed Beth a picture of the painting I'm working on, the one I may have sold, and she said it was 'cute.'" Sophie scoffed. "'Cute' is, like, the rudest thing a person can say to an artist. I don't even tell my students their work is cute."

"My friend Mindy's husband once called our house in Westfield 'cozy,'" Laura said. "I feel like that's the same thing."

"I keep trying to figure out what Mom would say about all this," Noah said.

"Doug wondered the same thing."

"I've been wondering how Mom would have spent the money if she'd been the one to win," Sophie said.

"Ooh, that's an interesting game." Laura tapped her chin. "Sylvia Jacobson with six million dollars . . . The possibilities are endless."

"Are they?" Sophie said. She pulled up a photo of their mother on her phone. In the picture, Sylvia was carrying three huge shopping bags from T.J. Maxx. "She loved a bargain way too much to pay retail for anything."

"I remember getting in deep shit for buying a Polo shirt for a job interview at the actual Polo store instead of the outlet," Noah said. "All I see her doing with the money is stuff for us and for the organizations she was a part of."

Laura plucked a piece of Sophie's muffin from the to-go bag and dropped it in her mouth. Their mother had loved sweets, especially cinnamon babka. Laura felt a welcome pang of hunger. "There must have been something Mom would have wanted to splurge on."

The three of them stood in silent contemplation.

"I'm coming up empty," Noah said.

"It's kind of like my students," Sophie said. "They can't imagine that I have a life outside of teaching. They believe all us teachers sleep in the school. Isn't that kind of how we saw Mom, like she existed only in relation to our family?"

"And now it's too late," Noah said, his voice catching.

"So if we don't know what she'd have bought, do we at least know what she'd have said about Matthew? I'm trying to channel her. We shouldn't have tossed the Ouija board when we were packing up," Laura said. When they found the game, the siblings reminisced about the way Sophie would push the indicator to scare Noah, sending him running to their mother's arms.

"Fair is fair," Sophie said, wagging her index finger like their mother used to when making a point. "That was one of her favorite lines. Though it doesn't actually mean anything if you think about it."

"If you're not going to share, I'm taking it away," Laura said. "She used to say that when Matthew and I fought over the Game Boy."

"Money doesn't buy happiness," Noah said. "She and Dad both said that."

"Of course, Mom also sang 'If I Were a Rich Man' from *Fiddler* at the top of her lungs whenever she had to do laundry," Laura said.

"She was a woman of contradictions, clearly," Sophie said with a guffaw. "I wish she was here now, even though she'd be pissed I'm not engaged. She liked Ravi a lot. Or she was terrified I'd become an old maid."

"She would hate my outfit. 'Beige does nothing for your complexion,'" Laura imitated Sylvia, pincering her sweater and growing wistful. "Yeah, I wish she was here too."

Several times over the past year, Laura had reached for her cell phone to call her mom, only to remember she was gone after dialing the first few digits. It was like phantom limb syndrome. Sylvia played a huge role in helping Doug and Laura buy their first home, the one they still lived in. The idea of buying a new house—especially a huge one—without Sylvia seeing it first didn't sit right. How would Laura know the mistakes she made if her mother wasn't around to point them out? She needed her mom to turn her new house into a home, dropping off picture frames she scored at HomeGoods and skillets on sale at Costco. The only silver lining of her mother's absence was that Laura didn't have to tell her about Doug's folly. Sylvia was loving and generous, but she did not forgive easily.

"I feel like if Matthew came to us and said he needed the money it would be different," Sophie said. "Or even that he felt hurt that we hadn't included him. What are we supposed to do with a cryptic group text?" Laura and Noah nodded in agreement. A pair of roaring ambulances rolled by and silenced them for a few minutes. When it quieted down, Laura said, "Can I show you guys the house we're thinking about making an offer on?" She pulled out her phone.

Laura and Doug were working with Nancy Ruben, a local real estate agent whose face was plastered on signs all over Westfield, to find a new house. They'd listed their home with her and were scheduling visits to houses three times the size of their current one in tonier towns, giddy to be upsizing as empty nesters. Real estate was a sound investment (hadn't her father said that?), and they agreed parking a chunk of their winnings into a house was a responsible choice. Their win wasn't meant to be public knowledge until the live TV broadcast the next day, so Laura and Doug were cagey with Nancy about why they were trading up, reveling in the suspicions she must have. Neighbors were similarly poking around, desperate to understand the story behind the For Sale sign staked into their lawn. It was deliciously fun to share a big secret with her spouse, even though Laura felt terrible keeping the truth from Mindy and her other friends.

"This one is our favorite," Laura said. "It's in Franklin Lakes. Kind of far from Doug's office, but he'll manage."

"Great landscaping," Sophie observed, leaning in close. "I'd love to paint those flower beds."

"Is that a six-car garage?" Noah asked, counting with his finger.

"Yep. Hang on, there's a 3D tour," Laura said. She took her siblings through the double-height living room to the regal dining room with a table set for fourteen and on to the basement, where an Olympic-quality gym was located.

"Is that your style?" Sophie asked. "I mean, it's obviously very special but it looks so different from your Westfield house."

"My style?" Laura laughed. "My style was whatever I could

afford when we bought furniture, even if it didn't match. I guess you could say we like gray, considering how much duct tape we have on the furniture. The only thing I'm sure of is that I want a lot of throw pillows in the new house."

"Why?" Noah asked.

Laura shrugged. "Feels like superfluous pillows are a thing rich people should have."

"Well, now I know what to get you as a housewarming gift," Sophie said. "I want you guys to visit my new studio. It's really bright and airy and super close to all the downtown galleries."

"I have some news too." Noah's blue eyes twinkled. "I'm buying a house."

Noah Jacobson, a homeowner? Laura was glad there wasn't a feather around to knock her over. "Congrats! Where is it?"

"Actually, it's Stanley Archer's place."

"Stanley Archer, as in our next-door neighbor? The guy who showed up in his undies?" Sophie was hysterically laughing.

"The one and only. I made Stanley and Ruth an offer they couldn't refuse. They're moving to Colorado to be near their grandkids. You guys know I love Beach Haven and this way I can keep an eye on our place. See what a wreck the new owners make of it."

"That's great, Noah," Laura said.

"Mazel tov." Sophie pulled her siblings in for a three-way hug as her cell phone vibrated. She looked at the screen and said, "Wow. Just got a text from my friend saying that budget cuts were averted at P.S. 282. We keep our jobs. But, wait a second, I guess I'm not going back anyway. Right? I'm done teaching." She shook her head wildly. "This is insane. I've been there for ten years. I gotta call Ravi."

"Speaking of your boyfriend, any news on this front?" Laura tapped Sophie's ring finger.

"Who are you, Mom?" Sophie pulled back her hand.

"Just kidding," Laura said, wondering if there wasn't something behind Sophie's quick dismissal.

After another round of hugs, the three siblings headed off in different directions. They would reconvene the next day at the television studio. On the matter of Matthew, it seemed a consensus had been reached without any of them having to say it out loud.

A FLATTERING OUTFIT AND A COHERENT STATEMENT OF GRATitude were essential ingredients for a successful lottery acceptance on live TV. Laura watched numerous videos on YouTube that lacked both of the above. She vowed not to fall victim to the same missteps.

After four hours patrolling the designer floor of Bloomingdale's with her daughters, both of whom Laura summoned home to help her find a dress, she purchased a navy shift with a bell sleeve and camel pumps with three-inch heels that brought her arches out of retirement. She needed to walk the knife's edge between looking responsible enough not to squander the money and appearing overly fashionable, which could suggest she didn't need it to begin with.

Predictably, the girls had shrieked when Laura and Doug dropped the Powerball bomb. The screaming eventually gave way to a flurry of questions. Emma: "Can I go to grad school now without taking out loans?" Laura: "Sure, if it's close to home." Hannah: "Can I get my highlights done by a super-famous hairdresser who only comes to the East Coast three times a year?" Laura: "Yes, if I can come with you."

Doug hit mute and turned to Laura. "Doing this over the phone was a mistake."

Laura unmuted. "Listen, girls, your father and I are much more comfortable than before. Of course, this will change some things in your lives, but we expect you to continue working hard and taking school seriously." The words were barely out of her mouth before Emma blurted, "Han, we should get tickets to see Taylor Swift. Remember when we saw her going into Black-Eyed Susans last summer when she was here for that wedding?"

"Duh, that was the most exciting thing to ever happen on LBI," Hannah said.

"She certainly caused the most traffic to ever happen on LBI," Doug said, but the girls paid him no attention.

"Maybe we're going to be invited to celebrity parties now."

"Totally."

"Do you know how much those Jennifer Fisher heart earrings cost? I've wanted them for ages."

Laura wasn't even following which daughter was speaking anymore. It was no use getting through to them when the shock was so fresh.

She and Doug tried not to worry. The girls didn't have access to the money, so they couldn't do any real damage in the short term. Upon returning from Japan, their chosen destination for a first luxury vacation, they would talk seriously about guiding Emma and Hannah through their new normal. Though Laura doubted anything would ever feel "normal" going forward.

"You look gorgeous." Sophie gasped when Laura entered the TV studio's green room. The sisters air-hugged and kissed to preserve their hair and makeup.

"So do you!" Laura stepped back to appraise her little sister. "Is that a pantsuit?" Sophie's typical style was a little bit hippie and a little bit rock-and-roll. She loved jaunty accessories, like a whimsical bandana tied around the neck or a silver cuff with turquoise stones snaking around her bicep.

Sophie laughed. "I had no idea what to wear. Ravi's mom helped. The suit is hers. I think she wears it to medical conferences or something. Do I look absurd?"

"Not at all," Laura said. She liked how Sophie had styled her red hair into a sleek ponytail, her curls blown straight so the light bounced off her mane. Laura couldn't do much with her boring bob other than add mousse for volume. "We're both wearing a lot of makeup though, aren't we?"

Sophie joined Laura at the vanity mirror illuminated by round fluorescent bulbs.

"Mom," they said in unison. Sylvia was forever after them to wear more makeup. At every special occasion, she'd chide them for trying to get away with the natural look. "You're pale as a ghost," she'd say to Sophie, swiping at her cheeks with the creamy rouge that just happened to be in her purse. "It takes ten seconds to put on lipstick," she'd admonish Laura, retrieving one of the many gold tubes that lived in the change compartment of her car.

"I just didn't want to disappoint her," Sophie said. "I like to think she's watching TV in heaven. She'd be so sad without *Jeopardy!*"

"She's definitely watching. And judging," Laura said. Sylvia's voice had buzzed like a mosquito in her ear as she readied herself that morning.

"Hello, hello. Looking great, both of you."

Noah had entered the green room with an unfamiliar woman whose face was half-hidden by rhinestone sunglasses. For the TV segment, he'd stuck to his regular well-worn T-shirt and jeans, into which his companion had her thumb tucked into a back pocket. He hadn't bothered to get a haircut.

"I'm Lisa," the mystery woman said through a mouthful of chewing gum. She extended a hand to Laura, then Sophie. She had long pink nails that ruled out any sort of desk job and a caterpillar tattoo on her inner wrist. "Noah's friend."

"Nice to meet you," Sophie said with a genuine grin. She was naturally less judgmental than Laura. That was something Laura admired about her younger sister. Laura, preoccupied by her own family, had neglected to consider how Noah was going to manage this massive change in circumstance. Gum-chomping, hot-pink-clawed Lisa was a reminder she'd have to keep a close eye on him.

"What's the caterpillar supposed to mean?" Laura asked, gesturing to the tattoo. She was trying to follow Sophie's friendly lead, but her inquisitiveness sounded naturally more judgy.

Lisa removed the gum from her mouth and attached it to her index finger. "Well, I always feel bad for the caterpillar because everyone just wants it to become a butterfly. And butterflies are pretty, but how cute are caterpillars?" Lisa spoke in a baby voice she was clearly faking, and Laura was sorry she'd asked.

"Granny, Granny, they gave us lollipops." A high-pitched child's voice rang out, followed by another, three octaves higher. "Granny Mabel, can I come on TV with you?"

A gaggle of small children charged for the catering table and began to stuff fistfuls of sugar cookies into their mouths.

"I'm having flashbacks of the art and baking unit I do with my third graders," Sophie said, lurching forward to catch a tray of falling brownies. "That I *did*."

"You okay?" Laura asked, catching Sophie's muted tone.

"Fine. It's just crazy I'm not going back to school in September," Sophie said.

"You must be Mabel Collins." Laura approached the elderly woman who trailed behind the swarm of children. Technically, their names had not been made public yet, but thanks to a sloppy production assistant at the local NBC affiliate, the Jacobsons knew the other winner from New Jersey was a grandmother whose main activities, according to her Facebook page, were baking, churchgoing and knitting custom sweaters for her bevy of grandchildren.

Laura had been tracking Mabel's posts since discovering her identity, but there was nothing to indicate anything had changed in the woman's life. Since winning, Mabel had posed a question to her knitting circle on Facebook (Laura had to join the private group to view the posts) about how to fix a mistake in a brioche stitch. She also posted a photo of a boy of about five in a Power Rangers costume blowing out birthday candles at a no-frills backyard party.

"I am, indeed. Are you one of the producers?" Mabel asked.

"No, I'm Laura Jacobson. My brother and sister and I"—she pointed out Sophie, who was bent over the craft table showing the children how to build a tower with Chessmen cookies, and Noah, seated on a plush couch next to Lisa, who was trying to feed him grapes—"are the other winners from New Jersey. Noah's the one who bought the tickets, but we went in on them together."

Mabel clapped a hand to her mouth. "Well how marvelous is that? What good fortune for you three. Your parents must be just overjoyed. You know, I'm one of three as well, but both my sisters have passed on." She crossed herself.

Noah disentangled himself from Lisa and joined their conversation, followed by Sophie.

"I was the middle sister," Mabel continued. "Which one of you is the middle?"

"That's me," Sophie said timidly. It was technically true of both she and Laura. They were both middles.

"Three is such a great number," Mabel said. "That's why I had three children myself. Two boys and a girl, opposite of you folks."

"Sounds like a lovely family," Laura said, reaching for a magazine to fan herself. What temperature did they keep the green room at? It felt like 110.

"Noah, don't you have a—" Lisa called out.

Laura shot her brother a look.

Noah glanced over to the couch. "Hey, Lisa, would you do me a favor? I think I forgot my driver's license at the security desk. Would you mind checking?"

"Of course, babe." Lisa stood and sashayed out of the green room with a pat on Noah's bum.

"You must be the baby?" Mabel said, looking at Noah. He nodded. "Did you wish you had a brother or were these two older sisters enough for you?"

Laura's face was on fire. Visible hives had ballooned on Sophie's neck, and Noah looked ready for a sinkhole to swallow him up.

"I, uh—" Noah managed.

"Noah's always had a special place in our family as the baby," Sophie interjected.

"So, how did you pick the winning numbers, Mabel?" Laura did her best to change the subject.

One of the children, a girl who looked about Austin's age, stopped fixing her hair and snapping selfies to chime in. "Granny uses the same numbers every week. She's been playing the lotto for sixty years," she said. "We even get scratch-offs in our Easter eggs."

Mabel smiled. "That's Ruby, my oldest grandchild. She's a real pistol."

"Tell them how you always use a three in your lotto numbers," Ruby said.

Mabel beamed. "I do. Three must be all of our lucky number."

"Don't forget you said I can interview you later, Gran," Ruby said.

Mabel blew her granddaughter a kiss. "I never break a promise." She turned to the Jacobsons. "Ruby has a video thing on that phone of hers with hundreds of subscribers."

"It's called TikTok, Gran," Ruby said. "And I hit a thousand!"

"TikTok, Schmick Tock. It's all nonsense. Anyway, I've played the Pick Six, the Mega Millions and the Powerball every week for as long as I can remember. Same numbers, same convenience store. The first kid to ever sell me a ticket has grown children now. He lives in my town. How about you? What's your lotto routine?"

Just great. Now they had to tell her they were undeserving, first-time players. Unless they lied—again.

"Well, we—" Laura began. If there was going to be a mouthpiece for their trio, it had to be her. Fortunately, a young man wearing a headset entered and saved her.

"We all settled in here?" the man said. "I'm Rich, one of the *Good Day, Garden State* producers. You've got about ten minutes until we go live. Everything will go just like I said on the phone. The state lottery commissioner will be on set, each winner will pose with the big check. Mabel, that's you alone, Jacobsons, the three of you, and then our anchor, Coralee Jones, will ask you how it feels, what you're going to do with the money, yada yada. Any questions?"

When no one said anything, Rich flashed a thumbs-up.

Laura heard her cell phone buzz from inside her handbag. It had been going crazy all day with texts from Doug and the girls, as well as Mindy and a few other friends she'd clued in that morning. Everyone was asking for pictures and demanding a play-by-play. There had been nothing from Matthew.

When Noah's phone rang, Laura hoped it might be their brother after all.

"It's Dad," Noah said. "Hey, Pops. We're at the TV studio . . . What? I can't hear you . . . You're where? Eating pickles?"

Laura took the phone. "Hi, Dad, it's Laura . . . Oh, you're at a pickleball tournament . . . It's windy . . . Yes, we're good . . . I called the financial planner you recommended. What's that? Oh, you have to go? Okay. We love you."

Laura handed the phone back to Noah, who shoved it in his pocket.

"Matthew always busted me for forgetting to say 'Uno,' remember?" Sophie was looking at Mabel's grandchildren, who had crashed from their sugar high and were crouched around a coffee table playing a civilized game of cards. "But then he'd always give me a second chance."

"This doesn't feel right," Laura said, lowering her voice. Ruby appeared far more interested in their conversation than the Uno game.

"I agree," Noah said. "I haven't been able to sleep." His normally bright eyes were dimmed by pillowy bags.

"I know Matthew and Beth are really comfortable," Sophie said. "Rich by basically all standards. But should that matter? Because nothing feels the—"

"They didn't have your license, honey," Lisa said, reentering the green room, her voice a purr. She looped an arm through Noah's. "Want me to check your wallet?" As she tried to slip a hand into Noah's back pocket, the producer burst in.

"Folks, it's time," Rich said. "We had to pull the cat food commercial due to an off-color pussy joke. Which means you're on in two. Follow me!"

The three Jacobsons locked eyes. What was happening? Had they just changed their minds about Matthew? Should they refuse to go on air without him?

"Let's call Dad back," Sophie suggested. Noah started dialing.

"We can't. He said he has to put away his phone," Laura said. "It's against tournament rules."

The three Jacobsons reluctantly left the green room. Mabel's granddaughter Ruby was walking in step with Laura down a long hallway covered with framed photos of Chiclet-toothed anchors. The girl touched each one as her fingers grazed the wall, knocking them off-kilter.

"I like your dress," she said to Laura and then stopped walking, her face suddenly serious. Laura stopped too and looked at the girl, unsure what was happening. "When I can't make up my mind, I flip a coin," Ruby said. "That's funny, actually, since this is about money. Anyway, see you out there." She dropped back to walk with her family.

"She's creepy," Noah said, looking at the teenager. "If we can't reach Dad, should we just—"

"Flip a coin?" Laura said as a chirpy voice rang out.

"Well, hello there millionaires," Coralee Jones said. The Jacobsons had grown up with her steady chatter as background noise, prattling on about local events, the constant inter-LBI battle over adding more dunes and the chipmunk who famously lived in the Brant Beach courthouse under the stenographer's desk. Now they were the story. "Sorry to rush you all. Jacobsons, follow me. You're up first. Granny, you're next."

The camera lights were blinding and hot enough to melt the skin off Laura's body. She couldn't make out anything other than a sea of blurry faces hidden behind gigantic cameras and boom mics. She felt Sophie's clammy hand in hers and reached her other hand to touch Noah's back, but his stage marker put him out of reach. She quickly scanned the wings for Mabel. The grandmother was now donning a floppy crochet hat that covered nearly her entire face. Could she be trying to show off her needlework on TV? Something about that didn't track with the woman Laura met in the green room.

Producer Rich approached.

"I gotta say, we sure were glad you all decided not to remain anonymous. Two winning tickets from New Jersey and both willing to be public," Rich said with a satisfied grin. "The winner from Idaho had to go public, but that fourth winner from South Carolina—crickets. You guys will be great for ratings. We're going to rerun this at eleven and then again tomorrow morning."

Laura didn't understand. This was a choice? Nobody mentioned that at the lottery office. The official who received them said someone from the local news would reach out to schedule the live check presentation, which happened the next day. Could there have been fine print in the nine pounds of paperwork they'd been handed, in the tiny text that required Leo's magnifying glass to decipher? Is that why Granny had thought to wear a hat that obscured nearly her entire face? Did she also not realize she had a choice to stay anonymous but knew enough to obstruct her identity? Why hadn't Laura thought to do the same instead of worrying about her makeup?

"Did he just say that—"

"We didn't have to—" Noah and Sophie were anxiously talking over each other.

By then it was too late. Coralee was live.

"Good evening, everyone. I'm Coralee Jones and tonight it's my pleasure to bring you a slice of Garden State history. Two of the four winners of a $261-million Powerball are from our home state and will accept their whopping $65-million checks right here, in front of your eyes. First up, we have the Jacobson siblings from Long Beach Island. Baby brother Noah bought the ticket, but sisters Sophie and Laura went in on it with him. Good thing because now they're all mega rich. Come forward, you three. Sheldon Mitchell of the New Jersey Lottery Commission would like to present the first check to you folks."

Coralee motioned for a suited man waiting offstage to come forward with the first of two giant checks.

"Sheldon Mitchell," Coralee said. "May I present to you Laura, Sophie and Noah Jacobson. Folks at home, you're the first to meet the newly minted millionaires!"

FANTASTIC FOURSOME 👥👥✡️👥👥

SOPHIE

I sort of hate that Snooki poisoned the Jersey Shore. All these peeps who saw our TV segment think we're from the same part

NOAH

Don't rag on Jersey Shore. that show gave us GTL

LAURA

What's GTL?

SOPHIE

OMG, are you even from jersey?

LAURA

M—do you know?

NOAH

If you don't know, he won't know. Matty—prove me wrong.

SOPHIE

Okay, we gave Matthew four hours to prove his chops and nothing. GTL stands for Gym, Tan, Laundry

LAURA

Ahh. I like it. Matthew—would you have known that?

NOAH

Matty?

SOPHIE

Earth to matthew

LAURA

Guys i found Mom's recipe book in one of the boxes. Matthew—her apple strudel you loved was basically a heart attack in a cake. So. Much. Butter.

NOAH

M—remember we begged her to make blondies and she asked if those are brownies for gentiles

M?

LAURA

I may try to make something from the book

SOPHIE

I hope the fire extinguisher is nearby

NOAH

Matty?

Three Months Later

7

Noah

ARGYLE SOCKS–WEARING, HEARING AID–PACKING, *60 MINUTES*–watching Leo Jacobson knew how to rock a tan.

It was all Sophie and Noah could discuss when they arrived at Boca Breezes and were greeted by their gilded father in the overly air-conditioned, white-marble lobby furnished in eighties mauves, teals and chrome. Three months in the Sunshine State and their father could model for a Coppertone ad in AARP magazine.

"Golf tan," he said proudly, lifting the sleeve of his short-sleeve collared shirt to show the contrast. "I'm terrible though."

"That's because you don't let me help you with your swing, Leo," a raspy-voiced woman with a helmet of platinum hair said as she passed through the lobby pushing a grocery cart filled with Publix bags. "See you at bridge later?"

"Save me a seat," Leo said, offering a friendly wave.

"You know I will." The woman headed toward the elevator but stopped short, her rubber soles screeching against the tile. "Oh my goodness, Leo, are these them? The famous Jackpot Jacobsons?"

"Two of them," Leo said, with more enthusiasm than Noah expected. "Kids, this is Roberta Rosenblum."

"My, oh, my," Roberta said. "What lucky ducks you are. I wish my kids had such mazel."

"Bridge?" Sophie asked Leo. Their mother was the card shark in the family. Leo refused to join his wife at the weekend canasta tournaments in Atlantic City, where she sometimes really cleaned up.

"I'm learning. We don't play for money," Leo explained. "Let me show you the grounds before we go up."

Noah and Sophie left their bags with the concierge and followed their father, whose step was noticeably peppier down south. Florida might as well have been a steroid. They trailed him to the golf course, tennis center, pickleball courts (where he pointed out his name on the bracket as the top seed), card room (the size of a casino) and the multipurpose room, shaped like an auditorium with rows of cushioned seats arranged in a U. On stage, a cluster of post-menopausal women dressed in black leotards, fishnets and tap shoes were performing a coordinated song-and-dance routine. Noah was reminded of his client Rita Harrison. She would fit in swimmingly at Boca Breezes.

"The gals are rehearsing for *Cabaret*," Leo explained. "It ought to be terrific."

"Hi, Leo," purred about a dozen voices, calling out to their father from the stage. His appearance brought the arthritic rendition of "Don't Tell Mama" to a standstill.

"Looking great, ladies. Can't wait for opening night." Leo thrust an arm around Noah and Sophie. "These are my kids, visiting from up north. They say they've got a surprise for me."

"Leo's lucky bunch gracing Boca Breezes," said a woman standing stage right with hair so black it looked blue. "I'm Donna, the director, which means I can reserve a front-row seat for your father opening night." She tapped her clipboard authoritatively.

"I'd love to have you all for dinner," another woman called from the stage. "You kids would love my pot roast. You certainly did, Leo." When she winked at their father, Noah nearly vomited in his mouth.

"I made a few kugels this morning so they should come to me," a different woman said. "Savory *and* sweet." Was she talking about herself or the kugels? Noah prayed it was the kugel.

"Leo, you promised to help set up my iPad." The lady requesting tech support propped one leg on a chair and attempted to touch her toe.

Leo's face instantly reddened. Electronics were his kryptonite. Had he feigned competency to get close to Stretch Lady? Or was he just too embarrassed to admit he didn't know how to help her?

"I got you," Noah whispered to his dad. Lately, he'd realized how much he missed his service calls on LBI. Passing Haymarket Hobbies in Ship Bottom, Noah wondered if the owner was able to integrate the sales software he'd contracted to use back in June. Seeing one of the island year-rounders, Lindsay McCauley, whizzing past his bike in her pickup truck, he remembered her request that he help her with a slideshow for her parents' fiftieth wedding anniversary party, which had to have passed by now. Since the Powerball, none of his regulars had been in contact. Even Robin, the client with whom he shared more than a tech connection, had laughed off his offer to tinker with her wireless printer when he ran into her outside the Surflight Theatre.

He still needed work, just not for the money. He didn't know how to communicate that to the community. Even the people he'd offered free tech support hadn't followed up to schedule appointments.

Leo was fumbling with his keys, looking more like the father Noah knew than the local Don Juan he'd become. It was a relief. "I'll be in touch about that iPad, Lydia."

Outside the auditorium, Sophie said, "Dad, you're a total fox here." She elbowed Noah in the rib. "Which one did you like? Leotard Lady was my fave. She was surprisingly limber. But I didn't care for the way the director tried to woo our father with good seats."

Noah refused to play along. "They were all the same to me."

"Let's go to the apartment," Leo said, clearly as desperate as Noah to change the topic. They passed through several buildings kept at meat-locker temperatures before they reached Boca Four, the residential tower where their father lived.

Noah wasn't sure what to expect beyond the front door. Leo had been managing largely on his own for two years, though Sylvia tried to arrange his meals and monitor the cleaning lady from her bed. While she was sick, he learned to grocery shop for himself and replace the soap and shampoo before he ran out. But to create a home in a new space, in a new state, was an entirely different undertaking.

"This is it," Leo said. He pushed open the door to a sunny apartment with views of a man-made lake and a putting green. He had leather furniture in varying shades of tan, a white kitchen with cookie-cutter appliances and the phone number for Boca Breezes' emergency hotline tacked to the fridge.

They followed him to the terrace. "I sit out here all the time," Leo said, sliding open the glass door. Noah put on his sunglasses and was walking toward the railing for a better look when he noticed two wineglasses on a small table, one of which had a deep red lipstick stain. Leo must have seen it at the same time because he ushered them back inside.

Sophie, who may or may not have seen the wineglasses, plopped herself on the sofa. Noah took the opportunity to poke around while his father went searching through his wallet for a receipt. The condo was a two-bedroom, two-bath. The rest of the furniture matched the living area in beigeness. His father had done alright. The swirly pattern on the hand towels matched the bath towels and shower mat. There was a neat line of pill bottles on the bathroom vanity next to a stack of paper cups. He snapped a picture for Laura. She would be pleased their father was on top of taking his medication. Still, something about the place irked Noah, though he couldn't put his finger on it.

"Holy cow!" Sophie called out. "Ravi just texted me. His 'Everyday Carafe' is in *Elle Decor*."

Suddenly, it clicked. It wasn't anything he saw in the condo that bothered him. It's what he didn't see. There wasn't a single family photo or tchotchke from back home. The shore house in particular had been littered with photographs, art projects, party favors, old invitations and refrigerator magnets from every spot on LBI. It bothered him to watch Sophie revel in Ravi's latest success, oblivious to the ways the Jacobson family unit was going extinct.

"Why are you staring at me?" Sophie tossed a beige throw pillow at Noah. "And what time is dinner around here? I could definitely hit up the early bird special."

"Do you notice anything missing?"

"Um, food that isn't supposed to relieve constipation? Dad has four bottles of prune juice in the fridge and six containers of dried fruit on the counter. Surprised I haven't found a bottle of castor oil."

Noah shook his head. "I mean photos. Of us. Of Mom. It's so sterile, like the rest of us don't exist here."

Sophie paused to consider and shrugged. "I think Mom did all that stuff back home. C'mon, let's go. I'm starving and I will literally ruin the plumbing at Boca Breezes if I eat any more fiber."

NOAH AND THE HOSTESS MADE EYES THE MINUTE HE WALKED into Fresco's, one of Boca Breezes' five on-premise dining establishments. When she said, "Right this way," with a hair toss and a light brush against Noah's arm, she might as well have handed him the keys to her apartment rather than a menu.

He'd been so preoccupied by the Powerball and its repercussions that he'd practically forgotten about sex, something he would have previously thought impossible. That wasn't to say he thought money was better than sex. Nothing was better than sex, at least nothing he'd encountered in his modest thirty years. It was that the windfall was proving extremely taxing. There were accountants and lawyers to meet with, decisions to be made about matters he knew nothing about. Stocks? Bonds? Mutual funds? What happened to a plain old piggy bank, metaphorically speaking? Then there was the onslaught of emails and physical letters he received from "long-lost relatives" and "old friends"—so lost and so old that Noah didn't remember them. Complete strangers contacted him to invest in their surefire businesses or to send money to patch them through hard times due to illness/fire/accident/layoff/you name it.

Noah felt like a fool. His sisters were not being similarly inundated. They'd had the good sense to change their mailing addresses to a P.O. box and create new email addresses. He was still using noahjacobson@gmail.com and his new address, the Archer house, was a click away for a modestly savvy person.

In the beginning, it was easier just to say yes.

He sent his ex a chunk of change in back rent and invested twenty grand in a high school buddy's microbrewery business. Another thirty thousand he'd given to Joe, his exterminator pal, to launch a bug-identification app. But there were others that made him uneasy. He was simply unable to say no to anyone asking for money to help a sick child and it felt perverse to ask for proof the child was actually sick, even if it meant he was being swindled. There were acquaintances who crept out of the woodwork, not all with sob stories like a sick child, but he still felt uncomfortable turning them down. And some presented with business ideas that Noah believed had promise, the kind he could imagine all five entrepreneurs competing for on *Shark Tank*. A peanut butter jar that opens from both ends, anyone? But more often than not, he heard nothing from these inventors and start-up folks after he sent the check, not that he was all that on top of following up.

He longed to do something worthwhile. To discover in the piles of mail a truly deserving person whose life he could meaningfully improve. Until that happened, he was glad to rediscover the joy of sex, the need for which now seized his body like a riptide. The hostess who made eyes with him reminded Noah of his before life— when he was just a good-looking guy who, despite having no stable income or personal property in excess of $500, could entice a woman to his bed with his looks and charm alone.

Sophie insisted on ordering the most expensive bottle of wine on the menu, even though Noah preferred beer and their father rarely drank (though the wineglasses on the balcony told a different story). After they each had a full glass of a dry red (the menu's description; Noah didn't understand how a liquid could be dry), Sophie's face grew serious.

"Dad, can we ask you something?" she said, setting down her fork. *We?* Noah and Sophie hadn't discussed anything. Maybe she was coming to see things his way. It was one thing to move to Florida and take up pickleball, but it was quite another to become the man whore of Boca Breezes without a single picture of his late wife on display. "It's serious."

"What's going on?" Leo looked up from his plate. Laura would not have approved of the fatty prime rib.

"Are you upset with us for not cutting Matthew in?"

"Is that why you're really here?" Leo set his cutlery down in an X across his plate.

"Of course not!" Noah said and glared at Sophie. She was ruining what was supposed to be a special night.

The impetus for their trip was to present their father with a new car, specifically a two-door Bentley Continental GT, retailing for $289,000. Leo was getting around on the BBB, the Boca Breezes Bus, a free transport service that took condo residents around the sprawling property and to the medical complex twenty minutes away. He claimed to have no need for wheels of his own, but they couldn't think of a single other extravagance to shower on him.

Leo wiped the corners of his mouth with the edges of a cloth napkin. Noah wondered if he was going to get up and leave.

"No, I'm not upset."

"Phew!" Visibly relieved, Sophie dug her knife into the butter dish and slathered a healthy dose on a roll.

"Hang on," Leo said, holding up a hand. "I'm not done. Matthew and Beth are very successful. They work hard and enjoy a nice lifestyle as a result. And it was their decision not to go in on the lottery. Adults need to own their decisions. You might be doing them a favor anyway. Who's to say they'd be any happier with more money? You've only been rich for three months. Let's see what happens over time."

In his lifetime, Leo had seen fortunes, modest compared to theirs, rise and fall. Noah recalled their father's first words after they told him the news. *Holy hell.* Had Stanley really fallen off the ladder? Yes, he had, they had all heard the crash. But it seemed as though Leo's reaction might have been the same regardless.

"You're not children anymore. You're fully grown adults. It's not for me to tell you what to do with your money. Or your lives."

At Beth David Memorial Park in Kenilworth, New Jersey, their mother had to be rolling over in her grave. Noah felt himself getting angry. When had his father done much parenting anyway? Leo was a backseat parent for as long as Noah could remember, and now, when they needed his assurance and guidance, he was throwing up his hands?

"These are on the house," the hostess said, appearing at their table with a tray of desserts. She set down a slice of key lime pie, a wedge of cherry cheesecake and a chocolate mousse. "I recommend the mousse. It's very silky."

"Thank you . . . Becky," Noah said, leaning over to read her name tag. An hour later, he discovered that Becky's panties were even silkier than the mousse. After two enthusiastic rounds of sex at her condo, Noah lay in bed with his head resting on Becky's bare navel.

"I think my father really liked the car," he said.

The Bentley had been waiting outside Fresco's with a giant red bow wrapped around the front hood.

"That's some ride," Leo had said with a nod of masculine admiration, walking past it toward the BBB stop.

"It's yours," Noah said.

For a man who didn't covet material things, Leo sure came around in the moment. The evening ended on a bright note, Leo revving the engine and lapping the parking lot twice before driving back to Tower Four.

"Who wouldn't? It's a hot car. Not to mention expensive as hell." Becky ran a hand through Noah's hair and pressed gently on his temples with her fingertips. His body relaxed into a familiar postcoital bliss.

"So about that car," he said. "My siblings and I kind of won the lottery. In case you were wondering."

"No way! For real? What's it like being a lottery winner?" Becky shot up in bed.

Noah found himself eager to speak candidly with someone out of his everyday orbit. At the shore, he was famous. He couldn't walk into the Holiday Snack Bar or fill up his bike tires with air at the gas station without being gawked at.

"It's not what I expected."

"What do you mean?"

Noah turned toward her. Without layers of makeup, most of which had faded during their romp, she was refreshingly pretty. "I guess my siblings seem to be handling it much better than me. My sister Laura and her husband bought a new house, joined a golf club and are traveling around the world. They're in Japan right now at some seven-star hotel. My sister Sophie, the one from dinner tonight, quit her job teaching and is painting full-time, which was her dream. I'm the only one who's sort of—"

"Floundering?" Becky suggested.

"Exactly!" That's precisely what he was and probably always had been. Even at summer camp, where the kids were grouped by age into the Snappers, Lobsters, Flounders and Starfish, Noah was a Flounder twice because he'd had to repeat kindergarten.

"You wouldn't believe the crazy letters and emails I get. I even had a guy camp out outside my house."

"What do these people want?"

"Money, what do you think? They all have some story. They claim we're long-lost relatives and my great-great-great-great-grandfather cheated their ancestor back in the old country. That they need money for their kid's cancer treatment, only I can't pay the hospital directly, I have to send the money to them. That they have an amazing business idea and I can triple my winnings within a year if I invest."

"God, that's awful. I'm so sorry you're going through that." Becky gently stroked the line of his jaw, which unclenched with her touch.

"Let's talk about you," Noah said. "How's working at Boca Breezes?"

"You mean Happy Endings?" She flashed a naughty grin.

It took Noah a minute to process the double meaning. When he did, all he could say was, "Yikes."

"The old people are a hoot. It's like watching a geriatric soap opera. The ladies cat fight about cards and are crazy competitive at tennis. The old dudes gripe about back pain and building assessments. The condo president was just caught embezzling from the lobby renovation fund, so that was a whole to-do. And don't get me started on the hookup drama. There was a recent chlamydia outbreak among the resi—"

Noah didn't need any more details. "Want to go for a walk?" He was headed home the next day and wanted to soak up the warm weather. Though maybe he'd be back soon. He liked Becky.

"A walk sounds great. Let me throw some clothes on." She walked to the bathroom, giving Noah a chance to admire her curves. She was shaped like a violin and was a hell of a lot more fun to play. He thought back to the lessons his mother arranged for him when he was about twelve. His older siblings were out of the house and she wanted him to have hobbies to fend off loneliness. She'd let him quit after a month when he demonstrated zero willingness to practice. The same went for Little League, Boy Scouts and surfing. The moment he complained, Sylvia let him beg off. His siblings lamented that their mother had been much harder on them, but was Noah really lucky? They all had their lives together and he was "floundering."

He lay on his back and shimmied into his jeans. The good wine, the sex and the unburdening had paid off. He was definitely in a better place than when he arrived in Boca.

Becky's phone dinged.

"Your phone," he called out, but she didn't hear him over the flushing toilet. He fished it out from the mess of covers. The screen lit up with a text message from someone called "My Boo."

How's it going with lotto dude? Did you tell him about our biz idea yet? Waiting up for u, sexy girl.

"Ready!" Becky emerged from the bathroom. Noah was already on his feet.

"I gotta get going," he managed to choke out, brushing past Becky and finding his way to the street outside her building. His father had driven off with Sophie in the Bentley. There was no BBB stop in sight.

He was stranded. Rich, alone and stranded.

"LAST CALL. DUDE, CAN YOU HEAR ME? I SAID, IT'S LAST CALL."

Noah picked up his head and touched a hand to his forehead. A sticky peanut fell off. His gaze narrowed in on a bartender wiping down a counter with a wet rag.

"I'll have another," he said, lifting his empty glass, unsure what it had been filled with.

"You sure?"

Noah nodded.

The bartender ambled over and poured him a finger of whiskey. "You gonna get home okay?"

Noah swung his head around and surveyed the empty bar. He wondered if he'd be allowed to sleep in one of the banquettes.

As if reading his mind, the man behind the bar said, "You're not staying here. But I can call you a taxi. You have money?"

Did he have money? Ha!

"I got millions, my brother," Noah said. He pulled out his wallet to prove it, but the cards and cash spilled out and dropped to the floor, landing in a puddle of beer. Trying to stand up from the barstool was trickier than expected, and Noah found himself splayed out alongside the contents of his wallet.

"Let's get you into a cab," the bartender said, extending a hand to pull him up. "You want some coffee first? I was gonna make myself a cup before I close up. I'm Dan, by the way."

"Nice to meet you, Dan. I'm Noah."

Dan took the whiskey glass and dumped it in the sink while Noah slumped into a more stable seat at a table.

"I know your name. You announced your name after you bought a round for everyone in the bar. Asked a few ladies if they would ever love you for the real you too. You've had a rough night. Let me get that coffee and call you a cab. Be right back." Dan disappeared through the barn doors leading to the kitchen and Noah pulled out his phone.

It was after one a.m. Noah scrolled past the text messages he'd ignored over the past several hours, stopping only to read the one from Laura.

> Greetings from Tokyo. I need a clearer pic of Dad's meds. I don't recognize the blue bottle and need to know what he's taking.

It was a sobering text, literally. Noah felt his surroundings come into focus, and with that, the reminder of just how shitty everything was.

Will do, he texted back and included a picture of Leo in the Bentley convertible from earlier. "Gift went over great."

"Your ride's here." Dan reemerged as a flashing pair of headlights gleamed from the parking lot. "Let me walk you out."

Dan helped Noah stand, again, and handed him a warm cup of coffee in a to-go cup. Outside, he opened the cab door and eased Noah into the back seat. Noah muttered, "Boca Breezes—Tower Three," to the driver. "No, Tower Four. Shit, I don't know. Just get me close, please."

"Take it easy, alright?" Dan said. As he started to retreat, Noah rolled down his window.

"Hey, come back," Noah called out. He pulled a hundred-dollar bill from his wallet. "Take this. Actually, take two."

Dan waved him off. "Buddy, some people just want to help."

Dan turned his back and walked toward the bar's entrance, where a partially burned-out neon sign read "For Old Times' Sake Pub." Sake. Like saké? Why was he thinking about Japanese wine? Laura was there. With Doug. *Greetings from Tokyo.* He was so tired.

Noah was still exhausted when Sophie interrogated him the next morning across the kitchen table. Their father was out with the "gentlemen's walking club," a group of men who gathered thrice weekly for a leisurely stroll to the Bagel Cove, where they sat and kibitzed for twice the amount of time they walked.

"So . . . how was your night with sexy waitress lady? What did she serve? Any specials on the menu?"

His sister's attempt to be cute was amplifying his hangover exponentially.

"None of your business," he said. "Do you have any Advil? Actually, that reminds me, I need to send a clearer picture of Dad's pills to Laura."

"I do." Sophie fished a travel packet of Advil from her tote bag and he swallowed three with a gulp of water.

Sophie followed Noah to their father's bathroom. The pills were arranged more or less the way Noah had seen them the day before, but with a glass of water next to the sink, a good sign he was taking them.

Sophie checked her phone. "It's only ten p.m. in Japan. Let's FaceTime Laura and see how her trip is going. We can show her the bottles."

"Good idea." Noah dialed their sister.

Laura's face filled the screen. She was all made up and wearing sparkly earrings that hurt Noah's eyes. Very un-Laura. He was used to her soccer mom attire. "Hi, guys! How's Florida? And Dad?"

"Dad is Bocatastic," Sophie said, crowding Noah to fit her face in the camera frame. "He really loves it here. You know how he didn't really have any friends when we were growing up? The only men he spoke to were Mom's friends' husbands? Here he's, like, popular. How's Japan?"

"Let me show you." Laura flipped the lens so they could see the opulent restaurant where she and Doug were eating. Doug was speaking to the waiter in a curt voice that Noah didn't associate with his brother-in-law: "No, we don't want any more saké. Or caviar. Just the check. Please."

Laura's face reappeared. "We're having a great time. This restaurant is really fancy so I shouldn't stay on FaceTime long. Before I forget, Myrna called me about the card party fundraiser on LBI. She told me that it raised $75,000 the last time it was held, so I told her we'd each send $25k. Assume that works for you two?"

"Yep," Sophie said.

Noah thumbs-upped.

"Great. I'll get the wire info when I'm back. Show me Dad's pills."

Noah panned to the bathroom countertop.

"What's the blue bottle? I can't read the label."

Noah lifted the bottle and enunciated each syllable. "Sil-de-na-fil. Looks like it was called in by a local doctor, Marshall Diamond."

Laura's features pinched together. "I think that's what he took when his liver function was off. Shit. Why didn't he tell me? I get that he didn't want to bother me while I'm on vacation, but I've handled his medical stuff since Mom got sick. Hang on one sec. Doug is trying to tell me something." Laura propped the phone in a way that gave Noah and Sophie a clear view of their table, where a sushi platter large enough to feed twenty and a hill of caviar lay on crushed ice. "Jesus," Sophie muttered. "Those two are living large."

Laura came back. "Guys, Dad's liver is fine."

"Phew," Noah and Sophie said in unison.

"Hang on. Those pills are . . . well . . . they're Viagra."

Noah dropped the pill bottle, as if it contained their father's actual erection and not just the means.

"Ewwwwww," Sophie said.

Noah felt a pit forming in his already upset stomach. "The waitress I, uh, met yesterday, the one who works in Dad's complex, said there was an STD outbreak recently among the residents. The staff calls the place Happy Endings."

"That's macabre," Sophie said, widening her eyes. "Oh, wait a second. I get it. Double eww."

"Do you think Dad is using protection? And do we know who he's shtupping?" Laura's voice was practically a whisper.

"Based on our walk around the property, it may be more than one woman," Sophie said. "One of us has to talk to Dad and make sure he's being careful."

"Matthew." All three said his name at once.

Their older brother was the only option. Laura handled Leo's medical care but she would never broach this topic with him. Sophie was too skittish. She got her period for the first time at Maizy Mandel's bat mitzvah and had to ask Leo to stop at a drugstore on the way home, an awkward experience neither of them wished to relive. It was understood that Leo didn't see Noah as an authority figure, on a medical matter or otherwise.

"I miss him," Noah said.

"Me too," Sophie said.

"He would find this Viagra thing very funny. Disturbing, but funny," Laura said. She had left the restaurant and was standing on a street brightly lit by a kaleidoscope of neon billboards. Noah's hangover was taking a second beating. "Let's text him."

Noah scrolled through his phone looking for the most recent Fantastic Foursome exchange. It had been a whopping two months since any of them used the group chat. Noah was in touch with his sisters on a separate thread. Sophie had named it JJ, for Jackpot Jacobsons.

"Yikes," Sophie said, eyeing her phone.

"How did we not realize Matthew would feel left out? Even if Dad isn't upset, I know Mom would be furious at the three of us," Noah said.

"It's not just about Matthew and Beth. There's also Austin to consider," Laura said. "Our nephew."

"I hope it's not too late to undo the damage." Sophie's eyes watered as she spoke and Noah handed her a tissue.

"I feel like a jerk saying this, but Doug and I just spent nearly half of the winnings on the new house," Laura said, rubbing her temples. "We thought it was a good investment, but now there's not that much cash left over . . ."

Doug's face appeared in the frame next to Laura's. "We'll figure it out," he said.

Noah assumed he had enough money to split the pot in fourths, but he hadn't really been keeping track of what he was spending. He too had dropped a hefty chunk of change to buy a home. He'd been giving handouts left and right.

"So are we doing this?" Sophie asked. "But do you think Matthew might be insulted? Too little, too late? Insult to injury? We should have called him right away after he texted us. Instead, we took the easy way out."

Noah hadn't thought of that. Had they let things get to a point where it would be impossible to make things up to their brother?

"We'll just be very clear about our reasoning," Laura said. "It's not that we were resentful about how they acted when we bought the tickets even if we— Well at least I . . . thought they were being haughty. We want our family to share this experience together. Which is the truth."

"Ditto on feeling annoyed about them acting haughty. But guys, I have to admit something. It wasn't even Matthew who called me Dopey Sophie. It was his friend Ricky—the kid who used to do the magic shows with him. I was feeling guilty about Matthew and thinking back to that day when we were all playing Monopoly, and I remembered that Ricky called me dopey and I was just pissed Matthew didn't stand up for me." Sophie cracked a wry smile. "It all sounds so petty now."

"I think we're all pretty stuck in our childhood ways when it comes to the way we interact," Laura said.

Noah agreed. He still felt the urge to pull his sisters' hair when they pissed him off.

"Speaking of childhood, think we can make the money conditional on Matthew and Beth spending a portion of it on fun stuff for Austin?" Sophie asked.

"Much as I'd love to, parents don't really love other parents telling them how to raise their kids," Laura said.

But that wouldn't stop Noah from stealing Austin away for a Disney weekend, he thought, hoping he'd be trusted to take the kid to a crowded park after the Fantasy Island fiasco.

"I hate to be the party pooper," Doug said. "But this will surely have negative tax implications. I still think it's the right move, just putting that out there."

"Man, can I just say Dad really dropped the ball with this whole lottery thing? He might have mentioned that back when we won,"

Sophie said. "It's like he stopped caring once we were too old to get allowance."

"Did we even tell Dad we were thinking of cutting Matthew in?" Noah asked. He, for one, was ready to make the call to his brother today, just as soon as he confirmed he was still liquid enough to write that check.

"We're all going to be together for Thanksgiving at my house. Let's tell Matthew and Beth we want to share the winnings with them at dinner next week. We should do it in person. And Matthew can speak to Dad face-to-face about—" Laura stopped.

"The boner pills," Sophie said.

"I like this plan." Noah's full faculties were returning. He was grateful to focus on reuniting with Matthew rather than on Becky, yet another person trying to take advantage of him. "Konnichiwa."

"That means hello," Laura said. "You mean 'sayonara.'"

"Close enough," Noah said. It was fine to be "close enough" when it came to speaking in a foreign language, but close enough was never okay when it came to his siblings.

8

Matthew

THE OFFICES OF MEYER, PACKER & DRISCOLL WERE UNUSU-ally quiet for a midday morning in fall. Normally the hallways were abuzz with the squeaky wheels of hand trucks piled with cartons of discovery, copy machines rumbling overtime and the constant dinging of email. Today it was nearly as quiet as Christmas. The lawyers and support staff were far too anxious to make noise. On a higher floor, the partnership committee was meeting to decide which associates, after eight years of indentured servitude, would be promoted to junior partner and which junior partners, the rank held by Matthew and Beth, would be promoted to full-equity partners.

"I'm so nervous," Beth said, making a meal of her fingernails as she paced Matthew's office.

"Me too," he said, though his reason for being nervous was diametrically opposed to Beth's. She was desperate to make equity partner, while he was terrified of it. They were already paid handsomely as junior partners, though the pay was less impressive on an hourly basis (divide anything by twenty-four and it's less grand). But their incomes were nothing compared to what they would make as equity partners, sharing a slice of the firm's profit pie. They both had excellent chances of promotion after years of glowing annual reviews and hearty client acquisition. But nothing was for certain until the partnership committee summoned you to the gleaming conference room on the twenty-eighth floor and put a glass of champagne in your hand.

Matthew believed they would both get promoted, after which there would be no turning back. It was simply too much money. Too much prestige. Nobody walked away from an opportunity like that. He felt like a prisoner facing the parole board, unsure whether to plead his case or ask to stay in.

"We're both going to get it," Beth said, trying to manifest their destiny. "There's literally no chance we won't. We're both whales. No, we're sharks. We're—"

"Octopi?" Matthew said.

"Sure, yes, we're octopi." Beth's face softened and a small laugh escaped her lips. She took a seat in the leather wingback opposite Matthew's desk. "Is it octupi or octopusses? Austin would know."

Matthew pictured their son at home. He was off from school the entire week for Thanksgiving break, overseen by a rotating cast of babysitters and tutors. How Matthew wished he had the freedom to stay with him, especially during a week when Austin wasn't being ferried between his chess tutor, piano teacher and robotics class on account of the holiday. His gaze landed on the family photo positioned next to his monitor. It showed the three of them beaming in a giant auditorium, Austin clutching a chess trophy bigger than him. In the picture, taken just a year ago, Austin's hair was closely cropped. Now it was floppy and constantly needed to be pushed out of his eyes. Austin resisted their persistent suggestions of a haircut until they finally coaxed out of him that long hair was "the style." It was the first time either of them could recall him caring about fitting in. Matthew worried Beth would try to squash this change, but she said, "Long hair it is," and asked if he wanted any new clothes. He turned over a wish list that included sports jerseys and a pair of coveted sneakers for which Beth had to hire a "line waiter" to stand outside the Nike store for six hours.

The maternal indulgence initially charmed Matthew. He liked that Beth was supporting nonacademic interests, even if $150 sneakers for a kid whose feet were still growing rubbed him the wrong way. Over time, he realized that Beth saw Austin's newfound susceptibility to peer pressure as just another achievement—*See how he's brilliant and developing socially appropriately! That's not a combo you find every day!*

"I'm curious to see Laura's new place," Matthew said, pivoting away from partner talk. Laura and Doug were hosting Thanksgiving dinner in Franklin Lakes. Emma and Hannah told Austin about the putt-putt course and the half basketball court at their new house.

"Me too. I asked Laura what I can bring, but she said just ourselves." Beth pulled a face. "She hired a chef, obviously."

"Well, that makes things easy," Matthew said. He and Beth rarely spoke of his siblings and their lottery win. They were too drained after work to talk about anything substantive, including Matthew admitting to Beth that he hated his job. That he sometimes fantasized about a scandal bringing down the whole firm (but leaving them unscathed) or a fire where no one got hurt but all the client files got destroyed. But he never confessed. They needed his income to support their lifestyle. Neither he nor Beth were overly materialistic—by New York City standards—but going backward was never easy. Beth signed on to marry a corporate lawyer. A corporate lawyer she'd formed from whole cloth. It wasn't fair for him to bait and switch.

"You know they love you," Beth said.

"I do. My last annual review was probably my best yet. Bringing over the Anderson business was huge. Plus I put in a good word for Watson's kid at Dalton." Matthew leaned back in his chair and let his eyes blink shut for longer than a normal beat. Had that all happened within the past year? For reasons he couldn't fully comprehend, time felt bifurcated between pre- and post-Powerball. It moved differently. Was it how little his cell phone dinged with messages on the Fantastic Foursome thread? Was it knowing that by abstaining from the lottery, he missed his chance to leave this rat-race life and spend more time with his son? Or that July Fourth weekend would hereafter be remembered for his siblings' lottery win, and not the weekend they mourned their mother?

"I'm not talking about the partnership committee," Beth said, taking the pencil from him. "I'm talking about your siblings. They love you very much and I hope you know that."

"Of course I do," Matthew said, perhaps a bit too defensively.

"You just haven't been yourself since the Powerball. I think from what your siblings see of our lives, they can't imagine that we want for anything. We have a gorgeous apartment, Austin's in one of the finest—and most expensive—private schools in the country. That place we rented at the shore was out of a movie. I wear stuff like this—" She paused to pull at her sweater and Matthew noticed the designer logo finely woven into the pattern.

Matthew was stunned. Normally he defended his siblings to Beth, not the other way around. He *had* been mopey, but he thought he'd done a good job concealing it from his wife and son. The Powerball changed him, but it wasn't in the way Beth thought. It brought into stark relief feelings he'd been hiding from her and, to a lesser extent, from himself. He shuddered to think of her reaction if he admitted that climbing the corporate ladder was making him sick, that he'd prefer to scurry down from his midlevel rung and never enter their office building again.

As for his family, Matthew didn't doubt his siblings loved him. If anything, it was his own fault for not being honest with them about his desire to leave his job and spend more time with his son. He'd done nothing to dispel the notion that he lived to work. It was true he already had the finer things in life and then some. On the other hand, when he sent the group text suggesting that his cash might have bought the winning ticket, none of them even called to suss out what he meant. Their mother's passing had already reduced the frequency with which they saw each other. The lottery was like a second nail in her coffin.

"Your siblings realized that even if we had won, we'd keep doing exactly what we're doing," Beth said.

Matthew felt the roof of his mouth turn to sandpaper. His wife didn't know him at all.

"Besides, I know I'm not the easiest to be around. They love you, but they tolerate me. If I'm being honest, I'm jealous when I'm around your family. There's so much camaraderie that I never had. I didn't have brothers or sisters, and you know how checked out my parents were. Watching you guys pack up the house together was hard. It seemed like every item had a funny story behind it or a cute memory. You guys were cracking up over a Custard Hut receipt. I've never seen people so excited to find old beach badges. Part of what drew me to you was that you came from this big, boisterous family and then I ended up being envious of it."

Matthew's head cocked so dramatically his ear practically hit his shoulder. This was the most vulnerable version of Beth he could recall. He took a swig of water from a glass bottle and felt the constriction in his throat ease up. "I appreciate you saying that. There are a lot of us Jacobsons. And not a lot of Moores. I realize my family has been this continual presence, between the holidays, the birthdays, the shore house."

"Exactly. But that's a good thing. In fact—" Beth put her hand on his desk. She twisted the gold band on her middle finger around to reveal a gigantic blue stone set amidst smaller, colorful gems. "I took this from the house that weekend. It was your mother's. It's just some silly piece of costume jewelry she probably bought on Long Beach Boulevard. I don't know why I took it. I guess I liked the idea of having a piece of her, and maybe more than that. It's a memory of you guys reminiscing."

Matthew was again surprised. Beth was not typically sentimental.

"Some woman in my barre class asked if it was vintage Bulgari!"

Matthew's office phone rang and he scooped it up. "Matthew Jacobson."

Beth flew to the edge of her seat. The family conversation was kaput.

"Yes, I can come up now. I've got Beth in my office . . . Oh, good news for both of us . . . Well, that's great to hear. We'll be right there." He placed the phone on its cradle. Beth was already on his side of the desk, squealing.

"We did it!" She grabbed his hands and squeezed them tightly. "Our dreams have come true!"

MATTHEW SAT ON HIS LIVING ROOM SOFA AND STARED OUT the floor-to-ceiling glass, looking directly into another glass cube apartment like his own. His eyes traveled from top to bottom of the neighboring building, watching the residents mill about. Some were sitting opposite wall-mounted, flat-screen TVs watching the news or football, others sipped wine while staring down at their phones. These so-called fishbowl buildings were controversial. Unless you drew the curtains and blocked the view, the whole reason you paid a premium for the apartment, your life was available for public consumption. But that only meant physical actions, the stuff you chose to show the world. For Matthew, that meant the magazine in his hand he wasn't reading, the show he wasn't watching and the smile he put on his face each time Beth walked by and said something about their promotions. His inner turmoil was hidden in plain sight. It was why he never bothered to look up Samantha Siegel on social media, though he was curious how his high school crush had turned out. He knew he'd only be treated to the parts she wanted to share, and that would mean knowing nothing about the real her.

Beth appeared at his side, sipping from a tumbler of whiskey with a giant, hissing ice cube. He drew up the corners of his mouth into another forced smile and clinked his water glass against hers. "Cheers," he said, remembering too late that toasting with water was bad luck. There was no point in pretending to be anything but thrilled. He'd consigned his life to the devil, a devil disguised as a law firm spread across ten floors in a Manhattan skyscraper.

"I feel like we should celebrate," Beth said. "Let's go out for dinner."

Matthew studied his wife, radiant in a sleek dress and high heels with sexy red soles that gave him a jolt when she crossed her toned legs. His mother's ring sparkled on one hand, her giant engagement ring shone on the other.

"Why not?" he said. He held back a snarky comment about this being the last time they might have time to go for a leisurely dinner that wasn't client-related. "I'll get Austin."

"Hey, bud," Matthew said as he pushed open the door to Austin's room. He wondered if Austin heard it the way it sounded in his head, like the greeting of a TV sitcom dad.

"Hey," Austin said. He was nestled in a bean bag chair, engrossed in his phone, which he immediately put facedown. Matthew wondered what he could be hiding. Maybe a girl? A boy?

"Mom and I want us all to go out for a family dinner to celebrate our promotions to equity partner." Now Matthew really hated the way he sounded. He'd rather be a cheesy sitcom dad than a corporate robot.

Austin shrugged. "I'm not really hungry."

"Too bad, you're coming," Beth said, appearing behind Matthew. "It's not a celebration without you."

"Fine," Austin said, his face hidden behind his phone screen again.

"And I have some good news for you too," Beth said.

Austin lowered his phone. He looked skeptical.

"Remember that grandmaster you met at chess nationals last spring? His schedule cleared up and he's finally able to give you lessons." Beth danced awkwardly, a combination fist thrust and booty shake.

"Great," Austin said. He might as well have been told he needed a cavity drilled.

"I thought you'd be happier. You said he was the only one who could really teach the Ruy Lopez opening."

Their boy shrugged. "I'm chill. Let's bounce." Beth and Matthew looked at each other, neither of them understanding the teenage vernacular.

Beth dominated the conversation at dinner. Matthew humored her by responding "Great idea" to talk of a Hamptons rental and "Me too" about hoping their promotion would mean moving to larger offices. Austin was sullen. Matthew grew worried. Their son was at a delicate age. The other day he'd noticed a few dark hairs on his son's upper lip. Once the boy started shaving, Matthew's window to get through to him would shut.

"Mom, can I talk to you for a minute?" Austin said when they returned home and Matthew was hanging up their coats. By the time he turned around, Beth was trailing Austin to his room. A moment later, the door clicked shut. He knew many children gravitated toward their mothers over their fathers. He need look no further than his own upbringing to see that. But that had never been the case with Austin. Now Matthew waited on tenterhooks.

"Everything's fine," Beth said when she finally came into their bedroom. She stepped into her walk-in closet and Matthew climbed out of bed and followed her inside. Beth was unclasping her jewelry. When Matthew went to help, he found his hands were shaking.

"What did he say?"

"I promise, it's nothing," Beth said. "Just some teenage social media nonsense that doesn't concern you."

Why would it concern him? He was about to say that when Beth preempted him. "Honey, I'm exhausted. I need rest before we see your whole family tomorrow. Let's go to sleep."

When was the Energizer Bunny ever tired? And why did she need to rest before seeing his family? She had no cooking or setting up to do. Beth switched off her night table lamp and their room fell into blackness. Matthew, still restless an hour later, realized how much he didn't like being kept in the dark.

"HOLY SHIT," AUSTIN SAID AS THEY PULLED INTO THE DRIVE-way of Laura and Doug's new house in Franklin Lakes.

"Language," Beth snapped reflexively, but as she lowered her sunglasses to take in the full property, she quietly echoed Austin.

"Parking won't be an issue," Matthew said as he drove their Tesla toward what he counted to be a free-standing six-car garage.

"This is a freaking castle," Austin said, his nose pressed against the car window.

"It's still in New Jersey," Beth said, clearly grasping for criticism.

They exited the car and stood in place gaping at the house, even though it was unseasonably frigid for late fall and a light snow was falling. The exterior was a combination of stone and stucco, with arched windows divided by crisply painted white mullions illuminated by iron lanterns. The roof was embellished with three turrets in a darker shade of stone and six brick chimneys. He immediately juxtaposed this mega-mansion with the Cohen family's former residence, a modest Colonial practically kissing the curb. It had been in stiff competition with the shore house for renovation needs.

A uniformed housekeeper opened the front door before they had a chance to use the brass knocker. Once inside, Matthew felt like he'd stumbled onto the set of *Clue*. He immediately thought: Mrs. Peacock, with the knife, in the billiard room. The entry was a cavernous two-story space with a domed ceiling and two grand staircases with gilded railings on opposite sides, curving to meet on the second-floor balcony. His and Beth's rental down the shore had been large, but it was still on a small plot of land and had a beachy sensibility that balanced its size. It was true the kitchen and bathrooms were tricked out with the newest appliances and solid brass hardware, but at least it didn't scream Versailles like this place.

"Austin! Finally!" His nieces, Emma and Hannah, flew down opposing staircases and tugged at their cousin. "You have to see the billiard room," Hannah said. Knew it, Matthew thought. But where did Mrs. Peacock hide the knife?

"Hi, Uncle Matthew, Aunt Beth," Emma said as both girls hugged them.

"Should we do billiards first or show him the screening room?" Hannah looked to her sister. The three cousins disappeared before Matthew could get a word in. He was curious to find out how the lottery was affecting the girls. Clearly, they were jazzed about their new digs.

"May I take your overcoat?" Matthew heard a cockney British accent from behind and nearly had a fit. His sister and Doug hired a butler? Wasn't that taking things just a tad too far? Laura used to rinse Ziploc bags for reuse. Doug had a conniption if his daughters threw out perfectly good food just because the "best by" date had passed. A hand patted his shoulder. Matthew turned and was relieved to see it was just Noah, goofing around.

"Hey, man," Matthew said. "You got me there for a second." The brothers each gave each other a back slap.

"Fancy a brew?" Noah asked, keeping up his act.

"Not just yet." Matthew took a step back to study his younger brother. Noah had been taller than Matthew since entering high school, but this was the first time he was ever wider. He tried not to stare at the gut bulging from his brother's midsection.

"I put on a little weight," Noah said, patting his belly. "And I'll be putting on more tonight." He pushed his shaggy hair out of his face and took a swig of beer from the glass bottle in his hand.

"It does smell amazing," Beth said. "I just hope Laura told the chef about Austin's dietary restrictions."

"The kid doesn't have allergies," Noah said. "You have to chill."

"Don't tell me what I have to do," Beth said, snappier than Matthew expected. "They're not allergies. They're intolerances. It's also about making sure our child doesn't consume carcinogens."

"Sorry," Noah mumbled. "Let's go to the den. Everyone's in there. We've been waiting for you guys."

Walking behind Noah, Matthew noticed his brother's unsteady gait. It looked like he was favoring one knee. He'd never seen Noah such a mess.

"You okay?" he asked, gripping his elbow.

Noah lifted the beer in his hand. "I may have had a few too many of these."

After passing a warren of rooms with Louis XVI–style furniture, they reached the den where all the Jacobsons were sunken into a leather couch and a football game played on TV.

"Are we late?" Beth checked the time on her watch and her iPhone. "It's only five after four."

"It was changed to three," Sophie said. "But no big deal."

"Nobody told us that," Beth said.

"Yeah, it was on the text," Noah said. He fumbled with his phone. "Oh, wait, never mind."

"What?" Matthew asked.

"Laura must have not realized she only texted me and Sophie," Noah said. "Whoops."

Matthew practically choked on the smoke coming out of Beth's ears.

He crossed the room to hug his father. "Dad, you've been getting a lot of sun."

"Pickleball," everyone said at once.

"He's pretty obsessed," Laura said, entering the den. "We've been hearing a lot about the tournaments."

"Number one seed," Leo said, reaching his hand into a bowl of gourmet nachos.

"Get it, Grandpa," Emma said. She, Hannah and Austin were at the game table, which had an inlaid marble chess board.

"Dad, I think you've had enough of those," Sophie said, pushing away the chips.

"Sorry we're late," Beth said to Laura. "Though I suppose we wouldn't have been if we'd known the time changed. Anyway, congrats on the new place." She produced a silver bag Matthew hadn't noticed earlier, adorned with tissue paper and ribbons. "Just a little housewarming gift. Though I'm afraid it doesn't quite match your style." Her tone was even enough, but Matthew heard the underlying sentiment: *I didn't realize you'd hired Donald Trump's interior designer.*

"I'm sure it's perfect," Laura said, retrieving a sleek candle from inside the bag and sniffing it. "Smells terrific. I'll go put it in the powder room."

"Who you rooting for?" Matthew asked Doug, gesturing to the TV.

"I don't even know who's playing," Doug admitted.

"They're pretty hard to miss on that screen. It's like a movie theater."

Doug reddened. "This place is a bit much, but Laura is happy. I think she is, anyway."

Matthew rewound to Beth suggesting there was marital discord between Laura and Doug and wasn't sure how to respond. Laura saved him. With a clap of her hands, she announced, "Time to eat. The turkey looks incredible."

The family filed into the dining room, where an ornately laid table set for ten awaited them. Thanksgiving was not always a holiday that brought all the Jacobsons together. Laura and Doug alternated years between their families. There were times when Sophie chose to go to a Friendsgiving or spend the holiday with a boyfriend. Noah was a wild card. Matthew was glad everyone was together this year. Even if the table setting was absurdly fussy—what was the purpose of four forks?—it was far preferable to a Thanksgiving party of three.

A full table in an echoey room and a robust waitstaff made a singular table conversation impossible. There was constant swapping out of china, including one shattered plate that might have been Noah's fault. Chef Francois, a heavily accented Frenchman, intruded each time a new course was set down to give an incomprehensible explanation. Matthew's concern for Noah escalated as the meal wore on. He never turned down a refill of wine and drained each glass in two large gulps. Several times Matthew thought Noah might fall asleep at the table.

Sophie told Matthew all about her new studio space, but when he asked what happened with the painting she was selling to the "suit," she changed the topic. Beth's numerous attempts to publicize Austin's latest roster of accomplishments went ignored. Laura and Doug, seated at opposite ends of the table like world leaders presiding over a state dinner, struggled to coherently rehash their trip to Japan and were constantly cutting the other off. Leo was quiet, even for him. Matthew caught him shaking his head when the chef described the first course as a foie gras pudding on a bed of edible flowers. Only the subject of pickleball ignited him, and there was only so much they could ask him about paddles and the two-bounce rule.

At the kids' end of the table, Austin and his cousins were giggly, sneaking glances at their phones and consuming unusually large quantities of food. Matthew didn't think Francois was anything special, but his son was shoveling forkfuls of turkey and cranberry sauce into his mouth in between fits of laughter. Perhaps he was just happy to eat a meal that his mother didn't sanction. Matthew reveled in seeing the cousins goof around. There was certainly no discernible distance between the girls and Austin, even though they were the children of lottery winners and he was not. It made Matthew nostalgic for the occasional week in August when schedules permitted Laura's family and his to vacation at the shore together.

"Isn't the stuffing delicious?" Doug asked, repeating the question three times before everyone quieted down.

"Is this supposed to be like Grandma's?" Emma asked. She lifted a fork of grayish-brown mush and eyed it with distrust. "She's the only person who put currants and hazelnuts in. Mom, did you give the chef the recipe?"

"Do you like it?" Laura asked.

"It tastes like dog poo," Hannah blurted and Austin started barking.

"I can't disagree," Sophie said. "The consistency is like tar."

"I think the currants may be rotten," Beth said.

"Your mother would spit in this," Leo said, pushing his plate away.

"I'll suggest a different recipe next year," Laura said quietly.

It wasn't that bad, Matthew thought, but before he could say so a parade of pies and cakes on silver stands came out. Once the desserts were set down, Laura asked the servers to step outside. They retreated, looking like marching penguins in their white-and-black uniforms.

When it was just family, Laura cleared her throat at the same time Doug dinged his water glass, and no one knew which way to face.

"Thank you all for—" Doug started to say just as Laura stood, winning the who-should-we-focus-on competition.

"Happy Thanksgiving, everyone. It's such a joy to have you all in our new home."

"It's very good," Noah said. "I mean gold." He took another swig of wine. "I mean nice."

"As I was saying, it's wonderful to be together. It's hard to believe how much has happened since the summer," Laura continued, locking eyes with Matthew in a way that flustered him.

"Powerball! Powerball!" Austin started chanting and Beth whipped around to shush him. She threw an accusatory look at Matthew, as if he was responsible for anything their son did that was less than perfect. Austin was not dissuaded by the ferocious look on his mother's face. Emma and Hannah quickly joined his cheer.

"Powerball! Powerball!" the three of them shouted in unison.

"Girls," Laura snapped. "Quiet! I'm about to make an important announcement."

Matthew noticed Sophie motioning frantically to Emma and Hannah, pointing at their eyes, then her own, then theirs again. What the hell?

"Sophie, what are you doing?" Laura asked, annoyed. "I'm about to tell Matthew and Beth the news."

"What news?" Beth asked.

"We're cutting you in," Noah slurred. He plunged his glass of wine onto the table and a splash of cabernet rolled down the white tablecloth. "You're gonna be rich like us. Whoop dee doo." He flung his napkin around like a lasso, smacking Sophie in the face.

"Hey, Noah, let me make you some coffee," Doug said, heading for the kitchen.

"Doug, someone can get that for him," Laura said stiffly. "Sit back down."

"Seriously, Laura?" Doug stalked out of the room.

"What do you mean, cutting us in?" Matthew asked, though Laura could only be referring to one thing.

"Why now?" Beth asked, an edge to her voice. Matthew was wondering the same thing. "I'm just curious why after all these months"—she slowed her pace to a crawl—"you decided to share your riches with us."

"Money, Money, Money" by ABBA suddenly blasted through the room, piped through built-in speakers. The three cousins were now hysterical, snort-laughing uncontrollably. It was then Matthew noticed his son's eyes were bloodshot. So were Hannah's and Emma's.

"Turn that music off," Laura said. "Who did that?"

"Emma," Hannah said, pointing at her sister through giggles.

"It was Hannah," Emma said, her bobbing head dangerously close to face planting in the pecan pie.

"What is going on with you three?" Beth demanded. "Austin, what did the girls give you?"

"Shit, you guys are high as fuck," Noah said. He sounded impressed.

"Seriously, guys? I warned you to get it together," Sophie said. Unlike Noah, she looked disappointed, like the younger generation was letting her down with their lack of subtlety. "Your grandfather is here."

"Can someone please explain what is going on?" It was the first time Leo had spoken since dissing the stuffing.

"What's happening, Leo, is that Emma and Hannah gave our son—a thirteen-year-old boy—drugs." Beth threw her napkin on the table. "Austin, come over here. I want you to drink some water while I call Dr. Fleishman's service."

Just what Fleishman needed during his Thanksgiving dinner, Matthew thought. Their pediatrician already thought Beth was loco for worrying that Austin's flu shot fatigue might interfere with his math test performance three days later.

"Girls, that's absolutely unacceptable," Doug said. He had returned with Noah's coffee in time to catch what was happening.

"How could you?" Laura glared at her daughters. "Emma, I'm canceling your trip to see Tomas. Hannah, you're losing your car."

"Who said *we* gave it to *him*?" Hannah said.

"Yeah," Emma chimed in. "Austin gave it to us."

"Are you insane?" Beth's rage, which Matthew didn't think could grow anymore, was taking on fire-breathing dragon proportions. "You expect us to believe an eighth grader gave two college girls pot?" She looked at Matthew. "Are you going to say anything?"

In fact, he was speechless. Not scared to speak, just truly at a loss for words.

"Can we go back to the part about us sharing the money?" Sophie attempted. "I think these kids need to, um, come down a little before we get into that mess."

"Aunt Sophie, it's fine," Austin said, speaking in a timid voice. "I don't want Emma and Hannah to get in trouble. It was me. I gave it to them."

"Aha!" Laura pointed a finger at Beth. "Turns out your perfect son is a troublemaker. What nerve you have, Beth. You should be thanking us for cutting your family in when you were so damn snobby about the lottery to begin with. Instead, you're accusing my daughters of corrupting Austin."

"Lower your voices," Leo warned. "We don't need the thirty people serving us dinner to know our family secrets."

"There are no secrets," Sophie said.

"Ha!" Beth said. "That's a laugh coming from you. From all of you."

"What are you talking about?" Sophie asked.

"Laura's right about saying thank you," Noah said. "You called us all stupid. I'm the only stupid one. I wasn't even supposed to buy a ticket that night. That's not why I left the house."

"You are not stupid," Leo said sharply. "But you are drunk as a skunk. Quit it."

"Hey, we were all there," Sophie said, speaking softly. "You guys could have gone in on the tickets with us. For fun, anyway. But it doesn't matter. Now we're all in this together. The three of us want to share."

"Is that right?" Beth said. "It's got nothing to do with a certain video Austin showed me? You guys just don't want the whole world knowing how selfish you are. Austin—give me your phone."

"Mom, no," he said. His blue eyes were watery, the whites less bloodshot than before. Matthew hadn't been high or seen anyone high in so long he didn't remember the tells. It explained the kids' uncontrollable laughter and munchies. A single tear rolled down

Austin's blotched cheek. "You promised you wouldn't tell. I never should have shown you."

"Austin, you are in no position to argue with me. I will deal with you later and you're going to tell me who forced you into drugs."

"What video?" Matthew asked, realizing this must be what Beth said about Austin and social media the night before. *It doesn't concern you.* The hell it didn't.

"Play it," Beth ordered.

The tiny screen forced everyone to gather in close.

Beth pressed play on the frozen video and a girl around Austin's age, with twin braids hanging over her shoulders, appeared.

"Hi, everyone! It's me, Ruby, the Ruby-roaster, the Ruba-thon, your favorite TikTok sensation. I'm coming to ya live from the Garden State, where I've been bringing you exclusive content on the Internet's most beloved Granny, my very own Grandma M, who won a whopping sixty-million buckaroos playing the Powerball. Like pop star Sia, Granny M won't show her face, but she has given me permission to tell you some of the things she's been up to."

"That's sixty million before taxes," Noah called out.

Ruby's face disappeared from the screen and the back of a tiny old woman dressed in a knit sweater and matching hat appeared. What the hell was going on? Clearly this was the other jackpot winner from New Jersey, but why were they watching this?

Text scrolled across the image of the old woman's back.

Granny Mabel's Adventures Since Winning the PB

1) Alaskan cruise
2) First concert (Coldplay with Yours Truly)
3) Mega donation to her church
4) Built a soup kitchen
5) Facelift (Granny looking hawt)

"Shit, we haven't done anything," Sophie said.

"Granny got us beat," Noah agreed.

"Quiet," Beth said. "Austin, turn it up."

Ruby reappeared.

"Today I have some juicy news to share with you guys, my beloved fans. But first, don't forget to like and follow @rubyrollercoaster and check out my YouTube page, which I've dedicated to my grandma. Anyway, get yourselves a big mug, because I have steaming-hot tea. You all know Granny M won the jackpot along with a group of siblings from Jersey. I decided it would be cool to see what they are up to and so I did a little digging. Watch this live footage of the day we met the other winners."

"Turn it off," Sophie said. She had her hand over her face.

"No," Beth said. "Keep going."

The video switched to a scene of his three siblings talking to Granny M, whose face was blurred.

Granny: "What good fortune for you three. Your parents must be overjoyed. You know, I'm one of three as well, but both my sisters have passed on. I was the middle sister. Which one of you is the middle?"

Sophie: "That's me."

Granny: "Three is such a great number. That's why I had three children myself. Two boys and a girl, opposite of you folks."

Laura: "Sounds like a lovely family."

Granny, looking at Noah: "You must be the baby? Did you wish you had a brother or were these two older sisters enough for you?"

Noah: "I, uh—"

Sophie: "Noah has always held a special place in our family as the baby."

Matthew's knees went weak. He was the oldest. He held Laura's hand when she was too scared to start middle school. He broke the news to their parents when she got pregnant in college. He did Sophie's math homework because numbers made her cry and threatened to beat up the guy who ditched her at prom. He taught Noah to ride a bike and babysat him even when it meant missing plans with his friends. Matthew couldn't believe his role in the family was so marginal it could be erased like a stray mark on a chalkboard.

Ruby appeared back on screen.

"Anyway, the tea is that these *three* siblings actually have a fourth sibling. Can you believe they lied to my poor granny? And they didn't share the money with their brother? You guys know me. Family means everything. I can't imagine not sharing sixty million dollars, can you? Drop your comments below and don't forget to like and subscribe. See ya next time. Ruby out."

9

Sophie

"COFFEE? TEA? ESPRESSO?"

"NO!" Every member of the Jacobson family, blood-related or in-lawed, shouted at the terrified server. The woman backed away quickly through the swinging door and Sophie wanted to escape right along with her. But she forced herself to stay put. It was obvious—at least to her—that she was the only person with a fighting chance of restoring order.

"First, we're going to start with sixty seconds of peace," she announced. It was how Sophie started her own days, with a brief meditation.

"I'm not hanging around for any Millennial nonsense," Leo said.

"Gen Zs are also into meditation," Emma said.

"Well, I'm not." Leo folded his arms across his chest.

"Fine. Can everyone at least take a deep breath and have a sip of water?" Sophie inhaled and exhaled loudly and brought her water glass to her lips. Lead by example, she thought. "There's a lot to unpack here but first we all need to simmer down."

"I knew this would happen," Leo said. He took no deep breath. Drank no water.

"Knew what would happen?" Laura was also not following Sophie's instructions.

"Problems," Leo said, shaking his head. "Only problems."

Sophie had an idea. "Everyone is going to have a chance to speak, but only if they're holding this." She reached for a knife on the table. "Well, maybe not this." She set the knife down and lifted a spoon. Back in Hebrew school, Morah Rachel used a Shabbat candlestick for these same purposes. "I'll go first, because I'm holding the spoon. Beth, Matthew, I can say with complete certainty that none of us has ever seen that video before."

Matthew snorted. Sophie decided it was not a technical violation of her silence rule.

"Gimme a break," Beth said. She refused to take the spoon when Sophie offered it.

"It's true. We decided, the three of us, that we wanted to include you guys when Noah and I were in Florida visiting Dad. Something came up that required Matthew's help." Sophie tipped her chin in their father's direction. "We were on the phone with Laura and we wanted to patch Matthew in, but it felt weird. It's obvious that our relationships haven't been the same since the lottery and we didn't want it to be a barrier between us any longer. We miss you, Matty Magician."

"Don't Matty Magician me," Matthew said, though Sophie could hear that his retired stage name had thawed her brother a bit. "It's not my fault we're distant. You guys didn't even realize I wasn't on the text changing the time of Thanksgiving dinner."

Sophie felt shame bubble inside her. How had none of them realized the time change was sent on the Jackpot Jacobsons group chat and not on the Fantastic Foursome?

"I'm sorry," Laura whispered.

"What did you need my help for anyway? What was so important it was worth cutting me in?" Matthew asked.

Sophie, Laura and Noah exchanged glances and looked over at

Leo, who was absentmindedly pushing a slice of honeydew around his plate. Sophie mouthed *uh-oh* to her brother and sister while Matthew looked bewildered.

"It wasn't like that," Laura said. "We did need your help. But that isn't the reason we decided to cut you in. It just made us realize there's been a rift among us. Not just with you. The three of us don't speak that much either. Noah's been . . . I don't know. Sophie has her new studio and Doug and I have been traveling and we're all having . . ."

"Trouble in paradise?" Beth's tone was icy.

"There's no such thing as paradise." Sophie hadn't meant to sound quite that incisive. "You've got to believe that video had nothing to do with our decision. We've never even seen it."

"I swear that's the truth," Laura said.

"Come on, Matthew," Doug said. "I don't think this family is perfect—far from it—and I don't agree with everything your siblings have done. But how would we have seen a video that some teenage girl put up?"

"It has three hundred views," Austin said.

"Now three hundred and fifty," Hannah corrected.

"And it's now an Insta Reel," Emma added.

"Noah?" Sophie appealed to the most guileless Jacobson. "Please tell Matthew what we're saying is true. He'll believe you."

After releasing a loud belch, Noah confirmed it. "It's true. S'cuse me. I ate too much."

"It's not the food," Leo said. "You've been drinking since ten a.m. And my grandchildren are smoking grass. What's gotten into this family?"

"There has to be a good explanation for that," Beth said. "Austin?"

"Hey, Beth, maybe that's more of a private family thing," Sophie said. "Let's get back to—"

"No, we're going to deal with this now," Beth said firmly, desperate to clear her son's name. "Austin, tell us who gave you the drugs. Were you lied to? Did you know what it was? I've heard marijuana can be very confusing for children. It can look like . . . well . . . anything."

"Promise you won't be mad?" Austin looked at both his parents. His lip was quivering. Sophie tried to catch his eye. She needed to get a message to him. *Don't believe them! Don't believe them! They will tell you they won't be mad but DO NOT BELIEVE THEM.*

"We promise," Beth and Matthew said at once.

Oh no. Sophie couldn't watch.

"I grew it," Austin said.

"Grew what?" Beth's face scrunched in confusion. Sophie knew exactly where this was going.

"The drugs. I grew weed with my friends and we made gummies with it. I used that candy-making set you got me for my eleventh birthday. The one you said would give me a leg up in chemistry."

"At least we know there's no fentanyl in it," Sophie tried.

"I told you not to buy him that," Matthew said to Beth. Sophie couldn't quite describe the look on his face, but if she had to, she'd say her older brother was just *done*.

"You told me not to buy him something educational," Beth fired back. "You wanted to get him that stupid rebounder when we don't even have a backyard. I didn't foresee that our son might use a candy-maker to make drugs!"

"I thought the rebounder would be fun to use at the shore," Matthew said.

"Oh please, we all knew that house was falling apart and would be sold the minute Sylvia died," Beth said.

"Watch it," Noah stuttered. "We love that house. Our best

memories with our mom are there. Besides, I live next door now. I would have stayed and fixed it up." Sophie had completely forgotten that Noah had bought Stanley Archer's house.

"You know, what Austin did is actually really impressive," Emma said. "It's not easy to grow weed. And then to grow weed and make gummies. That's like, very hard science."

"Em, I think we should stay out of this," Laura said.

"It does require a lot of knowledge about plants. Remember you signed me up for that botany class, Mom?" Austin said.

"Can we go back to my original question and discuss our son's drug business later?" Matthew said. "What problem was I needed for?"

"I don't sell it," Austin said, but nobody but Sophie seemed to hear him or care.

"I'd like to know too. What was this big problem that you three couldn't handle without Matthew?" Leo said.

"We found Viagra in your bathroom and we wanted Matthew to have a talk with you about STDs," Noah said, gaining coherence at the most inopportune time. "The old folks in your building all got chlamydia or something."

"Oh my God, Grandpa!" Hannah screeched.

"That's it," Leo roared, pounding his fist on the table. "I have heard enough and I have had enough. I should have done this an hour ago." He pulled out his cell phone.

"What are you doing, Dad?" Sophie asked. "Everything is going to be okay. We're talking this through."

"Leo, sit down," Doug said.

"Do you want to lie down in one of the guest rooms?" Laura asked. "I can have someone make up the bed."

"No, I don't want to lie down in one of the guest rooms in this fakakta house that looks like a gaudy palace. I'm getting an Uber, I'm going to the airport, and I'm taking the next flight back to Florida."

"It's late, Leo. You shouldn't travel this time of night," Beth said. She looked genuinely concerned. "This is all my fault. I shouldn't have played the video in front of everyone."

"I was ashamed of everyone well before that, Beth," Leo said. "The only good thing about this holiday is that your mother wasn't here to see what's become of all of you."

"Or taste that stuffing," Noah muttered.

"What do you expect?" Leo said. "Who the hell hires a French chef to cook for an American holiday?"

"I MADE THE STUFFING!" Laura burst into tears.

"It's true," Doug said as he rubbed Laura's back. "It was the one thing the chef didn't make."

Yikes, Sophie thought. Her poor sister. She hadn't even been good with the Easy-Bake Oven.

Leo's phone chirped. "My Uber's here. Emma, please get my bag and bring it outside."

"Grandpa, please stay," Emma said, but he was already ambling to the front door, which shut behind him a moment later.

Noah was the first to speak once their father was outside. "I wish we had never won the goddamn lottery. Laura, I'm sorry about the stuffing."

"I'll go after him," Sophie said. "He's got to be headed to Newark Airport."

"No, I'll go," Matthew said. "You'd have to Uber. I have my car."

"I can go. I have my car too," Laura croaked. "Cars. I have cars. Because I'm an idiot who ran out and bought a Mercedes and a BMW."

"Let me do it," Noah said. "I blurted out the Viagra thing."

"No way," Matthew said. "You've had far too much to drink."

"Well, someone needs to go. And soon," Doug said. "I'd go, but I think it should be one of you guys."

"I agree," Sophie said. "How about we all go?"

Nobody answered, but they moved in synchronized formation to retrieve their coats and bundle into Laura's Mercedes S-Class. Soon after, they were cruising down the New Jersey Turnpike.

They found Leo standing at the Spirit Airlines counter. Leo clearly wanted to get home, but he wasn't going to pay Delta or Jet-Blue prices to get there.

"He's on the phone." Noah pointed to their father's silhouette. "Who could he be talking to?"

As they approached, they heard him say, "I'll see you soon. Yes, I'm upset. And disappointed."

The siblings looked at each other. Perhaps their father had made a good friend in Boca, a Stanley Archer down south.

"Dad," Noah said. When he didn't turn around, Laura repeated "Dad" more loudly. Sophie tapped him on the shoulder and he finally turned.

"We don't want you to leave like this," Laura said. "It's Thanksgiving."

"I've already bought my ticket," Leo said, and he held up his printed boarding pass.

"So rip it up," Sophie said. "Come back to Laura's."

He shook his head. "I'm not ripping up a perfectly good airline ticket. And I'm not like your mother. I don't know how to fix everyone else's problems. I don't know what to say and what not to say. I think that's why God took away my hearing early on."

The siblings exchanged a look of shared anguish.

"That doesn't matter," Sophie said. "You don't need to fix us. Just don't leave."

Leo didn't respond right away and Sophie thought maybe she'd convinced him. She went to relieve him of his carry-on but he pulled it back. "No, I'm going back tonight. And my flight boards in fifteen minutes. It being Thanksgiving and all, I think you four need to spend some time thinking about gratitude."

"You're right," Sophie said. "You're absolutely right."

"And, speaking of your mother, her birthday was last month and not a single one of you thought to call me." With that, Leo walked off and quickly disappeared down the long escalator leading to security.

SOMETHING WASN'T RIGHT.

Actually, nothing was right.

Sophie made a slow 360 turn in her studio. South-facing, double-height windows bathed the room in sunlight all morning long. On the opposite wall, floating metal shelves held tubes and cans of premium paints lined up in rainbow order. There was a slop sink with neat dividers and space to soak even her largest rollers. Her other supplies—scissors of all sizes, paint thinners, sketchbooks, synthetic and natural hair brushes, sponges, scrapers and pencils—were organized with neat labels on three matching rolling carts.

And she had plants. So many plants. A five-foot Ficus with verdant leaves stood next to a lush maple with leaves like stars. Scattered around the studio were four stable, top-quality easels that didn't fall over when too much pressure was applied to the canvas. And yet.

The canvases, her new ones, were blank. Bare to the bone. Pure duck canvas, triple-primed, archival quality, purchased from an art supply store based in Florence that shipped internationally. Sophie used to loiter around her local Blick until the drool got to be too much, wishing she could buy the professional-grade supplies but settling for the lower-quality substitutes. Now she had a one-pound container of ultramarine pigment that cost more than fifty dollars and was still sealed shut.

Only one canvas was alive with color, her work-in-progress, *Look at this Stuff.* The one that was half-sold to the suited man who made her promise to contact him the minute she finished it. What had she done since that day? Added some detail to the steel office towers in the background. Layered a glaze over the bronze paint to make the Vessel more reflective. She'd done both of those things before the Powerball. Ariel's T-shirt was still blank. Her pose needed adjusting. But each time Sophie lifted a brush, a paralysis crept from her elbow to her wrists to her fingers.

Maybe it had been a mistake to rent this studio when there was plenty of room to work alongside Ravi. Shortly after the Powerball, Sophie had moved in with him. When there was no financial stress clouding her judgment, she felt better about the decision to live together. But both living and working together didn't seem like a good idea—not to mention that she had money to burn—so she rented the downtown studio to give herself the work-life and Ravi-Sophie separation she thought would benefit them all around.

She intended to complete the Little Mermaid work, deliver it to Suit, then tackle Belle on the steps of the New York Public Library. She'd render the princess's yellow gown torn and stained and pose Belle as though she were blowing a kiss to one of the famed lions who sat sentry at the library's entrance. It was almost too perfect—*Beauty and the Beast*, set in New York City, with a grunge slant. Maybe Suit would buy that one too. Then she would move on to an idea that had been percolating for ages.

When left alone to free draw, her elementary school students returned to the same subjects over and over. Rainbows. Puppies. Trees. Beaches. What she loved about the kids' drawings was how out of proportion everything was. The apples on the trees were twice the size of the branches. The eyes took up almost an entire face. She wanted to play with that mistaken sense of proportion. She would paint more mature subjects, but with wildly outsized or downsized features. It had been so clear in her mind last spring—she could remember staring at fifth-grader Olive Cantor's self-portrait and cracking up at the size of the freckles, each one practically a penny. But now all her attempts at translating this concept to her own work looked cartoonish and amateur. The wastebasket in her studio overflowed with crumpled paper.

Did she mention her workplace was also too quiet?

It was impossible to be creative when the dominant sound was the clomping of her clogs against the wood plank flooring. Every tap of her eraser against the drafting paper made her antsy. The sound of paintbrushes clanking around the metal sink basin was infuriating.

It was time to let the outside world rejigger her brain chemistry. She wrestled open a stubborn window and let Manhattan trickle in. The traffic horns and a one-sided phone conversation in a language she didn't understand helped settle her. She was overthinking things. Worrying unnecessarily that she didn't deserve the gorgeous artist's loft when her compatriots were still toiling at SHART, inhaling paint fumes and the stench of take-out food left out overnight thanks to a less-than-reliable maintenance crew. That's assuming her SHART friends hadn't been priced out altogether by now. The guilt was cramping her creativity. Who was she, Sophie Jacobson, to decide who deserved what? Did Ravi stay up at night guilt-ridden that he worked on his ceramics rent-free at his parents' place? No, sir. He conked out the minute his head hit the pillow.

Peals of laughter wafted through the open window and Sophie ducked her head outside. Uniformed schoolchildren were spilling onto the street from the red double doors of a schoolhouse. She eyed her watch. It must be recess. She was filled with a cavernous longing that drew her out of her studio and onto the street, into the cold December air.

She flagged down a taxi, lacking the patience to fiddle with Uber. "Please hurry," she said to the cab driver. If there wasn't too much traffic, she could catch the kids playing in the yard. She gave her notice to Principal Garcia in August and was no longer receiving school emails, but Sophie imagined the recess schedule hadn't changed.

Luckily, the cab sailed from Tribeca through the Brooklyn–Battery Tunnel and deposited her in Park Slope in a record twenty minutes. She felt alive at the sight of the familiar building.

"Senorita Jacobson, as I live and breathe. *Dios mio*, I've missed you," Ronaldo called from inside the yard, holding a litter picker-upper in one hand and a black garbage bag in the other. She rushed over, surprising both of them when she wrapped the man in a bear hug.

"You do know I'm holding a bag full of dirty tissues and half-chewed apples, right?" Ronaldo said. "A millionaire like you has no business near these things."

Sophie waved him off. "Nonsense. Let me help." Ronaldo resisted, but Sophie pried the stick from his hands and soon they were walking side-by-side, cleaning the yard in a brisk rhythm. It was a bright day and the sun bounced off the asphalt in a way that made it look like crushed diamonds.

"Where are the kids? I thought B recess goes until one. I'd expect a P.E. class out here on a sunny day like this."

"Holiday concert practice. Garcia is losing her *mente* because the superintendent is coming to watch. It's practice all day, every day. I've been cleaning backstage until eight every night. The missus is ready to kill me." Ronaldo stopped walking. "But you don't want to hear about that. Let's talk about what you are doing with all that *dinero*. What brings you back here? You weren't missing making me clean up your messes, were you?"

They were in a shaded part of the yard now, the brick three-story schoolhouse casting a gigantic shadow over them. Sophie's fingers were frozen and she couldn't grasp a discarded kombucha juice box lying under the basketball hoop.

"Just leave it," Ronaldo said. "Maybe they'll hire me an assistant if things don't look too good."

"Ha. And, yes, of course I missed you. Guessing you weren't missing me as much though?" Sophie gave him a knowing smile. She'd most definitely left a trail of glitter in her wake. "I wanted to say hi to Nora-Ann and the rest of the crew. See the kids. I have this great studio space where I paint, but it can get lonely."

Ronaldo nodded. "How's your man? Still no ring I see?"

Sophie sighed, her breath escaping in a white cotton puff. "Don't you worry about me. Let's go inside. I'm freezing my nips off." She started walking to the double doors that led from the yard to the cafeteria but stopped when she noticed Ronaldo wasn't in step with her.

"Come on," she said, beckoning him. "The yard looks spick-and-span. I'll kick the juice box under the fence."

He frowned and thumbed the identification card hanging from a lanyard around his neck. "Sophie, we have to go in through the main entrance. You don't work here anymore. I can't let you in unless you sign the visitor log."

She put a numb hand on her hip. Now that she took Ubers and cabs everywhere, she was accustomed to door-to-door transportation, which meant she'd left without a scarf, hat and gloves. The tips of her ears felt like they might snap off. Surely, Ronaldo had to be joking. She needed to warm up pronto with a cup of crappy coffee in the teacher's lounge. "Everyone recognizes me, Naldo. Besides, what will they think? That I'm here to rob the PTA fund? I'm a millionaire, remember?"

Ronaldo looked at the ground. "I'm sorry, Sophie. I could lose my job."

Then I'll hire you, she wanted to say. *I just really miss those damn kids, even Owen, who always made a mess. I want to hear one of Jayden's knock-knock jokes and check in with Ella, even if she was some other teacher's pet now. I want to see how the new art teacher is doing—is she up to the print-making unit?* How did she explain the concept of the horizon line?

Ronaldo spoke. "I have to go inside now. Garcia is having the kids practice the confetti scene so I gotta get the super-vac ready. It was good seeing you, kid. Next time give some notice and I'll let everyone know our big-shot celebrity is coming." He walked past her, pushing his utility cart toward the door. He seemed embarrassed. Not for himself, but for her.

A FEW DAYS AFTER HER FAILED VISIT TO P.S. 282, RAVI SURprised Sophie at her studio with Magnolia Bakery cupcakes.

"Cupcakes? What are we celebrating?" Sophie asked from her perch on a stool, where she had been aimlessly staring at her still incomplete Vessel painting for north of an hour. Her potential buyer, Tom, had contacted her the day before. His wife's birthday had come and gone but their anniversary was in January. If she wasn't ready to sell, he needed to look for an alternative gift. She assured him she would have it done by the end of the month. Tom seemed to know nothing of her lottery win and was clearly surprised she wasn't more desperate for the sale. Talking to someone who only knew before-Sophie was a rush, and she found herself trying to prolong their conversation with idle chatter. The weather was pretty mild for December, wasn't it? Did Tom know one of the curators at the Whitney Museum was under investigation? When she brought up the *E. coli* outbreak in Pennsylvania, Tom said his other line was ringing.

"I sold *Chalchiuhtlicue*!" Ravi tore open the bakery box and plucked a chocolate-frosted cupcake and tried to stuff it in Sophie's mouth.

"Huh?" It sounded like Ravi had said he sold Chipotle. Sophie wiped the frosting from her cheek with a sheet of expensive tracing paper.

Ravi's chin quivered. He returned his own cupcake to the box without a bite.

"My water jug. I named it *Chalchiuhtlicue* after the Aztec goddess of the river, remember? It's the largest sculpture I've ever made. I had to restart it six times because it kept collapsing. Is this ringing a bell?"

"Oh my God, yes!" Sophie hopped off her stool and swallowed Ravi in a hearty hug. From his limp response, she could tell it was too late. She didn't blame him. He *had* told her about the jug many times. Now that she had a studio of her own, she spent fewer daylight hours at Ravi's, which meant his artwork was less visible in her mind's eye. But that was no excuse.

"Ravi, I'm sorry. I've been so self-absorbed lately with all my family drama." Not only had cutting in Matthew not been the panacea Sophie had hoped for, it had also proven super complicated tax-wise. To think there was something called a gift tax? More like a Trojan horse. "I think maybe we were too stupid to win the lottery."

Ravi tugged Sophie over to the low-slung Barcelona chair and pulled her onto his lap. She picked at the dry clay around his fingernails as she wrapped his hands around her waist, realizing how much she'd missed the smell of his coriander shampoo.

"I get it," he said. "You've had a major life-changing experience and I can't even begin to understand what must be going through your head on any given day."

"Neither can I," Sophie said. She would have thought all the confusion, stress and shock would propel creativity and add depth to her work. Weren't most great artists tortured souls? But her scrambled egg brain did nothing but keep her up at night with a racing heart. All she knew was that she didn't deserve this man and, if she didn't get her act in gear soon, she would lose him. She had planned to meet up with his family for dessert in the city after her family's Thanksgiving feast, but instead high-tailed it to the airport to chase down Leo, dropping Ravi only a cursory text to explain. He'd emailed her sketches for a collection of candlesticks he was thinking about making and she'd written back "They look great" without noticing he'd asked for specific feedback. She'd forgotten to bring Iris a special bone and new chew toy for her birthday, which should've alerted her to how scatterbrained she was becoming, considering a month later she forgot to acknowledge her own mother's birthday. Ravi seemed content to accept this was a temporary fugue state. Thoughtful, attentive Sophie would return soon enough. She was just temporarily missing, like the winning ticket had been.

"You're not too stupid to win the lottery. Far stupider people have won. You should google it sometime," Ravi said. "Have a cupcake. We always have Magnolia when something good happens to one of us."

Sophie's sweet tooth normally crowded out other thoughts, but looking at the gooey frosting was making her nauseated. "Do you think it's a bad sign that we didn't get Magnolia after the Powerball?"

"What? No, of course not. Magnolia is our professional treat. That's what we have on your last day of school. And when we sell a work of art." Ravi's *we* was generous. "Besides, we were in shock after you won. You forgot to shower for three days, remember? I kissed the top of your head and it smelled like skunk."

Sophie jabbed Ravi's waist but her attempt at playfulness failed when she went in too hard and he clutched his ribs. She forced herself to take a bite of a vanilla-vanilla and say, "Yummmmm."

"Soph, I know you're still upset about Thanksgiving. You're worried about the rift with Matthew. That your dad thinks you've made a mess of everything. That Laura is spending money instead of dealing with her shit. That Noah's slipping and doesn't know who to trust."

"I don't think Noah has great judgment when it comes to people. He once said that the world could be divided into two groups. Those who pee in the pool and those who don't."

Ravi laughed. "Sounds like he's an excellent judge of character."

Sophie scoffed. "He's in the pee-in-the-pool group."

"Oh boy. Remind me not to swim with him."

"Tell me about your sale. I'm sick of talking about myself and the Powerball. Who's the lucky owner of your water jug?"

Ravi opened Instagram on his phone.

"This guy," he said, showing Sophie the profile of a well-known interior designer with more than a hundred thousand followers. "He bought it on behalf of a client, so I don't know where it's actually going. Harriet made it happen through her London gallery. The jug is going to be displayed at Art Basel next week even though it's already sold." Ravi had reposted it to his own account, which had an impressive five thousand followers. Sophie still kept her profile private.

"That is extremely cool," she said. Suddenly, she had an idea. "Let's go. To Basel. We need to see your work on display at the biggest art fair in America. I'd love to meet the famous Harriett anyway."

Ravi appeared taken aback by the suggestion.

"Really? Tickets to Miami are crazy expensive because it's holiday season and Basel and—" Ravi lived and worked rent-free, but that didn't mean he had unlimited funds for travel.

"Yes. I'm paying. It's for me as much as you. I've got to spend some time with my father. Find out what the hell the story is with that stack of paintings I found."

Ravi's dark eyes shone, as though he'd had the flash of inspiration she desperately needed. "I'll start looking at tickets."

A WEEK LATER, RAVI AND SOPHIE LANDED AT MIAMI INTERnational Airport, where the crowd was divided into the plastic surgery set rolling monogrammed Louis Vuitton luggage, the artsy types trying to one up each other in sartorial weirdness and the elderly rolling through the terminal in airport wheelchairs.

"Some melting pot," Sophie muttered. She could hardly blame her mother for resisting the southern migration.

"There she is," Ravi said, pointing to a chic woman in a white linen dress standing next to the baggage carousel. "That's Harriett."

Sophie was instantly intimidated as they drew closer. Harriett was everything Sophie was not. Her frame was tiny and lithe. She wore virtually no makeup, yet managed to have well-defined features and a dewy glow. Sophie instantly wanted to chop off her side braid when she saw Harriet's fringe of curtain bangs. Sophie casually removed her just-for-show plastic-framed glasses and slipped them into her bag, a tote that said "Art Is Free."

"My star," Harriett purred in an English accent, drawing Ravi in. "And you must be the famous Sophie."

Famous? As in the Powerball win? Or famous as in Ravi talks about you so much? Or famous in the way people just say that without really meaning it?

"That's me," Sophie said, instantly regretting her razzle-dazzle jazz hands. Harriett had definitely never jazzed-hands in her life. "I thought we were just going to take an Uber."

"I insisted," Harriett said. "The wait for an Uber in this zoo could be endless and I imagine you two want to freshen up before the party."

Party? Sophie looked at Ravi.

"Harriett's gallery is having a little shindig. I said we'd swing by," Ravi explained. Sophie had wanted to drop her bags at the hotel and go straight to her father, but she didn't love the idea of Ravi and Harriett gallivanting at a party together.

"Let's sort this out in the car," Harriet said. "Julia is going to kill me if she gets a ticket." She threw her head back and laughed as charming crinkles formed around her deep-set eyes. "My wife and law enforcement do not see eye to eye on traffic violations."

Wife? Wife! Sophie could have kissed Harriett. She would kiss Julia, whoever she was. She had been worried about Ravi stepping out for nothing. Why had Ravi never mentioned that Harriett was gay? He clearly overestimated Sophie's level of self-confidence.

After hot showers and brief naps at the hotel, Ravi was en route to a nightclub in South Beach and Sophie was facing her father on a pickleball court at Boca Breezes.

Sophie and Leo had never played a racket sport together in their lives, but that was just the tip of the current weirdness. When she visited her parents in East Brunswick or Beach Haven, it meant, until very recently, returning to the place where her height was etched on the inside of a closet and her gnarly high school retainer had fossilized in a medicine cabinet. Boca Breezes was an alternate universe that didn't house any ghosts of her childhood. She was reminded of what people said about visiting Australia, how strange it was to see the water in the toilet flush in the opposite direction. It was worse not having Noah with her this time. Despite knowing she inherited her artistic side from him, Leo felt more distant and unknowable than ever.

"Your grip is wrong," Leo called over the net. "Lower it. And less wrist when you swing, okay? Tennis and pickleball should not be confused." She didn't play tennis either, but her father didn't seem aware of that.

"I'll try." She didn't really give a fig how to hold a pickleball racket. She wanted to see how Leo held a paintbrush, to discover similarities in the way they applied acrylic to canvas. Was he also terribly impatient waiting for paint to dry? Did he ever work with gouache? Was he a sketcher? Sophie had spent her life feeling close to but different from her family members. When they made obligatory pilgrimages to museums, the other Jacobsons would look at a painting for at most fifteen seconds before someone would grumble "I don't get it" or "Where's the gift shop?" Their favorite works were always the ones with a bench in front. She tried to remember what her father had said on those sojourns, but all she could recall was feeling like an outsider. Where her family saw scribbles and random strokes, she found beauty. Where they missed meaning, she sussed out themes and intentionality.

"Actually, no." Sophie walked off the pickleball court and placed her paddle in a bin. "I really don't feel like playing right now. I came here to see you. To talk." She had told Leo she was coming to Florida to support Ravi's debut at Basel and said nothing of wanting to talk. It occurred to Sophie this was probably the first time in her life she'd requested a private audience with him.

She sat down on a bench. Leo joined. "What's on your mind?"

"I want to talk about your paintings. The ones we found in the attic. You totally brushed me off when I asked about them, but it's important to me. You and I have this thing in common—this huge part of my life—and you never even mentioned it." A lump formed in her throat. "Why didn't you tell me that you're an artist?"

A long silence followed. Her father's face was inscrutable. She pictured Ravi hobnobbing at the party in South Beach and suddenly wished she was there too.

"Fine. You want to do this, we'll do it." He leaned against the back of the bench, settling in. "I don't talk about it because it's a part of my life that dredges up difficult memories. And, unlike your generation, I don't feel the need to discuss every last feeling and emotion I have." The floodlights angled at the court cast him in an eerie spotlight. "But you've come all this way, so let's talk. From the time I was a little kid, I loved to draw. I spent all my free time creating these comic books. I was good. My teachers made a fuss about my art projects. I even won a few prizes."

Sophie looked at the scraggly hairs on her father's arms and tried to imagine him as a little kid doing a project, like the children in her classroom. "Dad . . . that is so cool."

Leo put out a hand. "Let me finish. You know I didn't come from much money. Your grandpa Jack had a decent job as a foreman but let's just say I never had a birthday party or anything like you kids had. One day, your grandfather came home from work all excited. He had this black satchel in his hand—I remember your Bubbe called it a 'valise—a filthy valise.' Anyway, he found this bag in an alley during his lunch break. Said it was abandoned in plain sight. He looked around for the owner, supposedly. When no one came forward, he opened it. Ten thousand bucks. That's what he found inside. Back in 1962, that was a life-changing amount of money. I don't need to tell you how that feels."

"No, you do not. And he didn't have to discount it for present value or pay taxes on it either."

"Correct, though he would have been better off with less. Your grandmother was very upset. The idea of keeping money that didn't belong to them, which wasn't earned, it didn't sit right with Bubbe. But my father was a persuasive man. When he wanted something, he got it."

"But Bubbe Esther was so tough. I feel like she and Mom were a lot alike," Sophie said. A section of her hair, frizzed from humidity, escaped her braid and she pulled out the elastic.

"Your grandfather was a redhead too," Leo said, touching one of Sophie's curls. "Before he lost it all."

"More things I didn't know." Sophie shifted back from the edge of the bench and felt a warm tingle when Leo put his arm around her. "So what happened with the money?"

"You're right your bubbe was tough, but only because she had to be. Nothing good came of the money. Your grandfather gambled a chunk of it away in Atlantic City and in underground card rooms. Bought ridiculous luxuries he had no use for. What does a shtetl boy need a crocodile belt for? He invested in ludicrous ventures that were probably fraudulent. Within two years, our family was in worse financial shape than before. Grandpa Jack owed money all over town. Bubbe Esther never forgave him. He died young. A heart attack that was no doubt caused by all the grief that money brought about."

"Wow." She resisted pulling out her phone to update her siblings. Her father was opening up and she wouldn't squander this moment.

Leo's grim face throughout Thanksgiving, well before the brawl, flashed before her. His declining to tour the second floor of Laura's house on account of bad knees, even though he was pounding the asphalt for pickleball daily, suddenly made sense. His anxious gaze every time Noah took a sip of beer or mentioned giving money to this person or that person. The I-knew-this-would-happen attitude when they all started fighting. Leo was having terrible déjà vu watching his children's behavior, and he no longer had Sylvia at his side for support.

"So it wasn't the pastrami that did Grandpa in," Sophie said.

"I'm sure that didn't help. Anyway, I—the boy who thought he'd draw comics like Charles Schulz or paint something good enough to hang in the Metropolitan Museum of Art—had to put down my pencils and go to work. I was fifteen."

"That's terrible," Sophie said.

"No, it's not," Leo said, his voice firmer than before. "I've had a great life. A stable career where I earned every penny I have honestly. An artist's life is difficult, and I wanted security above everything else. I put that part of my life aside, met your mother, had you four kids and never looked back."

"So you think a windfall is more of a curse than a blessing," Sophie said. "Ever since the Powerball, I can't paint a damn thing. Though it's probably because I'm actually a talentless hack. I used to think I could make it in the art world if I had the time to really hone my craft. But now I have all the time in the world, and I'm paralyzed at the easel." She bit down hard on her lower lip to stop a potential crying spell. "Dad, what do I do?"

"Ask your mother," Leo said.

Sophie gaped at him.

"Sorry, sorry. Reflex." He offered a chagrined smile.

"On that note, there's something I've been wanting to say to you," Sophie said. "Remember at the airport when you said you're not like Mom and you don't know how to fix everything?"

He nodded.

"Neither did she. She didn't always know what to say to us. Not all of her advice was correct. She begged me to date Ruben Cutler even though he was clearly gay. She convinced Laura to get bangs. Bangs were not a good look on Laura. The difference is that she was always there. No matter what, if we needed her, she was there. There were definitely times she steered us in the wrong direction. And that's okay. She wasn't perfect, but she did try her best. That's all we really need, the four of us."

Leo pulled Sophie in closer. "That, I can do."

Sophie walked her father back to his apartment.

"You're more talented than I was," Leo said. "Maybe that's why I didn't feel any pressure to share my past with you. I don't think I have much to teach you."

It was maybe the nicest compliment he'd ever given her.

She hugged him good night. As she was climbing into her Uber to go meet Ravi, she realized her denim jacket was still upstairs at her Dad's. She asked the driver to wait while she darted back inside. When she spotted her jacket resting on the arm of his sofa, she heard Leo's voice coming from the bedroom. She tiptoed down the hall and found him staring at a framed photograph he'd clearly retrieved from the open drawer in his night table.

"Oh, Sylvia," he was saying. "I thought I was doing the best I could. But I can do better."

She snuck out without him noticing, her heart fuller than when she'd arrived.

FANTASTIC FOURSOME 👮👮✡👮👮

> **SOPHIE**
>
> Dad is really good at pickleball

MATTHEW

I played with Austin. There are courts all over NYC now

> **SOPHIE**
>
> I sucked

LAURA

Our new golf club is adding 12 pickleball courts

> **SOPHIE**
>
> In actually important news . . . Grandpa Jack found 10k when Dad was a teenager and lost it all gambling. Basically I have a lot to tell you guys and we need sibling time ASAP when i get back

LAURA

omg—is that why Bubbe always called him a putz

> **SOPHIE**
>
> Assume yes

MATTHEW

It all makes so much sense. The way Dad is about money

> **SOPHIE**
>
> yep. Also he wanted to be an artist

LAURA

whoa

MATTHEW

Noah—I may be driving past the shore this wk en route to philly. Time for dinner?

LAURA

Noah—Hannah said you didn't snap her back

SOPHIE

N—Dad got some more furniture. Still all beige

LAURA

N, u ok?

NOAH

Yeah i'm good

SOPHIE

N—I almost forgot to tell u. Dad keeps mom's picture in his night table. He talks to her!

NOAH

Cool

10

Laura

"NOW I WILL APPLY A TWENTY-FOUR-KARAT-GOLD-ENRICHED body lotion to your back. Gold has wonderful properties, including increased circulation and evening of the skin tone. The antioxidants will protect your skin from free radicals and sun damage. There are jars for sale when you check out if you're interested."

"Thank you," Laura murmured into the headrest attached to the massage table, her voice muffled by a thick layer of fluffy white towel.

"For you, Mr. Cohen, we have an even stronger concentration of our Gold Dust Lather, specially formulated for men," the other masseuse said. "Please, try to relax your shoulders a bit more. This is your time to unwind and honor your body's intentions."

"Mrs. Cohen, you as well. Your muscles are very tight."

They were thirty minutes into a ninety-minute couples massage, and so far the two therapists working on Laura and Doug had chastised them for clenched fists, rigid jaws and hunched shoulders.

"It's Dr. Cohen," Laura said, though she rarely corrected people. "My husband. He's a dentist."

Doug lifted his head from the cradle and looked at Laura from his massage table a few feet away. Close enough that they could hold hands if they wanted, the spa manager had said as she led them to the treatment room. "Am I a dentist? I haven't been at the office for a full week of work since the summer."

"Of course you are." Laura raised her head and met her husband's eye. A couples massage was probably the dreamiest thing she could have imagined all the years she and Doug were in the trenches together, exhausted from frantic schedules and stressed about finances. In reality, the experience was proving a giant disappointment. Instead of unwinding, Laura was worrying whether Doug was enjoying himself. As the therapist tried to release the knots in her neck, Laura wondered if any couples actually held hands during the massage. Why would anyone do that? There was nothing romantic about getting lubed up by two complete strangers while trying to hold in farts.

"Is this your first time in Dubai?" Doug's therapist asked. *Good.* They needed distraction. The wind chimes playing through the speakers weren't doing much to decompress either of them.

"It is," Laura said, forcing cheer into her voice. "It's really something." Japan hadn't lived up to their expectations. It was too clean. Too much history for which they had no patience. Too many tours and hours on their feet. Too much raw fish. They spent gratuitously on things they didn't want (hand-embroidered kimonos for the girls and platinum chopsticks for themselves) and were so overscheduled they were rarely alone and too exhausted when they were.

And so, Dubai. A second chance at a fun holiday. They had expected a classier version of Vegas. More heart-stopping architecture, fewer prostitutes. Less all-you-can-eat buffet, more exotically spiced delicacies. More designer shopping with cultural modesty to suit Laura's middle-aged tastes, less Versace, tit-revealing glitz.

How wrong they were.

Starting with the gold. It was everywhere. Glittering, glinting and blinding them from the moment they stepped off the Emirates flight. Buildings were sheeted in gold. Cocktails were served in gold-rimmed glasses. They slept in gold satin sheets, ate off gold flatware and were now having gold rubbed into their backs at Au Spa.

A cell phone rang as Laura was being instructed to flip over.

"I have to take this," Doug said. A glowing light shone on his headrest. As he shimmied off the table, the sheet draping him fell to the ground. His penis flopped around like a beached seal until the masseuse, eyes averted, handed him a towel.

"Now?" Laura exclaimed, but Doug was already outside the treatment room.

"Relax, missus. Perhaps you two need some gold-dusted tea in the lounge after."

Doug never returned to the spa, leaving the remaining time for the treatment on the table, literally. It wasn't like him to be wasteful, even these days. When she got back to the suite, Laura found him showered and dressed. She rushed to ready herself for dinner, planning to interrogate him about the suspicious call once they were seated at the restaurant.

Dinner was at the top of the Burj Khalifa, the tallest building in the world and just one of many Guinness World Records attractions in Dubai. Throughout the eleven courses (excluding the amuse bouche and trio of palate cleansers), Doug swore up and down that the call was work-related. She wasn't buying it. He'd been furtive the entire trip, constantly checking his texts and taking long showers with the bathroom door locked. She didn't have a fancy job to speak of or a graduate degree to hang on the wall, but she was no fool.

"There is no other woman," Doug said. "I have no idea how I'm going to convince you otherwise." He had several dots of black caviar in between his teeth and a rogue patch of gray chest hair poking through the gap between his top two buttons. At that moment, it was hard to picture him as a sought-after heartthrob. He could be attracting women on account of his swelled bank account, but Laura's suspicions predated the Powerball.

"So then tell me about the call. What's going on?"

He took a sip of wine. The pours in Dubai were pathetic—the only small thing to be found in the entire place. "I'm thinking of selling my practice. The person who called is a dentist in Tenafly. He's looking for a second office."

"Oh. Wow." She was surprised Doug was eyeing retirement. After taxes and the future expenses of carrying their new home, car payments, golf club membership dues and the additional money set aside for the girls' continued education, there wasn't *that* much left. More to the point, he liked his work. Or she thought he did. "If that's what you want."

"It's still premature. Which is why I didn't want to discuss it," Doug said. "Speaking of topics we don't want to discuss . . . Beth."

"That's a person, not a topic," Laura said.

"This isn't Mad Libs. It's just you were a little harsh with her at Thanksgiving. Are you going to reach out?"

Jeez, this place was turning into a sauna. Laura tried to get the waiter's attention. The AC needed major cranking. Doug was still staring at her. "Yeah, fine, whatever. But she was harsh with me too."

"You can be the bigger person," he said. "While we're talking, I also wanted to say that I'm concerned that since the girls moved out, you—"

Laura shook her finger. "Nope. Our stressful conversation quota is full for the evening."

"Fair. What's on tap for tomorrow?"

Laura pulled up the itinerary on her phone.

"We're starting off at the Louvre Abu Dhabi. Then touring the campus of NYU's first outpost in the Middle East. We finish the day at the mall."

"So we're seeing a museum from Paris and a college from New York and ending at the mall? You know we have those in New Jersey. We're practically famous for them," Doug said.

"This one has ski slopes."

"Hm. Let's get the check."

"THIS . . . IS . . . SO . . . HARD," LAURA MANAGED TO SPUTTER through heavy panting.

"I know, isn't it the best?" Beth responded effortlessly from her neighboring Peloton. Bitch wasn't even sweating.

"Sure," Laura said. If you enjoy getting a stress test or running from a bear, she thought. She did her best to keep up, regretting that she didn't bring a change of clothes. But then again, she hadn't expected a cardio session when she appeared unannounced at Beth's office. It was Matthew's office too, though he was at Dalton for the science fair. Austin's class was studying climate change and he'd created a tornado simulator. Matthew had proudly shared a photo on the sibling chat earlier that morning.

With Matthew certain to be out of office, Laura seized the chance to speak to Beth, woman to woman. Unfortunately, she showed up at lunch hour, which turned out to be workout hour, which meant a trip to the law firm's in-house gym, which meant riding a Peloton with a lack of rhythm and a dangerously high pulse.

"So what brings you to Midtown?" Beth said, cranking up the resistance dial on her bike.

Laura had a rehearsed answer. She was in the city to meet with her estate planner and just happened to be walking by. Instead, she cut to the chase. "I thought you and I should talk about Thanksgiving."

Technically, the Jacobsons had agreed to put the ugliness of Thanksgiving behind them. Upon returning from the airport without Leo, they decided the least they could do was make peace between the four of them. The text chat was active again, but since spouses weren't on it, Laura and Beth's contact had been minimal.

Doug pushed her to speak to Beth in person. Laura didn't relish in-person confrontation; she preferred to hide behind snarky humor over text. In general, apologizing wasn't her strong suit. The closest she usually came was some version of, "I'm sorry what I said/did made you feel upset/disappointed/hurt." In other words, a half-assed nonapology. She gave so much of herself to her family that she believed her sacrifices entitled her to this one quirk. Well, maybe she had more than one quirk. Her competitiveness with Beth. Her resentment of Emma's independence and conversely her frustration with Hannah's dependence. Her inability to have fun until every item on her to-do list was checked off. She wasn't perfect, but neither was Doug! And he wasn't always right. Except in this case, about their sister-in-law, he was. She knew she had to clear the air between them. And, yes, maybe offer a teeny, weeny, itsy, bitsy apology. Like a yellow polka-dot bikini.

"Talk about what?" Beth's eyes were trained on the screen as she copied a jacked instructor peddling his heart out.

"I'm sorry." Laura blurted the words out quickly, zipping her lips shut to avoid a follow-up that would void her apology.

Beth hit pause and swiveled to face Laura, who had dismounted entirely. Apologizing while cycling was an impossible feat.

"Sorry about . . . ?"

"I was a jerk. At Thanksgiving. You were right to be upset about us cutting Matthew in months after the win. We've always prided ourselves on being such a tight family, but since my mom died, we've definitely had times where we've lost our way. And I don't blame you for thinking it was the video that pushed us to our decision, but I swear it wasn't."

Beth was quiet. Her comfort with silence probably made her an effective negotiator for her clients. Laura found even a momentary lull excruciating, which was why she continued. "It makes sense you thought my girls gave Austin the pot. I thought so too. I'm sorry for gloating when the truth came out."

A second sorry in one day. It had to be a record. Beth climbed off her bike and tossed her towel into a wicker hamper. "That was a seriously shitty night."

Laura had never heard Beth curse before.

"I want to say sorry too," Beth said as an older gentleman in a Harvard sweatshirt and short shorts entered the gym. "Don, just the man I was hoping to see."

Beth crossed the gym, leaving Laura dangling. She spoke to the man in hushed tones while he went through a series of calisthenics.

Laura made out only snippets, most of which sounded like gibberish. *Lis pendens. Discovery. In limine.* Whatever these words meant, they sidetracked Beth from apologizing to Laura.

"Great work, as always," Don said. "Let's reconvene after the Zoom."

Beth rejoined Laura. "Sorry about that. Big case."

"You were saying . . . before he came in?" Laura gestured to the old man lifting a barbell she was sure would crush him.

Beth furrowed her brow. "Gosh, I don't remember."

"Right, well." Laura started to collect her things. She'd said what she needed to say.

"Wait, yes. I was apologizing to you." Beth looked around. "Let's get out of here. There's kind of a church and state thing going between work and personal at our firm."

Laura followed Beth into the elevator and up to a different floor, this one lined with identical, pristine conference rooms. Beth opened the door to an empty one and motioned for Laura to take a seat. "I'm going to quickly change out of gym clothes."

She returned in a smart pants suit and took a seat opposite Laura at a shiny wood table that stretched across the entire room.

"Should I have my lawyer present?" Laura quipped.

Beth missed the joke. "Anyway, as I was saying, I'm also sorry for how I acted at dinner. But other times too." She tugged at a loose thread on her blouse. "The honest truth is that I'm jealous of you."

Laura was aghast. "Me? You're jealous of me? I'm a stay-at-home mom with modest to poor cooking abilities and a messy house." You got this all wrong, honey, Laura thought.

To her surprise, Beth's eyes watered, making them look iridescent. She was as beautiful as she was smart. It was easy to see why Matthew had fallen for her.

"Remember the night of the fireworks? Austin tripped on that loose deck plank. He was crying and I just froze. You immediately sprang into action, getting ice, Band-Aids, bacitracin. You distracted him and made him laugh while you fixed him up—and that's after you'd slipped in the kitchen and gotten hurt yourself. I just stood there like a bump on a log. I didn't know how to help my own child."

"I've been at this for a long time," Laura said. She didn't feel particularly proud of her maternal superpowers: making a brown bag lunch in under three minutes, knowing where the first-aid kit is in every room, erasing grass stains from uniforms like Houdini. Beth, who casually dropped legal lingo of the kind Laura only heard on TV, had no business envying her.

"Don't be modest. And how about the day after? When Austin got lost at Fantasy Island—" Beth broke off.

"Do you have any idea how many times I lost my kids at Fantasy Island? Both of them. And for way longer."

"I appreciate you trying to make me feel better. It's not just knowing what to do. It's knowing how to do it," said Beth. "I find all these programs for Austin and make sure he has access to everything that could help his future. But I don't even know how to get him to stop crying when he's hurt. Do you know he asked our au pair to take him for his checkup instead of me?"

Laura could imagine how that would sting. For years she wished she could have afforded more childcare, but it would have gutted her if the girls preferred their babysitter to her.

"If it makes you feel better, I'm jealous of you too," Laura said.

"Of course it does," Beth said, with a throaty laugh. "Can I ask why?"

"You know Doug and I got pregnant when we were still in college. I'm not saying I was going to be some major CEO or a partner in a law firm, but I definitely had bigger aspirations than carpool duty. I blamed Doug that I never got on the career track. I blamed the kids, the patriarchy, our inability to afford childcare, even the weather. Someone had to make sure our driveway was shoveled, right? Meanwhile, I watched you raising a genius while having this badass career and managing to always look great. Seriously, that Peloton ride nearly gave me a coronary. I lowered the resistance when you weren't looking."

"I saw."

"Of course you did. You see everything and you're on top of everything." Laura threw up her hands. "I have all this money now and I'm still not on top of things."

"Well, I didn't notice my son was doing drugs, let alone making them," Beth said with refreshing humility. "Why are we just now having this conversation? I've been married to your brother for fifteen years."

"I don't know. I think every family leaves a lot of things unsaid, for better or for worse. Personally, I've been in triage mode since becoming a mother, so it was easier to judge you from afar rather than make time for a heart-to-heart."

"Matthew and I try to be open with each other," Beth said. "Though I wasn't planning to show him that TikTok video." She picked up her phone, which had just dinged. "Look at this." She turned the screen so Laura could see Matthew and Austin arm in arm, Austin wearing a gold medal around his neck. Father and son both had windswept hair in the photo. Matthew's zigzagged across his bald spot like a lightning bolt. "Well done! I can see the tornado machine clearly worked," Laura said. "Look at my brother's face. I can't remember the last time I've seen him look that happy."

Beth's face darkened. "Why do you say that? Matthew is a very happy person."

"Of course. I only meant that he usually seems stressed. You know how when he's on a call he gets that foaming-at-the-mouth, rabid face and his eyes look sort of like he's dead inside? Adult Matthew is different from kid Matthew, that's all I'm saying." The minute the words were out of her mouth, Laura wished she could reel them back in.

"So you're saying he used to be happy but then he met me and he's not?"

"Not at all. In fact, I'm grateful that he met you. If he hadn't, well he might have turned out—"

"Like Noah," Beth said. "It's useful to have a fun-squasher around, huh?"

"Can we get back to the part where we apologized and admitted we were jealous of each other? That was nice." Laura put her hands up in prayer and Beth's grimace faltered.

"I think that's a good idea. One major blowout a year is about all I can take. There's something I've wanted to ask you," Beth said.

"Austin turned thirteen in June and I kind of blew it on the bar mitzvah front. Obviously, this isn't my milieu—"

"For what it's worth, your Passover seder is delicious. A-plus for the matzah ball soup," Laura said.

"Well, I just buy prepared food and serve it. Your feast is another story."

"Can I tell you a secret?" Laura said, dropping her voice. "I don't cook any of it either."

"I knew it!" Beth pumped a fist in the air. "I'm sorry. That wasn't appropriate. As I was saying, I always figured your mom would plan Austin's bar mitzvah but then she got sick and, to be honest, once she was gone I felt like I was off the hook. But now I think it's really a shame not to have a bar mitzvah for him. It would be nice for the family to get together and you did such a great job with Emma's and Hannah's that I thought maybe you could help?"

In hindsight, Laura would have said, "I think I can find some time in my schedule to help you with planning," but instead blurted out, "I would absolutely love that. You have no idea how freaking bored I've been."

STARING UP AT THE GIANT BLUE WHALE SUSPENDED FROM THE ceiling of the Museum of Natural History, Laura and Sophie were starting to get neck cricks.

"I get that Austin is into science, but I feel like I'm on a class trip," Sophie said.

"Agree. And it's way too lavish for a bar mitzvah. If you recall, Emma's and Hannah's bat mitzvahs were in the basement of the temple and the whole place smelled like herring. It was still good enough for a bunch of thirteen-year-olds to run wild."

"Can I answer any questions for you?" The woman from the private events department, a smug little thing named Arabella, approached. "We host events under the whale all the time. Mostly weddings, but we've had our fair share of religious milestones too. Seinfeld's son had his bar mitzvah here. I'm not supposed to say that."

"I think we've seen everything we need to," Laura said. "Thank you for showing us around."

"A pleasure. You're lucky the date is available. We just had a cancellation. But I suppose luck is normally on your side." Arabella gave them a knowing smile. Laura zeroed in on her Invisalign.

"Excuse me?" Sophie cocked an eyebrow.

"The lottery," Arabella said. "We google everyone who makes a private event appointment. Can I just say congratulations? I've never won anything in my life. How did it feel when you found out? What was the first thing you bought?"

A few months earlier, Laura would have gasped. By now, she was used to it. Winning the lottery had somehow made it okay for total strangers to ask them personal questions. It didn't help that the YouTube video of their televised win was the first return when their names were searched.

Sophie wasn't having it. "Would you ask any other person—let's say some hotshot CEO—looking to host a party here how they spend their money?"

Arabella, beet red, said nothing as she shuffled her feet.

"I didn't think so. We're all done here." Sophie tugged at Laura's arm and marched out of the cavernous space.

"Wow!" Laura looked at her little sister in wonder when they reached the steps of the museum. It had snowed the day before and the bare branches in Central Park were coated in shimmering white powder. It was a vista prettier than anything she'd seen on her recent travels.

"That felt good," Sophie said. "I have no idea where that moxie came from. Actually, I do. I'm at stress level ten thousand." She plopped down on the cold steps. Laura looked at her watch. If she left her car in the garage past six p.m., the rate would double when she dipped into peak hours. Two decades of a penny-pinching mindset were hard to unlearn. Oddly, splurging on two decadent vacations felt natural. It was the daily purchases that made her stumble, like buying organic fruit, even when they came in a peel, and coloring her hair every three weeks instead of every six. She looked at her sister's face, scrunched in despair, and said fuck it to the additional garage fee.

"What's going on?"

"I thought seeing Dad and finding out about his painting would help me. But I'm still blocked. When I was teaching all day, I had a zillion ideas running through my head. I kept a notebook on my desk to jot them down. Now I have all this time and my brain is an empty shell. I can't even finish the one painting that has a buyer waiting for it. I was glad to hear Dad's story and know we have this in common, but—like—now what? So we're both failed painters? He gave it up because he wanted stability and I was a hack all along. And I haven't even told you what a crap girlfriend I've been."

"Sophie, slow down. Stop berating yourself. You've had so much happen in the past six months, it's completely expected that you're unfocused. It'll pass. You'll get your groove back."

"That's what Ravi said, but I don't want people giving me a pass any longer," Sophie said. "You're not an artist. You're a mom. If I don't have inspiration, I have nothing. You still have your family."

"That was harsh. Just because I did carpool for more than a decade doesn't mean I can't understand other ways of being," Laura said. She didn't need to pay surge pricing at the garage to be talked down to. "Apparently, I'm more than just a mom. Beth said I'm a supermom."

"You totally are. See? I'm not just talentless, I'm also an asshole. Somebody else should have won the lottery, not me. I was supposed to make great art with my resources and it's just—" Sophie mimicked vomiting. "Let's talk about you. I'm being narcissistic. How was Dubai? How are things going with Doug?"

Now Laura really wished she'd gotten her car out of the garage. She could be cruising across the George Washington Bridge instead of being interrogated. The problem with telling people about the problems in your life is that you couldn't put the genie back in the bottle.

"Dubai was not my thing. Everything felt really manufactured. Like it was trying too hard to be amazing. The tallest this, the most expensive that. It was sort of like Disney meshed with Vegas meshed with Great Adventure."

"Wow, that's very specific. And you and Doug?"

Laura gritted her teeth. Lately her jaw had been aching something awful. Doug said she was grinding at night. He wanted to make her a mouth guard to sleep in. Just what she needed—something else to make her less attractive in the bedroom.

"It was fine. We've never spent this much time together. Once we stopped talking about the kids, there were all these weird silences. You know I can't handle that. I thought these trips would bring us closer. Or at least be more fun. I mean, compared to the vacations we used to take with the girls—driving to Florida to save money, the four of us staying in one room with a rollaway bed and one of the girls hiding in the closet when housekeeping came—you'd think we'd enjoy the good life a bit more."

Sophie's phone rang but she silenced it. "I'll call Ravi back. You and Doug are like Dubai. Trying too hard. Why don't you just watch a movie together on the couch rather than try to manufacture a perfect experience? That puts too much pressure on both of you. I read an article that said couples have less sex on vacation than they do at home. Isn't that surprising? But it's kind of a metaphor for life. The more expectations you have, the more disappointing things can be. Promise me you guys will do a takeout and movie night, in sweatpants, and see how that goes," Sophie said. "Then give me a full report the next day. Or right after the sex. Whatever."

"There's something else." Laura paused. "Doug was on his phone a lot during the trip. He even left in the middle of a massage to take a call. He said it was about selling his practice but . . ." Laura let her voice trail off.

"You still think there's another woman."

"I do. Or I don't. I have no idea. But it's freaking me out. What are you doing now?"

"Talking to you."

"No, I mean after this. What are your plans?"

"Oh. I was planning to go to my studio to stare at the walls instead of painting. Do you have something else in mind?"

"How would you enjoy a road trip to Franklin Lakes instead?"

"To give you a sense of my anxiety level when I try to paint, I'm going to say that yes, I would enjoy that very much."

"Excellent. We're going to spy on Doug."

Sophie pursed her lips. "For the record, I don't support that, but I'm in."

The Jacobson sisters stood with renewed purpose. Together, they bounded down the museum steps, gunning for Jersey and out for blood.

"DOUG TEXTED ME WHILE WE WERE AT THE MUSEUM THAT HE was going out for dinner with Dr. Bergson," Laura explained as they drove. Her hands were gripping the wheel at ten and two, white knuckles staring back at her. "He and Doug refer patients to each other. But I can't remember them ever going out for dinner."

"I know Dr. Bergson! He did my braces. That guy must be old by now. Did Doug say where they were eating?" She was noticeably peppier since finding an excuse not to return to her studio, even if her new plans meant trying to catch a cheating husband in North Jersey.

"No. But I did something clever," Laura said, giving Sophie the side-eye as she stepped harder on the gas pedal. They were cruising along the Palisades Parkway with the stereo on high volume, like a semitic Thelma and Louise. "I AirTagged his car!"

"What does that mean?"

"I got the idea from a website about how to find out if your spouse is cheating. There is so much online on this topic, it's incredible. Basically, I put a tiny tracker in his car and I can see where he is on my phone. I wish I had done this ages ago."

"First of all, creepy. Second of all, where is he?"

"When we got in the car he was driving, so I don't know yet. Here, you check." Laura handed Sophie her phone and walked her through the steps.

"Hm, it looks like he's in a shopping center in Tenafly. Nothing too sexy about that," Sophie said, zooming out.

Twenty minutes later, they were in the parking lot of a strip mall with a Chinese restaurant, an Indian place, a kosher cafe and a string of shops that included a dry cleaner, a nail salon and a kiddie gym called Totsercize.

"I'm not getting affair vibes," Sophie said.

"Me neither."

The seeds of Laura's migraine vanished. The pulse in her neck slowed to a normal tick. She smiled as she spotted Doug's car in the parking lot. "Let's get out of here before he sees us." Laura turned the key in the ignition and looked behind her before backing out of the parking spot. Suddenly, her heart dropped. There was a hotel across the street. The Jersey Garden Inn. Was it possible Doug was there? It was a nondescript building, a few notches above a motel but about nineteen tiers below the places she and Doug stayed in Japan and Dubai. "Look," she croaked, pointing the hotel out to Sophie.

"Don't be crazy, Laura," she said. "Let me check if he's inside any of these restaurants before we stake out a hotel, okay?"

Laura nodded feebly.

When Sophie returned to the car a few minutes later, Laura knew before she said anything.

"I didn't see him, but that doesn't mean anything. Maybe he was in the bathroom. He does pee, doesn't he?"

"We're going across the street," Laura said in a voice that gave Sophie no choice but to follow.

Together they straddled the tall divider bisecting the busy road and made it to the other side. Laura placed her scarf around her head like a babushka and motioned for Sophie to do the same with hers.

"There's a restaurant in the hotel," Laura said. "Let's peek through the window."

"Why are you whispering? We're outside."

"I don't know," Laura said, frustrated. Did her sister think she was some kind of pro at this? "I see him!" Laura pointed. "He's at that corner table. He's with a woman. I knew it!" The exhilaration of having her suspicions confirmed quickly gave way to anguish.

"Maybe it's not—" Sophie started to stay but Laura would not be talked off the ledge. She stormed into the hotel. "Where's the restaurant?" she demanded of a front desk employee in the midst of checking someone in.

"The Greasy Spoon? It's more of a cafe." He pointed to a door at the end of a carpeted corridor. "I recommend the chili fries."

Laura walked briskly down the hall, her fury intensifying with each step. She pulled open the door, setting off a clang of jangly bells, and watched Doug and his companion turn toward the noise.

His lover—lover!—was an Asian woman in a navy turtleneck, with side-parted, shoulder-length hair and minimal makeup. Wire glasses attached by a beaded necklace dangled on her chest. She was slightly saggy at the jowls. She didn't match the countless images Laura had concocted in her brain, but that was beside the point.

Indignant, Laura marched over to their table.

"Laura," Doug said. "What are you doing here?"

She scoffed. "What am I doing here? I think the better question is what are you doing here?" It was then she noticed their table was covered with papers, many of them printed with pie charts and graphs in bright colors. The woman, who Laura was quickly deducing was *not* Doug's paramour, had an open laptop next to her water glass.

"Doug, is everything alright?" The woman extended a hand to Laura. "Vivian Wanamaker. COO of SMILE. I'm going to go out on a limb and guess that you're Doug's wife?"

Laura reached a hand out to meet Vivian's. She looked at Doug, confused. "Isn't that the place you said was a fact— Never mind." She faced Vivian again. "It's lovely to meet you. I'm Laura. And I'm very sorry to intrude like this."

"Sorry I'm late," came a voice from behind. Laura turned to see Dr. Bergson arriving in haste, Sophie at his side. "I was just catching up with this young lady in the parking lot. Smile for them, Sophie. My handiwork really holds up."

Sophie did as she was told and Vivian silently applauded.

"Laura, it's been ages," Dr. Bergson said. "What are you doing here?"

"That's a great question," Doug said through a tight grimace.

"Long story," Laura managed to say. "I was just leaving. Um, enjoy your dinner."

A waitress arrived and set a tempting cheeseburger and fries in front of Doug. Last night Chef Francois, whom Laura hired to drop off prepared meals a few times a week at their home, delivered Chilean sea bass in a white wine reduction with roasted asparagus and candied turnips. Laura debated poaching a few fries from Doug's plate before she left. He couldn't get any more upset with her than he already was.

"See you at home," she said to Doug, but it came out as a question. A question for which she couldn't wait for an answer because Sophie was dragging her away like a madwoman.

"Why are you parked across the street?" Laura called back to Doug as Sophie looked on, horrified.

Doug glared at her, but then the oddest thing happened. He smiled. "They charge for parking here unless you're an overnight guest."

Laura smiled back. They were made for each other. Surely Doug had to see that, assuming he ever forgave her.

FANTASTIC FOURSOME 👮👮✡👮👮

MATTHEW

Laura I think Beth is cheating on me. Can you spy pls

LAURA

Sophie wtf???

SOPHIE

I'm sorry but i had to tell

LAURA

Want me telling your secrets?

SOPHIE

I have none. 😇

MATTHEW

We're family. No secrets

NOAH

Bulldozers coming any day

SOPHIE

Huh?

NOAH

Our house. New owners ripping it up

MATTHEW

Well . . . yeah . . . we figured

LAURA

R they nice?

NOAH

I dont think they have permits

MATTHEW

U gonna report them? 😬

NOAH

Maybe. Oh shit they r looking at the money tree now

11

Noah

THE SOUND OF JACKHAMMERS WOKE NOAH FROM A DEEP slumber. He rubbed his eyes, shaking the crust free from the corners, and rolled onto his back. Gradually, he sat up and rested his back against the faded silk headboard. He was still not used to sleeping in Stanley and Ruth Archer's bed, nor was he accustomed to living with this much pastel.

Buying the place furnished was his first mistake. The first of many, not least of which was grossly overpaying. The Archer's home was more dilapidated than his family's abode. Rusted pipes spewed brown water from the tap, loose screws in the cabinetry were a tetanus shot waiting to happen, and an infestation of ants required a legitimate extermination. Initially, he intended to fix it all. He contemplated doing the work himself. Noah thought he might enjoy working with his hands. The computer support had been brain work and he wanted outside of his head. Still, he'd yet to make it to Home Depot to buy caulk for the leaky shower, even after watching a painfully boring YouTube tutorial called "Look Who's Caulking." By now temperatures had plummeted, which meant exterior work would be hell. He could hire a contractor and work together from the inside out, but he couldn't think about negotiating a contract. Not with his scant knowledge of his financial condition.

He eyed his cell phone, which was lying face down on the musty rug. He had no recollection of dropping it. Today Noah would do what he'd been putting off for over a month. He would log in to his banking app and see just how much of his winnings he'd burned through.

At first, he was good about keeping track. He had a Google spreadsheet where he logged where his money was going. Twenty-five thousand to his friend Ancel, a dude he'd met when they worked the front desk at the same gym, to seed his sitting treadmill business (but wasn't that just a bike?). Ancel called Noah an "angel investor." He liked the sound of that, even if he didn't know what it meant. Another thirty-five hundred to Paola for what she claimed he owed her in "damages" to her apartment but was more likely remuneration for her broken heart. One hundred thousand to St. Jude Research Hospital. When a commercial came on TV, the bald kids pulled at his heart and wallet strings. That one he didn't regret. Then there was fifty grand, a loan he doubted he'd recoup, to Buzz Off Joe to convert his shed into a working beehive, on top of the money he'd already given him for the bug-identifier app that never materialized. Thousand-dollar tips left on bar tabs. There was also the million and a half dollars he'd sunk into the Archer house, plus the extra sixty grand to keep the furniture.

By November, Noah grew lazy about keeping track of his expenditures. But he didn't want his laziness to stand in the way of generosity, so he continued to write checks, send Venmos and hand out wads of cash.

He climbed out of bed and felt a twinge in his bad knee. He was shelling out four hundred bucks twice a week to a physical therapist who made house calls. Maybe he should have looked into the going rate for PT or driven to a rehab facility to avoid the house call overcharge. *Maybe. Should have. Would have. In retrospect.* These phrases were going to end up on his tombstone.

Outside, fat snowflakes were falling at a brisk speed. Noah squinted to look out the window. He must have removed his contacts at some point last night because his vision was a blur, though still sharp enough to make out the hard hats working next door. How focused were the new owners on stripping the house down to the studs that they had the crew working during a snowstorm? Well, maybe not a storm, but certainly inclement weather. He closed the shades.

A text message from his friend Paul dinged. He'd met the guy while jogging a few years ago in Hoboken at Pier A Park. He was about ten years older than Noah and they'd struck up a friendship that consisted of short runs and long talks about the Yankees. They'd lost touch after Paul moved to Philly. Then Paul reached out after the Powerball to congratulate Noah. They reconnected over beers and soon after their first hang, Paul shared that his wife, Talullah, had recently been diagnosed with Parkinson's. Noah hadn't even remembered that Paul was married, but in fairness their conversations were dominated by whether the Yankees had overpaid for their new pitcher. Her meds were working well, Paul shared. They would slow the progress of her disease and offer her a chance at a semi-normal life, but there were alternative treatments—expensive treatments not covered by insurance—that could really help. A vegan diet. Boxing lessons. Weekly sessions with a hypnotist. Noah offered to pay before Paul even asked. He read today's text. T is doing great with the boxing . . . 2x/week could be even more beneficial. Noah eyed his cell phone battery. It was at five percent. With the last remaining juice, he sent a thousand dollars to Paul through Venmo.

Downstairs, he fixed himself a strong cup of coffee and drank it black. It wasn't too late to catch a nap before the caffeine kicked in. He lay on the living room sofa, a bulky sectional covered in a floral slipcover, and tried to get comfortable. After wrestling in vain to drape a fuzzy afghan just so, he gave up and went back to the kitchen. There were several open boxes of cereal on the counter. A fistful of each confirmed they were all stale. Maybe he could Postmates a bagel, though the off-season delivery options were slim pickings. He couldn't check his bank account on an empty stomach. And now that the coffee was kicking in, he was jittery. He had a fridge full of beer and a bong on the kitchen table. He would wait until a respectable time of day and either have a drink or a smoke or both. When he felt more relaxed, he'd face the music.

Eventually, an infomercial about a nine-in-one home exercise machine eased him into a nap. He was roused some time later by a rapping at the front door. His mouth was too parched to greet whoever was on the other side. He decided to ignore the knocking until the person, probably someone delivering a package, gave up. The knocking eventually stopped, but was replaced by the Archers' doorbell, which chimed for a good twenty seconds as it ding-donged across eight musical keys. Noah shuffled to his feet, sidestepping a few discarded beer and soda cans and an open pizza box, to reach the door.

Robin, his erstwhile client and bedfellow, stood on the other side. She wore a thick green peacoat and a fuzzy wool cap pulled low. Her face was paler than he remembered. He realized he'd never seen her when it wasn't summertime.

"Can I come in?" Her breath came out as smoke.

"Of course." He stumbled backward into the foyer as Robin made her way inside. Noah touched his face and felt a scruff that qualified more as beard than stubble. But Robin wasn't looking at his unshaven face. She was taking in the house. He followed her gaze as it moved from the pizza box to the overflowing trash can to the stacks of unopened mail piled on a side table.

"Sorry, I wasn't expecting company."

"It's okay," she said. "Hang on a sec." Robin turned back toward the door and Noah wondered if the messy house and his unkempt face and gnarly breath had scared her off. She walked to her car and he fully expected her to drive off. Instead, she pulled out a cardboard container with two paper cups and came back.

"I thought you might want one," she said, handing him a steaming cup of coffee. Noah took a sip. It was much better than the sludge he made for himself, which tasted like tar because he never rinsed the coffee pot and the beans had probably been sitting around since Stanley Archer's military service.

"Thank you," he said. "Do you want to take your clothes off? Coat! I meant coat."

Robin laughed. "Sure." She slipped off the peacoat and placed it on the back of an armchair. "I'll bet you're wondering why I'm here. May I?" She gestured to the couch.

"Of course." He saw that the slobber from his nap was still visible on the cushion. She took a seat at the other end.

"I'll be right back." Noah took the stairs two at a time and flung himself into the bathroom. After a quick brush of his teeth and a disappointing confirmation that he looked as shitty as he felt, he rejoined Robin. What was she doing here? It was hard to fathom that she'd come all this way for a roll in the hay, not when they'd had zero contact in six months save for an awkward interaction in late summer at the grocery store. In the produce aisle, he'd asked if her software needed updating. It came out like the opening line of an adult film. It didn't help that they were standing between the bananas and peaches.

He remembered conversations they'd had, postcoitus, where

Robin shared the contentious legal battles she was having with her ex-husband over alimony payments, or rather the lack thereof. It dawned on him that she'd probably come to ask for money. He'd give her what she needed, assuming he had sufficient funds. At least they had a prior relationship, unlike some of the other termites coming out of the woodwork. *Termites*. What a bust The Plan had been. At least nobody had found out he was behind it.

"How have you been, Noah?" Robin asked, her voice soft and full of concern. He hoped after he gave her money, she might stay awhile. His adult conversations were limited to the FF chat and minimal exchanges at the quickie-mart where he picked up a week's worth of provisions: food for one, beer for a fraternity. Maybe he could convince Robin to go next door and pretend to be a local inspector, put a little scare into the hammer-happy owners. She was an LBI old-timer, like him, and didn't love their precious island getting overrun by new folks either.

"I've been alright," he said. "Thanks for the coffee, by the way. This is good stuff."

Robin smiled. "The only good thing about rich people buying up the houses on LBI is that some pretty bougie places have arrived. But you know that already."

He didn't know. He only went to the convenience store, notably not the 7-Eleven where he bought the winning ticket. The owner had received a thirty-thousand-dollar check from the state lottery commission for selling the winning ticket and had erected a virtual shrine to Noah above the coffee station. His only other regular excursion was to the liquor store. Still, he nodded and muttered, "Yep."

"There's a big storm coming tomorrow. I know it's only flurrying now, but we're supposed to get over ten inches." Robin clearly felt the need to make small talk before getting to the point. The letters and emails did the same. Usually a sentence or two asking after his well-being before the launch of a sob story. It's why he stopped open-ing the mail a few weeks earlier, though he wasn't bold enough to throw out the letters. What if somebody in the pile really needed him?

"Good thing I don't have any plans," Noah said, and Robin looked at him with sad-puppy eyes. Had he felt sorry for her once upon a time, a lonely divorcée passing the time with a guy too young for her?

"So you're probably wondering why I'm here," Robin said, fold-ing her hands in her lap. He took another swig of coffee, lukewarm and no longer as tasty.

"I think I know," he said, suddenly eager to get this over with.

Robin leaned forward on the couch so their knees were practi-cally touching. It wasn't necessary, Noah thought. There was no cer-emonial ass-kissing or flirting needed. He almost said, "How much?" when she said, "I've been really worried about you."

Huh?

"It's all going to sound very silly, but I've been trying to get in touch with you for the past six weeks because the Nicolas Cage prob-lem came back. Except this time it's the Rock. Everything I look up online just returns pictures of him from his movies. *Jumanji. Fast and Furious. Baywatch.* You name it. I went to the Apple store but they just tried to sell me another laptop. My kids have no idea how to fix it. Finally, finally, a friend from work came over and was able to get rid of the bug." She smiled sheepishly. He had forgotten how cute her elfin chin looked when she smiled.

"So it's fixed?"

"Yes. Now I'm able to look up pictures of my ex and his new wife again. I was probably better off seeing the Rock." Robin let out a hol-low laugh.

Noah noticed a half-full Amstel on the coffee table and picked it up. The beer was flat and tasted sour, but it settled in his belly more easily than the coffee.

"Noah, it's only ten o'clock in the morning," Robin said.

"That's five o'clock in—" He paused. Which time zone was ahead and which was behind?

"Anyway, of course you were my first call because you fixed it so easily last time. I texted you. Left messages. You didn't get back to me. And that didn't seem like you. I know you don't need the money anymore, but it's not like you to ignore a friend. So I started asking around. I know a few year-rounders and no one's seen much of you. I got nervous and decided I'd drive out and check to make sure you're okay."

It took Noah a minute to process. It was true that his email, voicemail and texts were clogged with unopened and unplayed messages. He choked out that he needed to get something from the kitchen. Tucked out of sight, he pulled open a mint-colored cabinet with the laminate mostly peeled off and took out his stash of weed. With shaky hands, he started to roll a joint. It was quicker than firing up the bong.

"Want anything?" he called out, buying some time. But Robin was already in the doorway, watching him fiddle with the rolling paper. The expression on her face broke him. He started crying like a baby.

"Let's put that down," she said, eyeing the joint. "How about we go back to the living room? Where's your phone?"

"Upstairs, I think."

"I'll find it," she said. And before he could protest, Robin was climbing the steps to the second floor. She returned with his phone. "You're almost out of battery but I brought a charger with me." She was so efficient, so determined, that a sinking feeling came upon him that maybe she would try to transfer money to her account from his phone.

While she searched for an outlet with her back to him, he finished off the Amstel. Once the phone was plugged in, she pulled Noah over and positioned his face to unlock the screen. "Thank you," she said, more to herself, and began scrolling through his contacts.

"Laura, hi, it's Robin Miller. From LBI." Noah, dizzy, stared at the fuzzy outline of Robin. She had his phone to her ear. "Yes, yes, everything is okay. Yes, I know this is Noah's number. Listen, I think you or one of your siblings needs to get down here," Robin said. "Noah's not in great shape."

"I CAN'T GET THIS FAKAKTA THING TO WORK," LEO SAID, TURNing his iPad upside down and giving it a shake. "Let me just share your screen." He crossed the room to where Noah was seated on the couch, a laptop open on the coffee table in front of him.

"Dad, I don't think that's how this is supposed to work," Noah said, though he didn't actually understand what was about to take place. His siblings insisted he be on a Zoom at a precise time, that he be sober, and that he give them at least a full hour of his time. As if he had other places to be.

The day after Robin showed up unannounced, his father arrived, also a surprise. He got the last flight out of Florida before Newark Airport closed. Noah knew things were serious when his father knocked on his door during a winter travel advisory.

The thing about "hitting" rock bottom is that the landing doesn't hurt. Noah thought this as he overheard his father on the phone earlier that morning with his siblings. He didn't suddenly crash into a hard place. The phrase should really be "sliding" to rock bottom. It was a far more accurate description of his descent into—madness? No, he had his wits about him. There was too much drinking, that was for sure, and a belief that nobody wanted him for anything besides money. What was that called? Loneliness with a side of bad habits?

"Why can't we share a screen?" Leo asked.

Noah shrugged. "Matthew said we should all be on our own computers. Here, let me take a look. I used to be pretty good at this kind of thing." Leo entered the code to wake the iPad and Noah immediately diagnosed the issue. "Zoom needs an update. And you're using a seriously outdated version of software. I don't think I can get this to work in time. How do you function in Florida with no computer and this clunker?"

Now Leo shrugged. "If I need to look something up, I use—" his father began to explain but looked down at his watch. "Isn't it time?"

Noah checked his phone. They still had five minutes. It was surreal, waiting around for his own intervention to start, helping with the tech. In the movies and TV, the person getting ambushed was taken by surprise. They came home after a long day at the office or a trip to the grocery store to find their nearest and dearest lined up on a couch somber-faced. In Noah's case, his dad was practically sitting in his lap to fit into the same camera frame; he'd had to walk Laura and Doug through a frustrating tutorial on how to reinstall Zoom and help Matthew connect to Bluetooth. He could have faked a service outage at the house or sent the wrong Zoom link, but he didn't. Noah made sure everyone was mic'd and ready to tell him just how poorly they thought he was faring.

Four Zoom squares appeared on the screen. Laura was in her kitchen. He remembered making many trips to that room over Thanksgiving to grab another beer, not wanting to trouble (or alarm) her numerous staff. Matthew was at work, bent over a desk overflowing with papers and file folders. Sophie was in her studio, wearing gigantic headphones and a too-clean smock. And then there was Noah, cheek to cheek with Leo. He had shaved for the occasion and put on a clean shirt. There was no garbage or beer cans in the camera's eye.

"How was your flight, Dad?" Sophie asked. Leave it to the teacher to nail the icebreakers. "You're lucky you were able to get in."

"Easy. I found an airline even cheaper than Spirit. Have you heard of Fly Zone? Thirty-nine bucks for my ticket," Leo said. "And one carry-on for free."

"Dad, those seats are like buckets. It's not good for your back," Laura protested. "I wanted to put him in extra legroom on JetBlue. It was only three hundred dollars."

"Only three hundred dollars." Leo scoffed. "I hope you hear yourself."

Matthew typed into the chat: I have more than 700,000 miles in my AmEx account from business travel. I could have booked you for free.

"How do I write back to that?" Leo asked, pointing to the chat box.

"You can just speak, Dad," Noah said. He was feeling antsy and wanted to get the show on the road. The sandpaper feeling in the back of his throat was back. If he ran upstairs to pop an edible, nobody would notice. He started to get up but Leo put a hand on his shoulder, firmly. "Sit," he said, as though Noah were a dog.

"We'll discuss your return flight later," Laura said. "I really don't like you in those hard-backed seats and I'm sure Dr. Rosen wouldn't either."

"How was Boston, by the way?" Matthew asked.

Nobody answered.

"Noah? Boston? How was it?"

Oh shit. Noah forgot that he'd told his brother he was going to be in Boston the day Matthew was passing through town.

"Uh, it was good," he said. "Nice to get away." When Matthew's text came in about the two of them possibly having dinner, Noah had just received an email from a man claiming to be seeking asylum in Boston. He needed $10,000 urgently to establish a new identity after fleeing from an unspecified dictatorship (spelled diktatership). Noah figured it was a ruse, but in case it wasn't, he Zelle'd $500. He didn't want dictator blood on his hands.

"Guys, this may be the teacher in me, but I think circle time needs to come to an end," Sophie said. "Noah, we're worried about you. Robin said you were a mess. You hadn't showered in a while. The house was a pigsty. She smelled alcohol on your breath. You hadn't returned any of her calls or texts. We love you, Noah. Please tell us what's going on."

Arrows appeared in the chat from Laura. Matthew followed with the same symbol.

"Up?" Noah was confused.

"That symbol means we agree with Sophie," Laura explained. "I learned it from the girls."

"And I learned it from Austin."

"Arrows from me too," Leo said.

"Guys, I seriously appreciate the concern, but I'm fine. Dad, you certainly didn't have to come up from Florida right before a snowstorm to check on me," Noah said, unsure whether to look at his dad in the flesh or his face on the screen.

"Yes he did," Laura said sharply. "But that's a whole other issue. Noah, you're not fine. You stopped seeing your clients, you barely text on the group chat, you clearly lied about going to Boston. You were drunk as a skunk at my house, which if it were a onetime thing, I could understand. But Sophie said you got wasted in Florida too."

He could have gone on the defensive and said that his clients stopped seeing him. That Laura was trying to use money to save her marriage. That Sophie was moping around saying she lost her mojo but doing nothing to get it back. That Matthew, despite now having even more money in the bank, was still toiling away at a job he clearly hated. Instead, Noah looked from one square to the next and said, "I've been going through some shit."

"We know and we get it," Matthew said. "This hasn't been the ride any of us were expecting."

"I wonder how Grandma Mabel is doing these days. Maybe it's better to get rich in your eighties?" Noah said.

Laura squealed. "You guys, I forgot to tell you, Mabel is a sugar mama now. Emma sent me a video from Ruby's TikTok. Mabel's got a new man and he's, like, maybe fifty tops. Noah—how do I stay on the Zoom but also pull up the video on my phone?"

Noah shook his head no. "Tech support is closed. Please call back during regular office hours."

"Maybe tech support shouldn't be closed," Sophie said. "I still remember how excited you were when you taught me how to digitize my students' artwork."

That was true. He remembered how grateful Sophie had been and how much fun it was to tackle the project together.

"I tried," Noah said. "Nobody wanted tech help from a millionaire."

"There's got to be something else that makes you happy," Laura said.

Noah was quiet for a moment, thinking. "There is. This place. Beach Haven. The sunrise and sunset. The sound of the ocean. The smell of the saltwater. The way everything is always sticky from bug spray and suntan lotion, even in winter. The fresh clams. The way I can bike everywhere. That's honestly the only thing that's been keeping me going."

"Well, none of that is going anywhere. No amount of money, won or lost, can take away the natural beauty of LBI," Matthew said.

"Matty, that was seriously deep," Sophie said. "Is there an artist's soul buried beneath your suit?"

"Soph, cut it out. Noah, one of us is going to be checking in on you every day from now on, whether you like it or not," Matthew said.

"You? Won't you be too busy at work?" Noah asked.

"Actually, on that front, I've got some news." Matthew cleared his throat. "I gave notice at the firm. I've got a month left to wrap up with my clients and then I'm out of here. I'm hanging up my suit for good, so I guess we will see what's underneath."

"Huzzah!" Sophie exclaimed. "It's about damn time."

"How's Beth handling that?" Laura asked.

"It's . . . an adjustment. She said you had a lot to do with it," Matthew said.

"Me? What'd I do?" Laura's eyes flashed with panic.

Matthew scratched at the back of his neck. "Apparently you said something about my smile that really got to her."

"Well, I suppose that's nice," Laura said. "Until she blames me for being the reason she has a stay-at-home husband now."

"I prefer stay-at-home Renaissance man," Matthew said. "It's temporary, anyway. I think."

"I have some news too," Sophie said. "Since we're all together."

She lifted a hand and showed off a deep-blue sapphire on her ring finger. "Ravi proposed and I said yes. He designed the ring and made the band himself. It's ceramic."

Everyone started cheering and whooping.

"How did you not tell me immediately?" Laura pouted.

"It happened last night. I'm still in shock," Sophie said. "Dad, I can't believe you didn't tell me. Ravi said he told you in Florida."

Leo smirked. "I can keep a secret. Mazel tov, honey. I wish your mother was here to see this."

The Jacobsons all quieted, thinking of Sylvia, and how she would have fussed over Sophie's wedding. Laura's shotgun wedding hadn't given their mother the necessary time to pull out all the stops, and Matthew and Beth had opted for a city hall affair because of the lopsided sizes of their families. As for himself? Well, Sylvia hardly held her breath waiting for Noah to tie the knot.

"There are good times ahead for all of us," Laura said, breaking the silence. "Which is why we need you well, Noah Jacobson."

"I READ THE YANKEES ARE THINKING OF TRADING FOR FRED-die Freeman," Leo said. He had the newspaper and his trusty magnifying glass in hand when Noah entered the kitchen. It had been a week since the Zoom-tervention and Noah was feeling pretty good. He liked having his father around again. It was nice to hear him whistle while he prepared his morning oatmeal. To cheer on the Knicks with him and scream at the TV when they missed an easy layup. To discuss dinner, even if it only meant a decision between scrambled eggs and frozen pizza.

"Freeman's a solid hitter," Noah said. "I could get behind that."

"Coffee?" Leo asked, lowering the newspaper with a devilish smile. He held a large mug that said "Sisterhood of B'nai Shalom

Spring Fling Honoring Sylvia Jacobson." Leo gestured to the counter, where a shiny new appliance made Noah do a double take. It was next to a new toaster in a reflective blue enamel with two slots for bread.

"Yes, please," Noah said. "Where did we get all this stuff? Who helped you do this?" He noticed new dishes, tea towels, flatware and glasses, all color-coordinated and organized neatly. "This must have cost a fortune. I need to pay you back."

"Can you not worry about money for a minute? I'm your father. And I wanted to help you get this place sorted. Open the fridge."

Noah did as he was told and was floored to see a fully stocked refrigerator, with yogurt, fresh produce, sliced meats, eggs, butter and a peach pie from Baked on the Beach.

"Wow. I have so many questions." Noah grabbed a perfect-looking apple and took a seat opposite his father, sliding out the business section from the paper. The cover story was about how non-chain restaurants and bars were struggling to stay afloat with rising labor costs. Noah thought of Dan, the bartender in Florida who'd helped him to a cab. He'd been offended when Noah offered him money. Maybe his father was right that he had become overly transactional. He wondered if the neon sign outside Dan's bar ever got fixed.

"I took a stroll next door yesterday," Leo said, choosing not to elaborate on the kitchen upgrade. "The new owner was meeting with the pool company. Dick really is a nice fellow."

"The new owner's name is Dick? You've got to be kidding me. And they're putting in a pool?" Noah gestured toward the ocean.

"Yes. And his wife, Sheila, is pregnant. I think you'll be happy having them as neighbors. They really love the property."

"Not enough to keep the house," Noah said.

"Well, the house wasn't going to last forever without a major renovation. If it wasn't going to be a new owner doing the place in, it would have been a termite infestation. Right?"

The apple slipped from Noah's sweaty palm.

"Noah, I know what you did. Your exterminator friend isn't exactly discreet. After you won the lottery, he started blabbing that story all over town."

"Dad, I'm sorry, I don't know why I—"

Leo put out his hand to stop Noah from blathering.

"Noah, I have something to tell you as well. Something even bigger."

"Yes?"

"We didn't have to sell the house. You know your mother and I lived very modestly. Even with four kids, we managed to carve out a decent-size nest egg for ourselves."

Heat was climbing up the back of Noah's neck. If his father could have maintained the house, then why was he living in Stanley Archer's hideous place watching his family home get demolished? "So, why the—"

"Your mother insisted we sell. She thought it was important for all of us that we not live in the past and—" Leo hesitated and looked at his mug. "She thought the house had become something of a crutch for you."

A crutch. He thought of finding Matthew's old crutch in the attic. Noah had used it for a few days after his bike accident, barely hobbling around since it was meant for a shorter person. To think the house was a larger, metaphorical crutch didn't seem that outlandish.

"Your mother had all sorts of ideas of how things should go after she went. She said I should refuse to let you kids hire movers. She wanted you to have the experience of packing up together."

Noah guffawed. "We assumed that was because you were cheap."

"Well, that too." Leo's face softened. He reached a hand across the kitchen table and rested it on Noah's. "Son, I'm going back to Florida at the end of the week."

He had known this moment was coming. The temperature had dropped to below ten degrees and Leo had taken a nasty spill on the icy front steps. There was an upcoming pickleball tournament and Leo was captaining the Boca Breezes team when they faced off against Turnberry Terraces.

"I appreciate you coming, Dad," Noah said. "Maybe I should go with you? Move to Boca Breezes. Whaddya think?"

"I think," Leo said, "that we both need to move on to the next phase of our lives. Why don't you show me your bank statement?" Leo tapped his head. "I still have my marbles, so take advantage while you can."

Noah groaned, realizing it was time to face reality. He might as well do it with his accountant father at his side. After retrieving his laptop, he logged into his account and turned the screen toward Leo.

"Well, it's not all gone," Leo said. "I was imagining worse. Get me a pen and paper. We're going to make you an old-fashioned budget, invest what's left, and get you back on track."

For the next two hours, Leo and Noah sat together, creating a financial plan that would ensure a comfortable lifestyle for Noah so long as he didn't keep giving away his money to every Tom, Dick and Harry who asked. "And for God's sake, make sure you deduct your charitable donations or you're going to give me a heart attack."

"I will, I promise," Noah said.

"Now that we've tackled the worst of it, have you given any thought to what you want to do next? It's fine to coast for a while, but no one can sit alone in a beach house forever."

Some of the weight Noah had felt lifted from his shoulders returned.

"What do you like to do? Why don't we start there?" Leo asked.

Noah thought for a moment. "I like what I used to do. The tech repair. Seriously, you recover someone's iPhone photos, you might as well have performed an organ transplant. You can't imagine the gratitude."

"It's nice to feel needed," Leo said. "Your mother fed off that. I did too, when it came to work. I understand the tax code, which looks like gibberish to most people. Tax season may have crushed my schedule, but it sure was nice to hear all those thank-yous."

"I get that. I really want to hear 'thank you' again," Noah said. "Speaking of, thanks for coming, Pops."

Leo leaned back and folded his arms across his chest. "To be honest, I should have been here sooner. I should have put off the Florida move the minute you kids won the lotto. Parenting isn't over when your kids turn eighteen, or twenty-one, or get a job, or get married or have a child of their own. Your mother knew that. She was parent enough for both of us and I happily slid into the background. But it's my turn to step up."

"To be fair, Mom took up a lot of space. It was hard to get a word in sometimes."

"Loudest librarian on the East Coast. And she coddled you too much and then wondered why you weren't acting more like an adult," Leo said.

"She told Sophie that if she wasn't married by thirty-five, nobody would want her," Noah added.

"And, yet. Sophie listened. She's making it just in time," Leo said. "That's your mother's hand at work, I'm telling you. She was a force."

"Of nature," Noah said. "Even if she hated bugs and dirt."

"A force to be reckoned with," Leo suggested.

"A tour de force," Noah said.

"A force feeder," Leo added.

"Speaking of, I'm hungry," Noah said. "Let's eat some of this incredible food that mysteriously appeared at my house. I still want an explanation, Dad."

"And I want my knees not to wobble and my back not to ache after pickleball, but we can't always get what we want."

FANTASTIC FOURSOME 🧑‍🚀 🧑‍🚀 ✡️ 🧑‍🚀 🧑‍🚀

LAURA

Do you like this dress for me?

SOPHIE

Meh. U look better in bright colors.

LAURA

This one?

SOPHIE

I'd prefer if you didn't also wear white to my wedding

LAURA

Oops. Sent wrong version. It comes in pink

SOPHIE

K, send that one

NOAH

Unsubscribe

MATTHEW

Can you guys include Beth in the shopping stuff? She would like that

SOPHIE

Definitely

LAURA

I have a call with her about Austin's BM later

NOAH

His sh*t?

LAURA

BM = bar mitzvah

NOAH

Oh. I met the neighbors

MATTHEW

And?

NOAH

We r better looking

SOPHIE

Ha! Maybe u r

NOAH

They r nice—as is their decorator . . . 🔥

LAURA

ooooh . . . deets pls

NOAH

Patience

12

Matthew

BETH LEANED ACROSS THE TABLE SO DRAMATICALLY IT WAS AS though she was contouring her body into a tablecloth. One more inch and she'd become the dinner napkin on Arnold Peterson's lap.

"So you were saying, Arnold, that you got on a plane to the CDC headquarters on March tenth and didn't return to New York for a year? That is just wild," Beth said, turning to Celine, Arnold's wife. "And you held down the fort at home while having your entire caseload moved online. Extraordinary."

Celine Watson, a federal judge of some renown, smiled politely. She had a regal bearing and ramrod posture. "There really was no choice," she said. "The real hero is Arnold, of course. I don't think my husband slept more than two hours a night until the vaccine was ready."

Dr. Peterson nodded. "That part is true. But a lot of credit goes to my team. It was a group effort."

"Modest too!" Beth exclaimed.

Good grief. Did his wife think she was at risk of drowning? Why else was she clinging to every word that Arnold Peterson and Celine Watson said like a life preserver? If Dr. Peterson wasn't pushing seventy and a good five inches shorter than Beth—a differential obvious even when they were seated—Matthew would think his wife was flirting.

"Boy, was my arm sore after getting the vax," Matthew said. "Not that I minded. Gave me an excuse to skip my workout."

"Matthew! That sounds awfully ungrateful," Beth said. The point of her stiletto jammed into his calf. He remembered her warning to be on his best behavior with these two.

"These two" were the power couple Beth had set her sights on from the moment Austin stepped into his kindergarten classroom at Dalton and was put at the triangle table with their son Theo. When Arnold was tapped to head the COVID vaccine effort, Beth proclaimed, "I told you they were winners."

"Of course I'm grateful. Watching Austin go to school online broke my heart. The kids need socialization, even more than we adults do. How did Theo handle lockdown?" Matthew looked from Celine to Arnold. He could feel Beth relaxing as he redeemed himself.

"Oh, it was rough. For all three of our children, actually. Theo probably handled it the best. Betsy had to evacuate her Harvard dorm during her freshman year and Sally was at that terrible preteen age where any setback is monumental," Celine said. "How about Austin? I know he and Theo were on FaceTime every day."

The boys were such close friends that Matthew had asked Beth if they should tell Theo's parents about the marijuana gummies. If Austin was mixed up in something, there was a good chance Theo was too. Beth immediately shot him down, looking at Matthew as though he were a two-headed monster. "We are not advertising Austin's mistakes," she'd hissed. "Besides, we have that under control."

Matthew hoped she was right. They had spent the rest of Thanksgiving weekend drilling Austin. He swore up and down that he'd only just started making the gummies. He wouldn't give up any of his friends who were involved. Matthew respected his son wasn't a narc, Beth less so. They searched his room, his backpack and his pockets for a month. He seemed so shaken up and embarrassed by the episode at the Thanksgiving table that they believed he would stay away from pot, at least for a while. The statistics about marijuana's effects on brain cells that Beth culled from the Internet scared the living daylights out of him. With a quivering lip, he'd asked how many cells they thought he'd lost from the six gummies he'd consumed in his lifetime.

"FaceTiming with Theo definitely saved Austin during lockdown," Beth said. "I always forget you have three children. You two make it seem so effortless."

Matthew suppressed a guffaw. Beth didn't forget anything about the Petersons.

Arnold waved off the compliment. "So Austin told Theo that you're no longer at the law firm, Matthew. How's that been?"

It had been two months since Matthew surrendered his ID badge, and the adjustment had been more or less a smooth one, for him at least. Matthew took Austin to school in the mornings and was home when he returned in the afternoons. They still had their au pair, but her contract was up in just two months. While Austin did homework at the kitchen table, Matthew peppered him with questions about his day, experimenting with different approaches to elicit the most detailed answer. The boy seemed to open up most when Matthew wasn't looking directly at him, so he busied himself rinsing fruit at the sink or flipping through the mail while he mined information. He also learned that nothing valuable could be gleaned from Austin until he'd had a large snack. As for the hours while Austin was at school, Matthew kept busy attending to projects that he never had time for before. Organizing the family photos into folders on his Mac. Filling bags of clothing for Goodwill. He had a pile of nearly identical navy suits, starched white dress shirts and patterned ties that he would have enjoyed incinerating, but knew they ought to be put to better use. He fixed the printer in the family room (with Noah's help on FaceTime) and collected all the unread *New Yorker*s around the apartment and dumped them into recycling. There was still the occasional call or email from a colleague asking for help deciphering his notes. He knew the tasks around the house and the work calls would eventually dry up, but for now he was sufficiently occupied.

For Beth, the change was another story. Moments after she returned from work, before she even set down her bag, she would ask him what he'd done during the day. "Done" really meant "accomplished." After every item he listed, she would respond, "And then what?"

"Yes, tell us how stay-at-home-dad life is treating you?" Celine asked, but looked at both Matthew and Beth to indicate she meant "you" plural.

Matthew put down the forkful of fish that was en route to his mouth. He wasn't enjoying the sole meunière (seventy-six dollars!) all that much anyway. Based on how much Beth was oohing and ahhing over the food and ambience, he suspected Celine had chosen the restaurant. "It's been wonderful to have more time with Austin. There were days when I was at work before he woke up and home after he was asleep. The biggest adjustment so far has been trying to stop myself from chunking my time into six-minute increments and reporting it on a timesheet."

Arnold chortled. "Boy, if we got paid by the hour for creating the vaccine, I'd be a very rich man. Like you folks. Austin told Theo you were cut in on the lottery winnings. Must be nice to relax."

Matthew filed talking to Austin about not repeating everything he heard at home to the list of father-son conversations that had to take place.

"It's been—" Matthew started to say, but Beth cut him off.

"Matthew's *not* a stay-at-home dad. He's just taking some time to plot his next steps. He has many interesting opportunities and it's important he explores them all before he commits to anything," she said.

"Ahh, well then you'll need to soak up all that time with Austin now before you get back to the grind," Celine said.

"I don't—" Matthew tried again foolishly.

"He will, of course. We both spend plenty of time with Austin," Beth said. "That child is probably sick of us," she added with a laugh Matthew detected as nervous but that probably sounded genuine to those who didn't know her like he did.

Somehow, Matthew managed to get through the main course by feigning interest in his companions' "grueling" apartment renovation and their charity boards.

"Can I interest you in dessert?" Their waiter reappeared holding four small, leather-bound menus. "We have an excellent souffle but it takes twenty minutes to prepare."

"Celine? Arnold?" Beth said at the same time Matthew said, "I think we'll just take the check."

"That was very rude," Beth snapped after they had air-kissed the Watson-Petersons goodbye outside the restaurant. "You can't decide unilaterally for the table whether we're getting dessert."

Matthew stopped walking even as the harsh February wind whipped his face. "And you can't decide unilaterally for me how I'm going to live my life."

Beth's face paled in the moonlight. He had struck the blow he set out to, but when it landed, Matthew didn't feel satisfaction.

Being honest and converting his thoughts into words wasn't cathartic. The only difference was that now two people knew instead of just one.

"Is that what you think?" Beth said. A look of disgust slowly moved across her face, shifting her expression like a developing Polaroid. "Do I need to remind you that you were a straight B student when we met with zero plans for the future? You grew up so coddled, so entitled, with your nice house in East Brunswick and your beach house at the shore. The irony of this whole lottery thing is the talk of your siblings becoming rich—you were already rich! All of you. You went to summer camp and had new clothes every year and fresh backpacks and tennis lessons and SAT tutors. So your sister needed to work a day job to pay her rent? Laura and Doug's house needed a new roof. Noah, who worked maybe an hour a day, still had a place to crash rent-free every night on the ocean. I helped you reach your potential. To make something of yourself. Because guess what? It feels good to be rewarded for hard work. Are any of your siblings happy? They had comfortable lives before the lottery. Now things are even cushier, but are they happier?"

Beth let the question dangle for a beat before continuing. "I want our son to have direction in his life. Structure helps—just look at Noah to see what happens without it. I really hope you don't plan on loosening up his extracurriculars just because you're home more. Listen, I've said my piece. It's late and I—"

Matthew's eyes watered, and not from the cold. "I'm sorry, let's go home. It's freezing." He pulled off his wool scarf and handed it to Beth, who had left the house with only a thin, silk one draped over her coat. She wrapped it around her delicate neck. He deemed the scarf an olive branch and her wearing it as acceptance. But then she turned in the opposite direction, calling over her shoulder, "I'm going out. And I forgot to mention this earlier but Polly got out of her cage and shed all over the rug. You need to clean it up."

Matthew watched his wife's retreating figure, her small waist cinched by the belt of her coat, her gait even sexier in high heels, one end of his scarf flapping in the wind.

BETH CAME HOME WELL AFTER MIDNIGHT. MATTHEW HAD gone to bed as soon as he cleaned the bearded dragon's mess. He slept in fits and starts, reaching his hand across the mattress to the cool spot where she ought to have been. He was awake when she entered their bedroom, but he didn't speak. He listened to her remove her heels, unclasp her jewelry and run the faucet over her toothbrush. *Do you hate me*, he wanted to ask, like a chastened Austin would mumble when he was a little boy and got in trouble. Eventually, she lifted the covers and climbed into bed. He kept his eyes closed but felt her gaze on him. Was she judging him? Was she wondering how he could be so ungrateful? Was she thinking about the hot young man she might have made out with at a bar earlier? Matthew couldn't gauge her mood. The next morning, he woke to her packing a suitcase. He slipped into a full-on panic until he remembered she was leaving for a scheduled business trip. Beth would be in Chicago for three nights to take depositions.

"Need help?" he asked, as she struggled to put two suits into a garment bag with one hand while holding her phone in the other.

"I got it."

"Let me at least make coffee," he said. Twenty minutes later, after a perfunctory kiss and no mention of their argument from the night before, Beth was in a town car en route to the airport.

Matthew eyed his watch. Austin would be late for school if they didn't get going soon. He rapped gently on his son's door before turning the knob. Austin was up and dressed, sitting at his laptop, which he quickly shut the minute Matthew entered. He was now used to his son's quick reflexes when it came to screens.

"We gotta go," Matthew said.

Austin swiveled in his chair. "No school today. Faculty development or something. But Mom is making me meet with Cantor Schwartz to practice my haftorah." Austin's bar mitzvah was still three months away but Beth was treating his preparations exactly like she'd managed studying for the LSAT. As many times as Matthew told her that nobody besides the rabbi and cantor would realize if Austin flubbed a line, Beth was not moved. "I gotta dip," Austin said.

"Dip" was teen speak for leaving.

"Like ranch dressing," Matthew said.

Austin grabbed his bar mitzvah folder and brushed past Matthew. "That's a really lame joke."

Alone in his son's room, Matthew was struck by the unfamiliar sight of Austin's unattended laptop. He brought it to school with him every day, an eight-pound contribution to a knapsack that had to weigh at least thirty pounds altogether. On the weekends, Austin remained glued to it.

Matthew edged closer, unsure if opening it was a violation of his son's privacy or the actions of a responsible parent. He supposed they weren't mutually exclusive. The screen prompted him for a password, naturally. Matthew knew he ran the risk of trying too many combinations and the computer freezing him out, thereby letting Austin know he'd snooped. Matthew decided to make two attempts. His siblings had certainly gotten lucky picking numbers; maybe he would too.

Austin was too smart to choose something obvious like his

birthday, or if he did, it would be the square root of each digit multiplied by the number next to it. He looked around the room for clues, his eyes narrowing on the glass case at the far end of the desk. The bearded dragon! He typed in Polly and clicked enter, his heart practically in his throat. The "incorrect" message deflated but didn't surprise him. He swept his gaze once more around the room. A poster of Shohei Ohtani gave him hope. Austin's favorite player wore number 17. Matthew entered POLLY17 and this time, the computer came to life.

His immediate excitement at cracking the code quickly gave way to nausea so extreme Matthew almost passed out. On the screen, a video was paused in a scene Matthew knew he wouldn't unsee for the rest of his life. He pressed play with a shaky hand and watched in horror as a line of girls dressed as cheerleaders took turns fellating a well-endowed football player on the fifty-yard line. He moved his index finger across the mouse pad to check the other open tabs. Orgies. S&M. And then a page with text that confused him. Refreshingly, it had no obscene imagery, but as he began to read, he grew even more unsettled. It was a chat room. Austin had apparently left his correspondent in the midst of a conversation where she (was it really a she?) was describing the size of her nipples. Oranges, as if that were even possible. He tasted bile as last night's dinner came back up on him.

Get it together, Matthew! You knew this was a possibility—it's why you looked! Clearly, he and Austin needed to have a serious talk when he came back from his lesson. From Torah study to a discussion of hard-core pornography—it wasn't the day either Austin or Matthew had been expecting. He knew being an involved parent meant more than going to parent-teacher conferences and making sure Austin remembered to wind his palate expander. But this. This was A LOT. He needed to loop in Beth, with whom he was skating on thin ice, and who would probably find a way to blame him.

Had his own father ever spoken to him about sex? Matthew couldn't recall any conversation of the sort taking place. Leo skirted the birds and bees talk, but the stakes were lower when porn to satisfy any fetish wasn't a click away, most of it free and quite a bit of it stomach-turningly sick. He'd been raised in a pre–social media world, at a time when Leo could respectably dodge parental obligations and with a wife who was happy to take over just about every facet of their lives. It might have been easier, but Matthew realized that he would not choose that same path. Even Leo, after forty-two years of parenting one way, seemed to be rethinking his role. He was calling more frequently and coming up the following week for Sophie's first solo art show.

Matthew was tasked with picking him up from the airport. The two of them alone in the car was the perfect place to tackle the Viagra and safe-sex conversation. Matthew and his siblings imagined Leo was not up-to-date on how easily things spread and how many new diseases there were to catch. It was a talk he'd been dreading, until finding porn on his thirteen-year-old's laptop, which now took first place as the topic he was least looking forward to discussing.

He shut the computer and sat down on Austin's bed, smoothing the Star Wars covers. Where had his little boy gone? Matthew wished, for the first time since giving notice at the law firm, that he still worked there.

His phone rang. It was Laura.

"I just got off with Noah," his sister said. "He sounds pretty good. How's the home life?"

"Well, I just found disturbing porn on Austin's computer, Beth thinks I'm a jerk and—if you could have Doug give me a call—I think I have an abscess."

"The stay-at-home-parent life not as glamorous as you expected?"

"Did I mention I have to take Polly to the vet? She has pneumonia."

"WHO'S THE PRESENT FOR?" MATTHEW ASKED HIS FATHER AS they sailed onto the Long Island Expressway toward Manhattan. Rattling around the trunk of the Tesla were Leo's carry-on and a large rectangular box wrapped in shiny white paper and a green bow.

"Austin. I got him a pickleball racket." Leo beamed. "Early bar mitzvah gift."

"He'll love it," Matthew said. That had to be the first time Leo had ever selected a gift for any of his children or grandchildren. Presents were strictly Sylvia's domain. She was more apt to know what everyone wanted and was less tight with the dollar. Matthew and his siblings were surprised when Leo remembered to call on their birthdays without Sylvia around to remind him. She'd probably drilled the dates into his head from her hospital bed. They all still felt like shit for forgetting to acknowledge Sylvia's birthday. Sophie made sure they put the date in their phone calendars and suggested a family get-together the next year.

"Sophie said she expects a packed house tomorrow night," Matthew said. "The gallerist is apparently a big deal and the RSVPs poured in. It was nice of you to come up."

"I wouldn't miss it," Leo said, and Matthew decided not to challenge the ridiculousness of that statement. He believed in second chances, and if the pot gummies and hardcore porn on his son's computer were any indication, Matthew wasn't in the running for father of the year either.

"So, Dad, I've been meaning to talk to you about something." The traffic had suddenly intensified, slowing their pace to a crawl.

Cruising at sixty-five, Matthew had every reason to look straight ahead. At fifteen miles per hour, not glancing over at Leo while he spoke was weird. "About, you know, those pills Noah and Sophie found."

"Oh, hell," Leo said, smacking his hand on his knee. "This again? Can't a man have any damn privacy? Don't I deserve a little respect?"

Of course you do, Matthew thought. I'm not enjoying this conversation either!

"It's because we love you so much—the four of us—and you don't have Mom around to look after you. I'm not sure you're aware, but at Boca Breezes, apparently—and I don't know when this was but I have it on good authority— What I'm trying to say is that—"

"Half the geezers in the place got the clap?" Leo finished his sentence with all the subtlety of a blunt force object to the skull.

"Yeah. That."

"I'll have you know the condo board made all the tenants take an online safe-sex course because of the outbreak. Listen, I was going to wait to tell you this. All you kids, actually. But I'm not really in the at-risk community. I've started seeing a woman. A pretty terrific gal. Believe it or not, I find myself thinking how much your mother would have liked her."

"Dad, that's wonderful," Matthew said, though his mind immediately drifted to Noah's reaction. His sisters would be judgy of their father's paramour, but they'd be happy for him. Noah, the mama's boy, was a different story.

"Don't get too excited. At our age, dating is mostly just accompanying each other to doctors' appointments. But it's nice. Annette is wonderful. I'm looking forward to introducing her to you all. Now, if it's alright with you, I'd like to close my eyes for the rest of the ride. And no more discussion about my pecker if that's okay."

The traffic eased and Matthew stepped on the gas, a smile on his face from ear to ear. He couldn't wait to tell Beth about this.

"SO MY DAD'S NOT AT RISK FOR GONORRHEA," MATTHEW SAID.
Beth didn't respond. She was in the bathroom applying makeup in her precise, no-time-to-waste fashion. It wasn't something Matthew would normally notice, the way a woman made up her face, but having observed Laura and Sophie get ready many times, it was hard to miss the stark contrast. Beth's products were arranged in an assembly line, each with its corresponding applicator behind it. There was beauty in her order, much like the beauty of her face.

"Did you say something?" Beth called out while simultaneously firing up the blow dryer.

"I said, my dad's not at risk for the clap," he repeated, this time much louder.

"Sheesh, you don't have to yell," Beth said, but she turned off the hair dryer and emerged from the bathroom smiling. Since she'd returned from her business trip, they'd been civil but overly formal, moving around each other like chess pieces wary of attack.

"He has a lady friend. I don't know what they do together. Probably Bingo. He said something about doctors' appointments."

"Matthew, your father had Viagra. They're playing more than Bingo. I'm happy for him. Sylvia's shoes aren't easy to fill." Neither are yours, Matthew thought, watching her step into heels that sharpened the muscles in her calves. "I've got to get to a meeting."

"Wait, there's something else," Matthew said. "Two something elses. The first is that I thought long and hard about what you said about my family. It was hard to hear, but you weren't wrong. I owe you a lot for giving me direction, even if ultimately I didn't love the path."

Beth sat down on the bed. It wasn't like her to be late, so he wondered if she had fabricated the meeting. "I was wrong, too. I could see you didn't love being a lawyer as much as I did. I saw a clear path for myself to become successful and I put you on the same track with virtually no consideration for what you wanted. You had the luxury of time to figure things out and I robbed you of that. Maybe you'd still be working if I hadn't put you on the legal hamster wheel."

Her last sentence stung. It was clear that a world in which he was a true stay-at-home-dad was not within her comfort zone. It wasn't necessarily within his either, but he needed a break. And time to straighten Austin out.

"Let's table that for now because the 'something else' is bigger. I looked on Austin's laptop while he was with the cantor. Not only did he have some really, um, explicit pornography open, he was also in a chat room with someone claiming to be a teenage girl but could be—"

She clapped a hand to her mouth. "A perverted man living in his mother's basement or worse," Beth said, her voice trembling. "This is terrible. What are we going to do? First the drugs, now this. What's wrong with our son?"

"I did some research. Apparently there's nothing wrong with our son. He's doing what most kids his age are doing. I even called Dr. Fleishman. But we clearly need to keep a very close eye on him. And he and I will have a very serious talk that hopefully scares the crap out of him."

"Both of us," Beth said. "We will both speak to him. I'll come home early today and we'll speak to him the minute he's back from school. Anything else happen while I was gone? Laura join a cult? Noah knock up a stripper?"

Matthew laughed. "Nope. You're fully up to speed as far as I know. At least tomorrow will be great. I'm excited for Sophie and it'll be nice to all be together again. We haven't seen her in person since she got engaged."

"That reminds me. I bought two of Sophie's artworks," Beth said. "I contacted the gallery and asked to hold the two best pieces, but not to tell Sophie who bought them yet. It ought to give her a nice boost of confidence before the show."

"She'll be so happy. And that was really nice of you." Matthew pulled Beth close and traced her collarbone with his finger. "I love you."

"I love you too." She reached into her briefcase and pulled out a file folder. "Take a look at these when you have a moment."

When she was gone, Matthew opened the folder and found dozens of brochures, business cards and floor plans. Loveladies. Ship Bottom. Harvey Cedars. Barnegat Light. All houses on Long Beach Island. All for sale. Each of them large enough to host his entire family. He dug up a picture from his camera roll of him and Beth playing with Austin in Beach Haven. It was taken at the beach in the spot where Austin took his first steps. He sent Beth the picture with a smiley face emoji.

Studying the different brochures and Beth's copious notes in the margins (*small kitchen . . . too few bathrooms . . . needs a new deck*), he felt renewed appreciation for his wife. He couldn't get over her thoughtfulness, buying two of Sophie's artworks in advance of the show. He hoped they weren't too risqué—he had little familiarity with his sister's recent work but was certain he didn't need a self-portrait of her private parts hanging over his dining room table. The storage cage in the basement of their building would come in handy if that was the case.

Just then, he heard Austin moving about the kitchen. He tabled thoughts of the laptop discovery and went to join him.

"Want me to make you pancakes?"

Austin brightened. "Yes, please. Chocolate chip?"

It was amazing how Austin could seem both like a small boy and a young man at the same time. Though maybe that mutability was universal. Matthew was a child around Leo, an authority figure around his son and something in between with his wife and siblings. Age, maturity, status . . . was it all fluid and impossible to measure? Not unlike happiness, he realized. Not unlike fortune.

FANTASTIC FOURSOME 🥷 🥷 ✡ 🥷 🥷

> **MATTHEW**
>
> Dad has a girlfriend

NOAH

NFW

LAURA

Whooooooooooo????

> **MATTHEW**
>
> Annette

SOPHIE

That's not helpful

> **MATTHEW**
>
> I'm sorry I was dealing with my son's porn addiction and talking to dad about condoms—didn't catch her last name

SOPHIE

Sheesh

LAURA

Does she live at boca breezes

SOPHIE

Wonder if she's hot

NOAH

Does no one else find this weird

LAURA

No

SOPHIE

No

MATTHEW

No; i'm focused on porn-gate

NOAH

Dude, let me handle this. I'm the cool single uncle. Let me take a crack at it

MATTHEW

Happy to abdicate if Beth's on board

SOPHIE

Guys! Harriett texted. Someone already bought two of my paintings!!!

MATTHEW

That's amazing

13

Sophie

"DOES THIS OUTFIT SAY I'M A RISING STAR IN THE ART WORLD?"
Sophie twirled around in Ravi's apartment—*their* apartment now—
and tada-ed with her hands.

"Absolutely," Ravi said, letting out a loud whistle. "And it's hot."

"It's also itchy as hell," Sophie said. "But I think a black turtleneck dress is the only way to go."

"You're the Steve Jobs of the art world," Ravi said. "And how
about my ensemble?" He popped the collar of his navy button-down
playfully. "The other half of a successful art duo or waiter at Apple-
bee's?"

"I'll have the quesadilla burger with fries and a Diet Coke," Sophie said. "Kidding, you look amazing. Besides, waiters don't wear
wallet chains." She firmly pressed her lips to Ravi's and lingered,
knowing they'd be pulled in separate directions at the gallery.

In the corner of the room, also making an adorable pair, were
Iris and Jasper, Sophie's new labradoodle. The dog was by far her
best indulgence since winning the lottery. His coat was a shiny
golden mess of curls, which Sophie compulsively tousled. Jasper (as
in Johns, her favorite artist) had a downward-curving mouth that
made him look like he was always begging for a tummy rub. She and
Ravi had started the search for a new apartment; a building that

accommodated a combined ninety pounds of greyhound plus labra-doodle was essential.

"How are you feeling?" Ravi asked. "Big night."

"Nervecited," Sophie said. She'd learned that word from the P.S. 282 kids. "Harriett is really optimistic. Did I tell you I tried to give her credit for giving me the idea in the *ARTnews* interview, but she was insistent that I say the entire concept is mine, from idea to execution? She knows best, I guess."

Ravi picked up the catalog for Sophie's show, which listed the pieces and their prices. On the cover it said "Emptiness" in small font, the name of Sophie's collection. The works were eclectic in style but uniform in theme. She thought back to the conversation that started it all, back in Miami during Art Basel. After her heart-to-heart with Leo, Sophie met up with Ravi and Harriett at her party. They stayed until the last guests left and it was just Harriett and the two of them drinking flat champagne and gossiping about the party-goers. Harriet knew who was buying what and for how much and which dealer was shady and which collector bought art to launder money. A little bit drunk and emotional from the conversation with her father, Sophie had a tough time pretending everything was copacetic when Harriett inquired about her work.

"I'm calling you next time I'm in New York to talk about this more," Harriett had said, which turned out to be a week later. Over double-shot lattes topped with Instagrammable foam art, Sophie confessed that her inspiration had dried up since winning the Powerball. That despite having a beautiful, temperature-controlled, well-ventilated studio, top-of-the-line brushes, imported paints and all the time in the world, her brain was a morass when she stood at the canvas.

"That's your story," Harriett had exclaimed, slapping her hand on the table and sending the flatware rattling. The gallerist then pulled a chic, Moleskine notebook from her menswear utility bag and started scribbling. Sophie peered across the table and saw a mix of random words. *Emptiness. Greed. Inspiration* (crossed out). *Loot. Winner. Loser.* "Your art should reflect how you feel. And you feel disappointed with how the lottery changed your life. How the reality was nothing like what you imagined. Tell that story."

Harriett's enthusiasm was infectious. Sophie did have something to say! Money doesn't buy happiness. It doesn't inspire creativity. Endless free time isn't a boon. How to translate those sentiments into art? Between her and Harriett, they came up with dozens of ideas, most of them Harriett's, but she contributed enough to feel ownership over the concept. She could barely wait to get back to the studio, her marching orders in hand. She started producing at rapid speed, the pieces accumulating at a pace she never imagined possible. Harriett checked in every day to make sure she was on track. It was like having a personal trainer, someone to hold her accountable and encourage her when doubt crept in.

Projecting her feelings about the money onto her art was cathartic in a way she hadn't expected. It made her rethink the purpose of creation. It wasn't just about sharing. It was transference.

"Listen, Soph, I want to talk to you before you become the hottest artist in New York City tonight and have no time for a proper conversation." Ravi pulled her toward the sofa. He took her left hand in his and twisted the engagement ring he'd made for her around in circles. "I know you didn't ask for this—yet, anyway—but I wanted to tell you that I'm completely prepared to sign a prenup before the wedding. I don't want your money to come between us. I loved you before you were a lottery winner and I love you now, regardless."

Sophie was stunned. She knew she would need to broach this

topic eventually, but they hadn't even set a wedding date yet. She hardly expected Ravi to raise it first, and so lovingly. With her show only an hour from starting, a fiancé who volunteered to sign a prenup and a puppy so adorable that even his slobber was pleasing, Sophie didn't think it was possible to feel any happier.

AS INSTRUCTED, HER FAMILY MEMBERS ARRIVED THIRTY MIN- utes before the show opened to the public. Sophie wanted time to walk them through. The gallery was located on a hip Lower East Side side street, sandwiched between an herbal apothecary and a tattoo parlor.

"I remember when this neighborhood used to be for knishes and pickles," Leo said, pointing at a store sign. "What in the world is Tibetan aromatherapy?"

Sophie walked Laura, Doug, Matthew, Beth, Noah and Leo through the two rooms of the exhibition, her toes tingling both from excitement and a lack of circulation from her narrow pumps. She had signed every piece in the lower right corner with her initials, SCP, Sophie Claire Jacobson, and seeing those three letters repeated on each of the twenty works for sale (technically eighteen since two were sold) was both humbling and surreal.

The first painting was a large white canvas filled with rows of dollar signs painted in black.

"S for Sophie?" Doug asked, confused.

"They're dollar signs, but I've subverted them by drawing the lines horizontally instead of vertically. Also, if you look closely, the dollar signs get marginally smaller in each row." Sophie watched Laura and Doug exchange a look. She wasn't discouraged. They weren't artsy people; their "collection" consisted of cartoon teeth posters hung askew in Doug's office. "Most people don't realize how much taxes diminish a lottery win. And that the prize is cut in half if you take a lump sum."

"You mean discounted to present value," Leo said.

"Exactly!" Sophie was pleased. "So it's about that, but also how the lottery can make life feel smaller."

She moved on to the next work, her first experience with papier-mâché outside the classroom. She had shellacked dozens of news articles in a soupy mixture of water and glue and arranged them in layers on a canvas. They were all about lottery winners whose lives were ruined by the windfall. Depression, divorce, substance abuse, fraud. In some cases, even suicide. "I call this one *Breaking News*."

Noah approached the work more closely, his eyes in a squint. "Is that a—?"

"A coffin? Yes," Sophie said. She'd been uncertain about using that particular image, especially in the center of the work, but Harriett said it would deliver the impact necessary to break out with a point of view. Harriett kept emphasizing that a successful art show sparks conversation and raises difficult questions. Didn't Sophie want to make waves? When Sophie expressed her uncertainty to Ravi, he told her to trust Harriett, that she was just having preshow jitters.

She walked her family to the opposite side of the room, where one of her two sculptures rested on a white pedestal. She had glued together 261 containers of gold glitter, to represent the $261 million jackpot, but emptied each container so that they were just empty plastic tubes with only the label remaining. It was her favorite work at the show. She could see her students' sweet faces in her mind's eye while she worked on it. Because it stood over eight feet tall, Sophie had expected it would be a tougher piece to move, but to her surprise and delight Harriett reported it was one of the pieces that had sold prior to opening night.

Beth was admiring the work, her gaze sweeping the sculpture. "What's this one called?"

Sophie beamed. "*All that Glitters Is Not Gold*."

"Hmmm," Beth said, looping her arm through Matthew's to pull him closer to the sculpture. "It's so . . . tall."

She overheard a muted exchange between Matthew and Beth. *Where would we . . . Shipping . . .* Sophie hated to disappoint them. "Actually, this piece is already sold," she said.

"Honey," Leo said. He had moved beyond the sculpture and was standing next to a photograph of Gin Lane, the most exclusive street on the East End of Long Island. Sophie had taken the picture a month earlier, in the dead of winter. The mansions looked barren and sterile, exposed behind anemic hedges, and the street looked far more spooky than glamorous.

"I'm still new to photography," she said to her father, anxious for his reaction. Sophie felt a different kind of pressure having her father there—like she was fulfilling both of their dreams. He'd never had the opportunity to pursue his art the way she was now.

"Can you point me to the restroom?" he said.

"Oh, um, sure. It's down that hallway, past the potato sacks with Monopoly money." Sophie watched him shuffle to the back of the gallery, disappointed. Perhaps he just needed more time to digest—the art, that is.

Harriet swept into the room, dressed in a smart caftan paired with shiny silver brogues. "Sophie, darling, I need you for a moment. One of my most important clients has arrived early and he'd like a private audience with you."

Sophie relished the triumph of being whisked away to speak to a VIP and was only sad her father missed it. The conversation with the high-end collector, a Russian businessman who jabbered "*Da*" into his cell phone and barely looked up, was a tad deflating. She tried to remain optimistic. She didn't know the rules of engagement among this milieu. For all she knew, the Russian had already wired money for an expensive piece to hang in his dacha.

Then came the appointed start time, and sophie's stomach was in fresh knots. Would anyone actually turn up, she wondered, as the memory of her eleventh birthday took hold. Sophie's birthday was in July, which meant she was always at the shore, away from her school friends. Emerging from the shyness that categorized her elementary school years, she had agreed to a party. Sylvia was overjoyed. Her party-planning skills were somewhat dormant during the summer season, so she relished the chance to choose invitations and color-coordinated paper goods for the occasion. For her theme, Sophie chose *Titanic*, the biggest movie of the year. All anyone could talk about was how hot Leo was. Sophie agreed, but couldn't fall head over heels for a heartthrob who shared a name with her father.

When the day of the party arrived, Sophie panicked. A sinking ship was an inauspicious choice for a beach party. What was she thinking? She remembered flattening the beach blankets and jamming the umbrella stands into the sand along with her mother, her eyes darting constantly to the planked stairs that led from the road to the beach. She was positive no one would come. The girls she played tennis with at the LBI Foundation weren't close friends. Sophie suspected they didn't even like her—she was a terrible athlete and nobody wanted her as a doubles partner. For sure they had better things to do on a Sunday afternoon, like hang around the Ron Jon Surf Shop where the boys clustered. "They're coming, honey, they're coming," Sylvia said, intuiting Sophie's nerves. And they did. The party was a great success. Everybody was impressed with the cake Sylvia had made to look like the blue diamond. Sophie channeled her mother's comforting voice now: *"They're coming. They're coming."*

And they did. Critics, artists, collectors and the young, cool set that gets invited everywhere for no actual reason turned out in droves for Sophie's show. Harriett and Ravi had been right. She was worried for nothing. The first hour passed in a blur. Sophie pingponged across the gallery, repeating "Thank you so much" over and over until her jaw locked and her tongue went numb. There was a palpable energy as the well-heeled rubbed elbows with the hipsters and everyone pounded the champagne and plucked goat cheese tartlets off shiny trays. Sophie couldn't recall the details of any single conversation. Had she been asked about individual pieces? Her process? What she was working on now? Probably all of it, but her senses had melded into one super-sense. She was smelling the conversations, hearing the champagne, tasting the colors.

As her body acclimated to the overstimulation and the opening moved into its second hour, Sophie felt the energy in the gallery shift. For one thing, it wasn't nearly as crowded as when the doors opened. And rather than being flooded by people wanting to talk to her, Sophie caught a few sets of eyes avoiding her gaze. She checked her phone to see if there was breaking news that soured the mood. The top two stories on the CNN app were about a congressman caught Snapping with underage girls and a protest outside of a McDonald's over a Big Mac price hike. Run-of-the-mill stories. Across the room, she saw Ravi huddled with Harriett. They stopped talking when she approached.

"What are you two scheming over here? If it's where to go celebrate after, the answer is nowhere until I get out of these heels."

Neither Ravi nor Harriett smiled. The crowd looked even thinner from their vantage point. "The champagne probably went flat.

This crowd wants IPAs anyway," Sophie said, but they still didn't respond. Sophie's underarms were quietly getting soaked. She cursed her choice of cashmere.

"Sophie, darling," Harriet began, although the "darling" was slightly condescending, not convivial. "The show is not being received the way I—well—what I mean to say is that your work is not being . . . I suppose in hindsight—" The normally smooth Harriett was flummoxed. Sophie looked to Ravi. Weirdly, he took a few steps back. She noticed his cologne grow fainter. Her senses were back in order, only now she wished she could turn them off.

"It's not good," he finally said. Fishing his phone from the back pocket of his black jeans, he opened Twitter and held the screen up to her face. Under "Trending" she saw a hashtag gaining traction by the second.

#poorlittlerichgirl

What? What did that have to do with her show? Why was Ravi showing her this?

And then it hit her, all at once, and she had to lean a hand on the wall for support because Ravi was too far away to grab on to.

BACK UPTOWN, SOPHIE PACED THE CREAKING WOODEN FLOOR, Iris and Jasper staring at her from their dog beds, confused by the change to their evening routine.

"They misunderstood everything I was trying to convey!"

"I was literally pointing out that family, love, the environment, fucking world peace are what matters, not money."

"Jeff Koons can take a crap in a glass jar and people applaud him. I try to say something and—"

From his seat on the edge of the couch, Ravi raised his head and spoke for the first time in a while. "That was Damien Hirst."

Sophie stopped pacing. "Huh?"

"The crap. It was Hirst, not Koons. It was a commentary on—"

She resumed her back-and-forth marching. "I don't give a flying fuck what it was a commentary on. There's a double standard in the art world. If a man had mounted this show, well, humph. Ravi, are you listening to me?" Her fiancé's face was buried in his phone.

"Yes. I'm listening. But I'm also combing Twitter and figuring out how we're going to get ahold of this situation."

Sophie softened. She appreciated the "we" like never before. Her problems were his problems. Ravi had been distracted from the moment her show went south. It was comforting to see his mood reflecting her turmoil, that he was already focused on finding a solution.

"What are they saying about me? On that." She pointed an accusatory finger at his phone.

"You really want to know?"

She nodded, bracing herself by taking a seat and hoisting Jasper onto her lap. Nothing could be that bad if she had Jasper to shield her.

"People don't like that a lottery winner is whining about having money. They're calling you tone deaf, entitled, out of touch, insensitive, ungrateful—"

She held up a palm. "I get the idea."

"Hang on. There's a picture of you from your old studio posted by @pierredelyon. He said you refused to share your paint with the poor."

God damn Pierre from SHART. She didn't refuse to share her paint. He was a petty thief.

"You know that it was Harriett who pushed me in this direction, Ravi. She practically designed the work and left me to fabricate it. It just felt so good to have some direction. I couldn't think of any ideas on my own, and I do really believe in the messaging of this show, and—"

"It's more than that, Sophie."

Sophie? Ravi always called her Soph.

"They think for someone who supposedly believes money doesn't buy happiness and causes more problems than good, it's interesting that several of your paintings were priced north of ten thousand dollars. Artists are upset because they're struggling to make ends meet and you're clearly not. Collectors are upset because they don't like thinking about their money in that way. And critics, well you know how they are."

Great, so she had offended the entire trifecta. Sophie thought about the way her family had responded when she toured them around. The looks they exchanged. Of all people, her father and siblings knew that winning the lottery was no panacea. But they had foreseen the reaction and she had not. If she had run the ideas by them while she was working on the pieces, maybe all this could have been avoided.

Her phone buzzed. She'd been ignoring the rings, pings and dings since getting home. Now she glanced. The most recent message was from Matthew: Beth and I are really excited about The Buck Stops Here and All That Glitters. We may need to crane the sculpture through the window, but it will look awesome in our living room. Great job, sis.

So it was Matthew and Beth who bought the two works. They had left the show early to get home to Austin.

"Ravi, this is so sweet. My brother was the mystery buyer."

"Nice," Ravi said absentmindedly. He was bent over his laptop with the same intense look he got when he fell into a bidding war for limited edition art on eBay.

"What are you doing?" Sophie took a seat next to him.

"Looking for new representation. Harriett is finished. At least for a while, anyway. I hitched my wagon to the wrong star, clearly. The sooner I extricate myself from this, the better."

"What are you saying? Harriett believes in you. She got your water jug in Basel for crying out loud. You can't just desert her."

He snapped his laptop shut and looked at Sophie like she was a foolish child. "This is my career. I can't remain loyal to her if she's tainted."

"Tainted." What a word. Sophie felt her heart muscle tensing. "And what about me?" she asked.

"Well, it's good we're not married yet. At least we don't have the same last name. I googled our names and there are only like three or four pictures of us together so I don't think it'll be an issue."

"An issue," she repeated.

"It's funny," Ravi said, wry half-smile on his face. "I was never a gold digger, you know that. When you won the lottery, it didn't change my feelings. That's why I wanted to bring up the prenup first. But I thought that the win would bring some benefit to both of us. The money would help us gain access to certain collectors. We could travel to the international art fairs and be at the right parties." He guffawed. "I didn't expect the money to do the exact opposite for my career. We probably need to keep our distance in public for a while."

She rose in spite of her wobbly knees.

"Jasper, come," she called to her dog, who had settled back onto his bed. She grabbed the leash from the coffee table.

"You're taking him out now? Would you mind walking Iris around the block while you're at it?"

Sophie looked at him in disbelief. "No, I'm not taking Jasper out. I'm leaving with Jasper." She pulled off her engagement ring and let it drop to the floor. "Have a nice life, Ravi."

"You're joking, right? Sophie, you need to get a grip. You're not thinking straight." Ravi sounded far more shocked than upset.

"I'm not joking. I need a partner who thinks about me before himself when I'm in crisis." She swung open the front door, tugging at Jasper to follow. Ducking her head back in, she said, "By the way, your water jug looks like a deformed penis."

FANTASTIC FOURSOME 🥷 🥷 ✡ 🥷 🥷

NOAH

Ravi Patel is dead to me

LAURA

Can I finally admit I hate his art

MATTHEW

Our housekeeper threw out the vase he made that u gave us for Hanukkah. She thought it was trash

SOPHIE

Awww, i love u guys. was his stuff really ugly?

LAURA

HE was ugly. on the inside anyway

SOPHIE

Sigh. He was so pretty on the outside

MATTHEW

Austin is working on something that may help you Soph

SOPHIE

Pot gummies?

MATTHEW

Ha, no.

LAURA

S—u r spilling popcorn in the couch cushions

NOAH

You guys r together?

LAURA

Same room

SOPHIE

R u going to cancel me too

LAURA

No. just make u vacuum

MATTHEW

Who's excited for Austin's BM?

It's really soon

Alrighty then

14

Laura

LAURA HEARD THE BLANKET RUSTLING AND A GLASS CLINK
against the coffee table, which meant her sister was up from her nap.
She'd grown accustomed to deciphering these sounds since Sophie
moved in "temporarily" after the art show debacle and her breakup.
After leaving Ravi's place, Sophie had taken an Uber to New Jersey,
arriving on Laura's doorstep at one a.m. with nothing but her purse
and a forty-pound mixed-breed in tow. Doug answered the door
wearily, hugged her, patted Jasper's head and said they could take
any bedroom in the house. Laura watched the scene unfold from the
second-floor landing with deep appreciation for her husband.

Sophie took over one of the main-floor guest rooms. Her stuff
arrived the next day in cardboard boxes shoddily taped up and left
haphazardly at the end of their driveway. Doug hauled them into
the house and left them outside Sophie's room. For a full twenty-
four hours after her arrival, they didn't see her face. The only sounds
from her room were Jasper's intermittent barks. When Laura and
Doug went to the kitchen on the second morning of her stay, they
observed with relief that the milk carton was lighter and the Cheerios
were in a different spot. Laura wondered if she should buy dog food.
Did Ravi send Jasper's food in the boxes? The guest room had a sliding door to the outside, which Sophie clearly utilized to let Jasper

out. The energetic way he dug up their shrubs coupled with the evidence that his digestive tract was functioning (discovered by a barefoot Doug going out for the paper) confirmed Jasper was being fed.

"Everyone hates me."

These were Sophie's first words when she emerged on day two, tossing her phone at Laura as evidence. "I can never show my face in public again."

She made Laura and Doug read through every vicious tweet and blog post. The haters had even come after Jasper. A lot of people were angry that Sophie hadn't gotten a rescue. #poorlittlerichpup trended for a hot second.

The online vitriol was real, but the hashtag #poorlittlerichgirl (and #pup) all but died out within forty-eight hours. The world moved on. Since Sophie's show, a Kardashian announced a pregnancy, a polarizing former president insulted a female world leader in Europe and Apple announced a new iPhone drop. Sophie's show was ancient history, at least in the theater of the Internet. Whether she had a chance at redemption as a professional artist, Laura had no idea.

"And Ravi? I mean, what the hell? I wasted almost three years with that guy. I know you guys trash talked him after the show, but you liked him before."

"But *you* had hesitations," Laura said. "There was a reason you weren't jumping to move in with him. You were just more intuitive than us. Must be your kind, artist soul."

"Ravi is an artist too," Sophie pointed out.

"Well, some artists can be dicks," Doug said. He had a higher tolerance for reading the cruelty than Laura did. Each insult lobbed at her little sister brought Laura back to the day she overheard a group of girls gossiping about Sophie at the Custard Hut. Laura was sixteen at the time, Sophie eleven.

"Eww, I can't believe the bathing suit Sophie wore to her birthday party," one of the brats said.

"I know, she looked like a mermaid. Oh my God—do you think she was trying to be the Little Mermaid because she's a redhead? That would be so lame," another of the mean girls said.

They giggled that smug, high-pitched squeal of girls ganging up on the vulnerable, momentarily emboldened by group think to forget their own insecurities. Laura let them go on for a few moments longer before she pounced. When she was called up to place her order (Muddy Sneakers—Laura's favorite ice cream flavor to this day), she turned around abruptly.

"I'm Sophie's older sister. And I wouldn't be caught dead going anywhere in what you girls are wearing. And you—" Laura pointed at the ringleader. "That tube top you're wearing is held up by pure desperation alone." She never told Sophie what happened, and she never would.

"We are passionate," Sophie explained to Doug. "Artists, I mean. It's normally a good thing."

Doug waved his hand dismissively. "I prefer dentists."

"Me too." Laura kissed Doug.

Slowly but surely, a routine took hold. Sophie would sleep late, have breakfast that she did a poor job of cleaning up, then camp out in the den, where she alternated long naps with reality TV. Commercials for diamonds and life insurance made her cry, so Laura set up tissue boxes on each side table. Laura didn't try to coax Sophie outside, even though developing bed sores (technically couch sores) was not an impossibility. She didn't want to rush her sister when she was this fragile. Besides, Laura liked having her around.

The new house was too big and too quiet with just her and Doug. In their old place, the heat rattled like a chainsaw and the refrigerator hummed out of tune, but the noises were oddly comforting. In fancy Franklin Lakes, everything worked just a little too well. Back in Westfield, they had lived on a quarter-acre lot where Laura could hear the neighbors' kids playing in the backyard and their phones ringing if the window was open. When she went to the mailbox, she inevitably got into a five-minute conversation with a neighbor or a friend driving by. She used to resent it—*I just want to get the damn mail without seeing Liz DiMarco gardening in her bathrobe . . . Peter Dubinsky talked my ear off about the new shopping center in town*— but what she wouldn't give now for a little friendly banter. Their closest neighbor in Franklin Lakes was a long walk away, and there were so many trees and fences dividing their properties each place felt like a fortress. She missed book club and the PTA and the run-ins at ShopRite. She missed texting her mom crew about Old Navy sales.

Laura liked having someone to care for again. She checked with Sophie every morning about what she wanted to eat for lunch and dinner, adjusted her blanket when it shifted during a nap and lis-tened to her ramble on about Ravi and her failed career, always quick to chime in with, "You poor thing." Then there was Jasper, another handful to dote on. At first Laura worried the puppy would soil the Oriental rugs and destroy the furniture, but he was easy to train— far more pliable than her daughters. A few YouTube videos were all she needed to housebreak him and he became pure joy.

Doug, Laura assumed, felt the same way about their houseguests. Surely he realized that it diffused the tension between them, still palpable even though three months had passed since Laura had crashed Doug's business dinner with the SMILE executive. The house would get even busier when the girls returned home for spring break in a matter of days. Laura was counting the minutes until she could hug them and grill them about school. It would be nice if So-phie could get her shit together a little bit before they arrived. There were no YouTube videos for that, and Laura worried the girls would be upset seeing their aunt in such a sorry state.

"How's our houseplant?" Doug came up behind Laura at the kitchen desk. She had plunged down an Etsy rabbit hole, searching for monogrammed towels for the girls' dorm rooms in a particular shade of ecru.

"Our what?" Laura looked up from the screen, surprised to see Doug dressed in scrubs. She hadn't laid eyes on the teal uniform in ages. He'd turned over his practice to SMILE in February and signed on as an investor and consultant. Most of the work he did remotely.

Doug gestured in the direction of the den, where the bottom third of chartreuse sweatpants was visible. "Wears green, doesn't move much."

"Ahh, you mean Sophie. I think she needs watering," Laura said. "But she'll live."

Doug smiled. "I should hope so. That room gets a lot of sunlight."

"Yeah, I think her head is starting to grow in the direction of the window."

"I heard that," Sophie called out. "It's my ass that's growing and it's in the direction of the couch. Francois drops off some seriously unhealthy food. We're not French. We can't eat that much butter."

Doug reached for a notepad and pen and scribbled *SHE HAS TO GO*. Laura's assumption that he appreciated the company as much as she did was obviously incorrect.

She nodded. He was still scribbling. *AND HER LITTLE DOG TOO.*

"Soph, honey," Laura said cautiously. "Can you come to the kitchen?"

"Why? I just got comfortable."

"Because you're squatting in our house and we asked you to?" Laura responded. Doug gave her a thumbs-up.

"Fine. I'm coming."

They heard her socks make the whooshing sound that announced her whereabouts as she moved about the house. She ambled into the kitchen, her hair piled to one side in a straggly bun. Jasper perked up when he saw his owner in an upright position and licked her ankles. "You rang?"

"Soph, you know we love you so much. And we feel terrible about what happened at your show and how Ravi acted afterward. There's no question you've been going through a rough time. We just think that—" Laura paused and looked at Doug, half expecting him to leave the room. When she disciplined the girls, even at his behest, she couldn't always count on him for backup. He liked being the nice guy. One tear from either daughter and he'd crumble like a cookie—the cookie he'd buy them to make up for upsetting his girls in the first place.

"We—mostly I—think you need to pull yourself together and move out," Doug said. "Yes, your life has taken a turn and I'm sure it feels like rubbish and we will always be there for you. But we raised two girls and it was bloody exhausting. We're done."

Laura stared at her husband. Who was this man suddenly willing to play bad cop? And why was his alter ego British?

"Sheesh. Is it that bad?" Sophie tried to take down her hair, but the elastic was tangled in her bun. Laura went for the scissors.

"There's room for improvement." He gestured to the capless Tropicana on the counter. "Emma and Hannah never replaced the cap either. Must be genetic. Anyway, my point is that we love those girls to infinity and beyond, but we've put in our time. They needed to leave the nest. And so do you. Laura and I want time to be together, just the two of us."

We do? Laura let the question swirl around in her head until it turned into a declarative statement. *We do!*

"Being splayed on the couch all day and seeing nobody but the two of us isn't doing much for your mental health," Laura said. "Besides, you don't want those haters online to have been right about you."

Sophie's expression went from downtrodden to confused. "What do you mean?" She scratched at her scalp, releasing a flurry of dandruff, and Sophie wondered if perhaps hair washing wasn't a part of her daily routine.

Laura felt her throat closing. She took the glass of water in Doug's hand and chugged. "What I mean is that your critics—I don't know what else to call them—thought you were unappreciative of the lottery win. And by sitting around all day watching TV and feeling sorry for yourself, you're not doing much to prove them wrong."

Sophie folded her arms across her chest defensively. "Oh, and you two are? Buying a monstrous house for just the two of you in some stuck-up town where you have no friends? Going on fancy vacations when you were both clearly miserable?"

"We have friends here," Laura said. "There's Karen, from Pilates. And Cynthia, who I always run into at the nail salon. And Debra—Doug really likes her husband—what's his name again?" Doug looked at Laura blankly. It had been less than a year since they'd moved to Franklin Lakes, but she knew it was past the time when their newness was an excuse for their lack of social life. It was unquestionably harder to make friends without having kids in the local schools, but Laura had made an earnest effort. Shown up to town hall meetings. Volunteered at the library. Used a reformer in Pilates class that looked like a piece of medieval torture equipment. She'd even borrowed Jasper to take to the dog park, but it was all part-time dog walkers half her age. The women were cliquey and only showed her the most basic courtesy. Franklin Lakes families had money from real-estate holdings and high-powered finance jobs, or, the holy grail, generational wealth, and they looked down at the Cohens' shortcut. As though their riches were ill-gotten.

"You're right," Doug said. "We don't have friends around here. And you're right about the dumb vacations. I just want to eat good food—three courses max—see some sights and sleep in a comfortable bed. I don't need an amuse-bouche or a palate cleanser or a bathrobe made from Himalayan sheep's wool. There's a point of excess. We're throwing the money away on gold-leafed food and sterile massages that don't mean anything. The truth is, nobody in this family handled the lottery particularly well."

"God, that's really true," Sophie said. "Do the Jackpot Jacobsons suck?"

Laura let out a wallop. "I think we might. To be honest, I feel kind of lost. I had friends where we used to live—good ones. And a purpose. Taking care of Emma and Hannah may not have been a lofty career, but I was a good mom. Am a good mom."

"So what should we do?" Sophie asked. "Not another tell-all art show, that much I know."

Doug pulled open the refrigerator, where the evening's delivery dinner was plated and awaiting warm-up later. Three lamb chops nestled on beds of sweet potato mash rested on bone china, asparagus stalks arranged in a crisscross pattern on the side. A mound of mint jelly glistened in a silver dish.

"We start by not eating this," he said. "How about McDonald's? I've got to see an old patient whose implant fell out, but we can hit the drive-thru first."

Sophie smiled for the first time in weeks. Laura admired her dazzling teeth. Doug had made her whitening trays after she got engaged.

"I would absolutely kill for a Happy Meal," Sophie said.

A happy meal. They needed it figuratively even more than literally.

"CAN WE KEEP HIM?" HANNAH WAS CROUCHED ON THE GROUND, practically French-kissing Jasper, her backpack and jacket still on.

"Yeah, can we?" Emma echoed, rubbing Jasper's tummy.

"He's not ours to keep," Laura said, though the childlike purity the dog brought out in her girls was reason enough to consider getting a dog of their own. A rescue, perhaps one of the dogs that Sophie had signed up to foster through a volunteer agency a few days ago.

"Can we hear about school? How were midterms?" Doug asked. He was at the game table, financial papers spread out in front of him. SMILE was seeing decent growth. Doug was relishing his role on the team, noting to Laura every time one of his comments on a Zoom was received with a "Good point" or "Great idea." After the failed attempts to expand his own practice, Doug needed this win. Laura was glad the lottery afforded him the opportunity to become a SMILE investor. It was doing wonders for his self-esteem.

"Pretty good. I think I'll have mostly A-minuses this term," Emma said.

"I didn't study," Hannah said. "Now that we're rich it doesn't really matter how I do in school."

Laura and Doug looked at each other, their eyes widening in horror.

"I'm kidding!" Hannah said. "Give me some credit. I'm doing really well. Actually, I have something to discuss with you both."

Laura couldn't help her reflexive angst. When she was not much older than Hannah, she told her own parents "something important." Technically, she made Matthew break the news first. She still owed him for that. That "something important" turned into Emma nine months later. She braced herself.

"Remember that program I did over the summer? The mentoring?" Hannah said. Of course Laura remembered the program that made her an empty nester two months ahead of schedule. "I've gotten pretty involved with the group that runs it on campus. They offer tutoring services during the school year too. I'm joining the executive board. It'll be a ton of work on top of my classes, but I really vibe with their mission."

Laura and Doug locked eyes again. It was hard to believe this was the same girl who once colored in a blank periodic table of elements with the NARS eyeshadow palette when she was supposed to be studying for a chemistry test.

"Anyway, the board's goal is to expand the program to other colleges in the area. Georgetown, American, Howard. Maybe even outside DC eventually. Emma said she could maybe bring it to Colgate. To grow, the program needs at least one full-time, nonstudent staff member. And someone to build and maintain our website. I was thinking that maybe you guys would want to help?"

"Han, I'm thrilled to see you so passionate about a good cause." Doug went to give Hannah a noogie, a tender gesture she loved or hated depending on whether a blow dry was at stake. "Mom and I will need to—"

"I'll do it," Laura said. Just then Sophie came through the front door, sweaty from a jog. She was slowly getting back to her old self, thanks to an all-nighter where she and Laura planned her immediate next steps: find a place to live, rent one of the private studios at SHART and create a dating profile on Hinge.

"Do what?" Sophie asked as she embraced her nieces.

"Hannah was just telling us that she's getting more involved with the mentoring program she did over the summer. They need a full-time staff person. I think I could do it. The train ride to DC isn't so long and I could stay over a few nights a week. If and when it expands to Colgate, I'll do the same there." Laura was flush with excitement, imagining working alongside her daughters.

"Um, Mom, that sounds really awesome, but—" Hannah was fiddling with the zipper of her hoodie.

"Laura, she was asking us to give money to pay for a staff member. Not to actually be the staff." Doug rested a hand on her shoulder.

"Oh. I mean, of course. I knew that. I was just thinking—"

"It would be a lot for you to commute and you'd get annoyed pretty quickly being around college kids all the time," Hannah said. "But I'm sure you could do great work remotely. I'd love you to get involved."

"I could," Laura said, trying to conceal her disappointment. "And of course I'd be happy to donate to such a worthy cause. It's just that if I donate, oh, I don't know, fifty thousand dollars, I'd need to be close to the organization so I know the money is being well spent." She clapped her hands together. "Enough of that for now. We can discuss the details later. Girls, what do you want to do for your first day of break? I thought we could get manicures, then drive into the city to do a little shopping, have lunch someplace fabulous. Emma, didn't you always want to try Nobu?"

Emma looked up from her phone. "That sounds awesome, but I have plans to meet Tomas. Our breaks only overlap a week."

"Yeah, actually, I'm not free either." Hannah chewed her bottom lip. "I'm going to Key West with my suitemates. Surprise! We planned a last-minute spring break trip so I mostly came home to get my bathing suits and stuff. And to see you guys, of course. We're leaving tomorrow so I've got to spend the day getting ready."

Laura was confused. "Wouldn't getting ready include buying new bathing suits and beautifying at that fabulous day spa in town?"

"I mean, I guess—"

Sophie interjected. "Girls, go do what you have to do. I need your mom's advice about something." Laura shot Sophie a not-now look, but it went undetected.

After the girls disappeared, Doug said, "Soph, you want me out of here too?"

"Actually, I think it's better you stay."

"What's wrong? What do you need to talk about?" Laura took her sister's hand.

"I just said that to clear the girls out. Now, please don't take what I'm about to say the wrong way." Sophie was staring at Laura, waiting for a response.

"Okay, I promise, even though I have no idea what you're about to say. I want to double check with Hannah about the spa and shopping before she runs out the door. Can we chat in a second?"

"Actually, that's what I want to talk about. I know it's been hard to have Em and Han both out of the house. But you can't use the Powerball to keep them close. You dangled that donation in front of Hannah. You offer extravagant gifts and trips to the girls but only if you're included. I get it. I swear I get it. But it's not fair to offer lavish gifts with strings attached, especially when those strings are doused in mommy guilt."

"Your sister's right," Doug said. "Even this house. We bought some crazy castle to entice the girls to visit, but the truth is they'd rather be with their friends in a youth hostel than with their boring old parents in a mansion."

"Well, I wasn't lying about wanting to get involved with Hannah's organization. I would love to have a project to throw myself into. Austin's bar mitzvah is going to be over soon and then I'll be back to trying to get these snobs in Franklin Lakes to like me."

"You absolutely should get involved. I'm sure you can do a lot remotely. Maybe organize a benefit or something. Rich ladies love parties," Sophie said.

A benefit! Yes. But not with these fancy pants women. Laura knew just who to call upon. Her friends from Westfield, the ones she missed terribly but rarely called. Laura and her mom friends had served on countless PTA committees, wrapped gifts for Secret Santa and Hanukkah Harry and made waffles for the teacher appreciation breakfast. They could stuff envelopes for the mentoring program while chugging wine. They could plan a fundraising benefit in their sleep.

"I'm on it," Laura said. "You know, you're pretty smart for a little sister. I'm going to miss you too."

Sophie was moving out that week. Which meant Jasper too.

"You had a good run," Doug said, his hand on Laura's other shoulder. "But now you're stuck with me."

APRIL TURNED OUT TO BE THE RAINIEST MONTH LAURA COULD remember. She hoped the downpours would yield spectacular May flowers, but wouldn't be surprised if nothing bloomed after taking such a beating.

The house was back to its quiet state, save the drops pelting the windows and the rainfall whooshing through the rafters. The girls were back at school to finish out their freshman and sophomore years. Laura heard from them when they needed an essay proofread or a FaceTime explanation of how to work the campus laundry machines. She ultimately created a Venn diagram of their various clothing items to explain what should go in gentle cycle/cold water and what needed hot water/heavy soil, disappointed she hadn't made the girls do more chores around the house. "Mom, the label says 'hand wash' but it has a picture of a washing machine," Hannah whined on FaceTime from the basement laundry room in her dorm. "I think the water temperatures are written in Celsius," Emma called to say that very same night, holding up a tag to the camera lens, as if Laura could read such a tiny font. She liked to think her daughters had coordinated their laundry schedules, with "ugh, laundry night" texts to each other. There were services that would pick up the girls' laundry on campus, wash and fold it, and return it within the week, but damn if Laura was going to tell them about it.

Sophie texted Laura with regular updates on her reentry to society. She ran into Ravi on the street and he already had another girlfriend. A guy she hooked up with on Hinge was perfect except for hairy toes. After an initial ribbing when she returned to SHART, her coworkers were kind enough (except for lying-thieving Pierre) to move on from the gallery debacle.

Everyone around Laura was getting their lives in order. Noah sounded happy and clear-headed on the phone. He was excited that Beach Haven was coming out of the off season. May was a sweet spot when LBI wasn't lonely and desolate, but the traffic on Long Beach Boulevard wasn't yet gruesome. Matthew was a few months into his sabbatical—or permanent work stoppage, Laura didn't know—and looked calmer and healthier than she could remember. Doug was tickled with his SMILE involvement. He didn't miss drilling cavities and performing root canals but was happy to keep his toe in the dental waters.

Now it was Laura's turn to carve a path forward.

Soothed by a glass of wine and a pep talk from Sophie, Laura reached out to her old friends from Westfield one by one to reconnect. She asked after their families and told them about Hannah's nonprofit, asking if they might want to join Laura in getting involved. She skirted the questions that made her uncomfortable with jokes:

SHARON GOLDFARB

How's it feel to be a rich lady?

LAURA

I don't miss washing dishes.

JANET BONAPARTE

How many pairs of shoes do you own now?

LAURA

I still have that awful bunion and mostly wear sneakers.

SUZANNE DAVIDOWITZ

Is it hard to keep the girls grounded?

LAURA

About the same as when we grounded them in high school.

Eventually, they moved past the awkwardness, and Laura and her friends were back to their old routines, gossiping about which teachers were diddling each other over at the high school and which kids were getting into which colleges and who actually deserved it. Still, a forty-minute drive separated them, and though she made it to book club each month (the benefit of a quiet house was that she actually read the book, making her mother proud in heaven), Laura was spending her days surrounded by too much silence.

Her anniversary—she and Doug had been married nineteen years—was coming up in a matter of days. It would be their first since he suggested the separation and their first since the Powerball. Previously, they marked the occasion with an exchange of cards, purchased at the dollar store. Because the selection there was slim, unlike the rows of five-dollar cards at Walgreens, they often gave each other the same card. They agreed flowers were where money went to die. Doug would never splurge on a bouquet, and Laura would kill him if he did. She was hesitant to mention the occasion this year.

"Morning," Doug said, ambling into the kitchen and filling up his mug with coffee. "Sleep well?"

"Yes," Laura lied. A crack of thunder had woken her in the middle of the night and she'd been up since, waiting for daylight. "What are we doing for our anniversary?" she asked. So much for letting it lie.

"Glad you asked. I was looking into different options. We can do a helicopter ride over the city. There's also a boat with a private chef that can take us around the Hudson. If you're up for travel, we can do a few nights at one of those chichi hotels that opened in the Catskills. Anything sound good?"

Helicopters made Laura nervous. Boats made her seasick. She was too loyal to the Jersey Shore to go to the Catskills. How could she say that to Doug and not sound like a huge pain in the ass?

When she didn't respond, Doug went on. "I'm open to suggestions. A redo of the couple's massage I ruined in Dubai?"

"What if we watch TV and order in Chinese?" Laura recalled Sophie's admonishment on the museum steps that they were trying too hard, that their romantic dinners were contrived, their luxurious vacations scripted.

Doug looked skeptical.

"It's not a trick." He wasn't wrong to worry. Historically, Laura wasn't above setting Doug up to fail. "I really think a relaxed night at home would be perfect. No meal delivery service. No housekeepers around. Let's eat lo mein out of the containers and watch a garbage movie we've seen five times before. What do you think?"

Instead of relieved or excited, Doug appeared somber. Laura's stomach twisted into a too-familiar knot. Now what?

"You're not happy," Laura said.

"What? No? I'm very happy. It's just that I want to apologize to you. I was going to write this in my card, but now seems like a better time. Last year—what I said about wanting time apart—I was an idiot. The girls were leaving, my practice was getting crushed by SMILE and I didn't want to admit it, and I just freaked. It was an extremely stupid way of trying to cope with a midlife crisis. A motorcycle would have been a better option. Or a tattoo."

"Please no. To both." Laura swatted Doug's arm. "I'm not getting on the back of that thing and tattoos are for people born in this millennium."

"Don't worry. I'm terrified of both. I just want you to know that when I—you know, did that thing—I wasn't feeling good about myself, but I blamed our relationship rather than looking in the mirror. And I'm sorry."

Laura patted his knee. "I have plenty to apologize for too. I was so focused on the girls for years I forgot you might need me too. I resented you for having a family and a career when I could have pursued something if I'd really been determined. And then, after the Powerball, I thought our problems could be fixed with gold massages and ten-course meals."

"And let's not forget the meals that had gold in them," Doug said with a playful smirk. "I don't blame you for trying that tack. That lifestyle sure looks good on TV and in magazines. And, mortifying as it was, I don't blame you for spying on me at dinner. I'm probably the first man in history to spontaneously ask for a separation from his amazing wife without another woman in the picture."

"I am curious though. Why the sudden watching your weight? The cooler glasses? The—" She stopped midsentence and reached for her phone. She hadn't even told Sophie about this. She found the photo she was looking for and showed it to Doug.

He let out a chuckle, not the reaction she was expecting. "Laura, I bought that for your father. He asked me to." It was a package of Just for Men. "When he came up for Sophie's show, he asked if I color my hair. I'm less gray than Matthew so I guess he figured I did. I told him if he wanted to do something about his gray, he could try Just for Men. He didn't know what that was and asked me to pick it up. I forgot to give it to him."

Laura was incredulous. She had been so sure the hair dye was a smoking gun. And since when did her father care about his appearance? This Annette must be someone special.

"As for the other stuff," Doug said. "I felt old and crummy. You look exactly the same as when we got married, I swear. So many women need to put on makeup and wear fancy clothes to look good, but not you."

Laura looked down at her sweats. They were a higher-end brand, but loose and elastic-waist all the same. She stood and placed her hands on Doug's shoulders, kneading her thumbs into the knots as he sighed with pleasure. "This beats a twenty-four-carat massage, no?"

Doug pushed back his chair abruptly. "Let's go do something that beats everything," he said and pulled Laura in the direction of their bedroom.

When they were done, Laura rolled onto her side and observed Doug lying on his back, his hands folded under his head, basking in the afterglow. Outside, the rain had given way to brilliant sunshine.

She reached her index finger over to his chest and made light figure eights, tickling the patches of hair.

"You know, I still worry about feeling lonely. You're busy with SMILE. The girls didn't last more than an hour at home. Sophie's back on her feet, which means I'll only hear from her when she wants to complain about her Hinge dates. I know I've got that mentorship program to focus on, but what if it's not enough?"

The corners of Doug's eyes crinkled. He turned on his side to face her.

"Yes, we can get a dog."

Laura beamed. Marriage got boring. It got tedious. It was often tense. But there was nothing better than having a partner who knew exactly what you were thinking before you even had to say the words.

SENSATIONAL SIX 🥷🥷🥷🥷🥷🥷✡

BETH

So honored to have made the group chat.

Though I feel like I wasted my first text saying that.

LAURA

Howdy

SOPHIE

What is dress code for the BM?

BETH

Festive. Summer dress, etc.

DOUG

It is weird to be on the chat. I'm nervous

MATTHEW

Confirmed w Dad. he's bringing annette

NOAH

What if we hate her

SOPHIE

Then WE don't date her. I'm bringing someone too

BETH

I didn't know that. I have to know these things!! The tables!

328 — *Elyssa Friedland*

LAURA

Beth, chill. This group chat is a relaxed space

DOUG

Beth let's start our own chat

BETH

Done. Check your WhatsApp.

LAURA

Ok ok we get it . . . S—who r u bringing to Austin's

SOPHIE

Not ready to jinx it

NOAH

U guys r all welcome to stay with me

BETH

We reserved a block of rooms at the Sea Shell.

NOAH

I fixed the place up

DOUG

I can't believe I was jealous of this text chain

BETH

Me either.

15

Noah

LEO, NOAH AND BARTENDER DAN WERE BENT OVER GIGANTIC
floor plans spread across Noah's kitchen counter, jotting notes in the
white margins and marking questions for the architect. They'd been
in this position for over an hour and Noah's knee was starting to
act up.

"Let's take a break. Dad, how are you still fine on your feet after
so long?" he asked.

Leo looked at his son. "My feet are fine. It's my back I'm worried
about. I think I'm stuck."

Dan and Noah eased Leo into an upright position. "Mine's kill-
ing too," Dan chimed in. "If we're going to do this thing for real,
we're gonna have to find a more comfortable way to review blueprints."

"This thing" had been Noah's obsession for the past three months.
He was opening a new establishment on Long Beach Island, with his
father and Dan—the proprietor of For Old Times' Sake in Boca—as
partners. The concept was simple. It was a combination tech-support
store and bar rolled into one. The name, which came to Noah while
walking on the beach, was his favorite part: Techila Sunrise. It was a
triple threat: his favorite cocktail, a tequila sunrise (though he now
drank far more modestly these days), combined with his favorite

activity (helping people with their tech support needs), combined with his favorite time of day, when the sun peeked over the horizon.

After his father returned to Florida, Noah paced the house for days trying to figure out what he wanted to do with his life. He was pessimistic about returning to freelance tech support. He had already seen that people felt awkward calling him to back up their photos, no matter how many times he assured them he enjoyed the work. The transfer of money, whether it was physical cash or a Venmo or Zelle payment, was always a source of embarrassment, unless the outlay was in the direction of him paying someone. He thought briefly about putting together a crew of tech support folks he could send out on house calls, keeping his own identity a secret, but management and scheduling weren't his strong suit. The uncertainty ruined his ability to sleep. He scoured the Internet in the wee hours, reading stories about lottery winners (most pretty depressing—he was reminded of Sophie's *Breaking News* artwork) and looking up pictures of his various ex-girlfriends. When he ran out of material, he remembered Dan's bar in Boca. He had meant to check on it weeks ago after seeing the newspaper headline about independent restaurants and bars struggling.

Dan, one of the few people who'd shown him genuine kindness in the last year, who'd swapped his whiskey for coffee and guided him into a taxi and refused his cash, stuck out in Noah's mind as a beacon of hope. He found the bar's Instagram account. The most recently posted picture was of Dan, wet rag slung over one shoulder, standing outside the bar next to a metal "Closed" sign. Noah read the caption.

After more than twenty years serving the Boca Raton community, I deeply regret that For Old Times' Sake is closing its doors. It's been an honor to know all of you that have come inside, in good times and bad, and I wish you all the very best.

Though it was three in the morning, Noah sent Dan a direct message through the app. He said he wasn't sure if Dan remembered him but that he was bummed to read the bar had closed. Dan wrote back at once, saying that of course he remembered Noah. He was already following him on Instagram. The two chatted through the app for an hour. Noah updated Dan on everything since his trip to Florida. Even online, there was a quality that Dan possessed— maybe all bartenders did—that made it easy to tell him things. Dan shared that his daughter was moving to Philadelphia for a job, and with the bar closing, he had no real reason to stay in Boca with the geezers. It was then Noah realized the bar's name was a nod to Boca's elder community. *Old* Times' Sake.

I love puns, Noah wrote.

Me too, Dan said.

We should go into business together. Just to have a clever name, Noah wrote.

Dan didn't write back. Noah had probably freaked him out.

Noah dragged through the next few days, saddened by how eagerly he had latched on to Dan, a man he barely knew. Not wanting to set off another intervention, Noah forced cheer into his voice whenever his family reached out. And he took long walks on the beach, where the granules of sand tickling his toes and the rhythm of the waves crashing on shore made it impossible to let melancholy take over.

His phone rang on a beach walk and Noah picked up the unfamiliar number without thinking.

"Is this Noah Jacobson?"

"Yes, who's this?"

"It's Paul, from Hoboken. I got a new phone."

"Oh. Hi."

"I'm calling to thank you. The extra boxing lessons and vegan meals have made such a difference for Talullah. Her doctor just gave her the all-clear to return to work. Which means we can finally start to pay you back. Noah, I'm so unbelievably grateful to you. I'm sure you're swamped but, if you have any time, Talullah and I would love to say thank you in person. Talullah wants to bring you homemade cupcakes in the shape of boxing gloves. She's very excited."

"Um, yes, that sounds great. I would love to see you both. But you are absolutely not paying me back." They arranged to talk again in a week to confirm a convenient time for a visit.

Later that night, Noah, feeling heartened, opened the well-stocked fridge and set about making himself a real meal, using the cooking tools furnished by his father. After a decent cheese omelet with diced vegetables, he picked up his phone to start another session of mindless scrolling. He was surprised to find a message from Dan on Instagram.

What if we actually did? Start a business together. Sorry been MIA. My daughter is a single mother and she needed a lot of help with her move. But I'm back and ready to talk about this for real if you were being serious.

Two weeks later, Dan was in Jersey spitballing ideas. Dan loved the idea of moving to LBI to be closer to his daughter. Noah loved having a partner, both to balance out his deficits and fend off the loneliness. The off-season, while slightly less dead than in the past, was still too quiet. Noah needed distraction. The two men hashed out different business ideas for a full day. Noah said he preferred a more behind-the-scenes role in whatever they did, but that he'd happily manage all the tech needs. "That's a relief, because anything having to do with the computer makes me need a drink," Dan said.

"That's it!" Noah said, jumping like Tom Cruise professing his love for Katie Holmes on Oprah's couch. "So many people feel that way. Half my clients are already half a bottle of wine deep by the time I arrive. Let's open a tech repair space that also serves drinks!"

Dan was immediately on board. Noah called Leo to tell him the news. "I want in," Leo said.

"Dad, c'mon. This is a risky venture. I'd love to hire you as a consultant though. You can manage our finances."

"Noah, do I seem like someone who would have left myself with so little? After all my years at the accounting firm, let's just say I planned for more than a rainy day. It's time I share the rest of the story with you kids about your grandpa and the black bag."

"There's more?"

Leo went on to explain that Noah's Bubbe Esther threatened to tell the police about the money in the bag if Jack didn't give her a portion to watch over. They settled on $2,000. She said she would use the money for family emergencies only. Bubbe Esther, unbeknownst to her husband, invested the money soundly—more than soundly.

"She was something of an investing genius. Coca-Cola, Xerox, IBM. Man, did my mother know how to pick them. But she kept that money far away from my father. And she didn't tell me or your uncle Morris about it, not until we were much older. When the money came to me and your mother, we treated it the same way. A rainy-day fund. Though I did buy her a few really special pieces of jewelry over the years. Made me crazy she never put them away in a safe-deposit box or even a good home safe. She swore nobody would take her stuff—they would assume it was costume." Leo laughed.

Oh shit, Noah thought, remembering his sisters combing through their mother's loot-filled shoeboxes, assuming it was junk.

"I probably should have mentioned that before you guys packed up." Noah sent an urgent text on the sibling chat.

> Guys, Mom's jewelry was real. Laura, pls say u didn't toss it.

Oddly, it was Beth who responded first. She sent a picture of her hand covering her face, a gigantic, colorful ring on her finger.

> Sorry! I didn't know. I didn't think it was worth anything and I just wanted to have a little something that belonged to Sylvia. I'll have it appraised right away.

Laura wrote back.

> Nonsense, keep it. It looks great on you. I know where everything else is. Also, WTF? She kept it in a shoebox!

Business papers were drawn up quickly. Leo, Dan and Noah went in as equal partners and Techila Sunrise was officially incorporated. It would take over the iconic Mustache Bill's Diner in Barnegat Light. Noah was happy to breathe life once again into the LBI icon. He promised locals he wouldn't change a thing about the facade except for the sign. Most of the islanders were relieved that a big-box retailer wasn't coming in. The lone CVS on the island was enough.

Thanks to his constant spying on the house construction next door, he had a crackerjack team in place for the construction and interior design of Techila Sunrise. Noah's whole family was arriving in a few days for Austin's bar mitzvah. He couldn't wait to walk them through the space.

WRAPPED IN HIS GRANDFATHER'S TALLIT, THE SAME ONE WORN by his own father and Noah at their bar mitzvahs, Austin looked like a man. He'd shot up four inches since the prior summer and had even started to shave—only once a month for a rogue chin hair, but it clearly made him feel more grown-up. His voice had dropped about three octaves overnight, but still cracked during the haftorah toward the end of the service. Noah loved that kid. He was still marveling over how mature Austin had been when he sat him down for the what-you-see-in-porn-is-not-real-life talk.

The family-only ceremony took place at the JCC synagogue. As was tradition, everyone chucked Sunkist jelly candies at Austin from the pews when the rabbi officially declared him a bar mitzvah. He dodged a few, caught a few and tossed a few back at them.

Afterward, the family headed to the Sea Shell hotel for a festive lunch with a DJ and games. Laura had helped Beth create the guest list, and they invited all the friends who used to attend Sylvia's July Fourth barbecue as well as Austin's school friends and a handful of their parents. Dan, thanks to years of barkeeping, had great connections in the food and wine world. The liquor at the party was top shelf, the catering superb.

But Noah didn't have much of an appetite. He was busy dodging one guest in particular. His father's "companion" was in attendance. Annette Feldman was a fellow retiree at Boca Breezes. She was widowed five years earlier after a forty-five-year marriage to a doctor named David. Annette had two grown children and three grandchildren. Noah learned all this from Laura and Sophie, who were hugging the woman within seconds. He realized it was Annette who had helped his father stock his kitchen and still it did nothing to endear her to Noah.

Giggling, his sisters came over to fill him in.

"She's exactly like Mom," Laura said. "Without even asking, she started fluffing my hair. Told me it had gone flat from the humidity."

"She said I needed more lipstick," Sophie said.

"I like the way she looks at Dad," Laura said. "She's really into him."

"Great," Noah said. His sisters were oblivious to his sarcasm. He turned to see Betty, Myrna and Arlene approaching, Matthew trotting uncomfortably beside them.

"Mazel tov," Myrna said in a raspy voice. "Rabbi Kaplan said Austin did a wonderful job."

"He did," the siblings said in tandem.

"We have something to give you," Arlene said. "Sorry it has to be now but we don't see the four of you at once all that often."

"Oh God," Laura whispered into Noah's ear. "Please don't tell me they're naming the kiddush room at the temple after us because we donated all that money for Mom's card party."

Noah hoped not. He couldn't imagine anything more embarrassing than recognition for writing a check that had taken all of ten seconds to scribble and wasn't even his idea.

Arlene fished in her purse and produced four checks, which she handed out to each of them with exaggerated fanfare.

"Why are you returning these to us?" Sophie asked. They were the checks they'd written to match the proceeds generated by Sylvia's fundraiser. "You sent a check too? When?" Sophie was looking at Matthew.

Matthew nodded. "After Mom's friends first approached us. I figured there was no way I could be helpful other than to send money. So I wrote a small check and mailed it to Myrna."

Myrna straightened her posture, bringing her to a total of maybe five feet. "Your mother gave her energy, creativity and time to the temple. She didn't just write a check. This isn't the way to honor her memory."

"We will manage without you folks," Arlene said. "My daughter is an event planner in Cleveland and she promised to help."

"If you recall, we asked you to help before you won the lottery," Betty said. "We weren't looking for a handout. It's not what your mother would have wanted. And neither do we."

The three women turned on their heels and spread out in different directions.

"Well, that sucked," Sophie said as Noah went to chase the women down to apologize. He spotted Betty first at the bar, ordering an espresso martini.

"Betty, I just want to say you're completely right about the check. It didn't feel right at the time and I wish I had said something."

Betty put a hand to his cheek, the inside of her palm warm and tender. "You're a very sweet boy, Noah. You always have been. We'd love you to come play cards with us again. I just want to know why you look so sad. It's a happy day."

Noah studied Betty's friendly face, trying to remember what his mother had said about her. All he could think of was that she was supposedly even better at bridge than she was at canasta.

"It's a little awkward with—" Noah gestured to where his father stood next to Annette. The two weren't engaging in PDA, but they stood close together and were clearly sharing a joke.

"That?" Betty asked. "Let me tell you a story. Did you know I lost my first husband when I was only fifty? Tragic heart attack took my Eddy, may he rest in peace. I told myself that I was done with men. I would focus on my children and be grateful for the years I had with Eddy. But it was your mother who insisted I not give up on that part of my life. She introduced me to Bernie and we've been married for twenty-five years. His children and grandchildren have become my family, and vice versa. If it wasn't for your mother's pushiness, I'd be a very lonely lady."

Noah, for the second time that day, was chastened. Betty kissed his cheek. "I'm going to make a plate for Bernie. He hates a long buffet line."

Alone again, Noah's eyes swept the dance floor. He saw Laura shimmying with her girls and Sophie attempting to extricate her date—a guy she introduced to the family as Divorced Dad Dave—from their insufferable cousin Edith. He tried to find Annette. Betty was right. He needed to be a man and warmly introduce himself to her.

"Boy, are you handsome." Noah spun around, finding himself face-to-face with Annette. "Leo told me you were a looker but he didn't do you justice. Are you single?"

Noah blushed. "Um, I'm not sure," he said. He was casually seeing Rebecca Anarak, the designer he'd spotted next door and hired for Techila Sunrise, though she had little commercial experience. Noah had invited Rebecca to Austin's bar mitzvah, but she was doing an installation in Cape Cod the same weekend. He wouldn't hold it against her that she wasn't fully committed to the Jersey Shore. If he wasn't ready to be exclusive with her, she shouldn't have to commit to working only in his preferred habitat. Now that it was summertime, Robin Miller was back on the island. She'd invited him over one evening and they had a long make-out session. After, he installed her router.

"Well, when you figure it out, let me know. I have a twenty-four-year-old granddaughter who would absolutely knock your socks off." Annette put out her hand to shake Noah's. "I'm Annette, your father's partner. But I'm sure you figured that out by now."

Partner. Noah didn't mind that term actually.

"It's nice to meet you," Noah said.

"We should hug," Annette said. "I'm not sure why I put out my hand. I'm much more of a hugger but I was a little nervous to meet you. I know how close you and your mother were."

He nodded to acknowledge that yes he was very close to Sylvia, but Annette took it as agreement they should hug. She embraced him, and Noah found that he didn't hate it. Annette had a warm touch and a pleasant smile. She didn't reek of old-lady perfume. He was kind of curious to see a picture of that granddaughter.

Someone dinged the tines of a fork against a glass and Noah and Annette turned to the DJ booth. Matthew was holding a microphone, flanked by Beth and Austin. Austin's blazer was ditched, his tie undone and button-down sweaty from a raucous round of Coke and Pepsi and an aggressive hora with his friends, who'd hoisted their pal up on a chair before the adults could even break through. It was exactly what Noah wanted to see.

"Thank you, everyone, for coming to celebrate our son's bar mitzvah," Matthew said. Noah's older brother looked healthy and restored in a white short-sleeve button-down and khakis. "Our son crushed it this morning and Beth and I couldn't be prouder. It's extremely meaningful to mark this milestone with all of you in this place that's been so special to my family for decades. Obviously, this has been quite a year for the Jacobsons."

The crowd cheered and Annette, instinctively sensing Noah's mixed feelings, touched his elbow gently.

"I would say more than anything, as a family we've thought about what it means to be lucky. And Beth and I are the luckiest parents in the world to have Austin as our son. My beautiful wife, who planned this absolutely spectacular event, would now like to say a few words."

Matthew hugged both his wife and son and handed the mic to Beth.

"First of all, I want to echo everything my husband said about how proud we are of Austin. He's always been a superstar. We've focused a lot on his academic achievements, but the bar mitzvah has shown us that he's also a superstar when it comes to character, values and appreciating his family."

Beth paused to look from Austin to Matthew and then back to Austin. She blew her son a kiss that he'd for sure give her hell about later.

"I also want to shout out my sister-in-law Laura, who helped plan today's festivities. As most of you know, we have asked for donations to a wonderful organization called Peer 2 Peer in lieu of gifts for Austin. Laura and her girls are very involved and I invite you all to learn more about it. Sophie, my other talented sister-in-law, created Austin's logo and designed the invitation for today. She's a brilliant artist and we're lucky she lent us her talents. Now, Noah."

Noah's ears perked up. Even though Beth had singled out his sisters, he hadn't expected to hear his name.

"My brother-in-law, Noah, loves LBI and the Jersey Shore more than anyone I know. He has a deep attachment to this place and what it has meant to his family for so many years, and I want to thank him for reminding us how lucky we are to be here together."

Noah shuffled on his feet. Annette whispered, "Your father said the same" in his ear.

"Finally, I want to thank my husband. For those of you who don't know, Matthew retired from the law firm earlier this year. The change was a big one. I won't get into all the reasons now, not when there's all this excellent food to eat and wine to drink. I'll just say that having him home more to spend time with Austin has been a gift, a gift I didn't understand the value of fully until I saw our son this morning in temple. Matthew, I love you. Austin, mazel tov! We love you and are so proud of you. Now, let's cut into that cake and get back to partying. *L'chaim.*"

Noah raised his glass. Beth had finally mastered the gutteral "ch" sound from the Hebrew language. He took a small sip of champagne and handed the mostly full glass off to a passing waiter.

The bar mitzvah cake was a two-tiered babka, with one chocolate layer and one cinnamon, decorated with blue icing and a Jewish star on top.

"The cake is amazing," Noah said. "Which bakery made this? I don't see the Crust and Crumb guys doing this."

"Yummmm," Sophie groaned with pleasure. She had a chocolate mustache above her lip, which Divorced Dad Dave wiped away for her.

"This babka, I'm sorry to say, is even better than Mom's." Matthew looked to the sky in apology.

Laura beamed. "I made it! I used Mom's recipe and embellished a little. I made ten practice babkas in order to pull this off. Turns out that I can't cook for shit, but I can bake!"

THE NEXT MORNING, NOAH WOKE TO A TEXT MESSAGE FROM Matthew on the sibling chat.

Change of plans . . . brunch will not be at Parker's Garage. Come here instead. He dropped a pin to a location in Loveladies. Noah couldn't figure out what this was about, only that the longer drive meant he had twenty fewer minutes to sleep.

At eleven, Noah reached the address that corresponded to Matthew's pin after driving by three times. Long Beach Island, despite its simple layout, could throw Google Maps into a tailspin. He was in front of a small, empty plot of land partly obscured by anemic shrubs and overshadowed by the large homes and tall trees on the block. He had just put his car into park when Laura pulled up and she and her family, plus Sophie, climbed out.

"I'm hot," Emma announced after standing outside for all of one minute and dramatically fanning herself with the program from Austin's bar mitzvah.

"Me too," Hannah said. "I'm going to text Uncle Matthew and tell us he sent us to the wrong location." Just then, another car turned down the drive and pulled up. A white rental car, driven by Annette, with Leo in the passenger seat. Noah signaled for them to roll down the window.

"We're in the wrong place," Noah said.

"I told Annette this couldn't be right," Leo said.

But then Matthew's Tesla came rolling down the street.

"There he is," Doug said. "Come to rescue my girls and their precious hair from the heat."

"Dad, you don't get it. I got my hair done for yesterday and I want it to last!" Hannah rolled her eyes.

Austin emerged from the back of the Tesla, which opened like the Batmobile, carrying a gigantic picnic basket.

"What the—" Noah said. As much as he liked the shore, he didn't care for picnics. His ant-phobic mother had prejudiced him against eating on the ground. And it was true that sand always got in the food. A peanut butter and jelly sandwich tasted crunchy when you ate it near the beach.

"Who's hungry?" Beth asked, easing herself out of the passenger seat with her hands full. She was holding a bottle of champagne and a second picnic basket draped in a red-checkered cloth.

Matthew got out of the car last, sporting a sly smile. Without saying a word, he went to the trunk and pulled out a skinny cardboard cylinder. Noah recognized that kind of tube. It held architectural blueprints, like the ones for Techila Sunrise.

"Morning, all. Everyone get a good night's sleep?" Matthew asked. He was acting way too coy. Noah knew exactly what was up.

"You bought this," Noah said, pointing at the patch of land covered with broken branches and sparse greenery.

"We did," Beth said. "And we're building a house big enough for everyone to fit comfortably. There will be a room for Emma and Hannah, Laura and Doug, Noah—if he gets lonely in Beach Haven—Sophie, Dad and—" She stopped short when the awkwardness was obvious.

"We won't crash there too much," Annette said. "Not to worry."

"You're always welcome," Matthew said. "I'm going to focus on building this place for the next year. That ought to keep me busy. After that, I may go back to school. Been thinking about getting a masters in psychology. This past year definitely got me thinking about relationships and emotions more than ever. Who knows though? Maybe I'll become a professional home builder on LBI."

"You'd be great at anything," Sophie said.

"Flattery will get you everywhere," Matthew said. "This place will always have a room for you and Divorced Dad Dave."

"Actually, there's good news on that front. Principal Garcia gave me my old job back. And because Divorced Dad Dave's daughter is switching to private school, we can keep dating and it won't be weird that I'm seeing a parent."

"That's awesome, Soph," Laura said. "Doug and I really liked talking to him."

"His sister's a dentist," Doug said approvingly. He patted his sister-in-law's head. "Soph, I'm so happy you're going back to teaching."

"Me too. I had this realization. The Powerball isn't the first time

I've been blocked. During the pandemic, when we had to go remote for three months, I couldn't paint a thing. I assumed it had nothing to do with the kids. That I was just overwhelmed by panic and worry that I'd get sick, that someone I loved would get sick, that the world was ending, you know."

They knew.

"But when I went back, even with the masks and the kids and parents being totally freaked out, my inspiration returned in full force. The kids are my source."

"Sophie, that's wonderful," Leo said. "I always said you should have a day job . . ." He winked playfully. "I must have known all along."

"Can we eat now?" Austin asked. "I was too nervous to eat anything yesterday."

"Not until I brag about your part in my reinvention." Sophie cupped his chin lovingly. "After Austin heard what happened at the show, he created a new social media account for me on Instagram and, somehow, I already have four thousand followers and a ton of content. Instead of highlighting my work, he started shouting out other artists. Turns out people love to be recognized and are happy to follow back. Now I'm ready to show off my own stuff."

"You did that?" Beth said, looking at Austin. He blushed with pride.

"He's a great kid," Matthew said. "Beth, we should start setting up."

Leo looked up at the sky. "Not much shade for this picnic. Annette, did you remember your straw hat?"

"Actually, we have plenty of shade," Matthew said. "Follow me."

The rest of them looked at each other in confusion. From the road, all they could see was a plot of land with low plants behind a chain-link fence. Matthew unlocked the fence and led them farther into the property. Their eyes were drawn first to the sparkling ocean visible beyond the dunes. White foam crested on the waves just before they broke on shore, sliding up the sand and receding in a soothing rhythm.

"Who's ready to eat?" Beth asked. Everyone agreed. They turned around and walked toward the spot where she'd spread the picnic blanket.

It was Noah who spotted it first.

"The Money Tree!"

"You moved it!" Sophie strode over to touch its trunk. "That's so awesome."

"I was wondering what happened to it," Noah said. "It's such a beautiful tree. I was surprised the neighbors didn't want to keep it."

"Let's just say they were well compensated," Beth said.

The three cousins, despite being too big, climbed it while the adults laid out the picnic.

"There's got to be a story here," Annette said.

The four Jacobson siblings shared knowing looks.

"Oh, there's a story alright," Sophie said. She pulled her sister and brothers in for a tight hug. "It's unpredictable, it's surprising, but it's all ours. We're living it."

ACKNOWLEDGMENTS

Another book, another opportunity to thank the people who helped make my professional dreams come true. Kerry Donovan, my editor at Berkley, may have moved across the pond, but that hasn't stopped our partnership from flourishing. Together we've put five novels into the world and she continues to elevate my work with her thoughtful suggestions and brainstorming sessions. She is also a trusted and compassionate friend.

Stefanie Leiberman is my rock-star agent whose staunch support and fierce advocacy assure me that my books will receive the greatest care and attention. She's also a terrific lunch date. Her team at Janklow & Nesbit, Molly Steinblatt and Adam Hobbins, is top-notch and I truly value their opinions and input.

Also at Berkley, Claire Zion has been a great advocate of my work from the beginning. I'd like to thank publicity powerhouses Craig Burke, Tara O'Connor and Chelsea Pascoe, and marketing magicians Jeanne-Marie Hudson, Anika Bates and Jin Yu. Without their hard work to bring *Jackpot Summer* to readers, this book would live merely on my shelf without any readers. Thank you to Lila Selle for another gorgeous cover—this one might be my favorite—and to my editor's trusty assistants, Mary Baker and Genni Eccles, for making the publication process a smooth one.

Though I'm a Jersey girl through and through, I had limited experience on LBI before writing this book. Sandra Caplan, Eva

Hoffman and Shari Garfinkel were excellent resources and many of the loving details they described are sprinkled throughout *Jackpot Summer*. An extra special thank-you to my new pal Lindsay Weiss, better known as @cocoincashmere, who showed me around Beach Haven—including taking me to her family home—and spent many hours answering my questions. I'm indebted to Lisa Jacobson, who detailed the life of a professional artist and art teacher with honesty and many "colorful" anecdotes.

Writer friends: Leigh Abramson, Corie Adjmi, Lisa Barr, Lauren Smith Brody, Laurie Gelman, Alison Hammer, Brenda Janowitz, Pam Jenoff, Jen Maxfield, Catherine McKenzie, Zibby Owens, Amy Poeppel, Jane Rosen, Allison Winn Scotch and Rochelle Weinstein . . . You guys just get it. I hope we continue to bitch about publishing for many years to come.

My family is my greatest source of joy and inspiration. Charlie, Lila and Sam, your mother the writer is at a loss for words to describe how much I love you. Your smiles and laughter are my oxygen. William, my loving husband, you certainly put up with a lot. Hopefully you get a lot in return! I appreciate your patience and support as I feverishly write and yell at you to help more around the house.

My parents, Rochelle and Jerald Folk, and in-laws, Marilyn and Larry Friedland, are constant sources of strength and love, as are my siblings-in-law and my nephews and nieces. Thanks, Mom, for the frequent trips to the Livingston Library back in the day. My love of reading is where it all started. I remember leaving the library with you, a tall stack in my hand, and chatting about which book I should start first on the ride back home.

Readers, I love you. It's a crazy world out there. Thank you for seeking solace in books. I appreciate you taking the time to escape into my work.

Jackpot Summer

Elyssa Friedland

READERS GUIDE

Discussion Questions

1. Which sibling in the Jacobson family do you relate to the most and why?

2. Did any of the Jacobsons remind you of someone in your own family?

3. Which sibling do you think had the best attitude toward winning the lottery?

4. How did this novel make you think about the role money management plays in marriage and romantic relationships? Where did you notice money playing an important part in the relationships of these characters?

5. What did you think about Matthew's choice not to buy a lottery ticket? Did you think his siblings should have cut Matthew in right away? Why or why not?

6. Have you ever bought a lottery ticket? How would you use the money if you won?

7. How did Leo change throughout the book? What did you think of his parenting choices?

8. Do you think children are always "kids" when it comes to their parents? If so, is that a good or a bad thing?

9. Sophie thought having more time to work on her art would be beneficial, but it turned out to be quite the opposite. Did that surprise you?

10. Sophie's art show turns into an epic disaster, thanks to cancel culture and online hate. Did you anticipate the negative reaction to her show? What do you think about cancel culture generally?

11. Matthew is afraid to tell Beth how much he hates his job. Could you understand his reasons? How would things have played out differently if he had been honest with his wife and family?

12. What did you think of Laura and Doug's marriage? Do you think she forgave him too easily?

13. Matthew felt caught between his siblings and his wife. Did you sympathize with him? How do you think he handled it?

14. After reading *Jackpot Summer*, how do you think you might change if you suddenly had a financial windfall?

15. LBI is so special to the entire Jacobson family. Does your family have a place—maybe a house or a vacation spot—that is particularly special to you?

16. Beth and Matthew and Doug and Laura have very different parenting styles. Do you think family members are inherently judgmental of the way their relatives raise their children?

17. How do you imagine the story would have played out differently if Sylvia Jacobson was still alive?

18. Do you think the Jacobson siblings are going to be closer or less close in five years?

19. What six numbers would you pick for the Powerball?

Keep reading for an excerpt from

The Most Likely Club

by Elyssa Friedland, available now from Berkley.

Prologue

THE SMART-BUT-SOCIAL TABLE IN THE LUNCHROOM WAS IN the back corner, underneath a row of wall-mounted pennants boasting victories in swimming, wrestling, and football, and kitty-corner from the hot-and-popular table, which was next to the cafeteria line. This ensured the jocks, and those lucky enough to orbit them, got first dibs on the sloppy joes and hash browns. Scattered in between were the artsy types, the nerds, the Phishheads, the goths, and the milquetoasts who defied classification.

Melissa Levin, Suki Hammer, Priya Chowdhury, and Tara Taylor had taken over the smart-but-social table during their sophomore year, inheriting it from students who'd graduated the year before. Bellport Academy, the tiny private school in their posh hamlet in Connecticut, had the usual Anytown, USA, teenage groupings. If the social cliques were any more stratified, it would be a pyramid scheme. Melissa, Suki, Priya, and Tara had been best friends since the eighth grade—a convenient time to fortify a social circle, or square, as in their case. They had agreed that upon entering high school they wouldn't attempt to penetrate the popular crowd, but they wouldn't fall in with the geeks, either. They'd occupy the precious space of honor roll students who still get invited to parties.

Their plan worked. The four of them stuck together, earning high marks—Priya always on top—and carrying enough social currency that the jocks and cheerleaders knew their names and the nerds knew better than to ask them to study. And now they were seniors. Graduation was only a month away. Today was the day they'd been dreading, anticipating, imagining and stressing over all at once.

It was yearbook day.

Yearbook day meant finding out if all their efforts had paid off. Having the right clothes (a fake Kate Spade could pass muster if the stitching was fine enough), devoting time to eight-minute abs (and buns!), leading the extracurriculars, maintaining GPAs above 3.5. College admissions season had already come and gone, arguably the more important barometer of success in high school. But the four friends were more anxious about the yearbook superlatives than whether the college envelopes in their mailboxes were thick or thin.

There were fifty superlatives each year and approximately two hundred graduating seniors. The entire class voted. Some results were obvious. Kim Konner would get Most Popular. She was a blond Jennifer Love Hewitt, tits on a stick with girl-next-door approachability. Lulu Anderson would clinch Most Fashionable; her collection of baby doll dresses was ripe for a *Seventeen* magazine spread. Charlie Rice would get Most Athletic, and Byron Cox would get Most Likely to Win the Lottery (and lose the ticket). Suki, Priya, Melissa, and Tara had agonized over what they'd get, silently fearing how it would affect their dynamic if they didn't each clinch something.

Melissa didn't say it to her friends, but she couldn't imagine getting skipped over. She'd made her mark. Student body president. Editor in chief of the newspaper. Honor roll every term.

Now she was headed to Georgetown, where she planned to study government and feminist studies. She figured with a track record like hers—not a single lost election for a leadership position—she might have a knack for politics in the real world. Most Likely to Be President had to be hers.

Suki was also feeling confident. She wasn't Melissa, with a list of extracurriculars that required an addendum on her college application. But she was well-known around the school. For starters, she was half-Japanese. And in a lily-white school community with a disproportionate amount of Mayflower lineage, Suki's heritage made it so every student, freshman through senior, knew her story. Her mother was Japanese, a former model in Tokyo aged into reluctant housewifery, and her father a white entrepreneur with a run of bad luck (or poor business acumen). He seemed determined to declare Chapter 11 eleven times. A solid student, Suki switched to Japanese when she wanted attention—and what high school girl didn't—and was rumored to have dated a college boy for the past year. She floated the rumor, but only Melissa, Tara, and Priya knew it. Suki was likely to get a superlative, but even she didn't have much of a hunch as to what it would be. Hopefully nothing dreadfully on the nose, like Most Exotic.

Then came Priya. Overworked, cautious, and brilliant Priya Chowdhury. Another student of color, but somehow it didn't ring the bells that Suki's roots did. Maybe her lack of mystique stemmed from her father being the preeminent pediatrician in town. In middle school, the boys used to joke about Dr. Chowdhury grabbing their junk when he examined them. Priya brushed it off as best she could. It helped that her nose was always in a book, and her gaze firmly planted on her future path. First stop Harvard (already accepted), then Harvard Medical School, then a fellowship in orthopedics—she'd always loved the intricacies of the human body. She would study the skeletons strung as Halloween decorations around the neighborhood while the others stuffed Blow Pops into plastic pumpkins.

Finally, there was Tara, who had (Michelin) stars in her eyes after an appearance in middle school on the *Today* show propelled her to local stardom. She made a duck à l'orange for Al Roker that made him weep on air. She'd learned to make eggs with shaved truffles and deep-fried Jerusalem artichokes at age five; for her eighth birthday she requested a rondeau. Her palate was supernatural—at least double the normal amount of taste buds resided on her tongue. She could detect the presence of nutmeg with her eyes closed and demanded her parents plant an herb garden so she could have fresh thyme and rosemary. She showed off the burn scars on her fingers like Girl Scout badges. There was little doubt she'd open a restaurant one day.

Of their foursome, Tara was also the most fearless. With the same bravado she used to wield chef's knives, she snuck into the guidance counselor's office to see where everyone was applying for college. She filched copies of the winter math final off the fax machine in the teachers' lounge and painted red lipstick on the school mascot. Nothing ever landed her in serious trouble—Tara's parents were hefty donors. With her moment on national television, and her family's last name gracing the athletic center, there was little chance Tara would be overlooked in the yearbook.

"I am wigging out," Melissa said. She was nervously eating fry after fry. "I saw the boxes dropped off this morning. What's taking so long?"

"Take a chill pill," Tara said. "It's out of our hands now."

"Oh my God, he's here!" Melissa said, jumping out of her seat so quickly her orange tray upturned. She pointed to where David Grossman, the yearbook editor, was walking into the cafeteria, pushing a hand truck piled high with books. As though he were tossing hundred-dollar bills in the air, all the seniors in the cafeteria charged at him. At least they weren't the only ones obsessing.

"He's coming straight here," Melissa gasped, her overly tweezed eyebrows twitching. She was white as a sheet. None of them wanted to be around if she got something beneath her, like Most Likely to Teach at Bellport. *Can you imagine never leaving this town?* There were even grumblings that this year there might be superlative burns. Kim Konner swore there was a Most Likely to Pull a Tonya Harding, and Eddy Falcon suggested Most Likely to Speed in a White Bronco. They doubted Mr. Mackay, the yearbook advisor, would let those slide. But a more veiled insult, something the students would understand but would escape the faculty's attention, was a possibility they were all dreading.

"Just like I told him to," Tara said, grinning. She popped a fry into her mouth and visibly enjoyed watching her friends' anticipation. "God, these are overcooked. I don't know why Chef Mick won't try peanut oil like I told him to. The food at this school is like one step below a Hot Pocket." She dropped the half-eaten fry onto her plastic tray and fixed her eyes on David. "I told Grossman he could squeeze my right boob if he brought the yearbooks here first."

"Tara!" Priya clapped a hand to her mouth.

"We'll see if I actually follow through. I bet he'll be satisfied with a look."

That was likely. David Grossman's raging acne hadn't quit since the ninth grade. There was little chance he'd seen a live breast.

"Why the right one?" Suki asked, clearly amused.

"Saving the left one to find out who the prom king and queen are going to be."

Melissa threw a Mike and Ike at Tara, though she was clearly grateful for the first peek.

"Oh, look, there's Josh," Priya said. "Right behind David."

Josh Levine was Melissa's boyfriend of the past two years. Their last names made an unfortunate combination—Levin-Levine—but it's not like she planned to marry him. They were an under-the-radar couple—a good thing because the rumor mill at Bellport could be vicious. Josh had an Adam's apple the size of a plum and teeth that couldn't be coaxed into submission despite years of braces, but he was sweet and dependable and put up with Melissa's exhausting schedule of extracurriculars. She just wished he would stop wearing carpenter jeans every single day. And making her mixtapes filled with Fiona Apple songs.

"Did Josh get new glasses?" Suki asked, cocking her head in his direction. She was remarkably observant. If any of them got new paper for their Filofaxes, Suki was the first to notice.

"Yes. I know, they're awful." Melissa shrugged. "He needs bi-focals because of his astigmatism." His inability to wear contacts meant he could never wear the sexy Oakleys worn by the cooler guys at school. "I wonder if he got anything in the yearbook." Josh teetered on the edge of the defy-classification group, something Melissa tried to spin into a positive. Everyone knew the jocks were jerks. The skateboarders were always high. The theater guys were too emo. Maybe she was the Rachel to Josh's Ross. Her haircut was even similar to Jennifer Aniston's and Josh prized his child-hood collection of plastic dinosaur figures.

"Hot off the presses, ladies," David said when he reached their table. Four hands grabbed at the top box on the pile, ripping into the packing tape.

"Got one," Suki announced, the first to pry a book free. She flipped ferociously until she reached the superlatives double spread.

"Most Likely to Cure Cancer ... Priya Chowdhury!" Suki announced. "Very nice, my friend."

Priya burned with pride. Her parents would like that. They would probably frame it next to her older sister's valedictorian plaque on the mantel.

Melissa cheered when she found hers.

"Most Likely to Win the White House," she said, the giddiness making her bounce up and down on her heels. She could practically kiss David, blistering pimples and all.

"Nice job, babe," Josh said, throwing a wiry arm around her, his gaze still searching the spread for his name.

"Suki Hammer ... Most Likely to Join the Forbes 400." Suki read her own aloud as her mind raced to make sense of it. She had turned the school bake sale profitable by swapping basic chocolate chip cookies for gourmet éclairs and apple tarts wrapped in paper-thin phyllo dough—she'd forced Tara to stay up all night baking. The triple profits came in handy when the student council was able to book the hottest ska band for homecoming that fall. Suki also got the student newspaper to source advertising from local businesses. And there was her Garbage Pail Kids side business dating back to elementary school. Yeah, her superlative fit. More importantly, she approved.

"And Tara Taylor gets Most Likely to Open a Michelin-Starred Restaurant," David Grossman said.

"The tire place?" Josh looked to Melissa for explanation.

Melissa looked at the floor. She wasn't about to admit she was confused, too.

"Yes. But they also award stars to the finest restaurants in the world," Suki explained in a voice that radiated maturity.

"I'll take it," Tara said, fastening the top button of her flannel shirt as David looked at her chest with laser beams.

"We did good, kids," Melissa said once David had moved on to another table and Josh had kissed her goodbye, clearly downtrodden about his absence on the pages.

"Think any of these things will actually come true?" Priya asked. Her dimples were out, loud and proud. It was obvious how badly she wanted to fulfill her destiny.

"Duhhhh," Suki said. The four of them clinked their diet Arizona iced teas together. "We're going to light the world on fire."

Elyssa Friedland is the acclaimed author of *The Most Likely Club*, *Last Summer at the Golden Hotel*, *The Floating Feldmans*, *The Intermission*, and *Love and Miss Communication*. Elyssa is a graduate of Yale University, where she returned to teach novel writing, and Columbia Law School. She lives with her husband and three children in New York City, the best place on earth.

VISIT ELYSSA FRIEDLAND ONLINE

ElyssaFriedland.com

ElyssaFriedland

AuthorElyssaFriedland

ElyssaFriedland

Ready to find
your next great read?

Let us help.

Visit prh.com/nextread

Penguin
Random
House